IN VITRO LOTTERY

Ed Ryder

Copyright © 2016 Edward Ryder

All rights reserved.

ISBN-13: 978-1523896189
ISBN-10: 1523896183

Dedicated to my family, friends, and anyone who decided one day to write a book just to see if they could.

Chapters

All the children from Emily's generation knew the story of Bjart Lorentzen, albeit a tale spoken in hushed tones and half-whispers, lest his ghost might hear and return to finish what he'd begun all those years ago. The rat catcher, the piper, patient zero of the Norwegian Death. The man who killed the world.

But the survivors of the plague, struggling to maintain their way of life in the chaos and aftermath, soon faced a new threat to the continuation of their species; a disease they called Infectious Embryonic Sterility. The virus buried itself secretly in their genome and made their children barren, with complex and expensive fertility treatment the only alternative. Some could pay, but most could not.

Thus in Britain, vigilant and isolated from the fragmented world beyond its shores, the In Vitro Lottery was born.

Walking wounded

England, November 2060

Emily shot an anxious look back to the hospital campus as she staggered towards the safety of the woods, the deep gash in her side burning angrily and threatening to overwhelm her. The clinic rose out of the landscape like a fortress, the scattering of surrounding trees and privet hedges failing to obscure the concrete walls and old rusting razor wire beyond. Its origins as a prison were unmistakable even now, decades after the Norwegian Death had all but emptied the place of any inhabitants. The guards remained, of course, but their main purpose now as they sat around the towers, smoking cigarettes and pointing their guns at the occasional wandering deer, was to keep people out rather than in.

Aptly it had been a women's prison in its day, famous for harbouring a notorious child killer who resided there long after her sentence had ended, primarily for her own protection rather than that of the public. Emily had been given the story during a tour of the site when she first arrived at the clinic, where the decay and neglect of the exterior thankfully stood in stark comparison to the gleaming corridors and state of the art facilities of the hospital hidden within. She had been so excited that first day, an Alice in her own Wonderland caught in the headlights of smiles, technology and promises. A new life would soon be growing inside her, not even from a donor but part of her, her own egg fixed just long enough to survive those first few precious days, which surely would make the bond between them even deeper when it was born?

But the dream had quickly turned sour. She'd been at the clinic less than two days before she heard of the discovery, a nurse with a loose tongue talking too loudly in the corridor outside. The news had shattered her, the walls of her room closing in and threatening to suffocate her, a prison cell once more. Her sister had often accused her of being weak, with her over-reliance on other people to aid and support her whenever things got difficult, and it was only then that Emily realised it was true. Now, though, she was alone and what happened next was up to her. She'd managed to steal an extra dressing gown from the bathroom that evening and a scalpel from a lab a few hours before that during another tour. Her clothes had been stored when she'd arrived, and a short surgical gown was all that was supplied in the warm surroundings of the Gamma block. Outside, however, it was late autumn and so far the English weather had not been kind.

What happened next was still a blur. She'd waited until the dead of night to make her escape and after years of struggling with work on the farm she was finally glad to be small, her light frame making her soft-footed and easy to hide from the patrolling night staff. It hadn't helped her navigational skills, however, and she'd managed to get lost twice before even reaching the stairs, the dim night lights obscuring the passageways and making them seemingly identical, with only the different coloured shades of floor tiles giving any clue to her location.

Getting out of the building without raising an alarm was one thing, but sneaking through the side entrance guard post unseen would be much more difficult. At least the security here was all focused outwards she reasoned, but it hadn't stopped a guard spotting her. Why he hadn't called for help she didn't know; perhaps a small young woman was something he thought he could handle himself, or perhaps the sight of her in nightclothes had stirred something in him where he didn't want to be disturbed by other people. It didn't really matter, he was on her in seconds, the flashlight shining in her face with a demand for identification. There had been a struggle, a pointed gun, a scalpel and a cry of pain from both of them. She'd broken free as the guard clutched at his groin and nose, and ran off into the night.

And it was here that she found herself, clutching the stab wound in her side while the sirens wailed and the torch beams came ever closer. Nature was her ally for now, at least, as warmer weather had rolled in, condensing the wet air and creating a thick fog around them. The woods, she remembered, were next to a road at the far end. If she could just make it there then maybe she would be lucky and flag down a late night traveller, or at least find somewhere to hide until early morning. The wound didn't appear deep or life threatening, but it did hinder her movement, causing a sharp intake of painful breath every other step and slowing her down. She wondered if the guard was okay. She hadn't meant to harm anyone, she just needed to escape.

The shouting and beams finally began to recede into the distance, the search dogs that would have been guarding the old prison thankfully absent now, and Emily allowed herself the luxury of hope for the first time. The fog that was concealing her from her would-be captors was also hiding dangers on the ground, however, and twice she tripped badly on an exposed tree root, quickly jamming her fist into her mouth to prevent herself screaming out in pain.

The deeper into the thicket she went, the worse the terrain seemed to get. As she struggled through the undergrowth, the low-hanging branches tore at her thin clothes and snagged her long curled hair, both of which were now soaked by the mist, making her body shiver and teeth chatter. Each movement made the pain even worse and it began to obscure her vision, making her wonder if perhaps the wound was more serious than she'd first thought, or had nicked something important? The thought of it made her laugh inexplicably. If only her sister could see her now, the little girl who would howl with pain from a paper cut now a desperate and injured survivor, clawing her way through a forest in the middle of the night.

Her humour was short-lived, though, as she suddenly came face to face with one of the clinic guards, his torch pointed at the ground allowing him to sneak up on her. It was the same one as before, a man not much older than her, with a balding head and bloody nose. This time, there were no attempted heroics on his part.

"I've found her!" he shouted, causing the distant beams to all focus their gaze on Emily's location. "You stupid bitch, what the hell are you doing? We're trying to help you! Thought you'd gone crazy or something?"

"Get away from me!" Emily screamed back, more in shock than anything else. "I know what you found, what you are going to do!"

"I have no idea what you're talking about. Look, my name's Sebastian. We're just here to get you back to your room and safe." He looked down and noticed the growing patch of wet blood on the side of her gown. "Sorry if I scared you before, but that cut really needs to get seen to."

Emily actually found herself believing him, but quickly realised it didn't matter if he was telling the truth or not, the result would be the same.

It was then she heard the noise, a distant rumble slowly growing in volume, followed by the unmistakeable sight of car headlights. The road! She was practically on top of it and hadn't even realised. Sebastian pre-empted her next move and made a lunge for her, missing her arm by fractions and cursing as his foot slipped on the sodden ground. Emily spun around and sprinted off as the man struggled to his feet, the adrenaline cancelling her pain for a brief instant. It was a debt that would be paid back in spades later she was sure, but that was a worry for another time. All that mattered now was getting away, back to Andrzej and the others.

She ran out into the road, lungs heaving, only a few yards in front of the car, causing it to slam on the brakes and steer violently to avoid her, before finally coming to a stop a short distance away. The front passenger door opened and a man in a large coat clambered out, his features obscured by the darkness and the peak of a baseball cap.

"Help me!" Emily pleaded. "There are men after me!"

"What's your name?" the man asked, which struck Emily as an odd thing to ask given her situation, but she answered him anyway. "Emily Palmer."

The man held a finger to his ear and repeated the name slowly and clearly, which made Emily even more confused. What was going on? Surely the guards would be on them both any second?

The man nodded slowly. "Sorry babe."

Emily's final memory was staring at the gun barrel in surprise, and the flash of light as the trigger was pulled. She was dead before she could hear the sound.

The Salesman

Victor's palms were sweating again. No matter how many experts he saw and coaching sessions he attended on public speaking, his hands always betrayed his nerves. The lights around the mirror on the dressing table weren't helping either; three were broken and one had started flickering with such migraine-inducing intensity that he briefly thought about smashing it just to put it out of its misery.

He had dismissed the 'hair and makeup' girl a few minutes earlier, tired of her prattling on while dusting his bald head with powder to stop the lights glaring off it, and her thinly veiled attempts to get a free session at the clinic. In the past, he had frequently acted on such offers from previously uninterested pretty girls, who would suddenly gladly accept his advances when they found out who he was.

But that was long ago, and these days, lust was more likely to be replaced with impatience and indifference. He pulled out a handkerchief from his jacket pocket and wiped as much of the powder as he could from his head, before shaking the cloth over the floor. His public engagement team had once suggested he wear a headpiece to make him more appealing to the public, but he'd resisted. Society liked their politicians young, vibrant with a strong hairline, he concluded, whereas scientists should be older, wiser and bald. One type for hope and another for reassurance, although he sometimes wondered which was which.

Letting out a sigh, Victor surveyed the small dingy changing room, which was in a similar condition and state of disrepair as the lights on the mirror. The mouldy and damp-stained wallpaper was barely hanging on to the rough plaster, and the musty sofa and patchy rug in the corner were both failing to hide a large hole in the floorboards. And apparently this was the best room the studio had! He sometimes forgot how normal people existed, and this local TV station was the epitome of normal.

Victor couldn't even remember why he was here in the first place. His diary was in the hands of others most of the time and often seemed to be a whirlwind of random events concocted by lunatics, intent on keeping him away from his job of running the clinics. He especially hated interviews, but even more than that he hated talking to the public, and the live element of today's broadcast made it even worse. The general populace had a nasty tendency of asking very elegant and complicated questions, even if they didn't intend to, and he was terrified of the feeling of helplessness as the cameras zoomed in on him frantically searching his brain for an answer.

Scientific conferences were easy in comparison, the questions technical and predictable from people more interested in the minutiae than themes and politics. His people, although he knew that they would probably refute that statement, that they distrusted him more than the public did, but for reasons of perceived integrity rather than intentions and power.

His old mentor, Tobias Heath, had once called him 'The Salesman', due to (what he believed anyway) Victor's unhealthy obsession with trying to patent and profit from every idea he came up with. It was supposed to be an insult, a joke to be whispered at tea breaks between conspiratorial grad students who fell silent when he entered the room, but Victor took it as a badge of honour. *Science was for mankind and the ages*, Tobias had told him repeatedly. It was an ironic statement considering what that man had done in the past, an act which made the idea of actually making some money out of research a laughably minor aspiration in comparison.

He wondered where Tobias was now? Probably rotting away in a nursing home somewhere, he guessed. That was if the old man still had any money left after passing the state care age limit, being almost certainly too cowardly to take Dignity and do society a favour. He made a mental note to look him up later to satisfy his morbid curiosity, but any further thoughts on the subject were interrupted by a loud knock on the door from one of the studio runners, the noise echoing around the spartan room.

"Five minutes, Dr Pearson."

"Okay just a moment," he replied shortly. His personal assistant Dinah had wandered off a while ago looking for some fresher tea, and he really needed her here now to go through the plan before he was due on set. He was considering firing her when she burst through the door, a clipboard in one hand and desperately trying not to spill tea all over it with the other. She put both down on the edge of the dressing table and straightened her skirt. "Sorry, got cornered by one of the production team." She was about to continue but Victor threw her a look that clearly said he didn't care. "Right. You wanted to go through the interview schedule?"

"Yes, there's three of us, correct?"

"No, two. You and some junior politician the Repro Ministry sent that I've never heard of. Probably seeing how he copes with a hostile audience." She paused, seeing the colour on Victor's face draining away. "Hostile to him of course," she quickly corrected, "considering the proposed extension to LockDown past the next elections. Which is fine, it gives you the opportunity to play good cop for once. But don't overdo it, these types can be prickly if you make them look bad."

Victor smiled. She had no idea how true that was. "Okay, and?"

Dinah looked confused for a second and then realised what he meant. "Oh yes, expect the usual debate show fluff. Lottery capacity, extortionate prices, questions about fairness and eugenics, just because some racial minority hasn't won anything for a couple of weeks. Leave anything about policy to the politician. You're just a businessman and scientist trying his best under the circumstances. Stick with the positives."

She was holding something back, he could tell, and it was starting to irritate him. There was precious little time left before the next knock at the door to play guessing games. "Sounds like something any of our press engagement people could have handled, I'm sure."

She adjusted her glasses, which Victor knew was never a good sign. "There's been a lot of noise from IVFree recently in the independent press and nightlife circuits, so Repro think it would be good for us to show a united front and bring out the big guns. They've even upgraded it from a local to national broadcast, so expect some sympathisers in the audience tonight."

Victor noted that the 'big guns' seemingly didn't include the actual Minister from the Reproduction Ministry himself, who was more than happy to send his junior to the wolves. He was glad, that was one distraction he could do without today. He stood up and Dinah patted down his suit, searching for stray fluff and hair donated from the chair. He could hear Tobias in the back of his mind gloating that 'real' scientists wore scruffier clothes.

"Just one more thing Victor, remember your accent."

Victor gave her a thin smile and thanked her for the reminder. Even after forty of his forty-nine years in this country, his American twang still permeated through particular words. The PR people suggested he suppress it, but he rather liked the slightly exotic aura it gave him.

The knock on the door was there again. Time to go and be a scientist again.

The drab and dark corridor was soon engulfed with new paint and carpet as Victor strode purposely down to the studio entrance, the doubt and trepidation replaced by excitement and thrill, as it always did when the time to act was finally nigh. The rest of the cast were already there waiting for him. The host, an attractive and sophisticated-looking woman in her early forties, with jet black hair and an evening dress to match, introduced herself as Astraea. She shook Victor's hand eagerly and kissed him on each cheek, before gliding off to check some details with the producers.

The politician, whose name turned out to be Caden, was about half Victor's age with a sharp suit, polished shoes and greased-back hair. He lounged back in his chair and didn't bother to stand up when Victor approached him, a sad attempt at some minor power play that betrayed his inexperience. Victor countered it by rising to his full height, and stood just far away enough that the politician had no other choice but to get up to reach his outstretched hand. Some of the more astute members of the growing audience noticed, which sent a small wave of tittering around the room. Caden's shake was oily, too strong and thankfully brief as they were ushered back to their seats. As the broadcast countdown began on an electronic clock in the corner, the remainder of the audience settled on the benches in front of the guests. The makeup girl Victor had dismissed earlier quickly ran up to the host and applied a final layer of lipstick to her, before ducking out of view just as the red 'live' light blinked on the studio camera.

"Welcome everyone to Talking Point!" Astraea announced enthusiastically. "Our main guest tonight needs no introduction."

Victor stifled a laugh, as the next line was usually an introduction piece. He wasn't left disappointed.

"Dr Victor Pearson, head of InVitroSolutions, and patron of the Lottery," Astraea continued. "The man who discovered the Infectious Embryonic Sterility virus and how to fight it, and some say the richest man in Britain." The crowd applauded as Astraea introduced Caden and the format of the show. It was the usual deal; a few friendly questions from the host about the Lottery format and how it might change in the future, the action of the virus and how the fix was only transient, before the floor was open to questions.

"If you can fix the gene, why can't you remove the virus?" a young man asked rather curtly.

It was a standard question which made Victor wonder if anyone actually bothered reading the information leaflets his company sent out. Still, at least it was an easy one. "As we explain in our primary literature," he replied in a patronising tone, "the IES virus makes thousands of copies of itself which then integrate into repeat elements in the human genome. Trying to cut them out would be akin to sticking your genome through a paper shredder."

He'd barely finished, when an angry obese woman began shouting and the microphone was quickly swung over to her, much to the indignation of the man trying to get out his retort. "Yeah, it's all fine for you to sit there taking money from desperate people and sucking them dry like a parasite!" she cried. "People like me! You took our life savings and I had nothing to show for it. IVF should be free to all! IVFree forever!" She began shouting and screaming the slogan over and over, even after the security guards grabbed her and started to wrestle her from her seat with Astraea gesticulating wildly at them.

Victor interrupted them all. "No, let her go for a minute, I'd like to respond to that if I may," he said, as calmly as he could. Time to earn his keep. He moved his gaze away from the woman, who had now fallen silent, to the audience as a whole. She was just an opportunity, nothing more, and there was little point trying to appeal to fanatics. "Is the treatment expensive? Yes, it is. Which is why we at IVS work with the Government on the Lottery and use the percentage earning system, which allows thousands of couples access to our system. Critical workers, who do so much for our society day after day, get donor-based treatments for free as is their right and reward. Do we guarantee success? If it's just due to the IES virus yes, we do. But sometimes it just doesn't happen. It's just nature's way, and those problems existed long before the virus." He looked at the woman again, who was having difficulty catching her breath after the altercation with the security guards. "And certain LifeChoice decisions probably don't help in that regard either madam."

Everyone apart from the woman, who now seemed to turn purple with rage, laughed at the observation, and Astraea took the distraction as a chance to get her evicted from the crowd as quickly as possible.

Victor turned his attention to the rest of the audience. "Of course, in addition to the actual clinics, we invest heavily in schools and universities to ensure that the skill base for the company I set up nearly twenty-five years ago will continue long after I'm gone. On top of that, we fund expeditions to the far-flung corners of the world to locate and trade in new sources of gametes to further bolster and diversify our stocks."

Caden, who had probably realised by now that Victor was stealing the show, quickly chipped in. "Yes, and everyone has to realise that the stocks of materials are a finite resource. We all remember what happened in France. The people demanded free treatment, so Government forces stormed the outreach clinics and took them over. The result? Queues a mile long, then riots and anarchy when the reserves ran dry. With IVFree's dogma, that would be our future too. And where are these people now? Thousands of them line up at our border control every day, desperate to get in."

"How many reserves are left?" was the obvious follow-up question that Victor really didn't want to be asked. Caden had walked into that one.

Victor, of course, knew exactly how much was left and how much was being generated down to the last vial of sperm in the cryogenic banks. But too much information was a dangerous thing; it made people think, calculate risk and panic when they came to the wrong (or correct) conclusions. "Well, the exact numbers are classified due to our national security agreement with the Government. But let me assure you that our stocks are plentiful, that our IES-clear teams of contracted donors are replenishing them, and we have our live donor first-generation infected programmes too."

That seemed to placate the audience, at least, and the conversation soon shifted to Government policy. There was general bad feeling about the continued use of LockDown, the Act which continued to promote self-sufficiency and keep the borders closed so many years after the Norwegian Death had run its course. It was originally designed to stop the plague getting back in, but now served mainly to keep people out. People who, according to the politicians, were only interested in themselves and not in helping the country and society as a whole. There was some immigration of course, but the requirements for entry were high and the process difficult.

Victor thought Caden had responded deftly to the questions about the continued use of Dignity, and how they'd managed to reconcile its use with Catholic doctrine. It was not suicide, he had explained, but a sacrifice for the greater good, no different from the soldiers who laid down their lives in battle. The world had been on the edge of collapse and even now, nearly half a century later, it was still recovering, clawing its way back by inches to the shadow of what it was before.

"We had to make some big decisions during and after the Death," the politician said, standing up and striding around the studio floor. "Strong decisions. Unpopular decisions. But look how far we've come, how we've risen from the ashes. While America fragmented, we held firm. When other nations were lynching minorities in the street, we stood side by side together in unity, striving to forge a better society. And look at us now, a beacon of hope, peace and security, the envy of the world. Now, as once long ago, Britain is truly great again."

The audience stood as one and broke into a rapturous ovation as Caden raised one hand in acknowledgement, soaking in the applause and basking in the adulation of the crowd. Even Victor couldn't help be impressed by the delivery, however well-rehearsed the scientist thought it sounded.

The rest of the show passed without incident and after some brief pleasantries, together with Astraea's phone number being slipped to him during an over-familiar farewell embrace, Victor slipped back down the darkening corridor towards the changing room. Dinah had disappeared again, but for some reason, the politician was rushing to catch up with him.

"Hey, Pearson!" Caden called, the smiles and polite pretence now gone. "I have a message from the Minister. It's about the incident yesterday at Highpoint."

"I told him it was under control," the Salesman shot back. "We analysed her sequence and couldn't find anything, and there was nothing else that suggested any outside influence."

"Yes, and now you have a dead body and the independent press sniffing around. Not my definition of 'under control' by any means," Caden replied sarcastically.

Victor lost his temper and grabbed the politician by the arm. "Who the hell do you think you're talking to?"

Caden knocked his grip away. "No, Pearson, who the hell do you think *you're* talking to?" He was staring right through Victor now, his expression severe. "Remember who I represent, what they represent, and what they can do."

Victor's relationship with the Government had always been slightly fractious, but until now he had never felt nervous around them. He swallowed involuntarily and felt his palms start to sweat again. "You're right, I apologise." His turn to reach out for the hand now.

Caden wasn't interested in the olive branch, though. "You will send us all of the data, samples and records. Everything. You will keep no backups and no copies. I presume you can handle your employees?"

"Yes. It's already been nipped in the bud," Victor replied, "they aren't going to risk their job and status over hearsay."

"Good, then we'll wait for the info from you," said Caden, patting Victor on the shoulder as the smile slithered back onto his face. "Enjoy the rest of your evening." He turned and swaggered off back towards the studio.

Victor made it back to the changing room and slumped into the chair alone with his thoughts, the dank surroundings reflecting his mood. Dinah appeared a few minutes later to arrange the driver to pick them up. "I saw that politician talking to you after the show, anything to report?" she asked innocently.

Victor tried to sound flippant and dismissive but wasn't sure he quite pulled it off. "Nothing of any note that I can't handle myself."

"Okay," replied Dinah slowly through narrowed eyes. "Hey I was chatting to Astraea and she seems completely into you. If you want me to arrange anything; dinner, or just anything, give the nod." She winked at him, completely oblivious to what had just happened. It was their little joke every time a woman threw herself at him.

"Of course she is, she's probably running out of Lottery time."

"Hey don't worry about it, have your fun with her and we'll just write off her treatment against tax. Cheaper than a hooker in real terms and she'll probably be a lot more grateful. Win-win!" Usually, Victor would have laughed but he couldn't raise the enthusiasm or desire, and Dinah finally picked up on it. "You sure you're okay? What did, what was his name again...Caden, want anyway? Did it have something to do with that girl?"

Victor turned away and looked at her through the reflection in the mirror. "I said it was nothing."

Her desk was cleared out the next morning.

First prize

Kate stared blankly at the wall as the door behind her slammed shut for the last time. She didn't know if she felt upset, angry or relieved, and the tear rolling down her cheek offered no clarification. It had been brewing for a while now, the pebbles slowly rolling and gathering into the inevitable and unstoppable avalanche. Too much had been said, words spat with venom that an apology and a hug could never take back, and no room left for a truce or forgiveness.

It boiled down to one simple fact; Kate did not want children. She had no maternal instinct to nurture and protect anything, apart from the stray ginger cat that occasionally wandered into the house, and no desire to spend sixteen years and beyond confirming that fact. To share that information, though, and admit the truth was heresy as far as Michael was concerned, so she kept it to herself. They had visited one of Michael's friends the previous year, who was eager to show off her expensive new toy to an envious and doting crowd of cooing women. Kate had spent the majority of the time hiding in the kitchen, pretending to be interested in the potted cactus plants. They had eventually tracked her down, and the overwhelming peer pressure had resulted in this small wrinkly baby being thrust into her arms. She'd frozen in fear and tried to smile through the grimace, until after what seemed like an eternity the mother had relieved her of the cargo and passed it on to the next eager recipient.

So, every Friday after work, she had done her duty and walked down to the shopping complex to buy her ticket. It was a simple enough system, designed to be random at three points and immune to cheating. There were always whispers and accusations of tampering with the results, of course, usually from some group desperate to feel persecuted about something, but most educated people knew it was physically impossible to fix.

Once at the shop, she would scan her ID card and the machine would dispense a ticket with a random eight-digit number printed on it; hope defined and reduced to a single point. The live draw was the following night, as thousands of women (for only women were eligible to play) huddled around their radios, televisions or each other in the public bars. Seven large machines, each containing a drum holding ten labelled balls, would whirl away, the rotating arms flinging the numbers around until one made its way into the collecting chute. The chosen numbers with a zero added in would then be randomly sorted by a computer, and the winning combinations displayed and recorded. Twenty winners would win the coveted top prize of zygote-repaired IVF, a child born of both natural parents. Two hundred more would have their own fixed egg fertilised with IES-clear donor sperm from the clinic archives, and a further two thousand would win a child derived from both donor eggs and sperm.

Kate would sit at home, listening to the radio or doing the same jigsaw again that Michael had bought her at one of the auctions while he made plans for what their child would be like, how it would be raised and what it would become. It was a fantasy, a myriad of quantum possibilities and dreams never to be made manifest. But then she had won, the wave function had collapsed and the dreams had become reality. Her reality. And to make things worse, she had won the top prize, which meant Michael got his possibly one and only chance to live on through their offspring.

They would be the talk of the neighbourhood, the lucky and deserved winners to be admired, respected and envied, which made telling him her decision even harder. She wanted to give her prize to her sister Emily, the delicate flower who cried herself to sleep when the emotional pain of being unable to conceive became too much. For Emily, it was an itch that could not be scratched, and a hunger that no amount of prayer or wishing could satisfy. It was in the rules of the Lottery that you could not sell a winning ticket, but you could give it to a family member in case of illness or injury. There were no rules banning a transfer out of personal preference, though. Presumably the concept of anyone just not wanting to win hadn't occurred to the organisers.

The news had not gone down well. At first, Michael thought she was joking, before dismissing it out of hand as the shock of winning. Then the arguing and campaigning had started, an endless wave of debate and counter-arguments about how this gift from God could not and should not possibly be passed to another. Subtle and friendly at first, then fiercer and more combative as time went by. She had tried reasoning with him to begin with, that the scarcity of children in the world hadn't stirred some dormant primordial urge in her to want to have them. Just because there was a current shortage of strawberries she'd explained, it didn't make her hungrier for one. Her irrefutable logic had just irritated him, though, resulting in more arguments and door slamming. After a while it seemed anything would set him off; an ill-judged comment, a word or an advert on the radio and the same conversation they'd had a hundred times before would start again, each more heated and angry than the last. She had even tried to break the cycle by just sitting in silence all evening rather than accidentally saying the wrong thing, but even that had stopped working eventually.

Kate never found out what had triggered it, but today he'd come home late from work spoiling for a fight which she'd gladly given him, finally sick of how things had progressed and spiralled down. Being called a selfish bitch, him being denied his God-given right to father a child, and the great opportunity they'd both been given to be a real family. She'd heard it all before, but this time, it didn't matter any more. She'd given the prize to Emily, and she was already at the clinic receiving the treatment. Michael had just stared at her, full of rage and an expression of utter betrayal. He'd not said another word after that, just gone to the bedroom, packed a bag and left without looking back, while she sat there scared of what he might do next.

She presumed he had run off to Becca, the bubbly young blonde that Kate had deduced he was having an affair with. The signs were subtle and he had done very well to hide it, but like any jigsaw the edge and corner pieces were there just begging to be assembled. She remembered that when the girl had first started at Michael's office, he seemed to mention her name constantly in conversation. Then one day, that had all suddenly stopped. She guessed Becca had quit, perhaps, but no she was there at the office party a few weeks later, wearing a tight short red dress and too much makeup, flitting around the groups and grabbing the attention of the male guests as she passed. All but Michael, who seemed to keep his distance all evening. The man whose open-mouthed gaze usually wandered to any pretty girl in the near vicinity, and he'd hardly spoken to the fantasy figure in front of him all night.

He'd played it too cool, though, too detached in case he said or did something to give the game away, but he had done so nonetheless. It wasn't enough to accuse him outright, and there was the possibility she was wrong, but it did explain the much-reduced demands he'd made of her in the bedroom in recent months. Kate had got herself tested for syphilis just in case, but it had come back negative, and she didn't feel the need to press the matter any further.

Kate looked around the lounge to evaluate what was left of her life. The broken television sat in the corner along with the computer, an old family heirloom of sorts, which too had failed to turn on for the last few years. She had been wanting to fix the machine for months, but just like all electronics new parts were expensive and the second-hand market nearly non-existent. Michael, however, had insisted that the car was a priority to fix and spent their savings on a new distributor and wiring for it. Quite why, Kate had never understood. They both worked in easy reach of the train network, which meant the car was a more luxury status symbol than a means of transport. Perhaps Michael had been planning an exit strategy before the news of the win, but it was more likely he just liked the attention it got him from others and the sense of superiority it clearly gave him when teaching her to drive.

He'd stormed out leaving the car keys on the coffee table, she noticed, which was still strewn with leaflets and booklets from IVS and the Lottery winner's pack. She had felt obliged to read them all, to help keep up the pretence at the beginning. It catalogued the changes in her body that would occur as the hormone treatments and pregnancy progressed, and a short biopic on the great Victor Pearson, saviour of the future who had first characterised the IES virus. There was further information on how the virus actually worked and how it only caused sterility in the children of those first infected, which was why it had gone unnoticed for so long.

No one knew where the virus had come from, only that it was spread through body fluids by sexual contact or exposure to infected blood, and that it had struck nearly everyone who had survived the Norwegian Death. Had the virus piggybacked within the bacteria that caused the pandemic, or had it been there all along, hiding in the human genome like a ticking bomb, disparate parts of a puzzle waiting to be rearranged by some external factor as humanity disintegrated? Or was it, as the preachers seem to prefer, a second great plague and further punishment from God trying to finish the job he'd started forty years ago?

Not knowing what else to do, Kate went back to her jigsaw. It was a landscape from Alaska, a small cabin overlooking a large and mirrored lake with mountains and the Mendenhall Glacier in the distance. She'd completed the puzzle a dozen times now and always did it the same way; edges first, the house, the mountains, the lake, the glacier and finally the sky. Michael would often mock her about it and 'help' by doing random parts that he happened to spot, which infuriated her and amused him no end. He couldn't understand what the difference was; to him, the end picture was the same no matter how it was put together. But the order was everything, the completed landscape a happy by-product of proper processes, pipelines and correctly followed workflows. The alternative was chaos and the final picture a corruption of its true self.

She was still sat at the table when the clock chimed twice, any attempt at adding more pieces long forgotten. The cat had appeared again (she must have left a window open upstairs) and made itself comfortable on the chair opposite, softly purring to itself and ignoring her. Kate smiled. Dogs loved you no matter what you'd done, whereas cats didn't care either way. She stroked it briefly on the head and headed off to bed alone.

Far too soon, Kate was woken by the bells of the old mechanical alarm clock in the far corner of the bedroom, a relentless ear-piercing screech whose sole purpose was to drag her out of bed to turn it off. She showered and dressed, tried to do something with her hair (she left it down in the end, adding a band to stop it falling in front of her face when she bent over), had a brief breakfast and left for work. She mused she should change the locks, in case Michael returned bent on some revenge or payback, but she dismissed the idea. For all his faults he was not a petty man, nor one prone to violence.

She glanced at the old houses down the street as she walked to the station. Like her home, they were all fairly nondescript terraced houses built a hundred years before the Death, their walls blackened from the exhaust smoke of a thousand vehicles and nearby factories that no longer exhaled poison into the sky. It certainly wasn't the most upmarket part of south London but it was okay, albeit slightly closer to the edge of the SafeZone than she would have liked. Faced with reduced policing and services capacity during and after the Death, the Government had sensibly targeted on focused areas to keep clear of crime and rubbish. The zones had increased in size and numbers slightly over the years, but there were still large areas of the cities and countryside which were now mostly left to nature to reclaim.

The rail station, however, gleaming with white stone freshly washed by the rain the night before, was a shining example of the Government's infrastructure projects initiated after the chaos. They were all perfectly designed, their purpose to get the maximum amount of people to work and back with the minimum expenditure of electricity. Although the rate had decreased in recent years, new stations were still popping up all over the country. It was a move that Kate agreed with wholeheartedly, especially as this particular one was well within walking distance, and the line stopped in Southampton near the power plant.

The station was fairly busy considering the early time of day, with the usual mix of people dressed in a variety of fashions, garnered from years of liberating wardrobes from empty houses and second-hand sales. But no matter the colours, cut or utility, there were three types of style for women as far as she could work out; frumpy, sophisticated and slutty. She tried for the second but always seemed to end up with the first once she looked in the mirror. She'd told Emily about the categories once and her sister had laughed at her, suggesting that Kate's version of provocative was the same as everyone else's normal, and perhaps she should dress like a streetwalker to rebalance things. Men, on the other hand, had it easy she thought; suits hadn't changed much in the last fifty years, and jeans and shirts were pretty much timeless anyway apart from the collars and tie widths.

So, dressed in a pair of slightly fading denim jeans and an old baggy sweater that was a size too big, she stood patiently at the platform, keeping a close eye out for the short man with the hat and umbrella who frequently took the same train as her. She had made the mistake once of telling him the time when he approached her and asked for it, which to him seemed to create some kind of social bond between them. Perhaps he was encouraged by the lack of a ring on her finger, or perhaps he was just lonely, but he had tried to strike up a conversation with her most days since. She'd ended up trying to avoid him, especially this morning when she had even less desire to talk to anyone. Luckily today he seemed to be running late, so she boarded the train alone and unmolested.

The houses and dirt of the city soon gave way to rolling fields full of oilseed rape and the biofuel plantations, as the train scythed a path through the countryside, the carriages gliding on the rails and sending sparks from the electric lines overhead. Kate stared blankly into the distance until her attention was caught by a collection of large information boards as they passed briskly by, giving those without a book something to read on the journey. She laughed to herself at the irony of the brand new 'REPAIR NOT REPLACE' poster, which showed a mother and daughter sitting around a fake open fire darning socks, while the husband could be seen outside from the window tinkering with something mechanical. There were a few advert boards about the upcoming LandFill Auctions-South, and finally a second Government board promoting self-sufficiency. The poster showed an endless field of yellow oilseed with wind turbines in the distance, composited next to a shoreline and tidal generator which looked suspiciously like the plant Kate worked at. To hammer home the message, a couple were seen tending their garden of vegetables in the foreground, whilst the chickens and a goat looked on.

The Government had championed self-sufficiency for decades now and seemed in no hurry to stop, for wastage was as big a crime as any when there were hungry mouths to feed. There were still some imports, of course, as some raw materials and goods could not be made in Britain; things like cigarettes, certain minerals used in construction, and, most importantly, tea. The wheels of bureaucracy were greased and powered by the leaf it seemed, the one luxury the British populace could not tolerate being without for long. Kate couldn't really understand why cigarettes remained so popular when smoking was considered LifeChoice, and any future disease that could be linked to it the responsibility of the afflicted to pay for. It created lots of tax income, however, which the Government could then spend on more discerning people and projects, without the extra burden of having to care for those who seemed determined to destroy themselves piecemeal.

Any further thoughts Kate had on the matter were shattered by the end door opening from the 'critical workers' carriage, as its inhabitants overspilled into hers. A couple of nurses were jabbering too loudly to each other about their portable phones, making the sure the rest of the travellers heard them and were suitably envious of their privileged access to technology. Mobile phones weren't banned, of course, but like everything else, the parts were expensive and difficult to come by unless the Government deemed them necessary for work. Critical workers were on call at all times in case of emergencies and needed to be contactable, which as far as Kate could work out was the only downside of being one. She went back to looking out of the window and tried her best to ignore them.

After what seemed like an age of half-overheard conversations, the train reached the coast and took a left past the docks and to the reception port, where every day hundreds of people disembarked from boats hoping to get into the country. The stark grey complex of high walls, long passageways with locked doors and barbed wire, was one of only four legitimate places in the country where visitors were allowed. The navy patrolled the British waters day and night, and anyone found deviating from the approved routes was shot on sight. It was a harsh but necessary measure, Kate thought. The main aim of the LockDown was to preserve bio-security and the society they had strived to create; the last thing they wanted was an influx of people with no sense of investment or responsibility, who would just take and not give in return. If they had something to offer then great, let them in and educate them. If not, then they should stay away and try to repair wherever it was they came from.

Everyone who entered the country was seen by at least two Reception Officers of either gender, who all had to agree on the application for them to pass through the large turnstile gates that welcomed them to England. It was a sensible idea designed to eliminate corruption, material or sexual, and was a highly sought after and respected critical position. Kate had wondered about applying for a job there in the past, but her education record highlighted her for work in other areas which put her at a disadvantage. Oh well, such was the way of things. She knew that almost all visitors were rejected on application and sent back on the boats they arrived on, their hand laser-barcoded with a serial number so the Reception Officers didn't have to waste time dealing with them when they tried again. She had heard rumours of some people burning or cutting off their own marked hands to give themselves another attempt, but wasn't sure she believed it. Surely people would never be so desperate they'd resort to self-mutilation for a one in a thousand chance of a different outcome next time?

A friendly female voice announced the power plant stop, and the train glided to a halt at the station terminal. It wasn't quite as shiny and new as the one near her house but it was clean and, most importantly, the trains ran to and from it on time and didn't break down. The Government knew the importance of the daily commute; society was a machine, and just like any other system, clockwork precision and reliability of the workforce being at the correct place at the correct time was paramount. No more was this true than the tidal power plant, a huge network of pipes, valves and turbines snaking their way from sea to shore, whilst the resulting electricity was transmitted from a vast array of pylons and cables to those who needed it. If God was an engineer then this was Intelligent Design in motion; order from chaos, entropy reversed.

The gas from the North Sea had run out years ago, and the reserves of coal belching out smoke from the huge chimneys that were old and decaying even before the Death, would soon follow. But even when the wind stopped blowing and the sails of the mills fell silent, the tide never stopped its flow of energy. The power plants had been one of the first large construction projects commissioned as the country clawed its way out of the catastrophe of the Death, giving hope and purpose to those that survived. That hope had been tainted by IES, of course, but the Lottery meant just enough remained for those who couldn't afford the treatment to function and work towards a better future.

The sea was a giver of life and power, but it also harboured the enemy; salt. The simple white compound that people put on their dinner to take away the taste of the food, played havoc with the metal pipes and fittings of the arteries of the plant, pitting and corroding them until they finally collapsed under the strain. It was a war without end, and as an Operations Specialist, Kate was one of the generals in the struggle. It was her job to make sure that sector A-9 ran smoothly; from the grills on the input pipes to the man-sized pressure control valves on the turbines and finally, the electricity entering the coils in the substation.

Every part of the pipeline relied on another, and all needed constant managing and troubleshooting in order to function. It was a role she was perfectly suited for, and her small corner of the universe ran better than anyone else's in the whole site network. A fact that even her boss begrudgingly admitted in their monthly assessment meetings. He had even offered Kate a promotion on several occasions, but she had declined. Advancement meant a sterile office instead of banks of equipment and displays, and even worse, managing people, with their lives and personal issues which had nothing to do with the job in hand. But most of all it represented a loss of control, independence and intuition, replaced by reliance and trust that someone else could do the job as well as she.

In the last year, there had been only one period of downtime and that had been out of her hands. A routine shut-down and maintenance of one of the input pipes had resulted in the downstream turbine failing and needing stripping down. The cause of the blockage had quickly become obvious, as red-stained water poured from the open seals. It was three bodies still mainly clad in diving suits, their limbs broken and contorted to impossible angles. They had waited for the shut-down (someone must have tipped them off for a price), and hoped to swim through the pipes and emerge on dry land unscathed and free. They'd either gotten lost in the maze, got stuck in the ever decreasing size of the pipes or it had simply taken longer to get through than they'd calculated. Whatever the cause the result was the same, the sudden surge in water pressure had forced them into the blades of the turbines and for them, that was the end of that. At least it would have been quick. Not for Kate, though, it had taken days to clean everything and get it working again, and the mass of paperwork she had to do afterwards had meant long nights working at home to catch up with it. All because some criminals wanted an easy shortcut into the country.

Fortunately, today was going better, and a lack of any major issues meant that morning break was more relaxed than usual. The water at work tasted odd and so she always brought her own tea from home in a silver-coloured vacuum flask, much to the baffled amusement of her co-workers. No one had asked her about how things were going with Michael and she hadn't volunteered any information. In fact, none of them even knew about the Lottery win or the eventual transfer, as the last thing she wanted was more opinions or unqualified punditry on how she should do things.

She was even more relieved as today one of the women from Accounts was throwing a 'no-vitro lottery' party at lunchtime, as they had just flipped over the maximum age for eligibility in the draw. It had become somewhat of a fad in recent times, similar to a divorce party or over-enthusiastic wake after a funeral, where people celebrated melancholy times as a way of over-compensating for loss, or to seek condolence and sympathy. It was an open invitation but Kate doubted she'd be missed if she didn't attend. She had always felt like someone on the outside looking in, and the others did nothing to alter that feeling. It was fine, she preferred it like that anyway.

Apart from a broken dial on a release valve, the rest of the day passed without incident. Kate even remembered to keep eye contact with her boss when he burst in asking for some data on turbine nine, although his gaze kept wandering down her body, she noticed, rather than paying attention to her responses to his questions. Most of the people in her area of work were male and even after seven years working there, she was still a novelty item to most of them. Looking through a self-critical eye, she thought she was pretty enough and very few people had naturally red hair these days, which gave her a slightly exotic look. Although she had maintained her looks and figure from her twenties through to her early thirties, there were certainly more attractive and probably more willing girls in the Admin department her boss could spend the day leering at. Still, if it became an issue she would deal with it, she just hoped he was big enough of a man not to let it interfere with her assessment scores when the time came.

*

The house hadn't magically cleaned itself or repaired any broken bits of equipment when Kate returned home, so she attempted to tackle the aftermath of the previous night by starting on the washing up she'd left scattered around the kitchen. She'd barely finished running the hot water when there was a knock at the door. She presumed it was Michael wanting something from the house that he'd forgotten to previously pack. After all, there wasn't anything else left to argue about now.

But it wasn't, it was a policeman.
He was there to tell her that Emily was dead.

The slope

Victor's temporary office wasn't the most opulent in the country, but it was large and spacious, with plenty of wall space to hang the paintings he'd amassed over the last twenty years. Most were Biblical Renaissance images on broad canvases, obtained on his travels when he was negotiating to open clinics and IES treatment centres around the city states of Europe. Well, those that still had enough of an economy left to bother with anyway. The paintings were a result of each town wanting to outshine the other with their gifts and platitudes, all of which were gratefully and enthusiastically received.

He had been entranced by the images and use of colour the moment he laid eyes on a painting in Vienna. The canvas was a three-panel epic showing Eden, Judgement Day and a fiery Hell, complete with Satan eagerly welcoming the eternally damned. The triptych took pride of place on the wall opposite his desk, which was currently buried under a pile of unread scientific papers and half-empty cups of cold tea. Even his picture of Susanna had fallen over from its fold-out stand, a situation he quickly rectified with a silent apology. He still missed her warmth every day, but especially now when her practical nature and way of seeing the big picture always provided comfort and a way forward. His passion for life, for anything really, had died that day too. He wondered what she would tell him to do today when he was having difficulty concentrating on his work, with the funeral of the girl coming up and the investigation still ongoing. He'd even moved up from Head Office in London to the Highpoint clinic to show willing and a spirit of cooperation with the authorities, even though in reality there was little he could do to help them.

There was a brief knock on the door and his new PA entered. He'd got tired of Recruitment's recommendations and had chosen this one himself; a large and fierce middle-aged woman called Janet, with nicotine-stained teeth and breath to match. She'd quickly acquired the nickname 'The Ogre' around the clinic, but her presence had already cut foot traffic to his office in half and her work was frighteningly efficient.

"Sorry to disturb you Dr Pearson, but there're some people here to see you and they won't take no for an answer. Guess they don't have phones where they're from, to, I don't know, arrange appointments or anything."

Her bluntness was refreshing and Victor was quickly learning she had a brutal turn of phrase. "Who is it?" he asked, dreading the answer.

"One of them looks like someone crossed the Cheshire Cat with a slug and poured it into a suit. The other one looks like some generic army meathead."

Well, the former certainly sounded like the politician at least. "Okay thank you, show them in please."

Caden strode in and shook Victor by the hand vigorously, while the other man stayed back at the doorway, chewing gum too loudly. What did he want this time?

"Pearson, good to see you again. Have you met Parker my security head?" said Caden, smiling while casually waving at the man to dismiss him before Victor had a chance to respond. "No hard feelings about last time I hope?"

"Of course not," Victor lied, pulling his hand away. Either Caden didn't pick up on it or he didn't care enough to make an issue about it. "What can I help you with today? I sent off all of the information as you requested."

"Oh yes, that's all good. We took the liberty and put some of our people in undercover to try to get the nurses to gossip, but they refused. You have some fine and loyal staff here Pearson, you should be proud."

Victor tried to hide his rage at this new revelation. How dare they leave him out of the loop on events in his own company? "As I said before, they know where their priorities lie, and the original source of the leak has been sanctioned. You should have told me about the agents."

Caden chuckled playfully. "Well they wouldn't have been undercover then would they?" he said, as he sat down and gestured to Victor that he do the same. "Nevertheless, it's all water under the bridge now and they caught the man who killed the girl. One of the security guards wasn't it? I actually wanted to talk to about something else."

Victor sat behind his desk, and roughly stacked the paper up into a loose pile. "Yes, a man called Sebastian, the other guards in the search party heard a shot and found him by the body. Apparently it was accidental, but the police are still questioning him." He had no doubt that Caden knew more than he was letting on about the incident, and that poor Sebastian was going to have to take one for the team on this one. Presumably, the accidental plea was the best thing on offer, and Caden's unreadable expression offered no suggestions. *He must be brilliant at poker* thought Victor, who was starting to realise he had seriously underestimated him on their first encounter. Caden had suckered him, playing the young inexperienced card whilst Victor had strutted about and left himself open to attack. It was not a mistake he would make again. "So, why are you here?"

"Screening."

Victor let out a sigh. Not this again. "I went through this with the Minister several years ago. I thought we had an understanding on this."

"We do, we do," replied Caden, holding up his hands in a gesture of surrender. "We're not talking some evil dark eugenics project here, just a quick screening of donor material to check for common disease genes. Imagine how much we can help society and also save taxpayers' money if we can filter out degenerative conditions before they ever become a burden?"

It sounded like a perfectly reasonable request, a good idea even. With resources so stretched and the population dwindling, why waste time and resources on the birth of a child who would never be a productive adult, if they even made it that far? But Victor had seen this road travelled by others too many times in his career. Scientists and doctors finding themselves in places and situations they never imagined, or would even believe from their high moral code at the beginning. It was a journey of small steps to be sure, each one pushing a boundary away slightly harder, and always accompanied with reasoned self-debate on why it wasn't such a big change, why their integrity was still intact and why their reputation would be left untarnished. A quick subtle slant on the conclusions to support the sponsor's views, or putting on a uniform just for show at meetings to gain favour with those in charge. Victor had done some very unreasonable things on his rise to the top, but those were usually business decisions and mostly only affected other unreasonable people. He was always surprised at himself when his slightly warped sense of morality sprang into life as it did now, especially given D336. Some things couldn't be helped and pragmatic choices sometimes had to be made.

"Yes, sure we can do that," he replied with a sarcastic tone, "or how about we screen out any female with BRCA mutations or sperm with specific CFTR haplotypes, you know, 'just in case'? Or go the whole hog and racially profile them all?"

Caden locked his fingers together and leant forward in his chair. "Putting words in someone's mouth? You should get a job in politics, Pearson. No one's talking about anything like that. We don't subscribe to the 'State of hate', as well you know, it becomes insular and self-defeating after a while. As with all things, there will be a line in the sand, of course."

"The problem with lines in the sand is that the tide comes in and washes them away," Victor retorted. "Anyway, it's a pretty moot point as I told your boss. We're not exactly overflowing with spare stocks and I can't start throwing them out based on percentages. We do a trisomy 21 screen and a small panel of dominant disease mutations already. There's just not enough time to test for everything before we need to implant, as we can't freeze infected embryos for storage."

Caden seemed to take the information on board, at least. "Well, as I said, something to think about. Nice paintings by the way." He pointed to one to the side of them, "Is that the Tower of Babel? Interesting choice, I thought you'd have a giant statue of Demeter or something."

Victor sat back as Caden laughed at his own joke. "It reminds me not to reach too far."

"Well I congratulate you on your collection, it's very impressive. Where did you get it all from, by the way?"

"Thank you," replied Victor feeling a flush of pride. "Here and there. It's amazing what a bit of power can get you."

"Influence," Caden corrected him. "Influence gets you paintings. Power gets you galleries." He stood up and adjusted his tie. "Anyway, I should be going, thank you for our little chat. Oh, don't forget my wife is booked in for our first pre-appointment meeting next week. It would be nice for you to greet her personally and answer any questions she may have."

"Of course," Victor agreed, rising out of his chair. "I'll see you then."

Caden got halfway to the door and suddenly stopped, turning his head towards Victor. "Pearson, have you ever heard of the King's Shilling?"

"No," Victor admitted, feeling his hands start to go clammy again.

"It was used by the English Navy several hundred years ago for recruiting sailors. You took the shilling and you agreed to serve, and take the glory and responsibility that came with it."

"Oh yes I remember now," said Victor, dragging out a memory from somewhere in his brain. "Not everyone did it willingly if I recall, or were drunk and unwitting when the press gangs came to town."

"Indeed," said Caden, with a thin smile. "Of course, that's not something anyone could accuse an informed and intelligent person such as yourself of."

Victor felt like a cow being lead down a slaughterhouse alley to the doorway with no exit. Wherever he tried to turn there was an electric prod pointed at him, compelling him towards the inevitable. "What's your point, Caden?"

"My point Pearson," Caden replied, all pretence at friendliness now gone, "is that there is change coming. The old breed is fading away, those too shackled to the past, those who remember the time before the Death and are too constrained by how things used to be. Still tiptoeing around the edge of the pond, scared to dive in and embrace the water because it might be cold or dark. Their time is almost at an end. The future belongs to my age, the next generation, and when we inherit power you might want to think a bit harder what side you are on."

"I'm part of the old breed too, you know," snapped Victor.

Caden snorted. "Oh, you've got a couple of decades left in you yet before Dignity comes calling I'm sure. You've done very well out of our arrangement, Pearson. I'm sure you've squirrelled away a bit for your retirement past the usual limit."

Now it was Victor's time to let out a laugh, although he found nothing amusing about the situation, "Scientists don't retire, we just work fewer hours."

"In any case, remember where your loyalties lie." Caden's slight frame relaxed a little, a cue Victor was quickly learning that meant he was putting his politician's mask back on. The CEO nodded, wiping the sweat from his hands under the desk.

"Those paintings are the wrong way around," observed Caden, pointing at the triptych as he turned to leave for real this time. "Eden should be on the right. Hell, Judgement Day, Eden. Matches the chronology that way."

Victor watched him go in silence, then stared at the canvases. No, they were definitely correct as they were.

Dust

Kate stared at the clock on the wall as the minute hand softly clicked over to five past the hour. Watchmakers were taught that time was a constant, a clockwork precision of gears and springs unwavering throughout eternity, but they were wrong. Time was an illusion of the mind, the brain's attempt to make sense of events from the chaos of signals and stimuli it received each day. It was also elastic, stretching out to infinity for the young, but condensing and becoming brittle with age. At the moment, it was nearly at a standstill, and she wished more than anything it would speed up or, even better, skip to tomorrow.

After spending ten minutes in the morning brushing her teeth until the blood in the basin shook her out of her trance, she'd tried to busy herself doing mindless chores around the house. It hadn't worked, the clock steadfastly refusing to comply and filling her head with pain and unwanted feelings. The house was silent, apart from the soft patter of rain against the windows, which didn't help either and left nothing to drown out her thoughts. She'd turned off the radio hours ago; music was associative, bringing old memories to the fore without warning or chance to prepare for their impact, and she wanted nothing to remind her of today.

The cat, who had come in again seeking shelter from the rain, stopped washing its leg, suddenly pricked up its ears and ran upstairs just pre-empting the knock at the door. It was Michael, carrying a wreath of flowers and a sympathetic smile. He had come over every day after he'd heard about Emily, when it hit the news a couple of days after the event. She hadn't told anyone about what had happened up to that point and had gone back to work the next day, thinking that if she didn't say anything then perhaps it wasn't real, just a strange figment of imagination or a dream she would soon wake from. But then the news reports had started on the radio, shattering her denial and making her violently sick in the kitchen sink. It had been the limit of her emotional response so far, apart from a guilty throb of feeling sorry for herself. She hadn't managed to cry or get angry despite her best efforts,

Emily was dead and there was no sense or justification she could make of that fact. Her mood this morning hadn't been helped either by the letter from IVS that had arrived late the day before, callously informing her that due to the death of the designated recipient the winning ticket had been returned to her for re-use.

"How are you doing?" asked Michael, placing the flowers on the table as he walked in.

His concern was genuine, all past grievances and transgressions forgotten for now. He was a good person Kate was realising too late. They had been together for over three years but she had never truly known him, nor in hindsight made any real attempt to. He was good company before all the shouting had started, someone to share experiences and secrets with, but she couldn't hand-on-heart say she had ever loved him. He had been a good choice from a limited selection, as although her looks and long fiery hair had given her plenty of admirers, they tended to lose interest when they realised she didn't have the girly and feminine demeanour they were looking for. Emily, on the other hand, just needed to twiddle her locks in her fingers and look bashful, and the men would come flocking to her and stay as long as she wanted them to. It was a gift that Kate was somewhat in awe of. *No one wanted to pick the fruit that had been left on the tree for too long* her mother had once told her long ago. Realising that time was lightly starting to make its presence felt, Kate had gone for the least-worst option when the opportunity had presented itself.

Perhaps if she had tried harder back then she might have wanted children with Michael after all, and the Lottery result would be a dream come true rather than a poisoned chalice. Emily would have never been at the clinic and would still be alive, shooting envious looks as Kate's abdomen blossomed with new life. It was a road not travelled, though, a thread cut a lifetime ago that no amount of wishing or regret would make come to pass. "About as well as can be expected," Kate replied, avoiding his gaze. "How's Becca?" She regretted asking the question as soon as the words left her mouth. It wasn't an accusation and she hoped to God he didn't take it as such. She couldn't handle another argument, not today.

"She's fine. How did you know?" was his confused response. He started to continue but Kate cut him off.

"It doesn't matter, sorry for prying. I'm glad you came."

"The car will be here soon with James and Rita, you need to get changed and ready."

Kate, realising she was still in her nightclothes, let out a sigh and felt even worse. She hadn't even spoken to James or his mother since the news, she couldn't handle anyone crying down the phone at her when she asked how they were. The longer she left it the worse it got, making her think it was better to avoid contact entirely and figure things out on her own, although that didn't seem to be working out particularly well either.

The short and silent journey in the rusting black limo from her house to the crematorium had been almost unbearable, but Kate was glad that at least the service wasn't hours out in the countryside. Emily had spent most of the time working away at the farm, but her husband James had remained in London where he worked as a scribe for the Government, racing to recover and archive to paper historical and cultural information from ageing and failing computer drives. It was an uninteresting job for an uninteresting person thought Kate, nothing more than regurgitating someone else's ideas or opinions and putting them in a box, where no one else apart from the odd academic would ever see them. He had spent the entire journey sobbing into a handkerchief whilst his mother, a tall spindly woman with harsh features, comforted him with hugs and kind words. Kate stared out of the window through the rain, feeling awkward and inappropriately attired. The only black dress she owned was a rarely worn party frock cut too short at both ends for such an occasion, so she'd just put on the darkest skirt and sweater she could find. It still looked like she was just heading out to the shops, though, and hadn't made much of an effort. The look Rita, resplendent in a large dark hat with a black crow feather stuck on the side, had shot her when they picked her up had confirmed that beyond any doubt.

The streets were nearly deserted, the rain forcing everyone inside or cowering in boarded-up shop doorways. She saw one woman up ahead struggling with a pushchair on the uneven pavement until a wheel got stuck in a hole, at which point a man came to help her. A few seconds later though he abruptly recoiled in revulsion and scampered off down a nearby alley, leaving the mother shouting at him between choking tears. When their car passed by Kate understood why. The poor child was horribly disfigured; its face and arms covered in swollen and vascularised red tumours. She'd seen this before on adverts for Victor Pearson's company in the newspaper, it was a common side-effect of unlicensed IES treatment and IVF from illegal backstreet clinics.

The alternative clinics were much cheaper, of course, and the treatments even worked occasionally, but the consequences of a botched gene repair could be disastrous for both the child and the parents. Getting the procedure done was not against the law in itself (it was only illegal to run such a clinic), as the Government sensibly didn't want to punish seemingly desperate people. It was, however, considered LifeChoice, and made you ineligible for approved therapy when they inevitably found you out at the first treatment. Plus, with no support for when things went wrong, the parents were often unable to meet the hospital bills and had the impossible choice between giving their child Dignity, or watching it suffer through painful illness and death. Kate couldn't understand why people would be stupid and selfish enough to take such a risk, but for today, at least, she felt sorry for those that had.

As the car reached its destination, Michael tried to hold her hand for support but she impatiently brushed it aside. Kate had wanted the morning and the journey over as quickly as possible, but now the time was finally here she would have given anything for the clock to stop forever. The others got out to mix with the rest of the congregation by the front entrance, but she stayed in the car until Michael returned. It was time, and she needed to go.

The crematorium was a converted medieval stone gothic church replete with large stain-glassed windows and towers with gargoyles at the corner, who were currently spouting the rain onto the path below. The only thing that betrayed its change in function from the outside was the large steel chimneys crudely bolted onto the clock tower, that ran to the multitude of ovens down in the crypts. The furnaces had worked night and day during the first few months of the Death, before the corpses piled up and overwhelmed them. It was a pattern that repeated itself as quickly as the Government and army could convert and build new plants to cope with the load. There were churches and services for the pious, and factory production lines for the secular. For a while at least.

Most were shut down now; turned back to places of worship, smelting plants or making mechanical spare parts, with just a few remaining scattered throughout the city, a remnant of a different age.

Kate walked slowly towards the arched entrance, her seldom-worn heeled shoes digging into her ankles and threatening to topple her over. She could hear the organ music emanating through the narthex, calling to her and drawing her towards the inevitable. She wanted to run, be somewhere, anywhere else but there was no point. The tide had brought her here through the open grill and narrowing pipes, and the roar of the spinning turbines awaited at the end. She got halfway through the doorway and the enormity of it all finally hit, wave upon wave of emotion crashing against her, the water electrified with memories of tragedy. Her mother, her father and now her sister were all gone, the profound sense of loss and grief flooding her body and threatening to pull her under, as she begged the absent tears to come and release her from the pain. Michael was there to catch her as she stumbled, his hand now gratefully received, helping her to the front pew as the rest of the flock looked on in silence unaware of her plight.

Time had finally granted her the morning's wish, and the service rushed by in a blur as the rain gave way to rare sunshine. The preacher's sermon was typically over-friendly and over-familiar, which grated slightly, but the words were kind and delivered with sentiment as the curtains slowly drew around the coffin. It was only afterwards in the memorial garden, a quiet green space full of cherry trees and weathered headstones, that Kate's senses returned enough to talk to anyone. She realised that she didn't know most of the people there, and they didn't seem to know who she was either, judging by the general lack of interest in her. Were they Emily's friends, colleagues or just curious bystanders wanting a day out? One of them definitely didn't fit. A rather scruffy-looking man in a long coat, his features slightly obscured by a mop of unkempt black hair, was loitering slightly away from the others, an unlit cigarette in his hand. He seemed to be trying to catch the eye of James to talk to him, but the opportunity kept eluding him as the queue of well-wishers grew. Kate never found out what happened next, though, as a young woman approached her.

"Hello. I'm sorry, are you Kate?"

Kate nodded. "How did you know my sister? I'm sorry I don't recognise you."

"I thought so, she told me all about you." The woman suddenly seemed to notice Kate's quizzical and increasingly impatient look. "Oh sorry, my name's Emma. I was Emily's care nurse at the clinic. I'm so sorry about what happened to her."

"What did happen to her?" Kate asked, sharply.

The nurse paused for slightly too long before answering. "We don't know. The police told us the guard said his gun went off accidentally when he was trying to fetch her."

"I don't understand why she was out there in the first place," Kate replied, feeling the anger rising within her.

Another long pause. Emma was clearly regretting having started this conversation and was starting to look flustered. "I'm sorry I can't tell you that either."

Can't or won't? thought Kate. She considered pushing Emma further but the nurse interjected.

"Dr Pearson is here too somewhere, perhaps he could help you?" said Emma as she scanned around, putting her hand to her brow to block out the sun. "Ah yes, there he is, talking to Kurt," she said, turning and pointing clearly to Emily's husband.

"Kurt? Don't you mean James?" asked Kate, rather confused.

"Oh! Emily kept mentioning someone called Kurt," replied Emma looking slightly embarrassed. "She said was glad that after this she wouldn't have to spend any more time with him, but he seems okay to me. Sorry, I must have been mistaken." The nurse tailed off at the last part, perplexed by her own apparent misunderstanding of the situation. Kate looked over the nurse's shoulder to the tall bald man in the expensive-looking black suit, and realised he was turning to leave. She'd seen enough of the IVS leaflets to know it was him, and this might be her only chance. She quickly barged past the young nurse without another word and headed off in pursuit, calling out his name as he headed off towards the exit and the car parked on the road. He was almost at the gates when Kate caught up with him, grabbing him by the shoulder and making him turn to face her.

"Who the hell are you?" he demanded, curtly brushing her grip away.

"Why did my sister die?" asked Kate, ignoring his question. The CEO looked shocked for an instant and then clasped her hand, which Kate quickly withdrew.

"Forgive my rudeness, this must be a harrowing time for you and your family. It's Kate isn't it? You were the angel Emily spoke of who gave her the most important gift in the world?"

Kate had been called many things in her life by her sister, but 'angel' was never one of them. She presumed this man had made it up to try and diffuse the situation. Still, at least he knew who she was, unlike most of the other guests. "I have no family left thanks to your clinic, Dr Pearson. Why is my sister dead?"

"I'm so sorry for your loss," he replied, shaking his head. "Apparently she was killed by one of our security guards in a dreadful accident."

"That's how she died," rebutted Kate, pointing her finger and making him step back. "Why is she dead? Why was she even out there in the first place?"

Pearson let out a sigh and looked genuinely sorrowful for a brief instant. "To be honest, I have no idea. It may be that she had a bad reaction to one of the muscle-relaxants we gave her, to help her sleep and prep her for the start of treatment. They have been known to cause hallucinations and feelings of paranoia in very rare cases."

"Why wasn't she watched then?"

"You strike me as an intelligent woman, Kate, so I won't try to placate you. We can't account for every single possibility or event. Nothing is without risk, your sister knew this and she went ahead willingly nonetheless. It was a tragedy and all of us at IVS will feel the burden of the guilt and the consequences, but it was an accident, and for that I am truly sorry." He bowed ever so slightly, turned and walked towards the car, wiping his hands down the trousers of his suit.

"WHY IS MY SISTER DEAD?" shouted Kate, shaking with rage and heading after him again, but she'd only got a few steps before Rita caught up with her, blocking her path.

"What are you doing?" the woman demanded, straightening her hat and trying in vain to get her breath back. "You're causing a scene and embarrassing yourself. And us. The great Victor Pearson comes here in person to share his condolences for my son's loss and you start a fight with him? What's wrong with you, girl?"

Before Kate could answer, Michael also appeared and took her gently by the arm, leading her away. "I'm sorry, it's been a terrible day for all of us," he said to Rita and the party in general, as they walked towards the end of the grounds. "We'll leave you all in peace now. Sorry if Kate's grief got in the way of your social climbing." They got to the iron gates at the entrance to the garden but the car and its occupant were long gone. "Are you okay?" he asked Kate, who shook her head.

"I want to go home," she stated. Home was familiar and safe, and she'd had enough of strangers and unwelcome emotions for today.

"Okay, there's an underground station not too far from here," Michael said, looking up at the sky which had begun to get dark and grey again. The wind had begun flicking up the leaves dropped from the nearby trees, suggesting that rain was not far behind.

"I'll walk, I need to clear my head," she replied. "Feel free to go if you want."

"Don't be silly, it's over an hour's walk from here and it's going to rain again soon."

"Good," said Kate, who headed off briskly, before stopping to remove her shoes and throw them into the road. Michael stopped to pick them up and followed her.

They walked in silence for nearly half an hour, following the route of the funeral car that Kate had memorised on the way out. The rain had returned with increased vigour, soaking them within minutes but Kate didn't care, although glancing across to a miserable-looking Michael he didn't seem to share that sentiment. Her mind was caught in an endless cycle trying to process the series of events that triggered Emily's death, but no matter how she replayed things in her head one thing didn't fit, and without that she couldn't interpret anything else.

"It doesn't make sense," she declared, more to herself than anyone in particular.

"What, getting soaked out here instead of sitting in a nice dry train carriage? You're right," said Michael, without a hint of satire.

"No, the security guard. Why did he have his gun out?" she asked rhetorically. Michael shrugged his shoulders, making Kate wonder if he hadn't thought about it or simply didn't care.

"They said it was an accident," he sighed, "you're going to have to believe them if you're going to deal with this."

"That's not the point," she replied, ignoring his second statement. "They said he shot her by accident. They could have said he was mad and shot her on purpose, or that he shot her after a struggle due to her delusions but they didn't. They said he was just trying to get her back to the clinic. So why did he have his gun out?"

"I don't know," admitted Michael, "but I do know you need to think about something else for a while." He knew her too well it seemed, how she got obsessively stuck on a problem and would omit sleep or sometimes forget to eat until she beat it into submission. "I don't want your next boyfriend to come to your house and see a big crazy-wall in your bedroom, it's not a good look."

Kate was surprised how deeply the words *next boyfriend* cut into her. Michael had moved on with his life and adopted the 'caring male friend' role, whereas she hadn't even begun to process their break-up yet. Still, she had to smile at his crazy-wall concept. She could just imagine herself sticking photos and scraps of information to a board, frantically joining them up with bits of string into a spider's web as the clues piled up. She tried to stop thinking about the gun but something else was also bothering her. "Have you ever heard of someone called Kurt?"

"Don't think so, why?"

"No reason, just something that nurse said," she replied, as casually as she could. Michael was clearly not interested in her so-called conspiracy theories and any further pressing would just irritate him.

The rest of the long walk home was mainly silent, punctuated with Michael trying to make conversation with fond and amusing memories of Emily, like the time they had all gone out to dinner and she had gotten so drunk on cider she passed out head-first into her dessert. Kate smiled and acknowledged the anecdote, but her head was somewhere else completely now. She made her living spotting patterns and predicting outcomes; how a sticky valve in one sector changed the voltage in a relay twenty metres away, or determining the optimal path of the water through the hundreds of pipes depending on the tide strength. But no matter how she tried to fit things together they fell apart. She was still deep in thought when they finally arrived at the house, dripping wet and shivering.

"I should go," Michael stated, looking at his watch. "Becca will be wondering where I've got to."

"At least come in and dry off before you catch a cold," said Kate, as she opened the door. "You still have lots of clothes here you can change into."

"That's actually not a bad idea," he remarked, before stepping over the threshold into the small hallway that adjoined the lounge, narrowly avoiding treading on a letter before picking it up. "What's this?" he enquired, turning the letter over in his fingers and noticing the stamp-mark in the corner. "It's got a police stamp on it."

Kate took it from him and ripped the top off urgently. "It's the police and coroner reports on Emily's murder. I requested a copy when they released the body."

"Why the hell would you want that?" He rolled his eyes, signifying that he'd answered his own question. He paused while she took out the letter and scanned through it. "So, what does it say?"

She handed the letter to him. "Read for yourself."

"Well, it seems pretty straightforward. 'We confirm that Emily Palmer died from a gunshot wound to the head, which caused a catastrophic haemorrhage and brain death, which was instantaneous.' That's something at least, that she didn't suffer," Michael said in a comforting tone as he continued to scan down the letter. "No toxins, poisons or illegal drugs were found in the body after chemical analysis. You see, it was as they said, an accident."

"There's no mention of the muscle-relaxants that Dr Pearson mentioned, though, that he said could have made her act strangely?" asked Kate which invoked another sigh from Michael.

"No, there isn't," he confirmed, "perhaps they didn't bother testing or reporting for routine medical drugs. There's nothing else, apart from a note about the presence of human chorionic gonadotropin and high progesterone levels as a result of the IVF treatment."

"What was that last part again?" asked Kate with wide-eyed interest. Something about that didn't sound right either.

Michael put the letter down on a chair as Kate stared at the stack of papers on the table. "Kate, you can't go obsessing over everything looking for something that's simply not there."

"Like you did with our imaginary children?" she snapped back, annoyed that he wasn't listening to her. Something was trying to worm its way to the front of her thoughts, something she'd read.

"Nothing ever changes does it," said Michael sadly, shaking his head. "Good luck Kate, I hope everything works out for you."

Kate was frantically searching through the pile of papers on the table and scattering them on the floor as he left the house still in his wet clothes. She didn't even register the door closing behind him.

Ah, that was it! Kate extracted the booklet from IVS she'd been sent after the Lottery win and flicked urgently through it, searching for the section on body changes. She focused her attention on the charts showing the processes and hormonal levels as the patient was prepared for the treatment, and afterwards as the foetus developed. Emily had been at the clinic for less than two days and would have only just started the initial treatment. According to the chart, Emily should have just begun the week of Follicle Stimulating Hormone injections. Gonadotropin wasn't produced at the levels the coroner found until after blastocyst implantation into the uterus, five to six days after the IVF procedure. *But the IES virus kills the embryo by day four?* thought Kate, now more confused than ever.

And then it suddenly all made perfect sense; why her sister ran, and why they killed her. Emily was already pregnant.

Little monsters

It was always the same dream; a memory buried deep in his subconscious like a tick, its pulsating black body feasting on sorrow and fear until it surfaced and expelled its stomach into his sleep. He was nine years old again and back at the airport, holding tightly to his mother with one hand and grasping his favourite Azami book with the other. His father went on slightly ahead, winding his way through the throng and clearing a path for them. The screening station outside had been abandoned after being overwhelmed by the surging crowds, and given the choice between firing at desperate people or retreating, the masked soldiers had wisely chosen the latter. As a result, the terminal was in chaos as an incomprehensible voice blurted over the public address system.

The barriers designed to separate and funnel the passengers to the check-in desks had long since been displaced and knocked down, causing arguments and fights as the groups of travellers jostled for position in the queues. His father finally got close enough to one of the big television screens to find the correct zone and directed them ahead and to the right with an urgent hand gesture. They had got held up in the traffic when a speeding driver, desperate to get his flight and weaving erratically through the congestion, had lost control of his car and crashed into a truck a few hundred yards in front of them. They had gone past the wreck with his father cursing the delay, the growing red patch on the airbag giving the only clue to the fate of the driver that no one had stopped to help.

The news reports had said that LockDown was likely to start today, causing panic amongst the remaining tourists and expats, and creating an unstoppable tsunami of vehicles racing towards the London airports. His father had used his business connections to get three tickets back to the United States at enormous cost, but it had apparently been worth it. They had been in England for nearly a year, a lifetime for a child but a blink of an eye for his parents, who now more than anything wanted to be home to the comfort of the familiar. It didn't matter where they flew to, any city would do as long as there were enough people left to keep the airport open.

Their plan of travelling light and beating the throngs to Security had backfired when they found the automatic machines either out of order or smashed beyond repair by a frustrated mob, so they eventually managed to get to the queue just as the staff arrived to set up the check-in desk and bag drops. His mother had begun to frantically pace up and down, counting the people in front of them, trying to gauge whether they would fit and ignoring his father's pleas to calm down.

"Those bastards oversold the flights as usual," she declared loudly. "We'll never all fit on the plane!" This caused a ripple of discontent through the surrounding group who agreed and added voices of dissent.

"Be quiet Mary!" his father commanded as softly as he could. "You're causing a panic and this isn't the time for one of your episodes. Don't worry, we'll all get on."

She let out a small scream and headed off towards the information desk, returning a few minutes later looking even more agitated and scratching at her arms. "The bitch at the desk just told me to queue up and wait my turn with everyone else. After we get out of here I'm making sure she gets fired. I just want to get out of here, I need to get home to Mum and Dad. Carl, I need to get home now!"

An old man standing behind them piped in. "I don't understand why there's the rush, surely after Lockdown they'll still let people leave?"

"I doubt the pilots want to get stuck away from home, though," his father replied, "and the airlines don't want to lose their planes." The old man gestured in agreement and fell silent once more.

There was suddenly a roar of angry voices, starting from one end of the bank of desks and rapidly flowing to their section, as the television screens above the walls all began to flicker and change from showing a green 'on time' to a yellow 'delayed' for flight after flight.

And then one after the other throughout the terminal, they all turned to red.

"Attention please!" came a voice over the PA system, as the airline staff grabbed what they could and ran at speed towards the safety of the secure access door at the back the desks. "Please be aware all airports and other entry and exit points out of the country are now closed by order of the government. Please return to your homes. If you have nowhere to go, please form an orderly queue in the main lobby and wait for processing."

There was a brief pause of silence, then all hell broke loose. People shouting, running, trampling over each other in all directions to race to the lobby or demand answers from the remaining and ashen-looking airline staff. He realised he couldn't see his mother and suddenly felt very scared, before spying her a short distance away. But something was very wrong. Her eyes were wild and wide open, and she was screaming and screaming about getting home, tearing chunks of her hair out with bloodying fingers and nails whilst looking frantically around her. He felt someone take his hand and turned to see his father.

"Come on Victor, we need to go now," his father said calmly, leading him away.

"What about Mommy?" he cried, pointing out where he had seen her and feeling stinging tears rolling down his cheeks.

"Mommy has gone, it's just us now."

***

As the dream started to dissolve, Victor could hear his name being called in the distance, getting louder and more urgent as he stirred from his sleep and into consciousness. For a second, he felt a brief panic of displacement, before realising he was still in his office at his desk and that he'd failed to go home last night. He had not slept soundly these last few days and decided he might as well work rather than stewing and churning in a sweaty bed alone, instead letting exhaustion and alcohol decide when it was time to stop. He soon located the source calling his name; it was his intercom flashing urgently red at him. "Yes?" he asked, trying to locate his suit jacket and tie, and narrowly avoiding knocking over the half-empty bottle of whisky on his desk.

"Oh good, you're awake. I came in earlier but you were passed out at your desk so I thought I'd leave you to it," Janet said curtly. "I stopped the cleaners coming in and vacuuming around you. Anyway, that politician just logged in at front security with his wife so I thought I'd better give you a heads-up."

Victor looked at his watch; it was 08:30. "Why didn't you wake -?" he began to demand but Janet cut him off mid-sentence.

"I got someone from HR to rush out earlier and pick up some clean clothes for you. And some breath mints. They'll be here in five minutes, which gives you fifteen to get freshened up and changed, five more to walk down and meet the visitors at reception, and still be a few minutes early to give them the impression you are busy but have made a special effort to meet them as soon as possible. Oh, and before I forget, I put the information on that man you asked about on your desk."

Victor spied the small file balanced on the top of his pile of research papers. "Thank you, Janet, I could kiss you sometimes you know that?"

"You'd be amazed how many people say that to me," the woman replied without a hint of irony.

Janet's timing was impeccable, and at 08:55 Victor came striding through the door to Alpha reception in a freshly pressed suit to find Caden and his wife sitting in some low cushioned chairs, chatting and drinking tea. Both of them rose to their feet in unison as he approached which pleased him immensely; this was his show and here, despite Caden's thinly disguised threats and attempts to undermine him, he was still king.

"Pearson! A delight to see you again," exclaimed Caden, obviously trying a bit too hard to paper over the friction of their last encounter. "I don't believe you've met my wife Rowena?"

"A pleasure," replied Victor smoothly, gently taking and shaking her hand. Rowena was probably one of the prettiest girls he had ever seen; a beautiful face with long blonde hair in loose curls and a youthful innocent expression. The picture was perfectly complemented by a slim hourglass figure, all slipped into a blue shift dress.

"Rowena is the daughter of Wayne Kirkland. We met at a presentation party two years ago and fell for each other there and then," explained the politician, as his wife smiled sweetly at Victor and nodded.

It had always amazed Victor that whatever the world threw at it, 'high society' always seemed to prevail and flourish, greeting people into their circle with open arms that a few years previously they would have crossed the road to avoid. Victor had met Kirkland only briefly a few times at various functions, but like most people knew the name. Wayne, a common northern scrap dealer had made a massive fortune since LockDown from a single idea. He was the first to realise that the cars of the time, reliant on computers to even start in the morning, were going to stop working when the complicated and imported circuits perished and corroded with age. He had therefore started buying up any deserted breaking yards he could find (and rumour had it, intimidating the owners of those that were still occupied to sell up), stripping out the engines from vehicles from the 1980s and 90s and charging a premium to retrofit them to the modern cars of the day. After a while, he had started making new combustion units under exclusive licence from the Government and his fortune was assured; there probably wasn't a car running today which didn't have a Kirkland engine in it. Where Victor had borrowed heavily in those early days, and consequently surrendered ultimate control of his company to others, Kirkland had done it all on his own. A fact that made him envious despite his own successes.

If Caden's boast about Rowena was meant to impress Victor or make him feel envious, it had the opposite effect instead. He knew that type of debutante; girls groomed at a young age at the best schools to behave, dress and speak like ladies regardless of their background, as long as mummy and daddy were rich enough to pay. Young women taught to keep their mouths shut and legs open; produced, packaged and finally presented to suitable men in power. The 'prep and finish' system his wife had once called it during a party many years ago, as she pointed and sneered at likely candidates. Victor had laughed and reminded her that she would have been one of them too had circumstances been different, which had prompted her not speaking to him for the rest of the evening. They could train, condition and suppress it, but somehow the original class always showed up. This was exemplified in the long black fur coat Rowena was carrying which reeked of new money, the hastily brushed-out creases suggesting she wore it more lying down than standing up. Victor couldn't help but be allured to the finished article, however, despite himself, and he could easily see why Caden seemed completely besotted with her.

The couple chatted amongst themselves and made small talk with Victor, as he guided them to one of the nearby vacant consultation rooms for the details of their appointment.

"Since it's Rowena's twenty-third birthday next week and she's desperate to start a family," said Caden enthusiastically as they sat down, "I thought we might as well go through the preliminaries now."

"Yes, of course," replied Victor, who managed to get two more sentences in before Caden's portable phone rang, resulting in a slightly heated discussion with whoever was on the other end.

"Politics!" exclaimed Caden, hanging up his phone and looking slightly flustered. "Sorry, where were we?"

"I was just saying that you'll need to provide a sample," Victor explained. "Unfortunately, because the virus kills any cells if we try to cryogenically store them, it will have to be on the day we perform the IVF."

"Oh that shouldn't be a problem," boasted Caden, leering at Rowena who giggled and looked away bashfully, before his phone rang again. "Sorry sweetheart I have to take this call somewhere private. Matters of state and all that," he said to Rowena in an apologetic tone, rising to his feet and looking genuinely sorry. "Why don't you ask Dr Pearson to give you a tour of the clinic campus and I'll catch you up later." He quickly kissed his wife tenderly on the cheek and hurriedly left the office with the phone stuck to his ear.

Victor and his visitor walked together down the brushed grey and tiled corridors, while he talked and Rowena greeted people as they passed by. The reception building was predominately offices and showrooms, which even he found pretty uninteresting, and so they soon stepped outside into the sunshine of the main site. The clinic campus was vast, and in keeping with its heritage, separated out into a number of large concrete H-shaped buildings spread over twenty acres of lawns, access roads and high walls. Each structure housed a particular area of patient care, class or science laboratory; a pattern which was repeated throughout the various clinics around the country and abroad. Highpoint was the first, however, and now the largest, having spread from its original single block into the surrounding decaying buildings, giving them new life and purpose. Ovaries, tubes and uteri for the eggs and knowledge safely flourishing within.

"So how is your father?" Victor asked through politeness rather than genuine interest, fearing that the conversation was beginning to dry up as they walked in an over-long silence towards the gleaming Alpha Patient Block, with its extensive glass facade and central atrium.

"He is fine, thank you," Rowena replied in an accent of pure English rose, as Victor held the door open for her to enter the infirmary. "Eighty years old, still working on his engines every day, and out on the town with my mother at night."

I bet he is thought Victor. Kirkland was on his third wife now, having dumped the first two long ago for not giving him heirs. Given Rowena's age, he presumed that the current one was a lot younger than her husband was. There was one thing that was puzzling Victor, however, about their application. "I'm sorry, but we didn't seem to note down your new family name at our preliminary meeting?"

The girl paused for a moment, before quietly saying, "It is Schoier," and adding, "Yes, Alfred Schoier was Caden's uncle," before Victor asked the obvious.

No wonder the young politician kept it under wraps. Alfred Schoier, the architect of Prisoners Dilemma, was still a divisive figure even to this day and tended to bring out strong emotions on either side of the fence.

"It is not that he is ashamed of his uncle's actions," Rowena added hastily, "it is just that it tends to dominate the conversation and derails the issues that my husband is trying to get across, so he does not like to advertise it to everyone just yet." She was clearly uncomfortable with the conversation and decided to change the subject, much to Victor's relief, who was now regretting raising it in the first place. "It must be amazing to be surrounded by all of this new life. Do you have any children, Doctor Pearson?"

"No," he admitted. "Well, technically I have several hundred I guess from live donor work years ago, but my wife Susanna died before we got the chance to have one together." He didn't really want to go into the details of her cancer with this stranger and a half-truth seemed like a good compromise.

"That is sad," said Rowena, not bothering to ask any follow-up questions. "Not much point having a statue of yourself if there is no one around to clean the moss from it."

Victor suddenly felt very lonely and decided to try and talk about something apart from family, but Rowena beat him to it. "Are these Government nurses?" she asked, pointing at the uniformed women pottering down the large open corridor, holding clipboards and chatting amongst themselves.

"Oh no, these are our own staff," Victor replied while Rowena nodded approvingly. "We train them up through university and the clinics ourselves. They're not officially Critical Worker status, but we give them the same perks. They're here to look after the patients like yourself, to make sure you're comfortable and that the treatments are correctly given."

"So what happens to me here?" Rowena asked, slightly nervously.

"Well, you'll be given a course of injections to boost your natural cycle and release multiple eggs," Victor explained, "which we'll then collect and fertilise in a dish. We then fix the gene the virus breaks using our special editing technology. The embryos are matured for a few days, and we'll choose one to re-implant into your womb. IVF technology has come on leaps and bounds thanks to the work we have done here, and our success rate for pregnancies is over ninety-nine percent."

"And then my baby will be cured? Normal I mean?"

"I'm sorry but no, we can only fix the gene for a short time before the virus reactivates at day seven and breaks it again, so your children will be infertile. But the gene is only required when the embryo is first forming and before we implant it, so it's enough."

"So why were the originally infected people not infertile straight away?" Rowena asked, rather more astutely than he was expecting.

"We did some extensive studies on this when we realised the scope and impact of IES," the Salesman boasted. "For people like me who originally contracted the disease, we found that the virus was dormant when it integrated into our genome. But in our children, your generation, the virus activates during embryonic development, fortunately when the gene it breaks has already been used, making your eggs infertile. The gene needs both copies intact to function properly too, which is why fixing the embryo is so much more expensive than an affected egg or donor sperm."

"It is funny, the whole of humanity nearly destroyed by such a tiny little thing," said Rowena wispily, ignoring the information about money. If anyone could afford it Victor imagined, it was her family. "Our country is lucky to have your company based here."

Victor felt himself flush with pride and continued the tour to show her the guest suites for the highest paying customers, who were spared mixing with the Lottery winners in the whitewashed walls of the functional Gamma building. Over there it was a hospital, but here it was more a hotel with restaurant food, gymnasium, a secluded indoor garden and entertainment on tap. Luck could get you the treatment, but money bought the luxury.

Rowena stared out of the window at the top of the atrium and pointed at the building on the far side of the site. A group of people had begun congregating outside it, prompting the politician's wife to enquire who they were. An entire building and sports field were reserved for the few hundred IES-clear donors Victor explained, who grew up, were educated, lived and died within the compound. For them, the clinic was still a prison, albeit a comfortable one, with a true life sentence and no hope of parole. It was an unfortunate situation but necessary, for they were the most important people in the world, providing hope to the country by topping up the banks of eggs and sperm in the cryogenic labs.

Rowena stared intently at the donor-block and the people jogging and laughing together. "If you can give me children, why are the donors needed?" she asked, her gaze on them unwavering.

"Economic really," replied Victor, wondering why she was so fascinated by the group. "We don't have the resources or trained staff to offer that many embryo treatments per week to the Lottery winners and low-tier clients, so they're an important stabiliser and insurance policy for the future of the population."

Rowena made a small noise of comprehension and seemed satisfied with the answer, as she turned away almost immediately. "I would love to see where you keep the donor eggs," she said eagerly.

"Of course," Victor agreed, pointing back towards to the reception building where a small unremarkable hut stood, surrounded by fan outlets. "It's just over there. It's mostly underground," he added noticing Rowena's rather unimpressed expression.

Rowena's demeanour soon changed, however, once they got through security, ventured down several flights of stairs and through the fortified access door into what Victor referred to as 'The Cathedral'. The room was an expansive open space scattered with round supporting pillars, with a high ceiling full of large extractor fans. On the vinyl tiled floor stood dozens of huge liquid nitrogen supply tanks, sample dewars, insulated pipework and gauges designed to keep the precious cargo cold and viable with minimum human intervention.

"This is very impressive, Doctor Pearson. There must be millions of samples here. Imagine all that life in one place!" a wide-eyed Rowena exclaimed, before looking upwards and pointing at the fans. "Are they for the air conditioning?"

"The fans are there for safety in case the tanks or pipes leak," Victor replied, carefully sidestepping her question about how much material was stored in the tanks. "If the level of nitrogen gas gets too high it will kill you before you even know there's a problem."

Rowena walked purposely towards the nearest cluster of tanks, tracing the piping with her eyes back to the connectors and valves, before putting her ear to the nearest dewar and cooing softly. "I can hear them singing!" she declared at a whisper, which Victor found curious, and slightly unnerving.

"So, is there anything you don't understand or need me to go over again?" He asked, trying not to sound patronising.

"May I ask you a question, Doctor Pearson?" she asked in a soft voice, glancing over to the entrance to confirm no one else was around.

"Of course."

"Do you think I am an air-headed whore?"

The question was without accusation, but Victor looked horrified nonetheless and attempted to stammer out a reply before Rowena quickly put him out of his misery.

"The look on your face!" she laughed. "Do not worry, we all do what we must in life to succeed and get what we want. I am sure there are a few skeletons in your closet too, Victor."

You have no idea he replied silently.

"Right, now that is out of the way we can talk properly rather than dancing around being over-polite to each other. We all have roles to play and appearances to uphold in politics, but they do so get in the way of getting things done. Caden will soon be the most powerful man in the country, and I will be taking over the family business and all its wealth."

Well, she's right on that point thought Victor. The Minister for Defence controlled death, but the Reproduction Minister controlled life; they could shape the population and the future demographic of the country. Prime Ministers, plucked from the ranks of the civil service came and went every five years before they could do any lasting damage or affect any real change, but the Departmental Ministers were there for life. Well, unless they lost the election, of course, but that was highly unlikely.

"I plan to build a dynasty that will last into perpetuity," she continued, "and for that to commence I need children. At least four and preferably more. Equal genders, of course, you cannot always rely on other people to have the right ones to marry to."

Victor was still slightly lost for words. "That's quite a punishment to put your body through at your young age. I presume your husband is okay with this?"

"Caden will agree to anything I say as long as I keep him well sated," Rowena replied, gently and suggestively sliding a finger down the side of the tank, which put an image in Pearson's head that he wished it hadn't, "and I have a team of doctors, personal trainers and makeup artists to deal with everything else. Anyway, things have come too far for something as minor as that to stop me. I have been chosen for this path."

"Chosen by who?"

"By God silly!" Rowena replied, giggling at Victor's apparent ignorance. "All that has happened is due to Him and His plans for me. He killed half the world and poisoned the other, just for me."

Victor was dumbfounded. "Why on Earth would you think that?"

"It is the only explanation for what happened, this path He set," she said, her accent slipping slightly. "Who would I be? What would I be otherwise? Some wretched northern lass scratching a living working in a factory, probably ending up drinking or smoking myself to death while my thug of a husband beats me? But now thanks to Him I can have everything I deserve."

"The dead in the pits might think that sounds like a very high price to pay."

Rowena pondered this for a moment. "Progress is built on the bones of the dead Victor, surely you know that? The bigger the pile, the faster the advance. The Great Wars taught us that if nothing else."

Victor listened intently. He didn't know why, but he found the juxtaposition of her innocent beauty, expensive perfume and unfeeling pragmatism incredibly bewitching.

"My children must be perfect," Rowena continued. "My family has a history of heart disease on my mother's side and Caden has bowel cancer on his father's. I need all of our embryos examined and only the best ones used."

Caden's last visit suddenly made a lot more sense now. Country-wide eugenics wasn't his primary goal, at least not yet, just his own. "I'm afraid that's not possible," said Victor, shaking his head, "numerous ethical reasons for a start."

Rowena paused to consider Victor's refusal, her expression hardening. "He does not like you, you know. My husband that is," she said frankly, turning her attention back to the storage tanks.

"Yes, I got that impression."

"He thinks you are an arrogant prick who believes he is better than everyone else just because he paid a bit more attention at school."

"I'm sorry he feels that way," Victor replied, biting his tongue to prevent himself from saying what he thought of her husband in return.

Rowena pivoted around, tipped her head slightly then walked slowly towards him, stopping inches away. She spoke in a soft, seductive voice, stroking his face with her finger, her touch electric. "But a quiet whisper from me in his ear at the right time could change that, smooth over the creases if you will. Like being wrapped in nothing but silk. You know I think he is just a bit jealous of you; he is just at the beginning of his climb but you have reached the pinnacle. Just imagine what you two could achieve, what we could all achieve together?"

Victor felt something intoxicating stirring inside him he hadn't felt for many years. Perhaps he was being too inflexible in his principles, too tied to the past like Caden had suggested? Perhaps just this once wouldn't make such a difference, and maybe Rowena would show her gratitude. Just put on the uniform one time in secret, where no one would see, and no one would judge.

"Leave ethics to the historians, Victor," Rowena said, taking a few steps back. "I do not remember the Americans worrying too much about Wernher von Braun's previous job when they put a man on the moon. Yes, I paid attention at school too."

"There's still the problem of timing, though," said Victor, desperately trying to regain his composure. "We only have a two-day window from fixing the faulty gene and growing the embryo before it needs to be implanted in the mother. There's only really time to take a few cells for screening basic lethal mutations and chromosome structure."

"Well, that will not do at all," Rowena said, folding her arms and pouting. "Surely with all of your money and resources it can be done?"

"Unfortunately, the equipment is getting harder to get hold of," Victor explained, "and every time something breaks we need to cannibalise others to fix them." This much was true, like many companies involved in high technology which depended on a few central brains to run and innovate, the manufacturers had not managed to survive for long after the Death. The collapse of the economy and paucity of materials were part of it, of course, but most of all it was that the patients, who had once paid handsomely for personal genomics and custom medicine, had come to realise that simply still being alive was quite enough to be getting on with. Victor had bought up all of the dusty DNA sequencers in abandoned research labs and biotechs he could get his hands on during his rise to power, but even they were beginning to run out. Machines with a five-year lifespan stretched to ten times that, well beyond their breaking point. "The only way we could even try and do it in that time is to pull all of our analysts from the other clients. We'd have to dedicate our entire genome sequencing capacity and informatics to just your embryos. And that will be very expensive."

"Splendid!" Rowena cried with a yelp and clap of her hands before Victor had a chance to continue. "A full screen it is."

"What about the others?" Victor asked, already knowing the answer.

"The Lottery winners should be grateful for anything they get, nothing is more important than this," Rowena replied, "and those who are wealthy enough to pay will, of course, have the intelligence to understand."

"Okay," said Victor meekly, suddenly feeling slightly sorry for Caden. The instant she had dug her claws into him the politician had never stood a chance. "If we manage to repair multiple embryos we usually offer them to other clients, to prevent wastage. We'll just need you to sign a standard release form."

"No, I do not think so," Rowena replied without hesitation, "I do not want inferior stock hanging around and potentially trying to claim what is not theirs later in life. Have the rejects destroyed."

Victor was thinking about disagreeing with her when he heard the entrance door opening behind him. It was Caden, carrying his wife's coat in one arm and spreading the other open which Rowena instantly ran to, giving her husband a hug and a kiss on the cheek.

"Sorry about my absence, work can be such a bind sometimes," he said primarily to his wife rather than Victor, before turning his gaze to the Salesman. "I hope Dr Pearson has been taking good care of you. Did you get what you needed?"

"Oh yes, he has been most accommodating," she purred.

"Excellent!" exclaimed Caden, walking over and patting Victor on the arm and pointing back to Rowena. "Isn't she something? Can you just imagine lots of little versions of her running about in a few years? Adorable!"

To Victor the very thought was terrifying; the siren and the snake, founding the future ruling class of the country, passing laws and shaping thoughts of the populous.

"Anyway, I'm afraid our time has run out. I'm needed at the Ministry and Rowena has a fund-raiser to attend," said Caden, passing the fur over to his wife. "We'll look forward to the first round of treatments as soon as possible. Goodbye Pearson." The couple turned to leave when Rowena leant up and whispered in her husband's ear making him stop in his tracks. "Of course!" he proclaimed, "how remiss of me. Go on then, darling."

Rowena skittered towards Victor and held out her hand, which was now holding a small ring box, and gently passed it to him. "A small token of our appreciation. No peeking now until we are gone! I will look forward to our next appointment." She returned to her husband, held tightly to his arm and skipped along laughing as they left, the door swinging closed behind them.

Victor looked at the small box and turned it over in his palm suspiciously before unwrapping and opening it.

There was no ring inside, just an old shilling.

Clues

Kate paused before finally deciding to knock on the door. She had phoned work the day after the funeral and requested two weeks' compassionate leave which, after some negotiation and poorly acted fake crying, had been begrudgingly agreed upon. She was glad of the break; her brain had spent the last few days stuck in a loop, the same questions raising themselves, again and again, racing around her mind with no way to shut them out. She often suffered from this affliction with work problems, or a line from a song that refused to go away, but they could usually be solved by logical thinking or playing the tune out loud until her cortex got bored with it. On this occasion, though, she didn't have enough information for either to work and despite the recent revelation, nothing made sense again. How Emily could have been pregnant and not known it suggested that it had happened very recently. If she'd done something stupid and gone to one of those back-street places, there would have been signs of the treatment and the clinic would have just thrown her out on the street. It was certainly nothing worth killing her for, so despite her reservations about the reception she'd get, Kate had made the journey to James' home in the suburbs near the edge of the SafeZone.

It was a large white semi-detached house with a garage, ornate porch and red tiled roof, each detail mirrored in the adjoining building. A suitably classed abode for a low-level Government worker and, with its sizeable rear garden full of vegetable patches, a farm employee thought Kate. She took hold of the ornate knocker but the door opened and ripped it out of her hand before she had the chance to use it. Rita stood on the threshold, her arms now folded and her face a picture of disapproval.

"Oh it's you," the older woman said scornfully, which struck Kate as a pointless thing to say, since Rita had obviously seen her approach by peeking through the net curtains. Kate wondered how much of the day her brother-in-law's mother spent doing that, and started to ask if James was in but Rita rudely cut her off. "Did you know Michael was here yesterday with his new fiancée?" she said, over-articulating the last word as to give the knife a sharper blade to twist. "Lovely girl, very charming and pretty. A nice warm disposition."

Unlike you Kate, you cold-hearted bitch, Kate silently added for her.

"Who is it?" a small voice from within the house asked, shortly followed by James appearing behind his mother. "Oh hello Katie, please come in," he said gesturing to her. "Mum, I'd love a cup of tea. Katie?"

Kate followed James into the house while Rita shot her a look and disappeared into the kitchen muttering to herself. Kate let out a gasp of shock at the scene that greeted her in the lounge. There were sheets of paper everywhere, either scattered randomly over the floor or loosely stacked in rough and unstable piles in the corners or on tables. Every wall she could see was covered in bookshelves, each shelf two layers deep with folders, books and crudely bound volumes.

"Work lent me some equipment, so I took a few journeys to the 'to do' vault," he explained, pointing at the computer and microfilm machine half-buried under reams of folded dot-matrix paper in the corner. "Thought I might as well do something useful. All of this information needs curating and sorting, so we can make sense of it and catalogue it. It's not just printing stuff out you know," he quickly added as if to justify his job to her.

Rita entered holding a tray of best-china cups. "He's been working day and night on this project," she said proudly, putting her arm around James who shirked slightly away from her. "What is it darling, some internet encyclopaedia?"

"Yes," her son replied and gestured to the near-collapsing shelf on the far wall, "and that's just AB to AC!"

"I had no idea how much space it all takes up," said Kate, surprising herself on how impressive it looked.

James put his cup on a nearby table and slumped down in his chair. "It's not the loss of people since the Death that's the problem you know, it's the loss of all the skills and knowledge."

Kate had to agree with him. Humans were basically still cavemen at heart, relying on the inspiration of a few individuals and an existing infrastructure to survive. Take those away and they were just scrabbling around in the dirt and excrement with the rest of the animals.

"We printed out the human genome a couple of years ago," James boasted. "You should have seen it, a thousand pages per volume, and two hundred volumes. The code of life preserved, for the ages. It could have been lost forever if not for us."

Kate thought about pointing out that the human genome was probably still on dozens of computers in various universities but thought better of it. She needed information and rubbing him up the wrong way probably wasn't the best way to attain it, so she just feigned interest and looked attentive.

"There's added urgency now since one of the remaining transatlantic links went down. There's only one left now, and once that's gone that's pretty much it," James said sullenly. "The internet is dying Kate, one server and one patch cable at a time. And when it goes, all of that information will be irrecoverable." He stared sadly at his untouched cup. "Oh well, keeps me occupied at least."

And that was the whole point of it, Kate realised. The best way to cope with the loss was not to cope at all, just keep busy and bury it all away until the grief hopefully slowly faded away by itself. She felt envious of him; James was trying desperately not to think about Emily, and think about her was now all she could do.

"Why are you here, Kate?" Rita butted in rudely. "I mean you haven't exactly bothered to pick up the phone recently, so why the sudden interest now?"

"Phones work both ways," snapped back Kate irritably. "Anyway, I thought I'd see how my brother-in-law was doing. Isn't that what you wanted?" She paused before adding, "but actually while I'm here, James do you know anyone called Kurt? Emily gave me a book of his to borrow and I'd like to return it." Kate tried to say it as casually and off-hand as she could, but she was a terrible liar and hoped they wouldn't notice her deception. Then again she couldn't exactly tell them the truth either; that Emily was murdered because she was pregnant, killed by probably the same people who she had trusted to take care of her. That this Kurt, whoever he was, was involved somehow, presumably in the conception. That fact alone would destroy James, and however dull he may be she didn't want to upset him even more, although the thought of the look on Rita's face if she did made it almost tempting.

James looked up and to the left as if searching his brain for a memory. "I'm not sure, but it does ring a bell somewhere. Ah yes, now I remember. I think there was someone at the farm called Kurt. He mucked out the pigs or something?"

"Thank you," said Kate, relieved and excited that the trail had sparked into life again. "I'm glad you're okay but I really should be going now." She turned to Rita and handed her back the half-empty cup as she got up and walked off towards the hallway. "Thanks for the tea."

"So that's it?" Rita demanded, following her out. "You've got what you needed and you're off? You've only just got here!"

"You didn't want me here at all a minute ago," countered Kate. She got as far as the lounge door when James slammed down the cup with a loud bang, stopping her in her tracks.

"Please Katie, stay for a while," he pleaded, wiping off the spilt tea from the table with his sleeve. "It's good to have someone else to talk to, isn't it?"

Kate wasn't sure if that was aimed at her, his mother or himself, but she apologised for her rudeness and sat down again, retrieving her cup from a gobsmacked Rita. She got so pre-occupied sometimes and focused on the task at hand that she forgot to be polite she explained, which by admitting blame defused the situation somewhat. So she stayed and they chatted about memories of Emily from childhood, things Kate had long forgotten until the retelling; the time she had to stop her younger sister from biting into a stinging nettle sandwich she'd made when doing her bit for self-sufficiency, or when they'd gone hunting for dragonflies once on holiday and ended up filthy and soaking, having fallen in a pond over-reaching with a butterfly net.

James laughed at the tales, and countered with some of his own about the working holiday he'd spent at the farm a few years previously. Emily was so at home with the animals; herding the pigs into the sty and manhandling grumpy dairy cows, while he spent the time trying, and failing, to tiptoe around the mud and dropping bales of hay when the twine dug into his fingers. He was lucky they'd met and fallen in love when she was visiting home for Christmas he grinned, as given his ineptitude with the countryside she would have just laughed in his face otherwise. It felt good to see him smile, and Kate felt a twinge of regret that it had taken such a tragedy to see him as anything else but a tedious bore. She had always held the opinion that James was not good enough for Emily, but would she have been happy with any choice? Kate had always played the protector, shielding her naive sister from the realities of life, and passing that obligation to another was a burden of responsibility almost too heavy to bear.

Their reminiscing was finally cut off by the phone in the corner bursting into life from under yet another stack of paper. Rita hurried to dig out the receiver, announcing it was the office enquiring about some of the information James had brought back to work on. Kate took the opportunity to quickly say goodbye. It had been a nice distraction, but a distraction nonetheless, and if she left now she should be able to catch the last train to the village nearest the farm. She felt Rita following her to the hallway, which was fortuitous as there was something she needed to say to her, although it came out as more of a command than the dispassionate statement she'd meant it to be. "James needs to grieve, and you need to stop distracting him."

"I didn't know you cared," Rita said sarcastically, folding her arms defensively as Kate opened the door to leave.

"It doesn't matter if I do or not, but Emily did, and so do you." It took a supreme amount of willpower to override her anxiety about touching others, but she managed to put her hand on the older woman's arm and clasped it gently. "So please, for her, let him deal with it and move on."

Rita started to say something in reply but then stopped abruptly and suddenly hugged her, much to Kate's alarm. "That was the first I'd seen him smile since it happened." She leant over to whisper in Kate's ear. "I don't believe what you told James in there about whoever that man was, but thank you for spending some time with him."

And for once when the door was shut behind her, Kate didn't hear it slam.

***

It was well past dusk by the time the ageing train slowly ground its way to the platform, the carriages creaking noisily against the rusty suspension and adding to Kate's already pounding headache. She had spent the last few hours sitting in a cold draught, made worse by the appalling burning rubber smell the brakes emitted every time they stopped at yet another station or red signal. It was a world away from the gleaming modern platforms and elegant high-speed waggons of the main lines she was used to travelling on. Here, everything was worn, grubby and grimy. She had originally presumed that the journey would take roughly the same time as her commute to work. What she hadn't factored in was the endless local village stops or the reduced speed of the train on the rickety track, which shook and vibrated the carriages around, threatening to derail them and plunge the passengers into the icy water-filled ditches below.

Kate realised that she had never travelled this far off the beaten track before, and was quite unprepared for what awaited her at what was optimistically called the rail station. Most people took the mandatory two weeks' holiday per year visiting the countryside or beaches, and the designated religious celebrations visiting family. Kate preferred being indoors, however, and there was no point travelling out to see Emily as her sister had always come back to London for Christmas. She'd seen postcards and photos of the Lake District and Welsh mountains, of course, but this looked nothing like the picturesque landscapes that her colleagues hung on the walls in their office. Here it was desolate and featureless, the flat treeless vista providing no break or protection from the squally wind or spitting rain that greeted her with horizontal enthusiasm.

There were only two passengers that had alighted with her, who not only seemed to know each other but were picked up by the same car, leaving Kate alone and stranded, frantically trying to keep the hood of her jacket over her head. The village was about a mile away up the road from the station, the women had told her before leaving without offering her a ride. Kate didn't really blame them; she probably wouldn't have done so either. As it looked like there were no taxis here either, walking seemed the only option remaining. In some ways, she was glad to be alone.

The only other occupant of her carriage had been a shifty-looking middle-aged man who kept staring at her from over his book, but who would then suddenly look away when she met his gaze. She was thankful he'd not got off the train at the same stop, for however nervous the dark and unknown made her, having some ogling weirdo to contend with would have been much worse. It was barely six o'clock in the evening but felt more like eleven at night as the operations specialist made the trek up the road, the slippery part-frozen mud sticking to her shoes and making progress difficult in the wind and dark. The village, when it finally crawled into view, was just a few dozen houses, a medieval church which looked far too grandiose given the surrounding population, and the most welcome sight of all, the Coach House Inn.

If the remote location reminded Kate of the end of the world, the interior of the pub was straight out of a tourist postcard, with wooden beams, stuffed animal heads and a few locals knocking back jars of ale or laughing and playing games. Kate was glad that the room she had booked was still waiting for her, as the owner of the place had such a thick local accent that when she had phoned the day before she wasn't sure if the message had gotten through or not. Unfortunately, when face to face the language barrier still hadn't gotten any easier and it took several attempts to extract the information about where her room was, much to his frustration and her embarrassment.

She stayed in her room the rest of the evening, only venturing down briefly for dinner before skulking back upstairs. She doubted that she would have any more luck communicating with the rest of the inhabitants than she did the proprietor and in any case, they would have nothing in common to talk about. So she practised the conversation she would have with Kurt instead; what she would say, the likely things he might say back, and her responses in return. It was an art she had developed over the years for guiding and winning task-related discussions with her work colleagues, but it appeared to work in most social situations just as well. Michael, though, had always hated it when she'd done it when arguing with him. Exhaustion from the journey soon began to overwhelm her, and coupled with a comfy bed and residual headache, sleep came easier than it had for the previous few nights.

Breakfast the next morning was probably the most impressive meal that Kate had eaten in years. The landlord's wife, a vivacious and buxom woman called Idell who was fortunately much easier to understand than her husband, had called it the 'full English'; a mammoth plate of eggs, sausages, bacon and mushrooms which would have probably cost a day's wages back in London. Kate hadn't told Idell her real identity and was instead travelling under the guise of someone looking for a job, which seemed safer somehow and gave her an unexpected buzz of feeling a bit like a secret agent in one of Michael's books. Idell had also been a veritable wealth of information about the farm, which was apparently built on the remains of one of the disposal pits, had its own private rail link and was the main source of employment for the surrounding villages. The train only ran once a day and she'd already missed it, but the helpful woman knew someone making a delivery run later who'd be happy enough to give her a lift from the village green.

The early morning mist was yet to clear as Kate stood shivering against the large granite memorial, using it as a makeshift windbreak to shelter her from the northerly wind. Just like every other village and town in the country, the monolith stood at the heart of the village, a monument to those unfortunates who had succumbed to the Death. The stones usually stood next to the plaques and statues listing those who had died fighting during the two Great Wars, often dwarfing them with their size, carvings and ornateness. Kate thought this disrespectful, relegating to the background those who had gladly given their life to the bettering and freedom of the nation, compared to those who just happened to die of a disease. Well, possibly not gladly, but for the greater good at least. Like most members of her generation born after the chaos, to her, the Death was a ghost story, a history lesson taught in draughty stone-floored classrooms by tutors that would suddenly stop mid-sentence and stare blankly out of the window. They had called it shell-shock long ago, then battle fatigue, then PTSD. The latest term was 'delayed-stress syndrome' but the effects and origins were the same; men and women thrust into raw survival situations and pushed far further than their terror, anxiety or sense of morality would allow, forced to live through it again and again for the rest of their days.

Still, it ensured that everyone knew the tale of the rat catcher Bjart Lorentzen, although the exact details had passed into fable and myth over the years. Some historians had painted him a lunatic terrorist bent on the destruction of humanity, others an unwitting victim who was just in the wrong place at the wrong time. Whatever his motivations, the results of the Norwegian Death, a highly contagious and antibiotic-resistant form of pneumonic plague, had been catastrophic. Just how he had caught it had been lost to history, but instead of staying at home or going to the hospital when he fell ill in the summer of 2020, he'd taken a flight and gone on holiday to Tokyo.

He'd gone to the Olympics.

And not just as an ordinary tourist, but a Games volunteer with access to the stadium and the world's best athletes at the opening ceremony. He'd shaken hands and exchanged welcome kisses with hundreds of competitors and staff, and breathed or coughed on countless more of those who had come to witness the spectacle of the occasion. They headed home with a slight cold, sharing the air in the planes with other passengers and spreading the infection to every corner of the globe. Lorentzen had killed the world, and for weeks, no one even knew there was a problem. The infected went through their daily lives, unaware of the bacteria slowly multiplying and spreading within them and expelled out through their lungs. At first, it caused nothing more than a bad cough and a raised temperature; certainly not anything worth going to the hospital for. But then people started dying, the surgeries and hospitals began to fill with the sick and doctors woke to the horrid realisation that their medicines weren't going to help them. Kate was reminded of a scene in an old film of men and women in suits and military uniforms, staring in horror as small red dots appeared on a map of America in front of them, which then grew and merged together as the country changed hue. It was a surprisingly accurate prediction. The world was a small place back then and travel was cheap, helping the bacteria spread all the quicker and wider.

By the time the governments and United Nations had woken up to the scale of the pandemic it was all too late, as one by one, the nations fell under the scourge. The flag-burning extremists on the news reports had sung, danced and fired their guns in the air with celebrations as America disintegrated, but the Reaper had come for them too nonetheless. In fact, if there was one good thing that the Death had brought, thought Kate, was a much greater religious tolerance from all sides and creeds. It was hard to take the righteous high ground when the churches, mosques and synagogues were rapidly emptying in equal amounts. The plague was indiscriminate and merciless, an end product of the endless war that humanity had waged on the bacteria, viruses and parasites of the planet, whose only crime was to have it as a host.

Britain had fared better than most, as the Government of the time had been preparing for such an outbreak since several false dawns had woken them up to the possible consequences. They had closed the borders and cleared the airspace to avoid the infection getting in again, whilst they battled to control the spread of the disease and an increasingly panicked populace. The politicians had wisely given the Armed Forces complete control of order, provisions and disposal. To stop the mobs killing each other over scraps of dwindling food, they descended in a fearful spectacle of uniforms, guns and gas masks; society's last hope against a tsunami of natural selection. They had performed their duties with ruthless efficiency, uninterested in pleas for extra rations, mercy journeys to the hospital for those with dying relatives or empty threats from an unarmed public. Yet Kate's mother and many others from that generation had nothing but praise for the soldiers who wielded absolute power over them for several years. It was always the same phrase they used to absolve the Government and military; 'tough but necessary', which seemed to excuse pretty much anything which would normally be considered an atrocity during war. Kate found herself using the same three words even today when the leaders talked about the continuing need for border control and treatment of people smugglers.

The army couldn't do it all, of course. The hospitals still needed staffing, fires needed extinguishing and the criminals they didn't shoot on sight needed processing. With what was left of the emergency services either too scared or unable to get to work and treat the infected, the Government tried rounding them up and forcing them to at gunpoint, hoping to lose a few dissenting hard-liners and bringing the others into line. It had been a disaster. With the rest of the country barely hanging on and starving to death, every extra loss of a medic or nurse was strongly felt. Having failed with the stick, they therefore tried the carrot, giving the newly crowned 'critical workers' and their families relocation to secure bases, extra rations and access to the best protective equipment.

The Critical Worker Act was still in force forty years later, and their list of benefits had increased substantially over the years. This was much to the annoyance of the rest of the populace, who couldn't understand why they were still more important than them decades after the last case of the Death, especially when it came to having children. Kate presumed that the Government, still so decisive and strong to this day, never wanted to be held ransom by a few individuals again, and found it easier to just pay them off with a few desirable perks. The workers had, in return, become their foot soldiers and mouthpiece for the cause, armed not with guns but knowledge and position, a new and highly enviable social class.

For Kate's parents, a newly qualified veterinarian and his young vet nurse wife, who'd just set up their own practice on in the Yorkshire countryside, the plague must have felt even more like the end of the world. With access to drugs and medical supplies, they'd barricaded themselves in at night and had their euthanasia guns clearly in sight during the day when, donned head to foot in scrubs, face masks and a caustic smell of carbolic acid, they greeted the startled clients. They'd dined on cat and dog food for a while, and then moved on to the animals themselves when the owners brought in their treasured pets to be humanely destroyed. It was always a heart-breaking scene no matter how many times they witnessed it; a final act of compassion, giving their animals the dignity that their families were denied.

They had sustained this way of life for a number of months, isolated in their own little bubble of survival and curious wedded bliss, until one day a man from the Government came knocking on the door, escorted by three burly-looking soldiers. The country needed her father's help in the 'clean-up', a prettified term they used to refer to the disposal of the corpses lining the streets and stinking out the houses. Specifically, in confirming end of life and identifying the cadavers. Most of the doctors and other human-focused medical professionals were too busy with the living for such menial and lowly work, but as a vet, he had just the right amount of knowledge they were looking for. It wasn't just him, of course, they were rounding up anyone they could find with a similar set of skills, desperate to find an answer to the unthinkable question: what do you do with thirty million dead bodies?

Kate was firmly of the opinion that it was good to die at the beginning of a disaster. The first casualties made the news, the families enjoyed an outpouring of public sympathy and a well-attended funeral, while those that perished later were left forgotten and nameless. This was no less true than with the Norwegian Death, for when the hastily built incinerators and crematoriums had become overwhelmed, they'd resorted to scooping up the corpses into open top lorries using excavators instead. The bodies were transported to vast wood-lined pits dotted around the countryside, and then finally doused in petrol. The pyres had burned fiercely for days on end, filling the air for miles around with billowing black acrid smoke and threatening to choke anyone who went too close; a final act of the dead seeking revenge on the uncaring living who had cast them aside.

When the fires had extinguished themselves, the soldiers simply covered up the pits and dug a new one nearby, repeating the macabre ritual until the dead finally stopped arriving. Her husband had returned from the pits a different man, her mother had told Kate, once she was old enough to understand the concept. The carefree jovial man had gone, replaced with a sombre and withdrawn doppelgänger who was prone to drinking and restless sleep. The plague had spared their lives but at the greater cost of his soul, and soon afterwards they'd taken up the offer to be rehoused in one of the newly designated SafeZones in London as a reward for their service.

Only once as a child did Kate ask her father about what he'd witnessed out there on the moors, a place he'd never returned to or even wanted to hear mentioned in the house while he still had breath. She had timed the question perfectly, to coincide with a big anniversary remembrance feature on the television. Her mother had gone out shopping with Emily and her father was just drunk enough to be coherent, but not too inebriated to be violent. So, as casually as she could make it, she'd gently asked him what it was like out at the sites back then. He'd looked at her, his eyes distant and filled with tears, and simply said, "I witnessed Hell, Katie. I saw it, I smelt it, I breathed it. I'd come home every night but no matter how much I bathed I couldn't wash it off. I'd shut my eyes but I couldn't stop seeing the bodies. I put my hands over my ears but I could still hear the bones breaking under the tractors. I prayed it wouldn't be me next, then after a while prayed it would be." He had begun to sob and hugged her tightly, the comforting parental embrace overriding her usual aversion to closeness. "The best part of me died out there Katie, and I'm sorry."

She had never asked him about it again.

Emily and herself had been lucky that both their parents had lived long enough for a cure to be developed, a revolutionary antibiotic created in a small lab in a rural part of Cambridgeshire. The politicians had annexed it under the guise of national interests and sold it to the rest of the world at a vast price, propelling the country from near bankruptcy to a rich and prosperous nation in a matter of months. They had invested this windfall wisely; if some money was squandered or went astray to personal accounts, there was still plenty left to filter down to every corner of the realm. The Government restored the rule of law and democracy, built power stations, expanded local rail networks and ensured production and fair distribution of food.

Slowly and surely, the nation had recovered from barely clinging on to the edge by its fingernails to being the envy of what was left of the rest of the world; from the independent fragments of America to the city states of Europe and the feudal countries of the East. Those early glory days of rebuilding had faded though as time went on, the advent of IES had seen to that. With a reduced and ageing population, the tax revenues were dwindling, and non-essential services with them as the lifeblood of the economy retracted inwards to the SafeZones to protect the vital organs within. Prices for items considered luxuries were going up too. Kate remembered her mother complaining that electrical goods and computers being ten times more expensive just after the Death than before, but these days it was more like twenty times, if you could get them at all. Thank God for the auctions!

If the independent gutter press were to be believed, only New Zealand had fared better than Britain in the new world order, mainly due to a series of earthquakes and a political crisis with Japan, which prevented travel to the Games and kept tourists away. It had been a blessing in disguise, for by the time the Death came knocking at their door they had already learnt from everyone else's misfortunes. Kate had also heard reports that they had a much lower incidence of sterility than Britain, although that was often claimed as just propaganda by the authorities as one of their former colonies flexing its political muscles. Whatever the case, it was the other side of the world, which was plenty big and empty enough now for the two nations to coexist peacefully, at least in her lifetime. The future generations could look after their own problems.

Kate's transport turned out to be in a very old rusty open backed truck loaded with straw bales, and a gearbox that screamed in pain every time the driver, an earthy woman called Charlie who liked to talk non-stop, wrenched the lever into position.

"Oh don't worry about that!" she laughed, having seen Kate wince in sympathy with the struggling motor. "Just needs a bit of warming up in the mornings is all. A bit like me really!" she joked, jabbing Kate in the ribs. "So what brings a townie girl like you out to the sticks?"

"I heard there was a job going, I'm looking for a career change," Kate replied, trying to sound convincing. Either she was getting better at lying or Charlie wasn't paying attention enough to call her out. Judging by the amount of awareness she was showing at what was optimistically called a road, it was probably the latter.

"Oh yeah, trouble with the boss was it? Bet it was! Get a bit handy did he the dirty old bugger? Am I right?"

Kate tried to correct her with her own concocted story but couldn't get a word in edgeways, and anyway Charlie's version of events was much more interesting than anything she could have come up with.

"With a pretty looking girl like you too - hope you kicked him where it hurts!" said Charlie in mock disgust. "So they're advertising for Emily's job already? That didn't take long, oh well life goes on for the rest of us I guess, and it's not like the pigs and cows are going to sort their own feed orders is it. That poor girl."

It hadn't occurred to Kate that the imaginary job she'd invented was actually Emily's, and it made her feel sick and hollow inside. "Oh yes I heard about that in the village," she said, looking down at her feet. "Did you know her at all?"

"Of course!" Charlie replied looking agape at Kate's apparent ignorance. "Everyone knew Emily. Lovely, friendly girl, always first to help out with anything and nothing was ever too much bother. Certainly rescued me and Bertha here a few times!" She laughed again and patted the dashboard. "It was such a shame the funeral wasn't out here you know, we would have packed our old church to the rafters and sung the roof off it for her."

For the first time since the cremation, Kate felt a real sense of loss and felt the emotion well up inside her again, threatening to overwhelm her. She'd become so obsessed with the clues, with piecing the puzzle together that she'd forgotten the reason why she was doing it. The young woman she'd often dismissed as fragile and inconsequential had touched and enriched the lives of more people than she could ever hope to. Would her own funeral be as well attended she wondered? Or would it pass unnoticed, a legacy of a solitary and insular life more concerned with the how and not the why, or whom?

"But that was her husband's choice I guess," the country woman continued. "Always seemed a bit useless when he came a visiting. Fish out of water, I suppose, but at least he tried and gave us all a good giggle." She paused slightly before adding almost as an afterthought, "Never met her sister, though, whatever her name was. Sounded a bit up herself by all and purposes, the silly cow. Didn't even ring or show up to congratulate her when Emily won the lottery."

Kate wanted to shout at the woman, to tell her she'd got it wrong, that it was she who'd won the prize and given the gift to Emily out of her love for her sister, and perhaps then Charlie and the others would see good in her. But it was a lie, a retro-fitted self-delusion constructed to reduce her guilt. She hadn't given the treatment to Emily out of love, it was a selfish act to get her out of a difficult situation and she deserved no credit or congratulations from strangers for it. Her spot in the memorial garden would remain unvisited, overgrown and forgotten, just as she deserved. She remained silent for the rest of the journey, occasionally nodding as Charlie carried on the conversation unabated, moving onto the punishment for the murdering clinic security guard which seemed to involve dismemberment and feeding him to the pigs.

The truck eventually pulled up to the main gate with a final crunching of the transmission. Charlie flirted briefly with the guards and dropped Kate off to report to reception, before heading off inside with her load now threatening to fall off the back. Kate was expecting the site to be a couple of fields with a few cows grazing in the background, but this was on a whole different scale. The farm perimeter was more reminiscent of an old medieval castle than an estate. A large deep moat, filled with water, encompassed high walls of concrete topped with barbed wire and security cameras, all of which dwarfed the small rustic cottage just outside that served as the reception centre.

The wall extended into the distance far beyond Kate could see, cutting off the fields, paddocks and barns from the rest of the countryside and those who might want to steal any of the thousands of animals within. She could only make out one other access gate a few hundred yards away where the railway entered and that too was heavily guarded by men and women with guns. Kate guessed the size of the farm was due to efficiency and economies of scale, as one of the side effects of self-sufficiency was that most of the spare fertile land was used for food crops or biofuel.

Animals, however, were an inefficient use of energy, and unless they were producing milk, eggs, wool or fur they were an unnecessary luxury. Meat was the by-product when all of the other uses had been exhausted making it tough, stringy, overly strong and best left for stewing. Only the pigs, whose myriad of parts and uses were nearly endless, were slaughtered when their flesh was at its most tender. Consequently, they were the most desirable and expensive of the domestic animals and a tempting target for thieves.

Considering fish were plentiful and cheaper, Kate couldn't see the attraction herself. The tales her parents' generation would often tell of juicy sirloin steaks and lamb shanks fell on deaf ears, and were filed under the things that old people were always going on about on how much better things were in the old days before the plague washed it away.

The farm owner, who Charlie had described as a 'jolly hockey sticks type', turned out to be a short broad woman in her early sixties called Amelda Sheriden. She rushed down to meet Kate as soon as Kate approached the reception desk and told them her true identity. "Oh my poor dear!" the squat woman exclaimed, dashing over and bear-hugging the breath out of Kate before she could object. "Just look at you, all upset. It must be a difficult time for you, what with your parents already gone from us and all."

"Being here, it's just beginning to sink in I think," Kate replied, extracting herself from Amelda's grasp. The woman's long dark blue wax coat was splattered with mud and what smelt like damp manure, which had instantly transferred its aroma to the London girl's clothes. She made a mental note to do some washing as soon as she got back home. "I'd like to pretend that I'm here purely on a remembrance pilgrimage, but I'm not," Kate explained. "Emily often spoke of a man called Kurt, would it be possible to meet with him, please? I need to talk to him about something."

"Kurt?" Amelda sounded surprised. "Why would you want to talk to him, my girl? He's just a farm labourer, and not a particularly nice one at that. I doubt he even knew your sister."

That was a good point. Why would she travel all of this way to talk to a dogsbody who in all likelihood would have minimal contact with an administrative assistant? Best to tell the truth, or at least enough of it. "I think Kurt was sleeping with my sister, and I want to understand why she would do that to James," she explained.

If Kate expected Amelda to be shocked she was disappointed, the older woman just shook her head and smiled in sad sympathy. "I heard a few rumours, you know what people are like for gossiping, but I never believed them. She wasn't that type of girl if you get my meaning." Amelda stopped for a moment before clearly deciding something in her head and loudly clapping her hands together. "Right! Probably all just a big misunderstanding and none of my business anyway. Well, you didn't come all this way just to talk to me, so let's go and find him and see what he has to say for himself. Just speak the words my girl and I'm sure we have some equipment for gelding horses around somewhere we can use on him!" She laughed too long at her own joke, before digging out a pair of muddy wellington boots from the pile in the corner and a thick waterproof coat for Kate to wear, which although too large for her slight frame and feet served their purpose. "Yes you look lovely dear," said Amelda dismissively. "I presume you can't ride a horse and I'm too old and fat to anyway, so the metal steed it will have to be. Come along girl, don't dither." She led Kate outside to where a small open two-seater all-terrain vehicle was parked, and gestured to her to climb aboard before slamming her foot on the accelerator and roaring off through the entry gate to the main farm within.

"I was so sorry to hear about Emily," Amelda said loudly, trying to make herself heard over the noise of the engine. "She was part of the family here. I know she joined us as a designated administrator but she was much happier getting muddy with the animals, so we let her do that whenever we could instead. In all my years I've never seen anyone so enthusiastic around the farm, helping out with everyone and everything. That's probably when she met Kurt, now that I think of it."

Kate wasn't sure she could handle another eulogy just yet and decided to try and change the subject. "Have you lived here long?" she asked.

"All my life dear, and my parents and their parents before them. It used to be a beautiful estate with wild deer, lakes and flower gardens before the Government came and turned it into human carcass dumping ground." She sighed heavily before sharply steering right and heading up a gravel path, "Then they levelled the whole thing and built that horrible wall around it. That cottage used to be the gamekeeper's back in the days and our family lived in that humble building there," she added, pointing back towards the reception building and then to the very impressive-looking large country home to their left. "Now I live in just four rooms of it and the rest is used by the farm staff, and when I'm gone the whole lot will go to the politicians to look after, God forbid."

Kate was shocked to hear someone of such standing openly criticising the Government after all of the good they had done for the country. She occasionally heard discontented voices on the train or out food shopping, but she always put them down as lazy embittered people with an axe to grind. Emily used to tell her that the agriculturalists had their own set of rules and axioms about countryside community, a sense of security which gave them a self-assuredness even so far from the SafeZones. So, rather than debate with the woman and risk stirring up a storm on something she knew nothing about, Kate let it slide. "Do you have any family left?" she asked instead, hanging on to the roll cage of the ATV whilst looking for a seatbelt.

"No, the Death popped by one afternoon and took Albert from me, and then came back a few weeks later for our children," Amelda replied almost matter-of-factly. "We managed to send off the little ones properly, but my husband, God bless his soul, is down there somewhere in the pits, poor bugger. He never had much time for other people and now he has to spend forever surrounded by thousands of them. Oh well, all good fertiliser for the grass!"

That final observation, Kate learned, was the main reason the farm and the dozens like it around the country were located where they were, apart from the benefit of having an existing train line in which send produce out easily. Amelda had scoffed when she asked why the farm was on prime crop growing land and made a scathing comment about city types not wanting to eat vegetables grown a few feet above mass graves. "I don't know why your generation are so squeamish about it," she said, sounding amused. "I heard that back during the outbreak, a lot of the townspeople had to eat their dead until the Government and army finally sorted themselves out with the food distribution, but no one wants to be reminded of that I suppose. I just hope they cooked them properly!"

Kate found the very notion repulsive, but then again she'd never been starving to death with a ready supply of fresh meat on the doorstep. People in desperate situations did desperate things, and she had to remind herself not to judge those who were forced to live by a different set of rules to their children.

As they approached a collection of large barns Amelda suddenly screeched the vehicle to a halt, resulting in a cloud of wet mud and forcing Kate to brace herself in the seat to avoid being thrown out over the bonnet. "Well, here we are! Kurt is on pig mucking duty in PB1 until further notice according to the schedule, and as the hogs are all now in for the winter he should be there somewhere," she said, before wandering off towards the nearest building and beckoning Kate, who was now very glad of the boots she'd been given, to follow her inside.

Although Kate had primed herself for the sight of hundreds of pigs cooped up together, nothing could have prepared her for the smell of the animals and manure, which was so strong she had to fight the urge to retch up her breakfast. Amelda pointed to one of the stalls where a rough-shaven young man, wearing a T-shirt and shorts despite the cold, was forking up soiled straw into a large barrow. The manual work had given him a physique that most of her male work colleagues would have envied, but his face was twisted and angry as he stabbed at the bedding and threw it up in the air, making little attempt to stop it falling all over him in the process.

"Well, I'll leave you to it dear," said Amelda heading for the door. "I'll be outside if you need me. At any point if you don't like something that man says, just scream and someone nearby will thrash the tar out of him for you I'm sure." She whistled to get the attention of a few of the other labourers and promptly left, leaving Kate to wonder if she was serious or not. Judging by the looks the others were giving her and Kurt, she guessed the old woman probably was.

Kate approached the man cautiously. "Kurt? My name is Kate; can I ask you a few questions?" she asked as politely as she could. Either he hadn't heard her or he was deliberately ignoring her, as the forking continued. So she asked again, louder this time with the same result. This was getting her nowhere, and she was rapidly running out of patience. "Hey asshole, I'm talking to you!" she shouted and grabbed the end of the fork just above where he was gripping it. The momentum of the swing nearly lifted her off the ground, but at least it got his attention.

"Who the hell are you?" he demanded, throwing the tool down to the ground aggressively.

She could smell alcohol on his breath. Perhaps confronting him like this possibly wasn't a good idea, but she'd come this far to back down at the first hurdle. "Kate Adams. Emily Palmer was my sister. I want to know if you were sleeping with her?"

"Yes," he boasted, "and before you ask why, who knows why girls do anything? Maybe she was a slut who needed it when she wanted it. She invites me round one night and throws herself at me. I guess she must have liked it, the number of times she called me over afterwards."

"Don't talk about Emily like that, she loved James," was Kate's rather weak retort. The conversations she had practised in her head the previous night had all started with him denying it, and her cleverly cross-examining him to finally admitting that he had forced or blackmailed Emily into it. The last thing she expected him to do was to be proud of it. "So why?"

He smirked at her, turned away and picked up the fork again before continuing his work. "So now you know. Thanks for coming," he said sarcastically.

Kate felt frustrated, she wanted to grab hold of him and shake the answers out of him, but he was much larger than her and probably more violent judging by his attitude so far. Perhaps the carrot was better than the stick after all. "You know how everyone here felt about Emily, and Amelda tells me you'll be mucking out the pigs in this barn for the rest of your life because of what you did," she said curtly. In reality, she had no idea why Kurt was relegated to this duty but from his reaction she guessed she wasn't that far from the truth. "A word from me, though, and maybe you can get out of here to, I don't know, herd sheep or something else that doesn't involve shit."

That got his attention back, at least, and he pondered the offer for a few moments. "Your sister had heard I was a first-gen infected apparently. I guess the old bat must have been gossiping in the office."

That seemed unlikely to Kate; he was barely twenty after all. "And were you?"

"Yes, but that's not the half of it." He stepped towards her and she instinctively took one backwards to keep her distance. "I used to be completely clean, IES-clear. Had me a nice room in the Highpoint clinic when I was a teenager."

"So what happened?"

Kurt looked down at the floor, looking ashamed and bitter. "Some nurse came on to me one day. I was sitting in my room in the block reading a comic, and she knocks on the door and walks in. I'd seen her around the clinic grounds, she made me hot looking the way she did. I guess she saw me watching her. So she leans over me and whispers into my ear there's some extra lessons the doctors want me to learn. The bitch told me she was uninfected. She told me it would be okay."

"And you believed her?" sneered Kate, wondering how he could have been so naive.

"I was sixteen years old. She was beautiful, she took her clothes off and offered herself to me on a plate. I would have believed anything she said."

"But why would she do that? Infect you deliberately I mean?" Kate often got confused by the actions and motivations of other people, but this was completely incomprehensible to her.

"Who knows?" Kurt replied. "Perhaps she was jealous, perhaps she was mental. Doesn't matter why she did it. She had her fun with me and they caught me at the next test." He looked up at Kate, his eyes full of resentment. "They just cast me out. I had my whole life set in luxury donating at the clinic and the bastards just threw me away. I had nothing. No home, no money, no career designation, just the clothes on my back. And so I wound up here, working on this Godforsaken shithole farm until I die."

"What happened to the nurse?"

"I don't care. Went to prison or down the mines I guess. But if what she did to me wasn't bad enough, the whore gave me syph as well so I couldn't even join the live donor programme." He laughed seeing the expression of alarm on Kate's face. "Don't worry I got it treated before I screwed with your sister. Not that it really matters now anyway."

The workers in the other stalls had stopped what they were doing and were now listening intently to the unfolding exchange. Kate hoped they didn't like what they were hearing, for if Kurt turned on her she'd be relying on them to come to her aid. Emily had once told her that most men couldn't resist a damsel in distress, and she hoped at least here she looked vulnerable enough to count as one.

Kurt, however, seemed determined to turn the knife come what may. "If it makes you feel any better she used to cry and make herself sick after we did it. I could hear her in the toilet gagging and sticking her fingers down her throat before she told me to get out."

"But you kept going with her anyway?"

Kurt moved closer and leered at her. "Your sister was pretty like you and she was easy, so yes I kept going with her. Tell me, does it run in the family?"

Kate felt physically sick at the thought and had reached her limit of her temper. "You're disgusting, you deserve to be with the pigs and the filth. I hope you rot down here!" she cried, her voice full of spite as she spun around and left him standing there, still mocking her. She got as far as the door, paused briefly and then screamed at the top of her lungs. She didn't turn around to witness the shouting and beating she could now hear occurring, but it made her smile nonetheless. Some people never learned from their past mistakes.

Kate met up with Amelda back at the ATV with a frustrating sense of disappointment. Kurt had merely confirmed the suspicions she already had, but Emily's motivations were still as oblique as before. The old woman had no more information to offer either, other than to request that Kate take a few personal items she'd found on her sister's desk back to James for her to save on postage. Almost everything else was either owned by the farm or had already been sent back to her husband. The small cardboard box, which was waiting for her back at the main reception building, contained a couple of pictures of Emily and James at their wedding, an old book with a picture of a horse on the cover, a few music tapes and a computer flash drive. It was the last item that piqued her interest; she picked it up and turned it around in her fingers.

Amelda looked away guiltily. "I'm sorry Kate, but I used that drive accidentally yesterday, I didn't realise it belonged to her. It looked like there were some personal things on there so I put it back in the box. I didn't open any of the files!" she hastily added.

That last denial was unnecessary, prompting Kate to presume that Amelda's curiosity had got the better of her and she'd found something inappropriate or provocative. "Can I look at it here?"

Amelda shook her head. "I'm sorry dear that's not possible, only authorised and cleared users are allowed to use the computers. Security you know, even I'm not allowed to break some rules."

It sounded like a flimsy excuse to Kate but there was no point trying to push the point further, so she thanked Amelda for her time and kind words about her sister, and finally for arranging a lift back to the station for her.

As she sat in the carriage on the way back to London, ignoring the buffeting of the tracks and water dripping onto the seat opposite, Kate stared intently at the old flash drive as if attempting to decipher its contents and what secrets it might contain.

But for that, she needed a working computer.

Foot soldiers

Joe Parker was used to being shouted at. A long career in the army with over-privileged officers barking orders, or drill sergeants shouting spittle into his face and down his squat frame had well prepared him for such things. He hadn't minded, he had even looked forward to it in a strange way, for it was a chance to learn from the best, to absorb their experiences and judgement for use in the future. As others had moaned and whined, he would be at the front of the pack, going the extra mile, carrying the extra weight and always first to volunteer when the chance came.

He'd been lucky in a way, a chance drunk encounter at the recruitment office had left his signature still wet on the paper when the first cases of the Death had started rolling into the hospitals. The army had taken him in under their wing, trained him, kept him safe from the chaos outside, and when it became their time to act he'd grabbed the opportunity with both hands. He had pitied the civvies, scrambling in the mud for food and drinking from dirty water that stank of sewage. He and his squad mates would ride in on the back of trucks and make them stand in line for the meagre provisions they were allowed to give out. The decree from above had been simple; keep order at all costs, putting the needs of the nation and the many before the few or any individual's sense of liberty. They all understood what that meant and to this day, he still remembered shooting a man who had pushed into the queue and tried to take what wasn't his from an old woman. The man had crumpled to the floor, blood frothing from his gasping mouth while everyone else had just stood there in submissive silence. No one else had tried to challenge their authority that day and he'd got a commendation for his quick action from his superiors. The chain of command was a wonderful thing, it entrusted soldiers like him to act on what needed to be done and took away the responsibility and the guilt of the consequences. It had made him feel powerful and protected, and the pretty girls offering themselves for an extra loaf of bread were just an added bonus to a contented existence.

It had been his life for over thirty-five years and he'd loved every minute of it; from the tense stand-offs and raids during the Jersey Rebellion to the routine border patrols on the sweeping vistas in the Scottish Highlands. But however much Joe wished it so, nothing was forever and the rigours he'd put his body through had eventually taken its toll, forcing him out into the real world. It was a rude awakening, making him feel directionless and adrift, so despite a generous early retirement package as an acknowledgement of his service, he'd taken a job with the Government on personal security detail for the Repro Ministry. It was mostly dull escort and protection work, but it got him out of bed in the morning, allowed him to wear a uniform again and gave him a sense of purpose. He was at ease again, at least until the day when someone had tried to assassinate the Minister. Parker had spotted the scruffy hooded man in the distance heading straight for them with a look of steely purpose, and recognised the danger immediately. Without thinking, he had dived in front of his charge as the man took out the gun and fired, the bullet striking him in the armoured chest piece and knocking him off his feet, as his colleagues had caught and beaten the assailant to death there and then.

For Parker, it had been a simple conditioned reflex born out of a lifetime of training. But the Minister had seen great bravery in his actions and seen it fit to advance him to the head of security as a reward, along with the pistol they'd torn from the dead man's grasp. But Joe was an infantryman, a ground pounder used to taking orders, not a leader giving them out and inspiring others to follow him. He'd felt a fraud, a pretender promoted far beyond his capability to do the job his superiors expected of him. For the first time in his life, he feared a task may defeat him. Military orders were easy to understand; take that bridge, secure that village, patrol that area, with rarely any room for interpretation or deviation. Politicians, by contrast, lived in the grey areas and shadows, always leaving themselves room to wriggle out of a situation should it go wrong, or sweep in and take the plaudits if things went their way. One minute he was berated for not making a judgement call, and the next lambasted for going over his authority and making ill-conceived decisions with far-reaching consequences.

And so this was where he found himself, three stories down underground in a bunker designed for a nuclear war that never happened, being yelled at by a couple of kids about the actions he'd taken in their name. He'd never seen Mr Schoier so angry, pacing around the room, shaking with temper and smashing a glass against a wall. All while the workers at their terminals outside tried desperately to pretend to be somewhere else, in case they accidentally met his gaze through the glass, or heard something they shouldn't above the sound dampening. Joe stood there at attention and said nothing while the younger man raged around him.

He deserved this verbal battering after all, and it even now it still felt like he was getting off easy. He'd done the unthinkable, he'd made a mistake and then lied about it to his bosses to try and cover it up, an indiscretion which would have got him the firing squad back in the forces. Perhaps he'd been around politics so much that the once inconceivable act of deception had seeped into his veins and polluted his blood, or perhaps after a series of failures he just wanted to not look incompetent for once. In any case, he had been found out by a few careless words to the wrong person and an increasingly conflicting set of reports. As he was rapidly discovering, when you told the truth you never had to bother about cross-checking your stories, but lying took constant vigilance and a good imagination to pull off. Otherwise, the inconsistencies began to unravel and uncover the obvious treachery within.

The politician's wife, who was wearing a plain black business dress and simple gold necklace, appealed for calm as her husband frantically ranted on about having to 'alter the narrative stream' and 'differential workflows', while continuing to pace around the room and counting scenarios on his fingers.

"Sit down please darling and let us talk about something else for a while," she said softly and cheerily, making sure it sounded like a request and not an order Parker noticed, deferring to her husband as any good woman should. "Do not worry about that now it will work out, you always find a way to turn these things around." She looked at Joe, her tone hardening slightly, "So Mr Parker, how is the IVFree project coming along?"

The security head felt chagrined at being addressed directly by Mrs Schoier, who wasn't actually even an official member of the Department, a point that everyone else seemed to have forgotten. To him, the woman's role mainly consisted of following her husband around like a lost puppy, and giving the men a reason to go into the office to ask questions as many times as they thought they could get away with. Just the type of girl who would have been on her knees during the Death and thanking men like him for the attention and extra rations the act would bring. But that was the long-missed good old days; she belonged to his boss, so he bit his tongue and played nice.

"Things are progressing, but slower than I would hope," he said vaguely. In truth things weren't really moving at all and, unfortunately, Caden saw right through his attempt at stalling.

"Don't use rhetoric with me Parker, I get enough of that from my peers. Facts and nothing else please." He sat down heavily in the seat next to Rowena. "Do you have any new information on the group structure or the backstreet clinics they help sponsor?"

"We've been unsuccessful in getting any of our agents into the group," Joe admitted. "They operate in a distributed network. The people they recruit to spread their messages know only their handler, and each of them have no idea of the rest of the structure or anyone else in the group. For all they know the contact could be ten levels down or the head of the organisation. There's a directional core obviously, but we've not got near it yet."

Caden looked frustrated. "So, no progress then."

"The main problem is exposure," Parker explained meekly. This wasn't going well either. "You can't seek them out, they come to you. The people we managed to catch and question gave up their contacts after some pressure, but all of the names were false and when we tried to use them as bait it never worked."

"To me, that suggests that the contacts have allies in the workplace who act as anonymous intermediaries with the targets," suggested Rowena, idly sorting through a pile of files on the desk and making Parker feel stupid for not making the connection himself. "I would guess that hauling them out of their workplace in front of everyone probably spooks and tips off the others somewhat."

Her husband nodded in agreement. "Yes, a bit more subtlety is needed I feel. Recruit a few female agents as low paid workers in the larger companies, get them to gently lament their dissatisfaction about not being able to afford treatment and see if that helps."

Right, so now they want a slow and deliberate plan instead. Joe felt the exasperation bursting out, prompting him to speak out of turn and immediately regret it. "I don't know why you think they're a problem anyway. It's only a bunch of liberals moaning and handing out leaflets."

Caden leant over the table, his stare burning right through Parker's skull. "It's sedition, it goes against the design of the Lottery and it's contrary to our plans," the politician fired back angrily. "For now, it's just leaflets.

Tomorrow it will be a few people with placards, then a demonstration in the street, and before you know it there'll be thousands of followers marching through the capital banging on our door demanding change. You were in Jersey back in the day Parker, you know how quickly these things can escalate."

Rowena had finally found the file she was looking for and was busy leafing through its pages. "Yes, it is much easier to stop a tumour before it grows and metastasises," she agreed, now too engrossed in the file's contents to bother finishing her train of thought. She abruptly changed the subject. "So anyway, this other business with the clinic. Is the sister going to be a problem?"

Joe mulled over the question for a second, trying to organise the information in his head to a logical outcome. In truth, he was still trying to work that out himself, but considering how the rest of the meeting had gone so far he didn't want to appear any weaker in front of them. "No, I don't believe so. I had one of the men tail her for a while. She spent a few days at home, then went to the farm where her sister used to work to visit someone, and since then she's been back home. As far as we can tell she's not done or said anything that would be considered suspicious, certainly not gone to the press or gossiped to other women at her workplace about it."

Rowena frowned at the response. "That is strange, these assessment reports suggest that she would likely pursue a private investigation. 'She doesn't like any strands left unexplained and gets obsessed over details' it says here," she added, browsing through some pages of the document and spreading them out on the desk. "I like her. I think she is wasted at that power station. Still, regardless of that, there was that incident with our good friend Doctor Pearson at the funeral."

That made Mr Schoier laugh at least. "I wish I'd been there to see that! Ran away with his tail between his legs I heard, with her chasing him back to his car screaming the place down!"

Joe joined in the laughing until a sharp look from Rowena made it very clear that he wasn't part of their private joke.

"Nevertheless, are you sure about this Mr Parker? The re-population plans are at a delicate early stage, and everything that happens from now on must do so in the right way and at the right time." She tossed the file back onto the desk and crossed her arms impatiently. "We cannot have unknown variables confounding our calculations, or people spreading falsehoods that may complicate things later on. So I will ask you again, is the sister going to be a problem?"

"No," the army man replied, making sure his voice sounded more confident this time, "she's not a threat." The power plant worker was just a woman, after all. They were occasionally a problem in the kitchen or spending too much of the man of the house's money out shopping, but certainly not capable of the kind of complicated inquiry work that the bureaucrats were concerned about.

"Okay then," said Caden, indicating that the matter was finished, for now at least. "We'll look forward to an update in two weeks on IVFree and I expect to see significant in-roads into their structure and location. And as for that other matter, be thankful that the Minister holds you in such high regard." His next statement was delivered with stark coldness; "Failure or mistakes I can work with and manage, deception I cannot. If you lie to me again it won't matter what the Minister thinks, you'll be paralysed with an injection and fed to the rats in the basement feet first as it wears off. Understood?"

Joe left the meeting room and walked straight through the network of offices and corridors without muttering a word. He got as far as the rear fire exit stairwell, the one they used to ferry suspects from the back alley to the holding cells for interrogation, before letting out a stressed sigh. He had no doubts about Mr Schoier's resolve and ability to act on his threat. He needed a result, and he needed it fast.

***

Victor had forgotten how much he enjoyed the hustle and bustle of everyday life back at the Highpoint clinic. The duties and responsibilities he'd found tedious or a chore on his ascension were now the ones he looked forward to most. The never-ending travel and meetings had been glamorous to start with, but had eventually disintegrated into a haze of spreadsheets, slide presentations and profit forecasts. He'd missed the personal contact with the staff and had even got back into a bit of laboratory work, much to the amusement of the technicians, whose deft hands could work at twice the speed that his rusty muscle memory could manage.

There was a problem, however, that being the current head of the clinic Dr Rama Chaudhri, a tall man of Indian descent who liked to show more of his heritage in his dress sense than most people found comfortable. At first, he'd welcomed Victor's presence and advice, but that had soon turned to thinly disguised irritation and enquiries on when the CEO was heading back to London. Victor had therefore done the only thing he could think of; he'd promoted him under the pretence of putting Rama on a sabbatical, to learn more about the company's structure and board-level decision making. Chaudhri was no fool, he knew he was being sidelined by a whim, but the increase in pay and perks was substantial enough to silence any of his complaints. He had emptied his desk and left for the capital without another word.

There was something else bothering Victor, though. He'd been acting restless and fidgety since Rowena's visit, eventually prompting Janet to ask him if there was something he needed to get out of his system. He'd dismissed her irritably, before sheepishly phoning her office a few minutes later and admitting there probably was. He could feel her rolling her eyes all the way from the next room, but she said nothing in reply apart to make sure he was back at the house by 9 pm. Having made the decision to extend his stay at Highpoint, he'd moved out of the campus guest quarters to a secluded cottage nearby. It offered him a comfortable space for entertaining guests and allowed him to feel more part of the establishment, rather than a temporary visitor peering in from the outside.

Janet, as always, was true to her word and at five past nine there was a quiet knock on the door. Victor opened it to reveal a beautiful blonde woman in a black fur coat and blue dress, holding a bottle of wine and a sly smile. It wasn't the politician's wife, of course, but it was a very close match and he couldn't help but be impressed by her attention to detail; his assistant's description must have been very thorough. But the fire that Rowena had started in him had gone out and the embers had cooled, and he'd sent the woman away soon afterwards with a large cash tip and a promise of discretion. Janet had not mentioned the episode the next morning nor had hinted it had even occurred which was fine by him; he'd had enough of running the events through his head and imagining a better outcome as it was, and was almost glad when the phone rang and a panicked voice at the other end demanded his presence immediately at Donor Block five.

Victor cursed as he made his way across the sports field and towards the large concrete habitation blocks at the corner of the site. In his haste he had forgotten to grab his coat on the way out of the office, an omission he was now bitterly regretting as the wind whipped around the grounds and trees, catching the leaves that the garden staff had neatly stacked into piles and teaching them a lesson in entropy. The donor accommodation buildings were not the most aesthetically pleasing on site, but in keeping with their heritage they were functional and, most importantly, secure. Each floor was built around a central stairwell and lobby with a thick steel door on each side, leading to a hallway with adjoining rooms for the residents and a kitchen recreation area at each end. It reminded Victor of his student digs at university, right down to the piles of washing up in the sink and posters of old films and pop bands on the walls. Even the older inhabitants seemed to act like they were still teenagers most of the time, trapped in an eternal loop of reduced responsibility and finding ways to fill time when they weren't on duty.

Men and women were housed separately for obvious reasons. The last thing the company needed was their main assets either potentially infecting each other, or being put out of action with unregulated pregnancies. Usually, this wasn't a problem; after two weeks on donation duty the last thing the men wanted to do was more of the same and, in addition, they were all given drugs in their food to suppress their natural urges. Judging by the content of the phone call, something had obviously gone very wrong.

He met two of the site nurses at the entrance to the second floor west corridor, one of whom was holding her arm and grimacing with pain, and both of them looked ashen white. They were soon joined by a small team of security guards who were red-faced and puffing for air, prompting Victor to make a mental note to increase their physical training regime. If they'd been fitter perhaps they would have managed to catch Emily Palmer before any harm had come to her.

"She's holed up in her room," said the injured nurse, trying not to wince when her colleague took a look at her arm and declared it needed stitches. "Jill here managed to get everyone else out after the mad cow came at me with that knife."

Victor gave them a sympathetic look in acknowledgement of their actions. "Tell me what happened here. What's the girl's name again?"

"She's called Ariane," the injured nurse, who introduced herself as Caroline explained. "She was due to start the donor programme next week as she's now sixteen, but she found out this morning that she was pregnant and then went berserk."

"How did that happen?" asked Victor. A 'surely you know that' glance from Jill made him realise what he'd just said, but this was no time for humour. "You know what I mean. Who's the father?"

"She's been close to Hugo these last few months, so we presume it's him," Jill offered. "I've been saying to Caroline here that we should keep an eye on those two. Donors aren't supposed to go off out of sight around the campus without an escort. We've had attempted assaults and kidnappings in the past here you know."

Victor didn't know that. There was a lot he was beginning to understand that Dr Chaudhri hadn't made him aware of in his monthly reports, and he cursed himself for not keeping a closer eye on things. "Do you think she was attacked?"

Caroline shook her head. "No, she said they were in love just before she went for me and there was no sign of any injuries during her routine examination last week. Actually, she must have stolen the pregnancy kit then. The janitor found it in the toilet this morning when clearing out a blockage. She'd tried to flush it down and it got stuck in the pipe. I guess she was late and got scared - as soon as I asked the group in the kitchen what they knew about it, she grabbed a knife out of the drawer."

Jill gave her friend a much-needed hug when the tears flowed as the shock of the situation began to sink in and she couldn't continue. "After she went for Caroline, she ran into her room and threatened to kill herself if anyone tried to get near to her. I got everyone else out and that's when I called you, Dr Pearson."

Victor turned to the head security guard, a stocky man about ten years older than himself, who looked like he was an ex-policeman who hadn't saved enough to afford a retirement. "Right, post guards at the entrance here and the fire exit outside, I don't want the girl escaping and doing any more damage. Do you have a remote stun gun?" he asked the guard, who pointed to the pronged trigger on his belt to confirm that he did. "Good, then come with me. I don't want her damaged, she's a company asset worth tens of millions so only use it as a last resort."

The lights in the corridor had been smashed and the blinds in the kitchen had been drawn down, leaving just thin open slits which illuminated the dust and made it dance around the men as they crept down towards the last room on the left. Once at the door, Victor realised that he had absolutely no idea what to do next and, judging by his hesitance to act, neither did the guard. It wasn't a situation he was familiar or comfortable with, so with no other solution presenting itself he knocked tentatively on the door. It brought an immediate response from inside.

"Go away!" Ariane screamed, "Leave me alone or I'll cut you like I did that nurse!"

Victor tried to sound as calm as he could, but his palms were sweating again and his response came out as more of a squeak than a command. "Ariane? It's Victor Pearson, can I come in please?" He hoped that his name would, at least, warrant an invitation.

There was a brief silence while Ariane considered the request. "Okay, just you, though. No one else. And keep your distance," the girl replied, her voice calmer now.

There was just enough light seeping through the thin curtains for Victor to survey the scene when he entered the bedroom. He expected to see the girl standing in the far corner crazed and waving the knife aggressively, but instead she was sitting on the bed holding her knees and clutching tightly to a small teddy bear, the blade discarded to her side. She may have been technically an adult in the eyes of the law, but here and now Ariane looked more like a desperately scared and lost child, and when she spoke it was more to herself than to him.

"You're going to take it from me, aren't you Dr Pearson?" she said, staring blankly into the mirror at the end of the room.

Victor ignored the question for now. They both knew the answer but she wasn't ready to hear it made manifest yet, so instead he perched on the end of the bed and glanced around the room, looking for a way to start the conversation. Common ground was always the most effective sales technique he had learned long ago; customers saw through flattery and usually went defensive on the hard sell, but a casual conversation always left their flanks open for a way in. He found what he was looking for on the bookshelf. The volumes were old and the spines badly cracked but he recognised the barely visible text style anywhere.

"Is that the Azami Chronicles?" he asked, gesturing towards the shelf. "I remember reading them when I was young, the adventures of the witch and her trials against the evil sorceress Shyla."

"It's for children," the young woman replied sadly, "I'm a grown-up now, I'm too old for those books."

Victor smiled sympathetically. "Nonsense, good stories don't have an expiry date just because we think we should be doing something more mature or important. Half of my staff still read them most likely." He paused briefly for thought, it was now or never. "You're a hero Ariane, just like the girl in those books, helping save the world and the future of mankind, even though most normal people might never know your name. But there's always a price the hero has to pay. Can you remember what happens to her at the end?"

"Yes," she replied, hugging the bear tighter and trying very hard not to cry, "Azami gives up her powers to Shyla to save her parents, but the evil witch can't handle it and the magic burns her from the inside out."

She was almost there, just one more nudge in the right direction. "I remember it caused quite a storm when it was first released," explained Victor, thinking back to his early childhood when such trivial things mattered to people. "The fans wanted a happy ending all neatly tied up, but it would have been a disservice to her character. Sacrifice is what sets heroes apart from the rest of us, not deeds of bravery or a show of kindness. Heroes know what has to be done, and they follow the path to the end no matter what challenges are put in their way."

The poor girl began to sob, tears rolling down past her cheeks and down her neck. She didn't bother to try and wipe them away. "It's not fair. Hugo and I love each other. Other people get to be happy, why can't we? Why can't I have my own children?"

For this exact reason thought Victor. The IES-clear women of the clinic were allowed to postpone the programme and have children on rare occasions only to help the continuation of the colony, and even then never their own flesh and blood. The true parents, selected to maximise genetic diversity, were never revealed to the surrogates or the children. The entire concept of the family unit was removed; no marriage, no relationships beyond friendship and under no circumstances any unauthorised reproduction. His company wasn't building the Ark, a point that Susanna had often made to him when he had doubts about what they were trying to accomplish here. The people here were product, and it was his detachment from them and their detachment from each other that made the donor system and D336 possible. He could not go down that path again no matter how much he wished it, and in any case, wishes had a nasty habit of coming true.

"No, it's not fair," he replied, "but you've been given a gift Ariane that most of those outside the gates would give all they had for. You don't realise how special you and the others here are. You'll live on through the children of others for all eternity, while the rest of us fade and die away. But there's a price to pay for that, just like for Azami."

Ariane caught his gaze and nodded through the tears, before picking up the soiled knife again. But this time it was just to pass it to him, her decision finally made. They emerged from the hallway together, Ariane still clutching the toy bear, and Victor with one arm around her. He passed the girl over to Jill and quietly asked the nurse to get her prepared for the required procedure.

Once out of view, he turned to Caroline and the remaining security guard. "This doesn't happen again, ever. If any of the donors even hold hands I want to know about it and them put on different rotation. I won't have all we've built up here destroyed because a couple of teenagers get a crush."

He looked out of the window to see the girl walking slowly with her aide towards the hospital block, the soft toy discarded on the muddy pathway behind them. As a boy, he'd often imagined himself as a character in the books fighting side by side with Azami against evil and oppression, but it had never occurred to him until now that he'd end up becoming Shyla.

The auction house

There was always a certain buzz that surrounded the days leading up to the auctions. The atmosphere became almost palpable with excitement as everyone turned their thoughts to spending what little disposable income they had, on whatever junk they could. The monthly sales up and down the country all happened at the same time and on the same day too, which just served to concentrate the anticipation and fervour. Some buyers ended up travelling far from home, just for the chance to bid on that one special item they thought they couldn't live without. Michael had always loved the pilgrimage and the sense of occasion that the auctions brought with them, meeting up with friends for drinks and the thrill of hunting a bargain. Kate had never really seen the point of them; she had the radio, some books and a few worn cassette tapes for entertainment. For her, being able to get luxuries more easily took away the special nature of Christmas and birthdays. Added to that, the large crowds of shoppers all scrambling for position put her off on the few times she had gone along to see what all the fuss was about.

This time, though, things were different. This time, she actually needed something, so she had made the journey south far beyond her local venue to the largest mine and warehouse complex in the region, one that had a reputation for selling what she needed.

Kate's grandparents and great-grandparents, just like everyone else of their generation, had spent decades throwing away perfectly serviceable possessions because they were slightly broken, out of fashion or simply because they needed to make way for yet more junk they didn't need. With nowhere else to put the waste, nor the inclination to sort the useful from the spoiled, they'd simply thrown the whole lot into a giant hole, covered it with soil and tried to forget it ever existed. And there it had stayed; buried, worthless and ignored, until the Death came and changed the notion and definition of valuable.

Harold George Watson and Dennis Jameson, who had been roommates at university studying economics if the official story was to be believed, came to realise that the hidden rubbish was worth far more than the now empty and derelict houses built on it. They made a deal with the Government to set up mining operations around the country, to reclaim and refurbish what they could and auction it off to the highest bidders. The authorities got their cut of the profits and first claim on any raw materials or precious plastic excavated, the public got a chance to obtain a slice of history or items they couldn't get elsewhere, and Watson and Jameson made a fortune off the back of it.

The excavation work was dirty and dangerous, with sharp metal and glass slicing at exploring hands and toxic gas build-ups threatening to overcome the workers, or cause an explosion. Consequently, most of the digging, extraction and sorting were performed by prisoners that the company had contracted from the Government's penal system. They worked exclusively with hand tools to avoid damaging the precious relics within the soil, a painstaking process any archaeologist would feel a flush of envy at witnessing. A lot of what the miners recovered was beyond repair, of course, but for every decomposed sofa or rotting mattress there was a stack of video cassettes still pristine in their cases, medical supplies with an expiry date that made no real difference, or a box of computer parts whose only crime was they weren't the latest technology.

Kate didn't have a lot of sympathy for the workers, especially when there was one-hundred percent employment for those prepared to do a hard day's work, rather than just take what they wanted from others. She thought that the convicts should, at least, be grateful they hadn't suffered the same fate as their predecessors had during the crisis. The liberal minority called it genocide and demanded recompense, but to most people it was simply known as 'Prisoners Dilemma'.

Faced with a large overcrowded prison population and a falling number of guards during the early days of the Death, the now notorious Minister for Justice, Alfred Schoier, had denied the criminals any medical attention and kept them locked in their cells twenty-four hours a day. The masked army relief guards did the bare minimum they could, occasionally tossing in a minimal amount of food through the bars for the inhabitants to fight over. The pattern was repeated across every prison throughout the country. When enough had died, the bodies and waste were cleared out and replaced by new inmates from a nearby facility undergoing the same reductive policy. The Death and other unsanitary diseases spread again, and the cycle continued. One-hundred institutions became fifty, fifty became twenty, twenty became ten, until only a handful were left.

Some said that Schoier had even deliberately infected the prisoners with as many sub-strains of the bacteria as possible to maximise the mortality rate, but that had never been proven. In the end, though, Kate couldn't really see what other choices he had. It wasn't like he could let a bunch of murderers, rapists and paedophiles out on the streets. Historians and commentators had the luxury of hindsight, and alternative ideas that would never have to be tested in the real world. It was easy to be right when no one could prove otherwise.

Hard work was rewarded as it always was, however, and the most prolific workers could look forward to a reduction in their sentence, and a good work placement when they got out. The Government was always willing to give a second chance to those who had earned it, a carrot which spurred on the workers to ever higher productivity, despite the dirty conditions.

Although Kate could see the operation in the distance from her train window on her daily commute to work, the scale of it wasn't apparent until viewed close up. The vast open face quarries, tunnels and transport lines all fed into the mammoth processing and sorting building named Warehouse One, where the auction itself was held. The simple name of the place did no justice to its neo-Victorian architecture; a magnificent unification of red brick, black marble, iron arches and glass, rivalling any of the Ministry buildings in the capital. A large annexe to the side served as a station and loading area, where Kate and a large group of other early risers disembarked and hurriedly aimed for the entrance line. The trains ran every fifteen minutes on auction day, and the big rush wasn't expected for at least another hour when the warehouse doors opened. Kate hated the crush of people even more than the raw temperature, so had set her bedroom alarm to wake her long before dawn broke.

Kate joined the queue of in the half-frozen muddy path by the side of the rail track, and was disappointed to see that dozens of people had got there already in front of her. Technically, of course, it didn't matter where in the line she was, but the early birds got the best chance of looking at the lots before the bidding started. As a result, they could spend their money more wisely, rather than trying to peek over the heads of a crowd six persons deep and guessing the condition of the products. The air was frosty and sharp on the lungs making drawing breath painful, and her feet were numbing quickly despite the thick tights and extra socks she wore under her jeans.

She grasped hold of the piece of paper in her coat pocket tightly, having already gone through several cycles of unzipping her pocket to check the note was there, zipping it back up, then anxiously unzipping it again to check it the paper hadn't fallen out the last time she checked it. Just keeping hold of it seemed like the best compromise in the end. Thankfully, the lonely man in the computer store had been very helpful. Kate had taken a leaf from Emily's book and simpered, twirled her hair and put on the best damsel-in-distress act she could muster when asking him to take a look at her broken PC. Luckily he'd taken the bait and ran some diagnostics on it with a hefty discount, before scribbling down on a piece of paper the part she would need to get it up and running again. Unfortunately, he didn't have any of the parts in stock himself (which was fine by her as she couldn't afford a new one anyway), but had offered to fit it for free for her if she managed to obtain one second-hand.

The auction queues had somewhat of a reputation of being a social hotspot, and listening in helped pass the time. It also kept her mind off her frozen extremities, as the minute hand on the large clock on the wall slowly cranked the hour gears towards nine. Friends and rivals formed small groups and told stories of previous encounters, what rare items they heard rumours that had been found, and psyched each other out on how much cash they had available to spend. Many of the locals had formed cooperatives and opened small stores nearby, competing out the casual shoppers and then selling their winnings on for a profit later. It was a risky business, as their competitors would often spread false rumours of demand and prop up the prices on what turned out to be worthless curios. As a casual buyer herself, Kate hoped they would all burn out each other's money before they got to her section of interest, but she doubted it. Computer parts were about as safe as it came for investments, and the meagre amount of cash she had got from selling the broken television, combined with what remained of her wages for the month, was looking more inadequate by the minute.

Kate scanned past down the growing line and briefly caught the glance of a shabby-looking dark haired man in the distance. She could just make out the flame as he lit up a cigarette, the cancerous smoke camouflaged by the condensing breath of the people around him. Kate recognised him from somewhere but couldn't place him, and before she had a chance to dwell on it there was a big roar up ahead, signalling that the doors were about to open. Fortunately, the British traditional sense of fair play and queue etiquette was one thing that had survived the Norwegian Death. The mad rush she had been dreading didn't occur, and everyone politely channelled into the main reception and exhibit hall instead.

Kate let out a gasp at what she saw on the other side of the doors. Just beyond the large buckets of bidding paddles there stood scores of glass covered cabinets and tables, full of goods diverse as watches and gardening tools, bike parts to cooking pots, and everything in between. All were neatly categorised, with large signs pointing to the relevant sections. Some of the larger items and furniture pieces were displayed behind red ropes, a boundary that everyone respected in fear of being evicted by the large security guards who stood watch vigilantly around the room. She made her way to the 'computers and electronics' area, just as some excited voices in front of her proclaimed that some working games machines had been found, causing a small surge as a crowd of thrilled men sped off into the distance.

If the power station worker thought the amount of paraphernalia available would extend to aisles and aisles of what she needed, the reality came as a disappointment. There were only twenty memory modules behind the glass screen, and some of them had reserve prices higher than she could afford before any of the bidding even started. She scanned the notepaper again, which told her she needed a minimum of two gigabytes of memory to run her operating system, and then checked the descriptions next to the items. Five were the wrong thing entirely, and five more were too small, meaning she would have to win multiple lots which seemed very unlikely. Three were exactly what she wanted, but the rest had a much larger capacity and were out of her price range. If she wanted to get one of the modules she desperately needed, luck would have to be on her side.

Half an hour later, the large crowd congregated in the glass-roofed atrium at the far side of the warehouse. The floor was clear apart from some benches around the sides and a large platform at the end, where the auctioneer and his agents now stood. The vendor, an old man in a black suit and top hat, stood stooped over the lectern and addressed the mass over an address system which fizzed and hummed with electrostatic feedback. "Welcome everyone to the Watson and Jameson Recycle Auction! Most of you are regulars and will be familiar with the rules, but for everyone else be aware that bidding will only be accepted by a clear raising of your number paddle." He pointed at someone Kate couldn't see at the front and added, "we don't have time to be messing about with winking and hat tipping," much to the amusement of the regulars. "Remember everyone this is a cash auction, so only bid with the money you have with you, and if you can't pay you'll be banned from future events. That said, good luck and God bless!"

The shoppers whooped and cheered as the first lots were brought on by two glamorously dressed women, who held them up for everyone to see. A revered silence descended on the crowd as the auctioneer described the items in the first category, which turned out to be entertainment. "Lot 001. A set of five records bundled by genre. Country and Western apparently! Let's start at twenty, any takers?"

The bidding was rapid and frantic for the first lot and all of those that followed. Spotters pointed out new punters to the auctioneer at an alarming rate, and any pause of more than a few seconds resulted in the gavel violently smashing against the block with a joyful call of 'sold!'. Despite the cold, the excited energy and heat from all of the people crammed into the atrium soon began to take its toll. Kate began to feel suffocated by those around her and became desperate for air, trying to escape the throng with ever more urgency. Her place near the back of the crowd meant that getting out was, at least, possible, and the others were more inclined to help people leaving than those trying to push their way further up. She frantically started to envision what would happen if there was ever a fire here, before putting the thought out of her mind as she reached the safety of the exhibit hall. She leant over an empty lot table to draw breath, unaware of the figure approaching behind her.

"Kate Adams?" the stranger asked, startling her and wrenching her out of her panic attack. She turned around too quickly and to her surprise found the voice belonged to the scruffy man in the queue.

"I'm sorry I scared you," he said, grasping her arm before she lost balance and fell. "Hey, are you okay? Women don't usually swoon at me after the first line. Takes at least three usually." He put on a warm smile at that last part, but his attempt to charm her fell flat and Kate snatched her arm away from him, taking a step back to get him out of her personal space.

"Who the hell are you? And how do you know who I am?" she demanded.

The man looked a bit taken aback, as if it wasn't usually the reaction he got from women he approached. "My name is Andrzej, I was a friend of Emily's," he explained, putting out his hand in greeting which Kate refused to shake. But at least now she knew where she had seen him before.

"You were at the funeral," she said, eyeing him suspiciously. "You looked to me like you shouldn't have been there but you wanted to talk to James. Why? Did you want to threaten him, blackmail him or otherwise you'd cause a scene? Are you a friend of Kurt's?" That made sense to her, with Kurt's free ride dead perhaps he wanted to extend the arrangement with extortion.

Andrzej, however, just looked mildly amused by the accusations. "That's a lot of questions in one go," he replied, "so to answer: Yes, I wanted to give him my condolences, no, no, no, and Emily spoke about him but I've never met him. I'm surprised she mentioned him to you, though. She said the two of you didn't get on." He threw up his hands in mock surprise before smoothly adding, "I can't imagine why not."

Well, he certainly isn't lacking charisma, Kate had to admit despite herself. On closer inspection he was quite handsome, and his scruffiness was the result of design rather than a lack of hygiene or proper grooming. It gave him the demeanour that he could probably blend into a crowd quickly, and his dark and nondescript clothes would fit in anywhere. Well, apart from a funeral anyway.

"So, how did you know my sister? She seemed to have a lot of admirers wherever she went," Kate asked, her voice trailing off sadly at the end, the usual guards she put up dropping for a moment.

"Emily and I shared a common cause, a way of looking at the world you might call it," he replied rather cryptically. "We both thought something wasn't quite right with the order as it is now. Not enough laughter, not enough sense of wonder, not enough innocence."

"So what do you want with me?"

"I saw you going toe to toe with Victor Pearson and thought you looked like someone worth getting to know," he said, sounding impressed at her exploits, "but you left before I could talk to you. It's lucky we bumped into each other." He looked around to survey their surroundings before asking, "So what brings you here? You don't strike me as a shopping girl who needs trinkets to make her happy."

"I'm investigating why Emily was killed," she found herself saying, shocked how easily this stranger had disarmed her with just a few words, "and I need a part for my computer to do it."

Instead of being aghast at this revelation though he just looked sombre. "I was never convinced by the story myself," he agreed. "If something doesn't make sense then it's usually not true."

Kate was just debating internally whether to tell Andrzej about Emily's pregnancy when she was shaken out of his spell by a loud ringing noise emanating from the atrium. "I have to go," she said hastily, running her fingers through her hair. "They're about to start the next session and I can't miss it. It was good to meet you." She hurried quickly away before he had a chance to respond or follow her, threading her way through a small crowd of happy buyers carrying their winnings, and headed towards the hall.

If anything, the atmosphere back inside the chamber had intensified, the buying fervour amplifying the excitement and feeding back on itself in a loop. The auctioneer struck his hammer loudly and appealed for calm before bursting out with enthusiasm. "And here's what you've been waiting for ladies and gentlemen! The start of the computer and spares section. Good to see you nerds still have plenty of money left after the sci-fi videos earlier!" He paused while everyone over about the age of fifty burst into laughter, leaving their younger compatriots confused and irritated about being left out of the joke. "So let's start with Lot 201," he continued as the noise abated. "Two gigabytes of DDR3 tested and fully working! I don't want to waste your time or mine, so let's start at one hundred and go up in tens please!"

Kate checked the note again to triple-check it was the correct thing, and was startled to hear the price had already doubled before she'd even got a chance to sort her paddle out. She quickly rectified the situation and thrust her number into the air, but her bid had been nullified by someone in front of her before she lowered it again. She tried twice more with the same result, and by the fourth attempt the price was too far out of her reach. The second module came up a few lots later and the pattern repeated itself much to her dismay. She wondered if the regulars were banding together against her or anyone else in genuine need. The woman next to her somehow read her thoughts and assured her it was always like this, but somehow that didn't make Kate feel any better as her chances of success continued to diminish.

The crowds had begun to thin out slightly by the time the final module, and Kate's last chance, came up for purchase. As she had predicted, the higher capacity ones were well out of her price bracket and she just hoped that everyone interested had spent their cash by now. She didn't even bother raising her paddle during the opening bids, hoping that playing it cool would deter others from joining in. It seemed to work; only two rivals were battling it out as the price edged up towards her limit. Seizing her chance, she casually lifted up the bat and registered her bid, triggering another round from the other two buyers. She raised it again, and to her surprise and delight, this time, they both fell silent.

The auctioneer sensed the pause and began to wind up the bids. "Once, twice, and..."

The wait for him to add 'sold' seemed to stretch our forever, and he got half way through the last word when another paddle far to the left of her shot up in the air with a shout of "YES!" from its handler. Kate instantly knew the bidder from earlier failures; it was one of the big buyers with endlessly deep pockets. She had one offer left before she ran out of money but that too was quickly overrun, leaving her out in the cold and swearing under her breath at the other buyers and her own lack of currency. Without bothering or caring who was still bidding or who would win her prize, she turned and stormed angrily out of the atrium, tossing her paddle forcefully into the collection bin as yet another new punter joined in the fray. That had been her last chance and she'd been deprived by some greedy bastard who didn't really care what they bought, only interested in turning a profit on it later. God only knew what she was going to do next. Perhaps it was a fool's errand, after all. Perhaps she should just give up and go back to her job at the power station and let things lie, as Michael had told her to from the beginning. Feeling thoroughly disheartened, she got as far as pushing at the main doors when a now-familiar voice called out behind her.

"Kate! Wait up!" Andrzej cried out, narrowly missing a display cabinet in his haste to catch up before she crossed the threshold. "Close your eyes, I have something you might be interested in."

"I'm not in the mood for games," she replied curtly. It had been too long a day and too stressful for frivolities and distractions, even from someone as charming as him. Not that her response seemed to put him off, however, as he slid his hand into his jacket and pulled out a small box.

"Consider it a gift. For Emily," he said simply, holding the package out towards her.

Kate accepted the present, her curiosity piqued on what could be inside as she opened it in front of him. Her eyes widened with elation as she realised that is was the memory module she thought lost moments ago. "I'm sorry I was rude just now," she apologised in a flustered voice, returning his smile with one of gratitude. "I don't know what to say. Thank you."

"People say that giving is better than receiving," he said smoothly, bowing slightly in recognition of her appreciation. "Seeing your face light up just then I'd have to agree with them."

Kate felt a shy blushing heat rising to her face as she tried in vain to think of an appropriate response, but her betraying mind went blank. It was all she could do to just thank him again for the gift.

Andrzej reached into his jacket pocket again and, this time, pulled out a pen. "I'm sorry Kate I have to head back to the auction, I still have some things I'm trying to get or the others will be complaining." He briefly took back the box and scribbled a number on the top before returning it to her. "If you find anything of interest you want to talk about, let me know." With that said, he turned and left back towards the auction room, leaving Kate turning the box over and over in her hands, feeling confused and conflicted. She'd always had a healthy distrust of strangers and as Andrzej himself had said, if something was too good to be true it probably wasn't. But then again, if Emily had trusted and confided in him then he couldn't be all bad, and despite her brain screaming out warning signals, part of her was desperate to see him again.

Secrets

Kate's hand was trembling as she pressed the power button on the computer and the fans whirled into life, waiting for the familiar error beeps to begin their mocking chorus of failure. The man in the shop had assured her that the new part had done its job, but it was still a relief when the operating system's desktop blinked into existence. Emily's flash drive went in next with crossed fingers, as the computer took what felt like an age to recognise it, before finally expunging its contents into a file window. There were a number of spreadsheet files about the farm and some home accounts, but the one that caught her eye was a text file simply labelled 'diary'. Kate clicked on it and scanned down, looking for anything that might offer a clue to her sister's fate.

"I sometimes feel we go through our lives thinking of things to do, to occupy the empty space in our souls or to amuse ourselves with distractions and pastimes. Some people work, some travel around the country and some fill their homes with ornaments and junk. I've tried all those and more, but it doesn't make any difference. The house is always too quiet, and the longing I feel to fill it with joy just gets more frustrating every day. The animals on the farm help ease the pain; seeing them born, grow and nurture their own, but it's not the same. Days tick by into weeks, and weeks into months and nothing changes. I feel I might go mad, trapped in an endless loop of expectation and false hope dashed with every cycle of the moon.

...

"I met a man called Andrzej today who stopped by the farm, looking to sell us some electrical equipment he'd bought at one of the auctions. We got chatting about the future and children. I can't remember now who brought the subject up. I don't know why, for some reason I really opened up to him about how I feel about things. He just had that

easy going manner about him you know, that makes you want to confide in him? I think even Katie would be dazzled by his charms!

"Anyway, as he was about to leave, he leant over and whispered into my ear what there were more people who felt the same as me. As he spoke I felt him press a piece of paper into my hand, and then he was gone without another word. I made sure I was alone later before I opened the note. There was the phrase 'the next generation is a right, not a privilege' and a phone number written underneath. Oh, how mysterious!

...

"My curiosity got the better of me today and I rang the number. Andrzej seemed pleasantly surprised to hear from me. He told me how special I was to make this leap of faith - I bet he says that to all the girls! We arranged to meet next time I'm back in London. I'll just tell James I'm going shopping and sneak away for an hour or two - he'll never know.

...

"I can't write much about it, even here, but my eyes have been opened! I had no idea the scale of their operation was this big. I have to admit I was nervous about accepting the request and it took some persuading, but I've agreed to do some spotting for them. Nothing serious, I just have to keep an eye out and report back if I meet anyone who feels the same way we do.

"After speaking some more to Andrzej, he says he feels very sympathetic to my circumstances. His intentions were to try and help no matter what my decision about contributing to the cause was, so I shouldn't think myself obligated to them either way. It was good to hear, but I would feel guilty just taking and not giving back.

...

"Andrzej knows of some places where it could happen, although he was coy about the actual location for secrecy's sake.

...

"I had my appointment with Isaac today. I explained I didn't want any injections, or anything that IVS could spot on an examination or screen that could

invalidate a Lottery prize. I'm on thin ice as it is, and James would never forgive me if I jeopardised the chance if we ever happened to actually win anything.

'I presumed that Isaac would just say it was impossible and that would be that, but he didn't! Apparently they've been working on a new method and I could be an ideal candidate, and because it's experimental the cost will be minimal compared to the other options. I have to admit, I didn't understand the specifics apart from the timing of my cycle is critical, but there are no needles required. All they need is a sample from James to kick off the procedure and we're good to go!

...

'I'll add this to the computer when I get to work tomorrow, but James is still asleep so I've sneaked downstairs with my notepad as there's something I need to tell you. I got the sample for the clinic today! I'd not been home for a couple of weeks so it was easy enough to set the mood with some red candles, my hair down and I put on that short slinky dress he likes me in. I had to do something in bed I normally wouldn't and I'm not sure God would approve, but it was the only way I could think of. Luckily James got very excited and it didn't last long, and while he was lying there with a big grin on his face I leant over the bed and dribbled it out into the collection tube they'd given me. I just hope that didn't damage the sample at all, and this will all be worth it.

...

'I told James I needed to leave early to get back to the farm, but I only went a couple of stops before I got off and met Andrzej at the station. I'd kept the sample in the fridge overnight just like they wanted me to, and put some ice into a pot to keep it cool in my bag. But the pot had a small hole in it and water dripped all over the floor in the carriage. Heaven knows what the other passengers thought of it! Luckily it wasn't too far to the clinic and Andrzej was full of conversation and ideas on the next stage of the campaigning. Support for the cause is growing every day, and it's just a matter of time before the whispered demand for change turns into a shout.

'To say the treatment was uncomfortable would be putting it mildly! Despite the anaesthetic, I could feel the cold of the metal as it slid its way up inside me to deliver its precious cargo. The follow-up a few hours later to take the biopsy, as they called it, was even worse. Still, it's over now and I'm sure it will be worth it in the end. I wanted James there to witness it, but there was no way he would approve and I don't want to put him in

that position. Oh, how am I going to explain it to him if it works? That it's a miracle, a gift from the Lord? No, he wouldn't believe that for a second. I just hope once he sees the new life we made together beginning to grow inside me his heart will melt, and he'll forgive me for what I'm doing.

'Now it's just a matter of waiting and praying.

...

'My prayers went unanswered. I bled today. I rang Andrzej and he gave me his sympathy which helped a bit. It was a long shot after all, being such an experiment but I'm still desperately disappointed and downhearted. Andrzej suggested I give it another shot but I'm not sure. Even though they are doing it at cost for me it's still a lot of money to find and hide from James, especially with the wage freeze situation at his office. I'm not sure how many times I can handle that sick sinking feeling of bad news either.

...

'I don't understand. I feel different. I can't explain it but something has changed inside me, making me feel whole, complete. Perhaps the treatment did something after all, but I don't know what or how? Perhaps I'm not half the problem now? All I know is that this yearning inside of me is now stronger than it's ever been. I need to do something or I fear it could consume me completely

...

'I heard something very interesting today while I was helping out with moving some silage bales for the cows. Apparently there's a man working here who's a first gen'er; infected but fertile! There are still quite a few around the country, of course, but most of them are as old as mum and dad would be if not older, whereas Kurt is younger than me! I asked Amelda about it, who said he was originally from the Highpoint clinic and warned me to stay away from him, but I'm intrigued by an idea that refuses to go away. If what I'm feeling is real, then Kurt could be a solution to my problems. If it works, I'll tell James about the clinic visit with Andrzej and pretend the process was successful. He'll never know, it won't make a difference to how I feel about him or our child. It'll be no different from a second prize win in the Lottery, I'll just know who the male donor was. I've got a couple of weeks now until I'm at my peak, which is plenty of time to strike up a conversation with

this Kurt and make some plans. I don't need to be lifelong friends with him or anything, I just need him to notice me.

...

"I've had a glass of wine before Kurt arrives to stop my hands from shaking. I'd never done anything like this before, gone behind James' back I mean. I don't want any emotion. It will just be an act of reproduction, nothing more. Kurt is quite young and I don't want to scare him off, so I thought a meal and some music would help set the mood. I don't think he's that experienced with women so I'll probably have to take the lead.

...

"I just made myself sick again but it doesn't help. How could I have gotten things so badly wrong? How could I have been so naive, so stupid?

"I could smell alcohol on him when I let him in. I'd barely had time to ask him if he wanted a drink, and he said I hadn't invited him for dinner and he knew what I wanted. Before I could say anything his hands and stale breath were on me. He didn't let me get as far as the bedroom or even take my dress off, just hitched it up and started his business with me over the table. At least he didn't try and kiss me, and where he was against me meant he couldn't see me crying. I tried to pretend it was James and this was one of the games we sometimes play, but it was impossible. My husband is kind, gentle and considerate, but Kurt was nasty, rough and selfish. When he'd finished, he just laughed and left me there as he sat down and started eating like nothing had happened. I feel dirty and violated, but it's all my own fault and no amount of vomit will cleanse me of this.

"And the worst thing of all? I've got five more days of this hell to go through while the window is open in my cycle. I don't want to and I hate myself for doing it, and what it would do to James if he ever found out, but I've started down this path and it's too late to back out now, otherwise tonight will have all been for nothing.

...

"Too upset to say much. I tried to slow him down when he came over this evening but he wasn't interested in eating or conversation. He seemed to enjoy it the more I struggled so I just lay still while he got on with it.

...

"All attempts at pretence were gone tonight, he was on me before we'd even got out of the hallway once I'd let him in. At least he left quickly after he'd finished, didn't even say anything, just left me on the floor sobbing and went. Is this what I have become? So obsessed and addicted with the idea of children that I whore myself out to anyone who I think might abet in my crime against my body and my soul? I'm ashamed, and I hate myself. I hate that man for doing this to me. And most of all I hate James for making me go through this because he can't give me what I want. What I need.

...

"I can't do this any more. He came again tonight but I pretended to be out. I closed all the curtains, turned out the lights and sat on the sofa hugging my legs and cried as quietly as I could, until he finally gave up and went away. I sat in the bath and scrubbed and scrubbed until I bled and the water was cold, and I had to stop myself from carrying on. I thought Katie was the only one who did things like that after copying daddy when she was little, but perhaps compulsion does run in the family after all?

"Mum always taught me to put my trust in God, but my faith in Him is running out. Surely this isn't His plan for me? To serve as a warning to others on giving into temptation, to become a subject for a sermon for bowing down to carved images of children? I've heard that addicts talk about hitting rock bottom, and after last night, I can't imagine things getting any worse than this.

...

"A new day today. I shouldn't have said what I did about James. I love him with all my heart and he's a victim in this just like we all are. I've still got years left before our time runs out, and who knows what promotions he'll have by then, and what I'll be doing here? Amelda seems to be grooming me to succeed her in running the business when she is too old and frail to carry on. Not that I can imagine her ever becoming like that, she'll be burying us all I'm sure! And who knows, I'll keep buying the tickets every week and maybe fortune will smile on me.

"No more Kurt, no more stupid behaviour, no more feeling sorry for myself and no more pointless dreaming about the future. Time to move on and enjoy what I have.

...

"The Lord tests us all. Some will fail and turn from Him and others grit their teeth and rise to the challenge. Perhaps miracles do happen after all, as it seems I passed the test! Sorry, I'm being unnecessarily cryptic. I got a call from Katie today and she gave me some amazing news. She won first prize in the Lottery! And even more unbelievably she wants to give it to me! Altruism and my sister don't usually go together and I don't know what this will do to her relationship with Michael, but I'll be eternally in her debt. If it's a girl, I'll call her Kate. I can't put in words how ecstatic I feel right now. My own child. Our own child. Our family. James must never know what happened, what I did, what I went through. When I get back from IVS I'm deleting you.

"Have faith, and hope will always win through in the end."

It was the last thing Emily had written. Kate tore the flash drive out of the computer and stamped on it repeatedly in a screaming rage until it was a meagre pile of broken plastic and silicon dust on the floor. Emily was right, James must never know what her sister had endured in her quest for family, and his memory of his wife should be left untarnished forever at any cost. She thought back to Kurt; however hard she thought she had screamed back at the farm, it hadn't been fucking loud enough for what that bastard deserved. Hopefully, Amelda was true to her word and he'd spend the rest of his days knee deep in pig shit where he belonged.

She glanced over at the number written on the memory module box before putting on her coat and slipping it into her pocket. If Andrzej represented what she presumed he did, it wasn't a call she wanted to make from home.

Political pressure

The engine spluttered and complained as Kate twisted the key in the ignition and held it there, while simultaneously pumping the accelerator with her foot. The car hadn't been started since before Michael had left, and the cold damp weather wasn't helping the already depleted battery spark any life into the old vehicle. She was about to give up when the slow turn of the starter motor suddenly sped to a crescendo and the engine roared into existence, accompanied by black plumes of smoke emanating from the exhaust pipe and cheers from a relieved owner. Andrzej had warned her that his new place was quite far from any station, so she had decided that moving under her own steam was probably easiest. Michael had usually driven if they needed to take the car anywhere, which made the first few streets and junctions a nervous challenge as she made her way carefully to the outskirts of the city, despite the lack of other traffic to crash into.

When she was growing up, Kate had always imagined the end of the SafeZones to be a vast concrete wall with checkpoints and armed soldiers guarding a post-apocalyptic wasteland beyond. The reality was much more mundane; apart from some rusty yellow signs warning the public and some ageing temporary barriers on the pavements that anyone could climb over, one would never know that the line even existed. Where the area had been once seen as a desperate last stand between civilisation and the chaos beyond, it now just separated off the more run-down part of the city, where the police presence was reduced and Government services harder to reach. In fact, many people even chose to live on the other side of the divide, or 'beyond' as they called it. The cheaper house prices more than offset the inconvenience of fewer rail stops, reduced amenities and an inconsistent electricity supply. Kate couldn't see the attraction herself, and preferred security and safety over most things, especially to a bit of extra spending money here and there. Or at least she thought she did, but the desire to know and to understand was a more powerful driver than either of the others, so despite a slightly sick feeling in her stomach, Kate weaved the car passed the broken barriers and drove off into the unknown.

A couple of miles down the road later, Kate spotted Andrzej exactly where they'd agreed to meet. He was gesticulating to a small group of women who looked to be exactly what their choice of clothes suggested they were. The number of workers walking the streets so early in the day was an unintended consequence of the Norwegian Death, a concept that had always fascinated the operations specialist. During the pandemic, both women and men had sold themselves in order to survive or feed their families, sex being the original currency that never went out of fashion to those willing to exploit the misfortune or desperation of others. It had become so commonplace that by the end of the crisis the taboos that had once surrounded the practice seemed outdated and old-fashioned, with both clients and sellers much more open about their deeds than would be acceptable previously.

This had been compounded by the discovery of the IES virus and without the danger of unwanted pregnancy, most people also stopped using protection. The result was a surge of syphilis infections and other sexually transmitted diseases. To combat this, the Government had legalised prostitution in an attempt to clean up the industry and provide a cleaner and safer environment for the employees. It hadn't worked, of course, but it gave an alternative career to those whose looks or talents in the bedroom were the only thing they had, and a precious tax revenue stream to the authorities. Looking at the state of the women, Kate doubted they were properly licenced workers, but this side of the SafeZone no one was really going to demand to see their certificates. Andrzej looked relieved as she pulled over and he quickly jumped into the car, much to the annoyance of the other women.

"Oi bitch, get back to your own patch!" one of them shouted as Kate accelerated away, leaving the angry crowd behind throwing rude gestures at her.

"I was trying to get them to move on," Andrzej said needlessly.

"Hey, none of my business," Kate replied playfully, enjoying him looking flustered. She'd only driven a few hundred yards, however, when she abruptly slammed the brakes on, causing her passenger to throw out his hands against the dashboard as the seatbelt dangled impotently by his side. "I need to ask you a question," she asked, cutting him off in mid curse. Something had been bothering her for a while now, and better to get an answer now before she got too deep into the situation. “I don't believe in coincidences, like our 'chance meeting' at the auction. Have you been following me?”

“Not directly.”

“What's that supposed to mean?”

“I was following the people following you,” Andrzej explained, rubbing his bruised wrist. “Did you know there were Government agents tailing you for a while?”

Kate was taken aback. “No, I didn't. Why would they do that?”

“Because they knew you were looking into your sister's death, or at least you were probably likely to,” Andrzej said, adding “Don't worry they've stopped now,” when he saw the concern on her face. “I'd imagine that your outburst at the funeral put you on their radar. I thought if you were interesting to them then you were probably interesting to me too, so I apologise for the deception to get closer to you.”

Kate, however, was now more confused than ever. “Why would they care? I was angry at Victor Pearson, not them.”

“Well, that is the question isn't it?” he added slightly cryptically. “So, did I pass? Can we get going now before those ladies catch up with us?”

“Okay,” Kate replied, putting the car into gear and heading off down the deserted road. She still didn't trust him enough to tell him about Emily's pregnancy. For all he knew, her sister witnessed some malpractice or industrial secrets which required her silence and that's what she was investigating. She couldn't understand why the Government would be sending out people after her in her quest about Emily's condition, though. In fact, she presumed they would be pleased with a potential cure, unlike Dr Pearson and his company who had the most to lose. It was a simple pipeline with obvious inputs and outputs; water to valves to turbines, cure for IES to loss of business to murder.

The change was almost imperceptible, but as street after street passed by the buildings and their surroundings became slowly more neglected, derelict and seedy. A few bin bags became a large pile of split-open decay surrounded by rats and hungry dogs, the potholes in the roads ran deeper and more numerous, and what few people there were looked increasing ailing and raggedly dressed. Kate couldn't understand why people even lived this far out; it wasn't as if there was a shortage of housing in the nicer areas nearer the edge of the SafeZone. Even though all empty houses were owned by the Government, the prices were reasonable for those willing to work for a living. If they were here by choice she surmised, then they were probably criminals up to no good, or on the run from the authorities.

"It's just up here," said Andrzej, pointing to an old disintegrating office building at the end of the housing complex. "Don't worry, someone will be out to look after your car while we're inside," he added, noting the look of concern on her face. She was glad of the reassurance, as for all its ageing faults her car was probably worth more than the buildings surrounding it. "So Kate, welcome to IVFree."

He led her through the main entrance lobby of the building, where two men stood guard with old hunting rifles slung over their shoulders. They greeted Andrzej warmly as he raced on ahead enthusiastically, leaving Kate puffing behind, following him up two flights of stairs and down a winding corridor. He grinned broadly at her like a child with a new toy, before flinging the doors open to reveal a large open plan space full of cubicles, many of which had been torn down and heaped in a corner to fit in the equipment they'd dragged up there. The windows had been hurriedly blacked out with paint which had sloshed over the frames and down the walls, presumably to hide the operations within, leaving only a few working strip lights which gave the expansive room a slightly dim and artificial gloom.

Everywhere Kate could see there was a bustle of activity; in one corner a young woman was designing leaflets which were then printed and assembled by her older male colleague, and in another at least ten of the cubicles housed workers on portable phones talking to their contacts. Kate fixated on a group of animated-looking people who seemed to be filming a protest video, where a slim attractive woman in a suit stood on a makeshift stage with a green background, gesturing at some invisible objects whilst quoting various statistics about treatment costs.

A multitude of questions came at once into her head, but her job at the power station had conditioned her too well. "How do you even have power here?"

"There's a petrol generator in the basement," Andrzej replied, letting out a laugh. "I show you the beating heart of our operation and that's the first thing you ask?"

A young man with short dark hair and a trimmed beard, who was wrestling a new tape into the camera, stopped what he was doing and walked over to join them, habitually cleaning his glasses on his shirt on the way. "This used to be a police logistics control centre if you'd believe it," he said and introduced himself in a strong Irish accent as Patrick. "Sorry to be rude, but who are you? Andrzej why have you brought a stranger here, especially with Aisha still missing? You know how close we are to a breakthrough here? She could be a Government agent sent to spy on us."

"You're correct, it was rude," replied Andrzej, chastising his younger colleague. "Kate is Emily Palmer's sister. She's investigating what happened to her so I've offered our services to help."

"Why are you so worried about the Government?" Kate piped in, cutting off the other man's apology. "They've said many times that IVFree isn't illegal, so why the cloak-and-dagger act?"

Patrick scoffed at the suggestion. "Oh it's not illegal, but the Government would shut us down and make us disappear in an instant if they ever found us."

The sense of instant dislike Kate felt for the man grew stronger with every word he said, prompting Andrzej to send him away on an errand before he did any more damage to the situation. "I'm sorry about Patrick," he said once he was sure the Irishman was out of earshot. "He doesn't mince his words when he is passionate about something, like we all are here about the cause. One reason he's behind the camera and not in front of it." His attempt to diffuse the atmosphere only half worked as he guided Kate to a small area at the end of the room, where a makeshift kitchen replete with a kettle, fridge and seating area had been set up. He poured them out a mug of tea each which Kate eagerly accepted before continuing his campaigning. "We give everyone a chance at happiness Kate. As we say here, the next generation is a right, not a privilege. We make people aware of their options and put pressure on the Government to change things. We're still at a whisper in the grand scheme of things, but our volume gets louder every day."

Kate looked around at the other members of the group, who'd now returned to busying away at whatever they were doing before she'd arrived. They didn't appear to be as concerned as Patrick was about outsiders which she was glad about. She suddenly felt very vulnerable; paranoid people were unpredictable, and the familiar comfort of the SafeZone was far too distant for anyone in authority to come and help her. "So do all of your members come here to help out?" she asked, hoping that expressing an interest in their movement would smooth things over.

"No," said Andrzej, shaking his head. "Most of our members just help spread the word - some leaflets, posters on walls, calling into radio shows, it all adds up. And we put people who want to go further in touch with alternative options and clinics they might actually be able to afford."

"So you take a cut of the profits?" Kate challenged her host, instantly regretting her question when she was supposed to be playing nice.

"Not at all. We're not like InVitroSolutions, feeding off desperation," he replied, sounding offended. "All of this you see here around you, it's all been donated to us by the men, women and couples who believe in us, believe in what we are doing. Hope is not a currency or a commodity to be traded amongst the rich and powerful. Everyone should be able to see the future in their children, not just the advantaged. Sure there's the salary scale the Government put in, but it's an illusion. How can you ever save up three times your salary if you need ninety percent of it just to survive day to day?"

"I guess that's true," Kate admitted. She'd never really given it much attention having no real interest in the subject, but now the thought of it had planted something intangible in her mind.

Andrzej took the moment and pressed his advantage, "I mean Emily and James both had jobs didn't they? But your sister was so desperate to have children the last thing I heard from her was that she was going to offer herself to a random stranger."

"She didn't get the chance, he attacked her before she could!" snapped Kate back angrily. She couldn't bear to use the word 'rape'; the emotion of discovering her sister's ordeal was still red-raw and she didn't want to cement the act in reality by acknowledging its existence.

Andrzej looked shocked at the revelation. "I didn't know, I'm so sorry. She didn't deserve it; no one deserves that."

"No, they don't," replied Kate. Andrzej's remorse was genuine as far as she could tell, but it did bring the original point back to the fore. "They would have saved the money eventually. Emily was just consumed by the idea of children, it wasn't her fault she couldn't wait. And there's still the Lottery of course that anyone can win."

The couple were interrupted by Patrick, who returned grasping a piece of paper. "The Lottery is fixed you know."

"That's impossible."

"Yes, it is, but it's fixed nonetheless," the Irishman replied, taking it as a cue for sitting down opposite them, even though no invitation was forthcoming. "I don't know how they do it, but I've been modelling the results from the last five years for months now," he said, gesturing at one of the computers whirling away in the background, "and they're not random. They're skewed."

"How?" asked Kate, now intrigued despite herself.

Patrick took a pen from his shirt pocket, turned the paper over to a blank side and proceeded to draw a set of crude scatter plots on it. "If you graph the winners next to age, it's random. Same with ethnic background and as far as we can work out from the yearly census data, it's true with location and wage levels as well."

"So what's the problem then?"

Patrick looked very pleased with himself. "No one who's unemployed has ever won," he declared. "Ever. We know they buy the tickets, though. No one with a criminal record or a recent family history of it has ever won. There's something else that doesn't fit too but I can't work out what the determining factor is."

"They're corrupting the Lottery somehow, Kate," said Andrzej, agreeing with his counterpart, "artificially selecting the winners and slowly selecting out what they deem as the undesirable parts of the population."

"But that's impossible, it's a random draw," Kate argued back. Water to valves to turbines, tickets to draw to prizes. There was no room for interference.

"Yes, as you said," Patrick responded shortly, "but the statistics don't lie. The odds against the patterns we see are millions to one."

"So say it is true," said Kate, confused at why this was even an issue. "Isn't that a good thing, though?"

Her response induced a look of shock and disgust in Patrick, who looked like he was about to unleash a tirade of abuse until a resigned-looking Andrzej calmly interjected. "The main problem Kate is what happens when they get to decide who's worthy, or when they simply get impatient." He took a big gulp of tea and put the mug on the table slightly too loudly. "Have you ever heard of Hadamar hospital?"

Kate shook her head, feeling she was about to find out.

"It was a mental hospital in Germany back during the time of the Nazis," Andrzej explained as Patrick nodded approvingly, making Kate wonder how many people he had told this story to in the past. "They decided that the weak and mentally challenged had no place in their society, so they decided to cleanse themselves of them. It started small at first, sterilising afflicted children so they couldn't reproduce and pollute the healthy population, and they moved on and did the same to the adult patients. But that wasn't fast enough, they got impatient, so they decided to just start gassing them instead. They'd bus them in from nearby hospitals for treatment, a hundred or more per day, but no one ever came out again."

Kate suddenly started to feel very uncomfortable. She wasn't used to having her opinions and beliefs challenged in this way, and had even considered herself a bit of a moderate compared to many of the people she worked with. On the other hand, she didn't appreciate being manipulated either.

Andrzej wasn't finished yet, however. "By the time the Allies liberated the patients the hospital had murdered over ten thousand men, women and children. And for what? Being a burden, being non-productive. My ancestors fled that part of the world, its ideology and persecution for a better life here. They'd be appalled at what's become of the new home they fought so hard to protect."

"You're being over-dramatic, that could never happen here."

"Possibly, but it's up to people like us to remind everyone that the right to reproduce is universal," countered Patrick.

"It's true," agreed Andrzej. "We are the last natural generation, Kate. What happens next is in the hands of others."

Patrick put down his pen, screwed the doodled paper into a ball and threw it at the litter bin, where it bounced off the rim and onto the floor. "You see Kate, you can control the populace either directly or indirectly, down the barrel of a gun or by guiding their behaviour. The first way will never work in the long term, a lesson that this Government seems to have learned at least, so they tried the second. So what then? You can keep the people down at heel or bribe them with luxuries, but oppression always results in revolution and decadence leads to entitlement and disillusionment. So you keep them in the middle, make them thankful for what they've got with the hope that things will get better in time. Make them work hard for everything they have and they'll love you for it, and have no energy to demand change."

"Look, I'm not interested in your crusade," said a combated Kate, who had decided enough was enough. "I just want answers about my sister."

Patrick leant back in his seat and let out a laugh. "You don't seem that interested in helping us, why should we help you?"

He did have a point, Kate supposed. If she wanted their help she would have to trust them, no matter how misguided she thought their views were. "Because I have some information for you. You want something to get everyone's attention, to get your breakthrough, then this is it. Emily was pregnant when she went to IVS, and I think Victor Pearson had her killed to cover it up and protect his company."

Patrick spilt his drink all over the table and Andrzej's eyes widened like saucers at the revelation. "Well, that certainly explains a lot. Are you sure about this?"

"Yes. She wrote in her diary that she went to see someone called Isaac and he did something to her."

"Yes, that's right," replied Andrzej, "I remember, I was with her for the treatment, but Emily said later that it hadn't worked?"

"I think it did, but not in the way she expected," said Kate. "Perhaps this Isaac could give us more information?"

Andrzej rose to his feet, pumped with excitement and a beaming smile. "Well then, let's go and ask him."

***

Isaac's clinic was only a couple of miles away, but the small side roads were so rutted and littered with debris that the car would likely get stuck or damaged, so Kate and Andrzej headed out into the depths of the old city on foot. The sun had passed its zenith now, and cast long shadows against the crumbling walls of the office block and terraced streets beyond, adding to the foreboding air and darkening the sinister-looking alleyways even further. Kate felt increasingly uneasy and vulnerable as they walked by a small group of old men, who stopped and stared at her as they huddled around a rusty incinerator with yellow flames licking at the wood within. Andrzej looked like he fitted in here, whereas her clean clothes and shoes were in stark contrast to the torn and filthy garb of the indigenous population, marking her out as a target for the nameless shapes at the windows.

"Why are all of these people here?" she asked her escort, as she stepped closely to him, the need to feel safe overriding her usual requirement for personal space. "Are they criminals?"

"Neither by choice," Andrzej replied, stopping briefly to light a cigarette. "The Government cares about you if you're useful, but once you're not they wash their hands with you." He pointed to an old woman across the street who was bent over a cane, being helped up the steps by a couple of young women to the house they had claimed as their own. "We kill our aged with Dignity, we discard those who become ill or injured if they don't conform to our rules, and call it LifeChoice. So they end up here living in condemned housing with no electricity, surviving by digging through the rubbish they dump from the SafeZones and eating what vermin they can catch."

Looking at these poor people, being confronted with them and their looks of despair as they scratched out an existence where they could, filled Kate with shame. These were not demons or lazy individuals lying around at home waiting for the Government to provide for them; they were her after a few wrong turns, they were despondent women like her sister who'd received a botched treatment with a dirty infected needle, and it made her feel rotten inside. "I didn't realise," she said, her voice dripping with guilt.

Andrzej turned to her and tipped his head in sympathy. "Of course you didn't, it's not something anybody thinks about until it happens to them. Before I started down this path I was just as guilty of the worst villainy in the world as anyone else: the crime of indifference."

It was true of course, the news often ran with stories of people in remote areas of the country that suffered from a disaster, quickly followed with an outpouring of sympathy and a cascade of donations and aid. But headlines were fickle things, quickly replaced with others when they started to stale and wane. The affected people were still there, though; still suffering, still in need, still forgotten.

"But surely these people still have a voice?" Kate pleaded, "We live in a democracy, after all, and they could vote for change. There are the elections in a few months' time."

Andrzej scoffed at the suggestion as he breathed out a lungful of smoke. "Well, they call it a socialist democracy but it's fascism pure and simple, just made softer around the edges to be more palatable to the masses. The Government talk about building a strong society, but what happens when you replace 'society' with 'state'? How long has it been since a different party was in charge? Not since before the Death. There's not even a proper opposition outside of a few independents campaigning on local issues."

Kate thought about arguing the point but decided against it. She felt awful for the people here, but they were victims of circumstance not a campaign of persecution from those in authority. The country had needed a strong Government to guide them through the bedlam of the plague and the rebuilding afterwards, and that had required some sacrifice of choice and freedom in all aspects of life. She granted Andrzej some degree of victory, however, perhaps though some of those rules that were so essential then now needed revisiting in more civilised times. She changed the subject instead. "So what's your story? How did you end up running the group?"

"I was a lecturer in humanities at one of the universities if you'd believe that," replied Andrzej. "I used to love it there; students are a bottomless well of ideas and dreams, and like sponges when it comes to absorbing new concepts and attitudes. We still have many contacts around there, spreading the word and gaining support. It's where I first made contact with Patrick actually."

Kate had never been a student, but she had always been envious of the extra years of carefree existence they enjoyed before joining the rest of the nation and contributing to society in a positive way. University courses were difficult to enter and even harder to pass, being saved for the elite while everyone else learned on the job or at local colleges one day a week. Growing up, she often thought she should have been on the academic ladder, but fate had guided her away from that path to something only years later she had begrudgingly admitted was much more suited to her. Even now the memory of that day was as fresh as last week; the cold exam hall and evaluation areas, where she and everyone else in the class who were aged eleven that year, performed the tests and tasks that determined the course of the rest of their lives. The assessment hall was impossibly large and dimly lit, the thin arcs of sunlight from the small windows near the ceiling giving the only clue that the outside world still existed. The floor was covered with small tables set far apart away from the prying eyes of her classmates, which she had been glad about. They were not kind to her and usually left her out of their play times, so the last thing she wanted was to help them now they were in competition.

The only obstacle between them and the friendlier practical tasks was a large booklet of puzzles, word games and strange questions. The puzzles and games had been easy, but she had struggled with some of the questions on facial expressions, and thereafter on any of the practical tests which involved interacting with groups of unfamiliar children a few years older than her.

From then on, the career paths assigned to them that moulded their education and experiences were split into three main areas; Academic, Services and Operations. Academia was reserved for the engineers, doctors, scientists, politicians and teachers, and carried the most prestige and responsibility. Services were for people who worked with the public or on the front line, and Operations was for those individuals like her who made sure everything worked how it should. The critical workers were drawn from all of three careers to avoid accusations of favouritism, for even the hospitals couldn't function without people like her to make sure the doctors had the equipment they needed, or the nurses had beds to house the sick. It was a system that worked perfectly, and meant that valuable education time was not wasted on those who had the ambition but lacked the intelligence or aptitude to carry it through. Engineers designed the railways, the operations staff made sure the network functioned efficiently, and the service employees drove the trains and ran the stations. A place for everyone, and everyone in their place.

Kate suddenly realised she'd been so lost in thought that she'd forgotten to continue the conversation, and Andrzej was looking strangely at her. "So what happened?" she asked hurriedly.

"My wife Lucja," he replied dolefully, looking away. "She was like your sister in a way; desperate to have children, to fill that void, that instinct. So we saved and saved, but it was to no avail in the end. There was an... accident, and I lost her."

"I'm sorry," said Kate, wondering what the 'accident' was but not asking out of respect. She knew from Emily's tragedy how eager the morbidly inquisitive could be for details, usually the more salacious the better.

Andrzej smiled sadly in acknowledgement. "So after her death I decided to dedicate my life to helping other people like Lucja, who wanted a family but either could never afford it or couldn't rely on the luck of the draw."

Although Kate still thought Patrick's accusations far-fetched, the idea had become a seed planting roots as it passed through her grey matter.

A few disparate pieces in the start of a new puzzle threatening to worm itself to the fore, when the existing one for Emily was not yet complete. Or perhaps it was all part of the same picture, a shifting maelstrom of images constantly splitting and merging in different forms, nearly impossible to decipher? Even if it were true, there was something missing, as even Patrick himself had admitted. If it were just about criminals or the lazy, the Government would have simply made them ineligible for the draw.

Her companion echoed her thoughts. "I know Patrick was a bit overwhelming back there and I'm sorry," he said, stopping in his tracks and turning towards her, "but I understand his concerns. We're at a crucial stage in our development, we're too big not to be noticed by those in power but not big enough to be missed by the body politic if we're cut down."

"He mentioned someone called Aisha?"

"Yes, she's one of our outreach agents but she hasn't checked in recently. It could be that she just got delayed somewhere, but it warranted some precautions at our end nonetheless," Andrzej explained, sounding to Kate like he was trying to convince himself of Aisha's safety rather than her.

They walked in silence as they went deeper into the city, more due to a lack of anything to say to each other than for safety's sake, as everyone they saw kept to their own business. Kate was glad for the respite, as having to constantly defend her opinions to apparently everyone she met was getting exhausting. The peace was broken, however, a few minutes later when Andrzej stopped at the entrance to a particularly dingy-looking alley and pronounced that they had arrived at Isaac's.

The alternative clinics and their practices were often referred to as 'backstreet IVF' by the press and general public, but Kate had never imagined that the term would be so literal. The street, with narrow Victorian terraced houses offset at slightly different heights to accommodate the hill they stood on, could have been the same as the one she lived in. But compared to her well-kept home this area looked feral, as nature slowly took back what humanity had stolen from it all those years ago. The planet played the long game and always won in the end, no matter what the dominant species at the time tried to do to it. A broken window, a cracked piece of concrete or a split in the tarmac was all the invitation it needed to encroach, spread and reclaim.

It had performed a remarkable job on the back of the house Kate now stood by.

"Did you expect a neon sign?" laughed Andrzej as he knocked quietly at the door. There was no response at first, then a sound of clomping feet, a twitching of the net curtain in the window, and finally the door opened and a figure emerged from the shadows.

Kate wasn't quite sure what she was expecting, but it wasn't a short man in his late twenties with bushy, curly hair and a bright blue Hawaiian shirt. Perhaps he was the assistant she mused, but this theory was dashed when he gave Andrzej a tight bear hug and introduced himself to her.

"Isaac Arrington at your service, proprietor of all your holistic second generation fertility requirements," he said with a beaming smile, posh accent and some over-dramatic hand gestures, "What can I help you with today?"

Andrzej interjected before she had a chance. "This is Kate; she was Emily's sister. We have some questions for you about the treatment if you have a few spare minutes?"

"I was sorry to hear about her death," Isaac said before looking suspiciously around down the alley. "This is probably a conversation to best have inside."

If the exterior of the building gave Kate little confidence, the interior was even worse, with what remained of the wallpaper peeling off the wall and the wind whistling through a large gap between the sash windows. The tatty and rotting floorboards were crudely covered by a series of mats and rugs that lead to a door at the back of the enclosed staircase across the far wall.

"Hmm, yes sorry about this, the cleaners couldn't make it this week for some reason," said Isaac, deftly bounding across the islands of mats like he was playing hopscotch, before reaching the door and twiddling the dials on a number lock hidden behind a small picture. "Anyway, the magic happens in the basement," he said enigmatically and disappeared through the now-open door.

They followed him down a dark stairway to another closed door which he flung open dramatically, instantly bathing them and the surrounding area in warm light. Kate peered through the entrance and was confronted by a very clean looking reception area complete with plastic chairs, a table stacked with magazines and an attractive young woman sitting behind a desk, pretending to look busy by idly tapping at a typewriter she clearly had no idea how to operate.

"There's usually a group of us here but we tend to not work on a Sunday, so Rafaela here was helping me with some paperwork," he said in a wholly unconvincing manner which fooled no one. "Whilst you're here, I might as well give you the tour. It's just through here."

About half of the generously-sized main treatment room was sectioned off with semi-transparent plastic sheeting where Kate could just make out a crude surgical bed and trolley, accompanied by a strong smell of industrial alcohol she recognised from the cleaning areas at the power plant. The rest of the space was given over to two folding tables upon which sat microscopes and stacks of lab glassware. A bank of under-bench fridges and freezers were tucked away in a corner, as was a small liquid nitrogen tank surrounded by blocks of polystyrene.

"Oh that reminds me, I need to get that refilled," commented Isaac following Kate's gaze to the tank. "Stupid thing only lasts about a fortnight. Anyway, so, how can I help you both?"

"I shouldn't worry about anything else Isaac until you tell Kate where you get the electricity from," quipped Andrzej, lightly patting her back.

Kate usually got annoyed by others mocking her, but somehow Andrzej managed to include her in the joke, which made it much less objectionable and even somehow endearing. The faint humming of a generator in a nearby room gave her the answer she needed, so she just grinned and gently elbowed him in the ribs in retaliation.

"Everything here has to be portable," said Isaac as a way of explanation for the scene in front of them. "We tend to move around a fair bit, always trying to stay a few steps ahead of the Repro Ministry." He moved closer to Kate and whispered conspiratorially, "Don't tell anyone else, but I don't think they like us very much!"

"We always put people in contact with this clinic above all the others when they seek us out," said Andrzej, making their host blush slightly. "Isaac here was one of Victor Pearson's brightest. Well, until they caught him, anyway."

"Caught you?" asked Kate.

"Yes," said Isaac, "the result of a misspent youth of theatrical histrionics and access to medicines during my education, unfortunately. I had quite the penchant for morphine you see." He winked at her before adding,

"Well that and one of my patients, and unfortunately I was apprehended in a compromising position with both at the same time, so they had to let me go."

Kate wasn't quite sure what to say at this revelation so just said she was sorry to hear it.

He grinned back at her. "Not as sorry as I was, she was stunning! They could have waited about five minutes longer at least." He glanced around briefly for dramatic effect, "Okay then, two minutes. Oh well, ships that pass in the night. After that, of course, with my powerful but rather unique skill set my employment options were rather limited, so I decided to set up my own business here in the bustling metropolis you see around you."

Kate tried to imagine Emily here, full of excitement and trepidation as they performed whatever mystery procedure it was on her. Kate had spent her life under-estimating her younger sister it seemed, a mistake born of burgeoning necessity as the innocence of childhood was replaced by growing pains, grief and responsibility. Kate had spent the time after their mother passed away busying herself, trying to organise both her sister's and their father's lives; a task that required practicality and detachment, else the magnitude of it would surely overwhelm her. She believed all choices in life, no matter how big or small, were governed by the three antagonistic actions of the head, heart and gut; logic, emotion and intuition. While Kate trusted logic over the others, Emily had always been the emotional one, driven by whimsy and her feelings above pragmatism and strong decision making.

Kate now realised far too late that regarding this as weakness had been an error of judgement. It had given her sister courage to follow her ambitions wherever they took her, whereas she had always played it safe, far within the boundaries of her limited comfort zone. This was now all changing, of course, as the recent journeys and discoveries attested to, making her wonder if this new-found fearlessness and determination was Emily's final parting gift to her. "I'm here to talk to you about the experiment you performed on my sister. It was apparently a new technique that you hadn't tried before?" she asked, before realising it sounded too much like a demand, a situation she quickly rectified. "Please, I've come a long way to find you."

Isaac strolled over to one of the tables and sat down on it, the extra weight causing the braces on the legs to creak and complain as he picked up a petri dish and held it up to the light. "The problem with IVF treatments is that they leave a mark. All those injections and hormone pills are like a beacon to anyone who knows what to look for."

"That's what Emily was afraid of."

"Exactly. All of the other alternative clinics out there either don't care or don't have the expertise, but fortunately, I have both."

"So what did you do to her?"

"Okay, simple version to put it in context. Victor Pearson's company fixes the gene the IES virus knocks out by doing a standard IVF, followed by a co-injection into the one-cell zygote of a CRISPR/Cas9 complex, and a single-stranded repair oligo template. The gene then functions normally until the virus knocks it out again a few days later, but by then the gene's job is done anyway so it doesn't matter."

"That was the simple version?" said Kate sarcastically.

"You should hear the complicated version!" he cried jovially, "Okay then, normally the gene gets fixed by InVitroSolutions shortly after the egg is fertilised in the dish using a puncture repair kit and an instruction manual."

"You could have just said that to start with," said Andrzej.

"Then I would have missed out on the chance to sound impressive to our guest here. Anyway, we tried something different." He walked over to one of the drawers in the corner of the room, and pulled out what looked to Kate like a metal syringe with a small flexible wire sticking out of the end. "It's a lot more complicated than it looks!" he declared, noting her distinctly unimpressed reaction. "Anyway, as I was saying, we tried something different. Instead of forcing biology to do what we want when we wanted it, we waited for nature to take its course."

"Emily indicated that the timing was important?" asked Kate, as Isaac nodded in agreement.

"Indeed. Whereas normally one would bring the egg to the party, we brought the party to the egg. We waited until Emily's body had released one naturally and injected a mixture of her husband's sperm and our own special repair recipe up her love tunnel." At that last point, he lifted up the syringe and made a high-pitched squelching noise for effect. "The real magic is in keeping everything all together. My contact in Cambridge tagged on a localisation sequence, adapted from their sheep work, to the complex that homes in on the egg in the fallopian tube. They then added another to allow everything to get through the cell membranes, so the repair could occur." He looked apologetically at them both. "It's a pity really it didn't work."

Andrzej glanced over at Kate and broke out a broad smile, "Actually, we think it did."

Isaac looked utterly shocked, which was instantly replaced by elation. "Oh my Lord, are you serious? But you told me it hadn't held?"

"It didn't, but she got pregnant later on after she was attacked by a first gen'er," Kate replied, dismissing with a wave of her hand Isaac's opportunity to offer sympathy. She'd had enough of reliving those scenes in her head after reading Emily's ordeal, and had no wish to go through them again. She wanted answers, not pity, but it did remind her of something at least. "My sister wrote that you did a biopsy a short while later. Could that have done something somehow?"

Isaac ruminated on this for a short while. "When we do a normal IVF session we keep a few eggs back in storage with our QC cell lines for R&D purposes; they're not viable, of course, but still useful. In this case, we took a sample of Emily's ovarian tissue to check for any off-target activity, but the results were fairly incomprehensible so we kind of just ignored them if I'm honest with you. The original treatment must have done something to an egg that hadn't even matured yet." He clicked his fingers simultaneously on both hands and then dashed off in the direction of a rusty filing cabinet, before delving into one of the drawers and pulling out a file with a cry of triumph. "Ah, here it is! Fortunately, our collaborator has access to a genome sequencer as well as being a handy person to sponge liquid nitrogen from, so we ran a bit of the sample through it. The counts and sequences were really odd, though. It's like the gene has been mutated and duplicated, but usually that's bad news and lethal for the cell."

Kate felt her hopes rise up. "So you can find out how it works?"

"No, sorry," Isaac replied. "Even if I did have that level of expertise, the amount of resources needed to crack it would be astronomical. Hang on I'll show you," He opened the file and passed them a large sheet of paper with a picture of lines and boxes at the top and various rows of tiny letters and numbers underneath. "The top part is a picture of the gene that the virus knocks out and below are the sequences we got back," Isaac explained. "The counts of sequences should be the same as the area surrounding it but they're not. There are several single base pair mutations in there as well, but not in all of the reads."

Kate studied the paper intensely for a moment before concluding she had no idea what any of it meant, and by the look on Andrzej's face he didn't either. She went to pass it back but Isaac refused. "You can keep it. See if you can find anyone who might be able to make sense of it, although to be fair that probably means my old boss. Nobody knows more about this gene than him."

Kate sighed, feeling too despondent to think straight let alone sound optimistic about the next steps. Whenever she got near to the answer it slipped out of reach, and each time the arduousness of the challenge to the next clue seemed to double, like a series of doors each exponentially distant from the last. She turned away from the two men as they continued the conversation on what the results might mean, pretending to examine the treatment room while she tried to compose herself before facing them again.

"Okay, well if you have any insights please let us know," said Andrzej in a disappointed voice, concluding the discussion. If he noticed that Kate was upset, he was polite enough not to mention it. "I'm sorry Kate, but I don't think there's anything more for you here. I'll see you soon Isaac, but we should probably be leaving now." He went to take Kate's hand and after initially shirking away, the gesture was reciprocated as they said their goodbyes to their host.

They were nearly at the door when Isaac gasped and leapt up from the table, sending a pile of flasks and test tubes crashing to the ground, and shouted to them to stop. "Hold on, I think we've all missed the elephant in the room here!" he cried, pausing briefly to pick up the few remaining unbroken tubes from the floor. "If the treatment worked on a different immature egg and managed somehow to fix it permanently, then Emily's child would have been immune to the virus. She'd be cured."

"Of course, you're right," said Andrzej, joining Isaac's growing sense of excitement. "This was never about Emily; it was about the future."

"I guess when she went to IVS for treatment and they couldn't work out how she was pregnant someone panicked. Wow, bet they were pissed off!" Isaac exclaimed, before apologising profusely to Kate and again offering condolences for her loss.

"It's certainly a good motive for murder," agreed Andrzej, turning to Kate. "So what do you want to do now?"

Kate held up Isaac's results and examined them again. "I want Victor Pearson. I want to show him this paper and for him to tell me what it means. I want him to look into my eyes and confess what he did to my sister. I want him to admit what he's done."

"Yes, and that he held the cure for humanity in his hands and scorched the earth," added Andrzej, "but there's no way though we can ever get near him."

Kate was about to agree with him when an idea struck her. "Actually, there may be a way. Emily didn't win the Lottery, I did, and when she died the prize got sent back to me. You know, I think it's time I made an appointment at IVS Highpoint."

Bait

The bulky and heavily tattooed sergeant, known simply as Harris, appeared suddenly from the murky darkness, almost taking Joe unawares. "Charges are in place sir, and we have a code green from the team up on the ground."

The old soldier acknowledged the report and felt his pulse quicken, the moment of anticipation a far greater rush than the adrenaline of the attack, or the thankful prayers of the aftermath. He glanced around to check the preparations unfolding, as the ten-strong unit did a final check on their own and each other's kit before showtime. Every day the Repro security force seemed to grow, not just in numbers, but in scope and specialities; a fledgeling private army spreading its wings as protection of the Ministry's interests began to turn to pre-emptive action. Joe had originally started training a small band of volunteers himself, but now he didn't even recognise most of them. That fun and rewarding task had fallen to another, while he focused on the much duller 'big picture' of planning and overseeing operations. Here was a chance to get his hands dirty again.

As the sergeant slipped off to get the rest of the men into position, Joe tried to work out what had annoyed him more; that the Schoier girl had spoken to him the way she did, or that her idea had actually worked. All it had taken was to plant some agents in some of the larger businesses around the city to spread some quiet dissension about the current order, and less than a week later IVFree had bitten at the hook. He felt almost sorry for the woman they'd caught when she made contact; anyone could see that she wasn't a soldier or spy trained in counter-interrogation techniques. She was just a scared little girl, playing at being a revolutionary. She had folded and spilt her secrets along with her bowels at the first hint of pressure from the questioner, a constant stream of information and reports jabbered out between tears of despair and humiliation. Although much of the intelligence had turned out to be useless and full of fabricated names that didn't check out, the insight into the structure and location of their base was eagerly received from his superiors, and their current mission was the reward.

Joe's patience, however, had been severely tested over the last few days by the constant unearned bravado from the unit he'd hand-picked for this mission. It was said that one could tell how much a soldier had witnessed and endured by how many stories he told. The animated characters at the bar who told tall and loud tales to the younger generation about the storming of an enemy base had, most likely, never even seen combat. Whereas the real heroes sat quietly in the corner, hunched over their whiskies and calling silent toasts to fallen friends. This cocky lot were unproven children, and when the bullets started to fly he would see who became men and who ran. The prisoner had told them that some of the group were armed which had warranted this cautious two-pronged approach; the front assault to keep them distracted and panicked, and the blitz from below to rout them to a quick surrender. The windows of the building had been blacked out but the thermal imaging showed it was leaking heat, so someone was at home, Parker just didn't know how many or exactly where the enemy was. So here he stood, in a cramped and damp abandoned sewer access tunnel that ran adjacent to the basement, ready to blast a hole through a wall and straight through the heart of IVFree.

Even though it was now over three decades ago, the gloom of the passageway and smell of damp brick and moss took Joe right back to the tunnels in Jersey during the rebellion. The small island had grown tired of the fortress mentality and trade restrictions imposed on it from the mainland since the Death, and decided on insurrection rather than compliance. It had started small at first, with a few demonstrations, but then the riots against military property had begun and organised armed resistance quickly followed. Joe had been stationed with the rest of his battalion at the Mont Orgueil garrison at the time, and their local knowledge had quickly resulted in them being deployed to the front lines of the assault, to crush the rebels before the idea spread to other parts of the nation. The populace was getting impatient, quickly forgetting why the country had almost perished like so many others. It was outsiders that had brought the plague to their door, and the rest of the world could keep their problems from now on.

The insurgents had set up base deep within the tunnels excavated during the second Great War, and with a newly-discovered cache of weapons and ammo from that period, they'd established a defensive perimeter and formed raiding parties in a frighteningly quick time. The guns may have been well over a hundred years old but an ageing MG 42 could still cut a man in half just as well as their modern equivalents, if not better. In the end, of course, the rebels were no match for a disciplined fighting force and although the defeat took much longer than expected, the eventual capitulation was never in doubt. To Joe, surrender was not a cowardly act, just one alternative outcome of a battle once the tide had turned beyond the ability to alter its flow. Fighting to the last man where there was no tactical advantage to be gained elsewhere was a worthless waste, at least in civilised combat where both sides respected the rules of engagement and treatment of prisoners. Only fanatics continued to fight when there was no more point, but since their kind usually had no place in any new order, the loss to society was minimal. Despite their lack of training, the fighters in those tunnels had been fierce but fair, and had earned the respect of Joe and the other career soldiers on the ground. The top brass had been so impressed, in fact, that many of the vanquished foes had later been offered roles in the armed forces. Most had accepted, their original point made and understood. The Government were all about second chances even back then, for talent was a thing to be nurtured, not punished because of a few misguided choices.

Joe paused for one last breath, the air electric on his skin, and gave the order to the crew on the ground. Two minutes to go, two minutes for the enemy to dig down in defensive positions and to have their backs turned on his own team when they advanced. He'd told the squad leader up top to go in guns blazing to panic the defenders, an order they'd obeyed with aplomb if the sounds coming over the radio were anything to go by. If IVFree lost a few in the fight then that would be no great loss, there'd still be plenty left for questioning and a nice public prosecution. That is, of course, if the people inside fired back. The Government liked to play at being within the law, and shooting a bunch of protestors in cold blood if they turned out to be just a group printing a few leaflets would be a hard sell even for them.

The explosion from the charges was small, but still sent a pressure wave that passed through Joe's body making him momentarily nauseous. The squad charged through the smoking breach and shattered bricks, and into the basement of the building. They were up the stairs in seconds, and burst through the door into the main floor shortly after as the shots from the ground team ceased, accompanied by shouting of ultimatums to lower weapons and waved guns from his soldiers. Joe stepped through past his unit to see two bodies, lying face down and riddled with bleeding holes. A small group of six people were huddled behind an old sofa, visibly shaking with fear. *So much for ideological revolutionaries* he thought, this bunch was no less cowardly than his prisoner back at base had turned out to be. He had hoped for at least a decent challenge for his men, and it was only when he strode over to the crouched figures that he realised that something was terribly wrong. These weren't the young and passionate idealists that had been described to him; they were old, bedraggled and stank of piss.

The sergeant strode over to the quivering group and grabbed the nearest one, a skinny man with a long white beard who looked to Joe like he should have taken Dignity and done the world a favour about ten years ago. Harris threw the man hard up against the wall by the throat and held him there up so high that his feet were off the floor, his legs dangling uselessly as he attempted to struggle free. "You, answer our questions or you'll end up like them," the sergeant demanded, turning the man's head towards the fresh corpses on the floor.

Joe strolled over to them and indicated to Harris to release the man. "Why are you here?"

The vagrant coughed violently as the sergeant let him go, clutching at his wrung neck and massaging it back into life. "There was heating, light and food, why wouldn't we be here?" he spat. "Can't we even have that now?"

Harris stepped in and punched the man hard in the face, breaking his nose with an audible cracking noise and sending him crashing to the floor unconscious. Swearing loudly, the sergeant marched over to the rest of the captive group, who were staring at him in with a mix of disbelief and horror. He plucked out the next detainee; a woman with scraggly black hair and draped in a long torn coat. "How about you? Are you going to be more helpful than he was?"

Joe realised a change in tack was needed, and ordered Harris to let her go before he abused the woman or shot her as another example to the others. He was in charge here, not the sergeant, and it was vital that discipline and a proper chain of command were maintained at all times, otherwise the whole system would collapse into anarchy. Parker had seen the effect that combat could bring out in others many times throughout his career and it usually wasn't pleasant. There were a few amongst his squad mates back in the day who seemed to be addicted to death, keeping score of how many lives they had ended in the name of war, but Joe couldn't see the attraction himself. Killing was simply a part of the job, not something to be feared or relished but simply an order to obey. If Harris acted like this after a simple raid operation, God knows what he'd be like when the enemy started shooting back. Thugs could be useful and had their place in any unit, as long as they were kept on a very short leash.

"Who are you people?" the woman, who looked about the same age as her captor, asked defiantly with a shaky voice. "You're not the police, they don't bother coming out this far."

Joe ignored the question and instead wondered what it was about women which made them always talk out of place, even with several guns pointed at them. "Look, I'm not interested in who you are or what you're doing here," he stated clearly, "I want to know what happened to the people who were here before. Or should I just let him beat the answers out of you?" he added, pointing at Harris who grinned manically at the woman, "because don't think for a moment he'll be squeamish about hitting a woman."

The threat seemed to have the desired effect as she opened up immediately. "If you're after the dreamers you missed them, they left a few days ago," she said, her eyes darting around at the rest of the security force as they busied themselves turning the place upside-down looking for clues. "And no they didn't tell us where they were going, so there's no point trying to beat it out of us. They just left some fuel and food in payment for us hanging around for a while. I suppose they wanted to know if you were after them or not."

And what we'd do when we caught up with them: guess they just found out Joe added silently, as he felt a sudden sinking feeling in his stomach. He hadn't surprised the enemy at all; they'd set him up, playing him for a fool presumably since the moment he'd arrested the Aisha girl. They were cleverer and more organised than he'd given them credit for. He turned his attention back to the old woman, "Anything else?"

"That's all I know," she replied, bending over the man with the beard, who groaned with pain as he regained consciousness. "So, if you've finished killing or beating my friends half to death, can we go now?"

"Sir? Should we leave any witnesses? We don't want them blabbing," Harris interjected, causing some frightened gasps and sobs from the rest of the huddled prisoners.

"Who the hell are they going to tell?" exclaimed Joe impatiently, before receiving the unwelcome confirmation from the rest of the team that there was nothing in the building to further the investigation. He swore and gave the order to withdraw. He had enough blood on his hands today as it was, without adding to it with more needless slaughter. Still, despite today's failure, he was getting closer to the prize, he could smell it. He just hoped there was enough time left before he gave the politicians even more rope to hang him by.

Planning

The market street was busy with shoppers as the couple weaved their way through the stalls and bustling crowds of people. The throng was, at least, fairly polite, despite the people jostling in front of them, intent on getting the pick of the fruit and vegetables for their dinner that night. Kate, dressed in an old dark brown coat that blended well with her partner's shabby leather jacket, stopped at a random vendor under the pretence of browsing, but it was really to catch her breath. The close proximity of so many other bodies still made her feel claustrophobic, despite the reassuring presence of Andrzej by her side. She picked up a green apple and turned it over in her hand, before biting hungrily into it and handing the merchant some loose change. They were here under a pretence so she figured they might as well blend in, plus the journey from the IVFree base had been tiring and she was hungry. The sight of her eagerly devouring the fruit must have reminded Andrzej about his own grumbling stomach. He quickly followed suit, dropping a nearly-finished cigarette and extinguishing it with a twist of his foot, before announcing that their destination was just around the corner.

After her incorrect assumption about the appearance of the backstreet clinic, Kate had learned about not accepting things at face value, but the newsagents she found herself in front of just looked like any other shop on the high street. "We're a few minutes early," she said, checking her watch and noticing the sense of unease in the air, "Do you think Aisha will turn up?"

Andrzej made a face that indicated even saying the name in public was a risk. "No, that was never the plan," he replied slightly irritably, "There should hopefully be a message here somewhere. Why don't you pop inside and buy a paper and I'll meet you out here?"

Kate felt slightly annoyed at being dismissed in such a way, but decided to forgive him and let it pass. Andrzej was obviously very worried about the woman, which was affecting his usual polite manner, so she did as he asked and entered the shop.

The sign outside said 'newsagents' but inside there was very little news to be had. Most of the shop was given over to cigarettes, children's sweets or hobby magazines about gardening, crafting or home improvements. There were also several publications dedicated to providing tips and formulae on winning the Lottery, cashing in on the gullible readers who thought that the result of one draw had any influence on the next. The actual newspapers were at least given pride of place on two turnstile racks by the counter, with more stacked in piles on the floor in the corner by the entrance. The right stand housed the administered broadsheets with their serious issues and informed debates, whereas the left contained the independent press. Those papers (or rags, as they were often referred to), were more concerned with gossip about radio and film stars Kate had never heard of, than anything of worth.

Both types had one thing in common, however, they contained predominately good news about her homeland and bad news about everywhere else. For every uplifting story about the Navy bravely boarding and neutralising armed people smugglers, or scientific breakthroughs like the genetically engineered bananas that could one day be grown in England, there were several more downbeat ones about the misfortunes of the rest of the world. Her eye was drawn to the headline article in one of the serious publications, proclaiming that even with the IVS outreach centres at full capacity, many of the major city states in France and Germany were doomed to fail within the next generation or two. Even Strasbourg and Frankfurt, the relatively successful examples of European political restructuring in the years following the Death, were vulnerable they explained, completing the rest of the front page with graphs and tables to illustrate the point. Intrigued by the story, she took a copy from the stand and, after placing the correct money on the counter to avoid the small queue in front, walked out to see how her ally was getting on.

Not very well it turned out. Kate pretended to look interested as Andrzej stared intently at the large display of small postcards stuck onto the shop window. There must have been hundreds of them, all placed at slightly odd angles to each other, which made her feel very uncomfortable for reasons she could never explain. Still, at least they were organised into categories, and as her companion scoured over the 'lonely hearts' section, Kate couldn't help but feel a little jealous despite herself.

"Ah, there it is," Andrzej finally proclaimed, pausing for a few moments to read whichever card it was that had piqued his interest, before letting out a large discontented sigh. "Come on, let's go," he announced rather too loudly, "they don't have the paper I want after all."

The two had walked for nearly ten minutes before Andrzej broke the uneasy silence. "I'm sorry about that," he said, "and for my impoliteness earlier. You never know who's around listening and it was the news I was dreading."

"That's okay," replied Kate, still feeling inside that actually somehow it wasn't. "What happened?"

"We have a system for communications that can't be traced to the receiver," Andrzej explained, "it's very useful when one of us thinks they've been compromised. Aisha left the message, 'Sorry I got my head turned by the stranger on the train. Missing you already, Ais.', so either they got to her or she thought they had her marked. I knew it was odd when she didn't check in on time, which is why we moved HQ so quickly afterwards. None of us are professional agents and it's a given assumption that anyone caught will talk eventually, even if we mix truth and lies to confuse those who would harm us."

"I'm sorry," said Kate as sympathetically as she could muster, but a part of her that she rarely let out was intent on a fishing expedition. "Were the two of you close?"

Andrzej's expression suggested that he was far too shrewd for his own good sometimes, but his answer was diplomatic. "As much as I am with any of the group, we're all family here." He stopped briefly to light another cigarette before adding, "Yes, even Patrick!" The accompanying laughter from the both of them lightened the mood as they made the journey back to base.

The comfortable peace was shattered the instant they entered the old office building, however, by the sounds of a very heated argument emanating from within the IVFree headquarters. Kate recognised the Irish accent of one of the voices even before she saw the owner.

"It doesn't matter if I asked or not, I saw it with my own eyes!" Patrick shouted across the desk to his opponent as Kate and Andrzej strode in, catching the eye of the tall blonde woman he was disagreeing with.

"Great! You're back, Andrzej," the woman who Kate remembered as being called Brianna said with some relief. "This moron could have just compromised our entire operation!"

Patrick started to argue back again, but Andrzej held up one hand and the two fell silent instantly at the gesture. "What's going on? Brianna first," he asked in an even tone.

Brianna, who had apparently been on a break from her usual post fronting the propaganda videos when Patrick had returned, took great delight in depicting his alleged crime. "He vanished soon after you'd left to see if Aisha would make contact," she explained, as she fiddled with her necklace nervously. "Apparently he went back to the old HQ to satisfy his curiosity."

"I just wanted to see what had happened, if they'd got to Aisha and if she'd been cracked," Patrick replied. "It seemed like the quickest way."

"You're an idiot!" the newswoman cried. "What would have happened if they had been waiting for you? You put us all in danger! We have our messaging codes for a reason!"

"Brianna is correct, that was a very foolish thing to do," Andrzej said, chastising the Irishman, "but since you were there, what did you find?"

Patrick threw a pompous look of triumph at his opponent. "Lots of holes, smashed glass, some blood and a shit-load of bullet cases. The Repro police did a hell of a number on it. I'm glad we moved on when we did."

"We don't know it was anything to do with the Government," Kate piped in, much to the incredulity of the others. "It could have been criminals fighting over the fuel and food Andrzej told me you left behind."

"Well anything's possible, I guess," Patrick said as he sneered at her, "but most likely is that Aisha told them where the base was the instant they captured her. She always did have a sponge for a backbone."

"That's enough!" Andrzej snapped at him angrily. "We have no idea what they did to her when they got her. And since no one's asked, yes she did make contact with us, through the proper channels I might add Patrick, and she'll never be able to come back to us again. So please both of you, show a bit more respect."

"I'm sorry," said Brianna before turning back to Patrick, "and if they'd caught you, we'd be having this conversation in a questioning cell. I doubt that they'd wait as long before striking our base next time."

"Interesting choice of paper," remarked Patrick snidely as he pointed at the publication Kate was holding, presumably changing the subject because he was losing. "You do realise that's State edited and sanctioned?"

"Well it's Government approved," replied Kate correcting him, "but the truth is the truth, surely?"

Patrick looked like he was about to launch into another of his tirades, but Brianna took advantage of the brief silence to continue her cross-examination and his opportunity was lost. Kate was glad of the interruption, but she noticed that more than a few of the people in the room were giving her some odd stares. She folded the newspaper up and slid it under her jacket. She thought about reiterating her point about the perpetrators, but held her tongue and instead walked over to the kitchen area, where a small group of campaigners were huddled around the chairs trying not to be drawn into the discussion by the senior members. Judging by their whispered comments, it was a fairly regular occurrence.

"I wish those two would stop shouting at each other and just have sex and get it over with," said a young man with a shaved head and a goatee beard, much to the amusement of the audience, who all fell quiet with a few elbow jabs as Kate approached.

"Is it true?" another of the crowd, a woman twenty years Kate's senior with weather-bleached tattoos up her arm asked. "Are we really going to make an assault on IVS Highpoint?"

"Not quite," said a voice from over Kate's shoulder as she sat down at the small table. The three combatants had apparently finished their argument and decided to join her. Andrzej took the opportunity to call the rest of the group together from their various stations around the office area. "I see the rumour mill is alive and well, and you have my apologies for not sharing things with you earlier. I don't want this organisation to hide secrets from each other but we also have to be careful. But rest assured, we're not planning to attack any institution, that would be suicide and go against everything we've built here together. We are, however, going to use an opportunity that's arisen to make contact with Victor Pearson and ask him a few questions about his business practices."

"He won't talk to us," said the man with the shaved head, "even if we camp outside the clinic with placards for a month."

"Oh he'll talk," replied Kate, "one way or another. He'll be a captive audience, after all."

A few comments and murmurs erupted all around her, although Kate couldn't make out if they were positive or negative. Gossip was one thing, but nothing tipped over the apple cart like a dose of truth.

"Hopefully, it won't come to that," added Andrzej reassuringly which seemed to quell some of the naysayers, even though Kate thought it almost certainly would come to that. "I know some of you are nervous. You feel that something like this will put our head over the parapet, make us too big, too much of a threat to those who would silence us. But I'm afraid we're already past that point. Patrick has just returned from our old base and it's been decimated in an attack." The revelation sent a wave of shocked and worried gasps around the room, as the inhabitants began to realise the reality of the situation, that the fun game they had been playing had suddenly turned deadly serious. Andrzej appealed for calm but Kate could see his eyes were fired up with excitement, and he spoke as if this was a moment he had been longing would come. "The only way now for us is forwards," he continued, "to make even more noise, to turn our ripples into a tidal wave they can't ignore. If we want to change things, then this is the only way. We're going to dig out Victor Pearson from his hole and hang out his dirty secrets for everyone to see. They think he's their saviour? It's time we let the world know the truth, let them know how he just murdered their future."

The speech was greeted with a euphoric cheer, the shock news of the attack replaced by applause and shouts of encouragement as the crowd latched onto the triumphant words emanating from their leader. Kate was glad; she might need all of their help by the time this was over, and division in the ranks only lead to distrust and split loyalties.

As impatient as Kate was to get things started, her fever was soon cooled when Andrzej announced that the planning would not start in earnest until the next day. It was too soon to start now he explained to her, better to let people get used to the idea first before overloading them with details. She had to agree with him but it was still disappointing, and with nothing else to do she made her farewells instead, feeling the pull of the familiar back home. She only made it as far as the foyer main entrance, though, when Brianna came sprinting up behind calling her to wait up.

"I've not seen Andrzej so passionate like that for a long time, not since I first met him at the beginning," Brianna said, catching her breath. She then moved to in front of Kate, blocking her path, her expression now hardened with concern. "This path you've set us on Kate, I hope you're right, I really do. Because if you're wrong, you've just condemned us all to death."

Infiltration

The old laundry van pulled up to a stop on the street opposite the rail station, the metal hubcaps scraping along the kerb and sending sparks up the rusty wheel arch. Andrzej cursed and pumped the brake pedal, as Kate lurched forward against the seatbelt and made a curt comment about a bad workman and tools. She smirked to show it was in jest, a gesture which he returned in kind as he gently brushed a few loose red hairs from her face to behind her ear. They had become close in the past few weeks, the physical proximity of her visits to IVFree matched by the emotional connection she now felt towards him. Andrzej's presence had become an extension of herself, and as such she now no longer tensed at his touch or shied away from his gaze. He accepted her for what she was, not like the men back at the power plant who enjoyed the look of the fruit but recoiled when the flesh inside wasn't to their liking.

Even Michael had tried to change her with his campaigning and subtle ways, but the IVFree head was different. He revelled in her faults, like gently mocking the continued use of her vacuum flask instead of their kettle, and for some reason unknown to her, she enjoyed all the attention. During one of the early discussions they had toyed with the idea of stealing a uniform, but Kate had been concerned that it might not fit her, causing a charmed response from her co-conspirator.

"It's one of the most sought-after jobs in the country and most of the managers are men," Andrzej had said, "so nearly all of the nurses will be slim and attractive. Don't worry, you'll fit right in. Just remember to smile when Brianna takes your photo."

The statement had caused her to blush cherry red and turn away, much to her embarrassment and his amusement. It was an episode he would later bring up regularly whenever tensions rose with the rest of the group, as the various strategies began to come together. The attack on their old base had spooked many of the members, despite Andrzej's rousing speech afterwards, and a few had left as a result, the fear of retribution winning the battle against a half-hearted belief in ideology. Kate didn't blame them, they didn't have the same personal connection to the mission that she had.

The issues had been compounded as she had been compelled to return to work after her compassionate leave had ended, a distraction which had made the planning frustratingly slow. Each day she went through the motions at her old diagnostic station but the joy had gone, replaced with monotony and a realisation of how insignificant it all felt. Her eyes had been opened and her old life seemed small and inconsequential in comparison. She spent the days staring into the distance, longing for the evenings with Andrzej and the others; pouring over maps, bouncing scenarios off one another and mocking her compatriot for his new temporary job as a 'washer-woman'. The plan still left too much worryingly to chance for her liking, but it was the best they could do with the constants and variables they had available. Patrick had observed pointedly that they could plot and conspire in the safety of the IVFree base until the end of time but, ready or not, eventually they would have to pull the trigger if they wanted answers. Kate had begrudgingly admitted that he was right, although it wasn't him putting his head in the lion's mouth. It was now or never, the board was set and the pieces were in place. All they needed now was the courage to play.

Her train of thought was interrupted by the radio, which had ceased playing some old jazz music and was now on the news.

Andrzej turned up the volume excitedly. "Hey it's us!"

"The statement released by IVFree, reports of an armed attack on an old campaign headquarters by the Ministry of Reproduction's security force several weeks ago, in which unarmed civilians were allegedly killed," the reporter said in an articulate voice with no discernible accent. "The new Deputy Minister for the Department, Caden Schoier, was quick to deny the accusation, calling it a work of fiction designed to undermine belief and trust in the Government, and that IVFree should stick to handing out leaflets rather than slinging mud."

"Well he's quite witty, I'll give him that," admitted Andrzej, turning off the radio in disgust, before turning towards her with an uncharacteristically serious look. "There's still time you know, to back out if you want. Go in, get the treatment and have the child that Emily always wanted, for her."

Kate appreciated the sentiment, giving her a way out even now, but her decision was made. "I can't. I have to know."

Andrzej took her hand softly in his. "Okay, but know this, once you make that first step there's no going back, it's all in or nothing. You can't just kidnap the head of IVS and go back to your old life afterwards. I just want you to be sure."

"I am," she replied, before hesitating briefly. "I'm just scared I'll be caught at the first hurdle. I'm not good at lying and I'm not good at fitting in anywhere like you."

"I'll tell you a secret, it's easier than you think," said Andrzej in a conspiratorial tone. "Seriously! People ignore most things that they think don't concern them. Just dress the part, look slightly annoyed at everything you see, and always look like you know where you're going even if you have no idea."

"Really?"

"Yes. The first part we have covered, the second one comes naturally to you, and the third is just acting."

Kate made a mock *humph* sound, pretending to be offended but feeling comforted nonetheless. Thinking back to her daily grind it was completely true; she had little idea about most of the people she didn't work directly with. They were just a parade of faceless roving mannequins, instantly forgotten once out of eye or earshot. All she needed to do was not look out of place.

Andrzej looked uncomfortable for a second, like a man trying to work out how to deliver some bad news. "I've left Patrick in charge of things while we're away," he said, sparking a hostile look from his passenger. "Yes, I know he's not your most favourite person in the world, but he'll get things done. He's already got everything packed up for moving to the new base. We can't risk being caught and giving the rest of the group away, so best not to know the location in the first place. I've told them to stop using the newsagents for any communication from now on in case it gets compromised, and they're going to pick up Isaac on their way out as well," he added, letting out a sigh. "I'm sure he'll love that, almost as much as Patrick will enjoy lugging all of his equipment about I'm sure, but it's for his own safety."

Kate looked at the clock on the van dashboard. It was time to go. She paused for a brief moment, wanting to tell Andrzej how she felt but the emotions would not form and the words would not come, replaced instead by awkward silence. The next time they met she would be a criminal and nothing would be the same again.

As she turned to open the door Andrzej caught her arm. "Just remember that the access door and lift from the laundry is locked from the other side, so I can't enter the main complex until you let me in," he reminded her. You'll need my help for the second and third phases."

Kate knew why he was so insistent, but echoed his words back anyway. "There's still time you know, to back out if you want."

Now it was his turn to act offended. "Now, how chivalrous would that be? Come on let's get your bags out before you miss your train."

Kate turned and watched as Andrzej slowly drove away, and suddenly felt very alone. They'd chosen a station on the main East Line a few stops from the clinic to help coordinate their efforts and, in case anyone was watching, not risk raising any suspicions of her turning up in a logistics truck.

She needn't have worried. The brief train journey was uneventful, and as she waited in the main reception for a nurse to escort her to her room, everyone else ignored her. The staff were busy with whatever tasks occupied their time, and the other clients were either chatting to their partners or had their heads buried in a newspaper. Kate hadn't really known what to expect as she made the short walk up the main drive to the clinic campus with its high walls, stern-looking armed guards and razor wire. Although she hadn't presumed that a large parade of doctors and nurses would be waiting for her to offer condolences for her loss as she approached, a total indifference to her presence came as a shock. Perhaps they were being polite, or had been told not to bring up the subject in case it upset her, but the most likely explanation was that they didn't even realise who she was. Emily did not share her surname, after all, and as far as any of the staff were concerned, Kate was just another Lottery winner showing up for her free treatment; lucky for sure but otherwise unremarkable. In many ways, it made her mission here much easier, but she couldn't help feeling hurt nonetheless. Her sister had been murdered by this place, and no one seemed to care or even remember.

The appointment had been set for 10 am, but the clock on the wall went beyond half-past the hour before her name was finally called by the stroppy-looking receptionist, who was sitting behind a large and expansive pine desk. The area behind the counter was raised slightly, making the workers there appear much taller than everyone else. It gave them a self-styled aura of superiority as they looked down their noses at the thankful clients. Kate noticed that the paying customers across the room had a different area to wait where the juxtaposition was the opposite, not to mention that at least ten of them had entered and been greeted with smiles, drinks and polite conversation in the time she had been waiting to be seen. The winners were supposed to be grateful just to be there at all, she surmised.

A harassed-looking young nurse with an arm in a sling met her at the desk, clumsily fiddling with some paper on her clipboard with her one useable hand. "Kate Adams? I'm here to escort you to the treatment block."

Kate was about to ask her about the injury but the girl pre-empted the question. "I had an accident, so I've been relegated to meet-and-greet," she said and introduced herself as Caroline, before looking to her sling and adding "I'm sorry, you'll have to carry your bags yourself."

"Are you my treatment nurse?" asked Kate, as she threw the knapsack over her shoulder and picked up the suitcase full of clothes she would never use. She felt guilty about what would happen next if this innocent girl, who looked barely out of her teens, turned out to be responsible for her care.

"Oh, no not for a few years yet, I'm afraid," replied Caroline, shaking her head. "It'll be a while yet until I'm qualified for that. I'll introduce you to the senior nurse in charge of your comfort and treatment when we get to Gamma Block."

Kate tried to imagine how Andrzej would handle the situation, and how he would get the nurse to open up and trust him. She didn't have the advantage of his rugged looks and easy-going charm, and unless Caroline liked girls, flirting wouldn't help either. So she decided to go with flattery instead. "Don't worry I'm sure you'll get there," she said in an encouraging tone, patting the nurse gently on the upper arm. The words produced the desired effect and the young girl smiled as she relaxed her frame slightly, giving Kate the opportunity to press the advantage. "So what do you do here, when you're not injured and escorting fortunate people like me around?"

It all felt so long ago now, but before her life was changed forever and she worked contently at the tidal plant, Kate had considered herself one of those rare people, at least in her direct experience, who were genuinely enthused about the work they did. As she toiled diligently at her post, those around her appeared to be motivated only by the payment at the end of the month, or what they thought they could get out of the company. Luckily, she had found a kindred spirit in Caroline. The nurse was more than happy to give a detailed description of her duties with the donor colony, as they walked together down past some offices and laboratory showrooms.

"As well as the general wellbeing care of the people, I'm involved in some of the donor functions too," the nurse said as modestly as she could, whilst at the same time beaming proudly about it, "although that part can be a bit intense sometimes."

"That sounds like important work," said Kate encouragingly, waiting for the girl as she paused at a set of hooks to collect a coat.

Caroline blushed slightly at the compliment. "I'm very lucky I was trusted with it, most of the other nurses who get assigned donor duty so early have been transferred from one of the other clinics on placements."

"Oh yes, I read that the all of the IES-clear donors live here," said Kate, as they exited from the rear of the building and onto the campus grounds. The dark and heavy clouds overhead had begun to sprinkle a dusting of snow around them, causing a flurry of activity from the ground staff as they raced around with bags of salt, casting the contents liberally over the paths.

"That's right," agreed the nurse, "this is the safest place for them. All of the other smaller clinics are in city centres and not as secure. This was once a prison after all!" she added with a slight laugh.

Kate joined in the humour and continued to play the part of the bewildered and impressed guest, even pointing to Alpha Block and asking hopefully if she was staying there, knowing full well it wasn't the case. Best not to ask pertinent questions that might arouse suspicions, where ignorance might offer the answers anyway.

The nurse shook her head apologetically. "Sorry no, that's the Alpha Block for the paying customers. Not even we get to stay there for our own treatments."

"Are you keen to have children?"

"My boyfriend wants me to, tells me he'll propose when I do," Caroline replied, "but I want to wait a while, work my way up the ladder a bit first. Also, being surrounded by the reality of things each day kind of takes the glamour off. It can all get a bit gooey and disgusting sometimes if I'm honest."

A look of horror passed the girl's face as she realised what she'd just said, but Kate quickly alleviated her fears. "Well as my father used to say, 'no one who works in a slaughterhouse ever eats sausages'. We all have the temptation to peer into the magician's box occasionally when we know we shouldn't."

"You have no idea," Caroline whispered under her breath a little too loudly as they reached the plain and uninspiring entrance of the Gamma Block. "Well here we are," she announced with a slight apology.

They entered the stark reception hall where about thirty other women were sat on hard-looking wooden chairs. A radio was set up on the wall to provide some background noise, but the volume was set too quiet to hear properly. What sounds it did produce echoed around the vinyl floor and painted brick walls, making them even muddier and difficult to distinguish. A nurse about Kate's age was standing guard by one of the doors, which had a sign above pointing to the wards. She approached Kate and greeted her, dismissing her junior colleague who said her goodbyes, before vanishing off back to her duties. Andrzej was definitely correct about one thing, Kate thought; Michael's new love would have looked positively plain and unremarkable in comparison to most of the women at work here.

If the nurse shared her junior's looks, however, her personality was the complete opposite. "Right. Kate, is it? Congratulations your first prize means you jump the queue and get me as your treatment nurse," she said sternly and without humour. "But don't worry I can do all this in my sleep. I don't usually do such routine duties, but I've been re-assigned here, to," she paused briefly trying to find the right words, "refresh my skills."

"That's reassuring," said Kate flatly. "Sorry, I didn't catch your name?"

"Bethany," the woman answered. "Come with me please. I'll show you to your room."

Kate followed the nurse up several flights of stairs, wrestling and levering her complaining suitcase as she did so, and down a series of dimly lit corridors with doors evenly spaced apart on either side. The sporadic iron radiators barely took the edge off the rapidly falling temperature outside; apparently the heating had broken that morning but Kate wasn't really listening to the details. Was this the beginning of her sister's last journey she mused, wandering around this building frantically looking for a way out? The floor and signs had a colour system, but in the dull light, it seemed impossible to follow them unless you already knew where you were going. The only change to break up the pattern of doors, hallways and stairwells was a large room they walked passed optimistically called 'Entertainment Room 5', which looked to consist of a small library and an even smaller collection of board games. Bethany explained that due to security measures, the patients (which was the first time Kate had heard herself described as such since her arrival) were confined to their rooms or the social areas during their stay.

"I thought IVS were rich? Why does everything look so utilitarian?" complained Kate as she glanced at her surroundings. She didn't actually care one way or the other but it seemed like a good enough way to start a conversation.

Bethany sighed in a way that suggested that the question came up a lot. "You won the greatest prize of all; children. For free. At least allow the paying customers some sense of satisfaction in their investment. Right, your place is just up here."

Kate's quarters turned out to be a room just about large enough to fit a bed with itchy-looking blankets, a small desk, an even smaller wardrobe and a health monitoring station standing silently in the corner on a wheeled trolley. The only attempt at decoration on the stark white walls was a small painting of a dog lying on a beach, and a large mechanical clock hanging over the bed. A freshly pressed nightgown had been placed on the bed, along with a towel and basic washing essentials. The inhabitants weren't expected to stay there for their entire pregnancy, of course, just a few days a month to check on progress. Even so, the lack of space was making Kate feel claustrophobic even without crowds of people around her.

"I'll leave you for a few minutes to get unpacked and into a gown," said Bethany, "and then we can start your initial health assessment before the tour later today. Can't start any treatments without that! Someone will be along later to take your clothes into storage," she declared before heading out, closing the door behind her.

Kate waited a few seconds and sprang into action. She took a small box from her rucksack and placed it carefully on the bed, before extracting the contents and hiding it under the covers. Everything else could wait until afterwards, so she quickly got undressed and into the cold gown, leaving her clothes in a heap on the floor.

She'd just managed to get into bed when Bethany returned, holding a glass and mercury thermometer. "Don't worry!" Bethany laughed, the event obviously being an in-joke amongst the nursing staff, "this is just an oral one."

Kate breathed a mock sigh of relief as the nurse grabbed the health station trolley and manhandled it into position, before attempting to connect various parts of it to her patient. Kate was compliant as she could muster, asking questions about each device in an effort to calm herself, but she could feel her heart pounding in her chest, threatening to burst and betray her intentions.

"Okay, this will only take a few minutes" Bethany explained, finally flicking the switch and watching as the machine whirled into life. It was only a few seconds before the nurse let out a gasp of alarm when the heart rate readout shot up into triple figures and started to beep uncontrollably. "Oh my God are you okay?" she cried.

"Yes just a bit nervous about the treatment," Kate replied unconvincingly.

Bethany saw right through that one. "No, this is something else, maybe a medical condition. Let me get a doctor, I'll be right back!"

During the planning of the operation, Kate had often thought about would happen when the time to act finally came. Would she freeze? Would time stand still and allow her to weigh the pros and cons before finally committing, or would it pass so quickly the opportunity would be lost before she'd even realise it was there? As it turned out it was none of those things, as a part the brain once thought long lost to civilised society took over and made the decision for her.

The act of instinct.

The will of survival.

As the nurse turned to leave Kate made a grab for the glass syringe hidden under the covers, flinging them aside as she lunged towards the woman, who had no chance to cry out before the needle was deep within her neck and the plunger pressed against it. The drug within was thankfully as powerful and fast acting as Isaac had boasted it would be, and Bethany instantly fell silent back onto the bed.

Kate stared in shock at what she had done until the tangled wires attached to her arm sent the health station crashing to the floor and shook her out of her trance. She'd made the first step, gone beyond the point of no return and nothing else mattered any more. Her initial fears about the noise the health monitor had made were thankfully unfounded; no one came to investigate the noise as she quickly manoeuvred the unconscious nurse fully into bed and under the covers. It would be hours before the woman woke up, more than enough time to complete their mission. Kate grabbed the security badge from around the woman's neck, placing it over her own before delving into her suitcase and retrieving the spare uniform and hair band that Andrzej had procured from his job. Finally, she retrieved the small ID photo from between the pages of the old book she'd packed, licked the back of it and stuck it over the picture of Bethany's. It wouldn't pass a detailed examination close up but it should be enough to fool anyone at a casual glance. Tying her hair back in a ponytail, she let out a large sigh of relief, before recomposing herself and heading out into the thankfully still empty corridor.

It was time to pay Dr Pearson a visit.

Donors

The sense of purpose Kate felt was soon replaced by the feeling of being lost in a labyrinth of incomprehensible signs and different coloured floor tiles, which blended and blurred together in her adrenaline-clouded mind. The plan of heading off in one direction and taking the stairs down whenever she could was thwarted by a large locked security door that refused to budge. She eventually realised that she needed to swipe the stolen security card against the box by the side of it. She didn't get the chance, though, for it opened from the other side, revealing a suspicious-looking nurse of Indian origin with light brown skin and thick dark hair.

"Who are you?" she demanded while glaring at the interloper, "and where are you supposed to be?"

Kate froze, fear suddenly taking over her and forming beads of sweat down her arms. This wasn't someone she could surprise and subdue, the syringe was empty and she had no idea how to fight. In any case, a struggle would cause an alarm and the operation would be over before it began. She thought back to Andrzej's words earlier; at this point anything was worth a try, so she looked the woman straight in the eyes and pretended to look really annoyed at life. "Oh good! At least *someone* actually works in this bloody building! I've been wandering around here for ages and I couldn't find anybody!" she complained loudly, taking the other woman somewhat by surprise. "Bethany was supposed to be giving me a tour before I started my placement, and then she disappeared somewhere to get something. That was about half an hour ago!"

The nurse rolled her eyes in sympathy, her guard dropping along with her formal demeanour. "Oh yes, that sounds fairly typical of her. She's been a right mardy cow since she got dropped down the order for whatever reason it was. Probably went off for a smoke and lost track of time. Where are you supposed to be?"

Time to see if Caroline's as useful as she is friendly thought Kate. "I'm here from London on a placement," she explained, "I'm supposed to be learning about the donor procedure, but I'm apparently spending my time wandering aimlessly around here instead. Sorry, my name's Kate by the way." She had originally thought about using a fake name, but the amount of concentration it required to keep up the pretence didn't seem worth the effort. She wasn't on the clinic staff register and if anyone thought to check it wouldn't matter what she called herself. Better to sound convincing and not give them an excuse to bother.

"Sharmila," the woman said in reply and held out her hand. "As a matter of fact, I'm heading out there myself if you want to tag along, I'll leave a notice in the staff room for Bethany when she comes back." With that she disappeared back behind the door, re-emerging a few moments later and beckoning Kate to follow.

Kate checked her watch nervously as the woman turned her back to her. Andrzej should have arrived by now, and he couldn't wait forever without raising suspicions on what should be a quick unloading job of fresh linen to the clinic. He had devised a backup plan to prevent the van from working, but that was a dangerous option, especially if someone knowledgeable came to help him or the operation went wrong and they had to make a run for it quickly. Nevertheless, she'd spun the tale to Sharmila and she couldn't change it now without blowing her cover, so her co-conspirator would have to make do with his own devices for now. At least they were heading towards the correct building, and a well-timed trip to the toilet would hopefully allow her to slip away unnoticed.

The snow had thankfully stopped for now, giving the grounds the impression of being bathed in icing sugar, the grass poking its head out just above the flakes. Kate knew exactly how they felt and became acutely aware of the silence around her. Better to make conversation, to fill the vacuum with a pointless noise like the people in the offices at the power plant, so her new colleague didn't feel the need to with questions she couldn't answer.

"So, will I get to meet the donors?" Kate asked, suddenly dreading if that was something she should have already known.

"Yes sure, I'll arrange that if you want. Most of the interns don't usually bother actually talking to them, they're just interested in the overall picture," Sharmila replied, making Kate wish she hadn't asked. More delays. "Oh, one word of warning, if Chrissy tells you that you need to take the sample manually don't believe her, she does that to all of the interns. It kind of stopped being funny about three years ago to be honest. And obviously, don't believe it if the donor asks either," she added with a wink. "It's instant dismissal to even touch them."

"Of course," said Kate in mock agreement. She had no idea who Chrissy was but was grateful for the information anyway. Looking like an idiot or getting instantly fired, with the subsequent tricky questions from the security guards about just who the hell she was, would not aid in her attempts to blend in or contact Andrzej.

"You'll be able to tell Chrissy," said Sharmila as if reading her thoughts, "she's a redhead like you. I didn't know they made that many of you any more."

"Guess the managers must like us," Kate replied with a mischievous yet sarcastic tone.

"Yeah, lecherous bastards," Sharmila agreed as they reached a large solid steel door with a security box on the side. "Come on, it's just through here. Welcome to the wonderful world of Gamete Production Central!"

More corridors, but at least here the layout made a bit more sense and the signs pointed to something Kate could recognise. In contrast to the borderline squalid conditions of Gamma Block, everything here was bright, clean and spacious. Large white strip lights bathed the area in a warm daylight glow, giving the inhabitants a soft aura as they glided down the reflecting polished floors. Large potted plants and flowers at every junction added to the atmosphere of peace, reminding Kate of less of a hospital and more of the church she was pressured into going to as a child. Her mother would send her there every Sunday to help out to set up the communion before the preacher started with his traditional brimstone and hellfire sermons. The serene and reverent quiet of her new surroundings was occasionally permeated by announcements over the address system, but even they were soft and clear. "So what happens here?" she asked Sharmila as they reached the male donor block.

"What do you think? I'm not going to draw you a picture!" laughed the Indian nurse as they entered ward MD1, only to be confronted by a buzzing security turnstile gate blocking the entrance to the rest of the area beyond. To the side of the gate was a small desk, behind which sat a red-headed woman that Kate presumed was Chrissy, and an older male colleague dressed as a porter leaning casually in front of her. The man, who stopped talking and blushed with embarrassment as soon as he laid eyes on the new visitors, made his excuses and left promptly.

"Interrupting anything?" asked Sharmila.

"Hardly. If he was a doctor then you might have been," the woman replied slyly. "Anyway, I'm a good girl really. And betrothed," she added, holding up her hand and jabbing a finger at an antique-looking engagement ring. "Look, but don't touch. No one ever mentions not allowing friendly conversation."

"You'll have to forgive Chrissy, Kate, she's a relentless flirt," said Sharmila to her charge in a lightly accusing tone.

"Well, you can't be surrounded by all these hormones and not get affected by them," replied Chrissy defensively. "And anyway, my boys down the hall here like a bit of dirty talk now and again. Helps them if they're having trouble."

"Yeah, I think the drugs probably help with that more; I don't think being a slut is officially in your role profile. Chrissy, this is Kate; an intern from London. Will it be okay for her to meet with one of the donors? And before you say it, I've already told her about your jokes."

Chrissy ignored the last comments and instead looked surprised, which was not a good sign. "Really? I don't remember anything on the schedule about anyone coming. I thought the last batch just finished and went home?"

"I was ill and missed the trip, so they sent me separately," explained Kate feeling the blood pumping through her again, the sweat of her body betraying her deception from every pore.

"Okay, still I'd better confirm. If you could wait here please for a few moments, I'll check with HR." She went to pick up the phone but Sharmila reached out and stopped her, much to Kate's relief.

"No need. One word; Bethany."

"Oh right," said Chrissy in a resigned fashion as she moved away from the receiver, "she probably forgot to file the paperwork through again. You know, it's one thing being upset for being told off for gossiping about things that don't concern you, but she's going to get herself fired if she's not careful. Talk about cutting off your nose to spite your face." Kate must have been looking impatient because Chrissy immediately cut herself off from her next sentence. "Oh yes, sorry, you wanted the tour blurb. Okay, well, there are twelve wards here split into twelve rooms, each with one supervising nurse per ward. Don't ask me why, I guess the designers liked the number twelve for some reason. Anyway, each donor has two weeks on here and two weeks off back at the block to recover, before the process repeats. If you want to meet with one of them be my guest, just press the button on the door and give them a few moments to prepare." She glanced briefly at the timepiece on the wall before sighing quietly, "Now I think of it, Hugo's probably finished his session by now. He's like clockwork usually. Actually, you might as well collect the result while you're in there. Pass me your card and I'll buzz you in."

Kate handed over the card as casually as she could, desperately hoping that Chrissy wouldn't look too closely at the crude forgery. But luck it seemed was on her side, as Sharmila distracted her colleague with some more gossip, and the donor nurse swiped the stolen card over the console with only a cursory glance. "Last room on the right."

Kate left the two nurses chatting and joking about the luckless porter as she made her way past the desk and through the gate, which lit up green and hummed approvingly. The ward consisted of a long corridor, with one large window per room offset from each other on either side. The lighting here was slightly dimmer and softer, Kate noticed, as she peered through the windows as she passed. Each small and sterile-looking white room contained one male, from teenagers up to middle-aged men, all wearing identical blue T-shirts and surgical trousers. Some were watching videos, others were playing games on a computer or just sleeping lazily on the small metal bed in the corner. One of them, however, a man maybe a few years younger than herself was sat bolt upright on the edge of his bunk, staring intently at the large digital countdown timer on the wall of which fifteen minutes remained. None of them seemed to notice her presence but she felt odd watching them, a strange voyeuristic sensation she often got observing animals in the local zoo.

The patient in the last room on the right turned out to be a young man in his late teens with short dark hair, sitting against a pillow on his bed and quietly reading a book. Kate tried the door to his quarters but it was locked, the red light at the top mocking her attempts to open it. She was about to give up when she noticed the intercom button to the side of the handle and pressed it sanguinely.

"Hello?" a voice emanated from within a small speaker on the wall.

"Hi, Chrissy sent me down. I'm here to collect your sample."

"Oh okay, hold on a second."

There was a brief pause, before the light above the door flicked over to green, and the mechanism behind the door slid open the lock with a satisfying *thunk* sound. Kate entered the room, only to be confronted by the sight of the boy with his arms now raised above his head, his wrists bound up in metal restraints connected to the wall above the bed. The large window on the wall was a mirror here she noticed, giving the inmates some privacy from each other, if not the clinical staff.

Kate tried to ignore the boy's current predicament. "Hello Hugo, my name is Kate, I'm a visiting nurse from the London clinic. I'm -"

Hugo laughed and cut her off mid-sentence. "No, you're not," he declared as if the statement was the most obvious thing in the world. "I don't know who you are but you're definitely not a nurse. Are you a journalist? A spy?"

There seemed to be little point in arguing the point. "No, I'm not a nurse," confirmed Kate, "but I'm not a journalist or a spy either, I'm just here to try and talk to someone. Are you going to turn me in?"

"A while ago I might have done, before they took Ariane away from me. But no, don't worry, your secret is safe with me," he replied with a conspiratorial wink.

Kate felt herself relax a little for the first time since entering the clinic. It was good to be herself again. "How did you know?"

Hugo gestured with his head at the book strewn aside on the bed. "I'm studying psychology and body language in my ample spare time, to keep myself occupied. Even when I'm not on duty there's not exactly a lot to do around here, apart from watching people and trying to guess their motivations. I'm hoping to be a counsellor for the others one day, to help them deal with it all." He slowly looked up and down Kate's figure, making her feel self-aware and uncomfortable at his gaze. "You gave yourself away the instant you came in. All the people we get from other clinics put on certain subtle airs and graces, because they feel inferior to everyone here where the real work is done. That, and you looked surprised at my confinement when you should have been briefed in your training before you left London. The instant primal reaction is the hardest to hide, you might want to work on that."

"Thank you, I will," said Kate, more coldly than she anticipated, the result of being chastised by someone nearly half her age. "Why are you in restraints?"

"It's to stop me attacking and raping you," Hugo replied nonchalantly, "but don't worry I would never do anything like that," he added quickly, as if to set her mind at ease. It didn't work. "It's the chemicals we have to take; they can send people a little lust-crazy."

"That's reassuring for the staff here I'm sure."

"No, you don't understand, it's not to protect you," Hugo replied. "It's to protect us from getting ourselves infected if we violate you. A few years ago, one of us couldn't control it and forced himself on one of the nurses. Since then, well as you can see, they took precautions," he said, waving his hands through the restraints to illustrate the point. "They won't unlock until after you've left."

Kate had a pretty good idea who that person might be but didn't pursue the matter further. She wasn't even sure why she was even here. This wasn't getting her to Andrzej, but something compelled her to find out more, to understand, to peer behind the curtain despite Caroline's cryptic warning. At the very least it would be more information or ammunition for IVFree to use for the cause. "So what are these drugs they give you?" she asked as she made her way across the cold vinyl flooring and towards the bed. It seemed strange to her to incarcerate someone and then make them sexually aggressive towards the staff.

"It's to boost how much sperm we can supply," Hugo replied. "Usually, it takes a couple of days to get a full barrel-load, so to speak, but the drugs they give us sends everything into overdrive and takes that down to four hours. The public need their children after all, or so they tell us. Luckily they give us other medicine to suppress the desire otherwise, the wait can be, well, frustrating to say the least. Unfortunately, they don't always get the dose right for that one."

Kate thought back to the man in the other room waiting frantically for the clock to count down. "What's to stop you acting on your urges before the timer runs out?"

"Cessation of entertainment, double dose of suppressant and, of course, the restraints," said Hugo. "After a while we all learn to wait for the bell like good little salivating dogs, stuck in a purgatory of anticipation."

"I know a lot of men that would consider this heaven," retorted Kate half-jokingly.

"Yes, it probably sounds to most guys on the outside as an ideal job right?" replied Hugo irritably, clearly taking offence at Kate's flippant comment. "But what if that job never ends? That it's your life from the age of fifteen until you die? We can't leave this campus, we can't fall in love or have a family of our own, ever. I read books to pass the time, but I'll probably never be able to use much of the knowledge inside them. So instead, for two weeks per month, every four hours, day and night, when the timer hits zero I get to do it with that."

Kate looked at the tubular cylinder on the brushed steel table by the bed that Hugo was staring accusingly at. The tube was tapered towards one end with a clear collection vial sticking out of it. She knew what it was, she remembered as a small child her father bringing one home from one of the farms and leaving it on the kitchen table, much to the annoyance of her mother. That one had been much larger of course as it was designed for bulls, but she imagined the premise was pretty much the same.

"Oh well, at least compared to what the women go through we have it pretty easy, I guess," said Hugo cheerlessly.

Kate was about to ask what happened to the female donors when Chrissy's disembodied voice drifted across the room from a hidden speaker. "Kate? A porter is here to collect Hugo's sample to take it to storage, can you hurry it along please?"

Kate swore under her breath; her time was up. Hugo pointed her towards the small fridge in the corner of the room, which contained a chemical cooling block with the precious cargo of a full collection tube housed inside.

"See you, Kate, it was good to see someone different for a change. I hope you get to talk to whoever it is you've tried so hard to meet," said Hugo with a hint of sadness.

"Thank you," replied Kate as she carefully picked up the container and headed for the door. She was just about to leave when Hugo called out to her.

"Just remember what I said. Watch out for your reactions, they'll tell people things about you that you can't hide, even if they don't realise or pick up on it instantly."

Kate joined the others back at the gate and handed over the sample block to an impatient-looking porter, who then vanished down the hallway, muttering loudly to himself. But it wasn't just him, Sharmila was also pacing around. "Kate, I've just been paged that a parturition is about to occur and I'm needed in D section asap, but as Bethany is still missing if you want to tag along that's fine."

Kate had no idea what 'parturition' even meant, but heeding Hugo's advice she agreed to the invitation without missing a beat, still playing the role as best she could under the pretence of gaining experience first-hand. Andrzej had been waiting this long, a few more minutes wouldn't hurt.

Sharmila's demeanour turned from jovial cordiality to steely professionalism the second they entered the room with the sign D201 over the door. The parturition chamber was empty apart from a metal surgical table covered in blue cloth, and a large glass box on a wheeled trolley in the corner. The clear casket had a lid on the top and contained several rubber tubes, which were connected to small gas cylinders bolted to the side. A young assistant nurse dressed in green scrubs was carefully laying out tools on the table, which looked to Kate more like salad tongs than surgical instruments. The set of doors at the far end of the room turned out on closer inspection to be the entrance to an elevator, the glowing arrow on the wall and a faint hum of pulleys and chains signalling an imminent arrival.

"You can stand over there in the corner. Just don't try to help out because you're not experienced enough to," Sharmila ordered Kate. "If you need to rush out then do it quietly; the toilets are down the hall if you make it that far. If you think you're going to pass out lean back against the wall and someone will wake you up after we've finished. There's a big difference in hearing about it in lectures and seeing it up close and personal."

Kate nodded her head in confused agreement and stood where she was told, feeling nerves and a cold sweat build up inside her. What the hell was going on?

Her question was answered almost immediately as the doors of the elevator glided open, and out of the darkness burst a nurse in a burgundy uniform and greying hair. She was pushing a trolley, on which a woman in her mid-thirties and wearing a short surgical gown lay motionless, her arms connected by sensor wires up to a monitor by her head.

"Sorry for the lack of warning, the misoprostol kicked in early," the nurse explained as she screeched the trolley to a halt next to the surgical table and passed a clipboard to Sharmila. "She's had one sac break but the others are intact."

"Okay, thank you," replied Sharmila, flicking through the pages and glancing at the charts within, while the nurse who had been laying out the tools checked the readouts on the monitor. "Right," she paused briefly to confirm the name on the list, "Haleigh, you know the drill by now. We'll try and get this over and done as soon as possible for you, and you can get out of here and home."

Kate stared at the woman on the trolley as the red-clad nurse strapped Haleigh's legs to each side to the bed. The lower half of the frame then disconnected and split out, spreading the woman's legs wide, high and bent at the knees. "She's five centimetres," the nurse confirmed.

"That's wide enough," replied Sharmila, placing the clipboard on the table. "Haleigh, I need you to push with the contractions. It'll be quicker, I promise."

Kate had presumed the patient to be unconscious but on closer inspection she was awake, her head tipped away from the bustling nurses. Her eyes were glazed and distant, seemingly disconnected from the unfolding events around her. The only acknowledgement of Sharmila's request was a slight nod of the head. To Kate, however, something seemed very odd even if the professionals surrounding her took no notice. Sure, the woman looked pregnant, but her swollen belly was nothing like as large as the women in the instructional films that Kate remembered from her childhood. Her thoughts were interrupted as Haleigh appeared to grimace slightly, and a clear fluid tainted with red suddenly gushed from her and splashed onto the floor, followed quickly by two more of the same.

"Well that's all of them I guess, nearly there dear," Sharmila said, moving to stand between the patient's legs as the assistant handed her some of the surgical instruments. "I can see the first one, keep pushing." She took hold of the spooned tongs and reached inside the woman, slowly drawing out the handles.

And with them came out a tiny child.

Sharmila worked quickly, cutting the umbilical cord a few inches from the baby's belly and sealing it from bleeding with a clip, before passing the newborn to the assistant. "Incubator. Quickly please."

The nurse in green rushed over to the glass box in front of Kate and placed the baby inside. Her colleague quickly joined her, working around the controls by the gas cylinder. But something looked very wrong. The baby was less than ten inches long and covered in a white sticky substance, its minuscule and barely-formed fingers grasping at the air as it struggled to breathe through weak and premature lungs. What was left of the umbilical cord hung limply by its side as the burgundy nurse worked quickly to insert the tubes into its nose and give it a chance of life. Kate stood transfixed in repugnant fascination as the child was soon joined by another, and then two more. All were girls, and all looked too young and underdeveloped to survive long outside of their mother, even with the help of the incubator.

"Well done Haleigh, all finished," said Sharmila, lowering the trolley's outstretched frame and placing a large cotton-wool padded dressing between the woman's thighs, before turning to her assistant. "Can you phone this through to Collection, please? I'd like to-"

She never got the chance to finish, however, before her patient let out a scream of pain and a large patch of red began to seep across the dressing. It soon overwhelmed the absorption and continued to run down her legs, creating a rapidly growing puddle on the floor.

"Oh shit!" exclaimed the young assistant, turning a similar shade of green to her uniform.

"Calm down girl," said Sharmila in a composed tone before addressing her patient. "Don't worry, Haleigh, it's just a small tear in your uterus where one of the placentas has detached. The bleeding will stop in a minute." She looked across the room to the others, and a look of grave concern shot fleetingly across her face as Haleigh let out another scream. "Can we get some sedation here, please? And ring through for a doctor in case this gets worse,"

The assistant rushed over, picking up a syringe on the way and clumsily burying it in the patient's arm. Haleigh winced briefly before falling silent as the senior nurse chastised her younger colleague for a lack of care.

"Well, that's another one off the programme for God-knows how many weeks," Sharmila exclaimed, looking down at the now-sleeping woman as the puddle of blood on the floor grew steadily larger, congealing slightly around the metal rear wheels of the surgical trolley. "I keep telling the management they need to ease off a bit and give them longer to recover between each cycle, but no one ever listens. Perhaps next time I should invite them down to watch the results."

The commotion, coupled with the increasing smell of the blood, snapped Kate out of her trance and back to the reality of why she was there in the first place. If there was any opportunity to get away and back on her mission, then this was it. "I'm going to be sick!" she cried suddenly, which wasn't that far from the truth, and ran past the incubator with its writhing and gasping cargo before making a dash to the exit. She could hear Sharmila reminding her the toilets were down the hall as she left.

Once outside, Kate quickly orientated herself, locating a sign to the logistical and sanitation section before marching off purposely in the indicated direction. But she'd barely managed ten yards when a cursory glance at a small group of staff members in the near distance produced a shocking jolt of recognition. Amongst the chatting and laughing company was Emma, the clinic nurse she had spoken to at Emily's funeral, and she was looking straight at her. Kate spun away, frantically searching for something to look busy doing, to not look out of place, to blend in as she felt Emma's gaze as the group walked slowly towards her. She found her salvation in a door to her left, taking her badge in hand and quickly swiping it desperately across the security panel which refused point blankly to cooperate. As a last-ditch attempt, she placed it right up to the panel and held it there, praying under her breath for the God she didn't believe in to intervene. Luckily, it seemed someone was listening, as the door finally relented and opened up the tiniest of cracks, allowing her to push it open and dart through just as Emma and the others walked by unaware.

The door was labelled D336.

Catching her breath, Kate took in her new surroundings. It turned out to be a spacious, brightly lit but windowless research lab separated into three bays of benching and strange-looking equipment. In the nearest bay sat eight scientists in white lab coats, hunched over large microscopes and deftly using manipulators with small scalpel blades and tweezers attached. On closer inspection they appeared to be slicing up something in a glass dish, carefully placing the carved strips into liquid-filled wells of a small oblong plate. *Is this one of the IVF labs or where they fix the virus?* thought Kate, but any further investigation was curtailed as she was suddenly aware someone was looking at her. It was a short, portly man, whose stomach was straining against the belt that was optimistically trying to hold his trousers above his waist. "Can I help you?" he asked as he moved towards her, his open blue lab coat swishing like a cape behind him.

Kate quickly glanced around the lab for something to catch her eye and found salvation up on a shelf in the far bay. "Yes, we've run out of surgical gloves," she said confidently, pointing her finger in the air and guiding it along the distant shelves in a searching motion. There's a patient bleeding in one of the parturition rooms and this was the nearest lab."

"Sure, take what you need," the man replied in a bored tone before turning his attention back to his work. Kate wondered why he was adorned in a different colour uniform to the others in the laboratory, presuming like the nurses it was a sign of rank or to differentiate the role they performed. Judging by his manner and the others' deference to him, he seemed to be the one in charge.

Kate thanked him and made her way to the back of the room, passing a group of people sat at open cabinets and a bank of what looked like small ovens (although the temperature gauge at the top showed thirty-seven degrees) with glass doors. Curiosity getting the better of her, she surreptitiously peered inside, but any great revelation she may have expected was tinged with disappointment. Each oven just contained racks of the small plates that the workers at the microscopes were filling. Any other investigations were cut short, however, when the door to the laboratory suddenly swung open.

A man had appeared, pushing a trolley that Kate instantly recognised, its precious contents still twitching as he brought it to a halt. "Sorry for the lack of warning; some fresh lambs for you," he announced, before handing over a clipboard to the lab head.

"Great, had we known earlier we wouldn't have bothered thawing out a sample this morning," the plump man in the blue coat complained, as he signed the form before returning it to the porter.

The porter shrugged his shoulders in a complete lack of sympathy. "Sorry, not my department," he replied unhelpfully as he turned and left, clipboard in hand.

The lab head spied the incubator contents with a critical eye. "Let's see what we have here then," he mused, reaching into the glass box and pulling the tubes from the nose of the nearest child, before separating it from its siblings. "Larry can you take notes please?" He gently held up the baby to his eye level, supporting its neck with his thumb and forefinger as he examined the tiny form more closely. "Female Caucasian, North-European heritage," he declared, continuing his assessment as his assistant took detailed notes in a book, taking care to fill any blank spaces in his work with a neat pen line. "Judging by the developing bridge on the nose probably the offspring of MD#122. Busy chap that one. Give it a few generations and most of the population of the country will have that phenotype."

As the man's colleagues laughed at the quip, Kate stopped her pretence at collecting some gloves and instead stared intently at the scene unfolding in front of her. Couldn't the rest of the people in the room see how distressed the baby was acting without the warmth and oxygen of the incubator? She wanted to cry out to the man holding the child, to warn him of the danger but she never got the chance.

"Time of nullification, 11:35," he announced in a manner so matter-of-fact that to Kate it made his next action seem even more inexplicable. He slowly increased his grip around the baby's neck, pressing his thumb on its spine with ever increasing pressure until the bones made an audible and appalling cracking noise. The child let out a small cry and then fell still.

The man passed the lifeless body over to one of the microscope scientists who placed the body in a large metal dish. Acting swiftly, he picked up a scalpel and begun carefully slicing at the small cadaver near each hip, folding back the flesh like butterfly wings and securing them with surgical clamps. Next came a smaller scalpel and a set of fine tweezers. The operator dug into the hole he'd created, pulled out a small lump of tissue and passed it to a colleague, before repeating the procedure on the other incision. Satisfied with his work, he casually tossed the tools into a bowl of clean water, the blood swirling from the blades and mixing with the pure liquid within.

The others stared down their eyepieces and began slicing the parts into thin strips. Kate stared in unblinking horror as the man in the blue coat extracted another child from the safety of its glass cocoon and repeated his assessment, before the grim dissection began again. The first corpse was slung uncaringly into a large yellow-lined cardboard bin to make way for the new specimen.

She had wanted to know, and now she knew. And the revelation sickened her to the core. She turned and ran, shoving through the surprised-looking scientists on her way out the door. Sprinting now, she desperately swallowed the saliva rushing into her mouth as her brain and stomach tried to expel the images she had fed them. She no longer cared about her maintaining her pretence and blending in as she tore past nurses, doctors and porters alike. She needed to get away from this ghoulish freak show and she needed to do it now.

Inquisition

Victor could tell this was no ordinary sleep. Usually, in dreams he was a passenger, a slave to his subconscious playing a role in someone else's macabre theatre. But here things were different, a vague sense of self-awareness giving him a fragmented comprehension of the images and scenes swiping across his mind's eye. He was nine again and back at the family home, sealing his parents' bedroom door with electrical tape to stop the smell of his father's death permeating through and contaminating the rest of the apartment. The soldiers breaking in as he swore and waved a blunt kitchen knife at them. His first day at the orphanage, smashing in the nose of a bully who'd tried to take his books from him. Love, hate, envy, desire for knowledge all its forms, a cacophony of emotions and snapshots on a zoetrope revolving with ever increasing speed. They were soon joined by echoing distant sounds that grew ever louder, then the sudden pungent odour of ammonia.

He snapped awake with a jerk as a blurred figure, holding a pot of what Victor guessed were smelling salts, disappeared into the shadows to whisper something to an accomplice. He tried in vain to piece together how he had ended up in this windowless, humid and dingy small dark room with pipes on the ceiling and rusting metal shelves adorning the walls. The only light he could make out was coming from small red bulbs on a bank of electrical breaker circuits in the far corner, giving everything it touched a fiery glow. It was then he realised he couldn't move, but his brief moment of panic was tempered by a quick glance down at his body. He hadn't been paralysed in some accident, he was tied to a chair at the wrists and ankles with duct tape.

An abrupt pounding in his head shocked a remnant of memory to the fore; he had been at his desk when Janet had rushed in, announcing in an alarmed tone that there was a nurse outside who needed his help for an emergency in one of the parturition rooms. He'd thanked her and promptly left, dashing by a porter pushing a large laundry trolley (which was odd in retrospect - what was a porter doing in the office section?) in his effort to catch up with the nurse, who was now walking away from him. That was strange too, as was the lack of anyone else around. Had the corridor been shut off as the closed doors at either end suggested? Slightly out of breath, he'd caught up to the nurse with red hair who'd spun around to face him as he reached her. She was somehow familiar but the memory was hazy, her face mixed with other women he had known making her identity a mystery. She had called him by his full name, her voice full of hate as he felt the presence of a figure behind him, quickly followed by a sharp scratching sensation on his neck.

And now he was here, wherever here was. Victor had taken kidnap training a few years previously, but however realistic the drama his brain could never get over the fact it was all make-believe. No matter how much the men in masks shouted at him and demanded answers, he knew they would never actually let him come to any harm, making the whole drama seem a little pointless. Luckily, he had paid attention in the lectures, which outlined various scenarios and outcomes but came down to two simple determinants; amateurs or professionals, and money or information. Amateurs could be bargained with, confused and even manipulated into a release, but professionals were a different matter. If they wanted money, it was best to cooperate and keep your head down. And if they wanted information? Well, you'd better start talking now and save yourself a whole lot of pain. The very thought of it sent him into a panic, his palms now dripping with sweat, quickly followed by an urgent burning feeling in his bladder as he fought to catch his breath. Showing fear was also a no-no according to the trainer, but that was easy to say in the comfort of a classroom where his autonomic nervous system wasn't screaming at him from every synapse to run. But if he couldn't be confident, at least he could try and act it. "You do know I have a tracker implanted?" he said in his best attempt at a mocking tone, although the wavering in his voice betrayed his anxiety. "In a few minutes that door will smash open and you'll be shot to pieces. So let me go now and you can just disappear back to where you came from."

One of the figures, a scruffy-looking dark-haired man dressed like the porter Victor had rushed past earlier, approached him from the gloom and into clear view. "Oh, I shouldn't worry about that," the man replied, "no one will come for you. By the way, are you left or right-handed?"

"Right," said Victor without thinking, as he focused on something gleaming slightly in the man's grasp.

"Okay, just so we're clear where we all stand," the porter stated, holding up a small surgical needle with a wooden handle to Victor's eye line. Slowly, he turned it over in his fingers, letting the dim light dance on its reflection. Then without warning, he grabbed Victor's left hand, pinning it to the chair arm as the prisoner struggled vainly in his restraints.

Victor had often heard people speak about imagining pain when describing an incident or a scene in a movie, but he'd always dismissed it as a misnomer. Pain could not be imagined, it could only be felt, be endured. Once it had passed, only the memory of the mental trauma of the incident remained, and a sickening feeling of not wanting to suffer through it again. None of which was any comfort, however, as his assailant pushed the needle hard under the nail of Victor's left index finger and deep into the flesh, making him scream out in agony, all pretence at bravado now gone.

"I can do that all day," the man stated impassively, slowly removing the needle from Victor's hand, "but feel free to holler, the doors and walls here are very thick."

"Who the fuck are you people?" Victor demanded, tears of pain rolling from his eyes as snot ran uncontrollably from his nose and blood oozed from his injured finger.

"IVFree," the man replied simply. "My friend here would like to ask you some questions," he added, gesturing to his partner who moved out from the shadows. It was the nurse with red hair.

"Hello Dr Pearson, remember me now?"

"Kate?" Victor answered, the memory of their meeting at Emily Palmer's funeral coming into sharp focus. For the first time, the seriousness of his situation truly hit him. These weren't trained professionals or amateurs looking for a quick score, they were a fanatic and a vengeful woman seeking recompense for the crime of neglect she thought he had committed. He wasn't going to be able to pay or talk his way out of this one.

"What happens in that room?" Kate demanded.

"Which room?"

"Don't play games with me or I'll stick the next needle in myself, and I won't be as gentle," Kate shot back angrily. "The room with the microscopes and ovens. The room where you take the babies and cut them up."

Victor felt a sickening feeling in the pit of his stomach. Context was everything in D336 and Emily's sister had none of it. "You saw?"

"Yes, I saw. And I wish to God I hadn't."

Well, she wanted an explanation, so Victor put on his best lecturer voice and reeled off the spiel they gave to the new medical staff. "It's the most efficient way of collecting donor eggs. By the time the female foetus reaches twenty weeks' gestation it contains millions of primordial follicles. The egg that made you Kate, existed when your grandmother was pregnant with your mother. Most of them are reabsorbed by adulthood, though, so we induce birth halfway through the second trimester, harvest the ovaries and culture the eggs to maturity *in vitro.* It's a very complex protocol, and even then only a fraction of them survive and grow to be of any use for IVF."

"You have banks full of eggs, or so you keep telling everyone. So why?"

"You wouldn't understand."

"Try me."

If a part of Victor thought that the next cut would be less painful somehow, he was deeply mistaken. The weapon was pushed under the nail of his ring finger this time, making him jerk his head backwards violently against the wall as he shrieked out once more. "There was nothing left!" he cried, letting out a sob as the needle was withdrawn again. "Nothing! Your generation doesn't understand. You think you do, but you don't. You never could. The world was ending, just trying to survive day to day was nearly impossible, so you can guess how much attention got paid to fertility clinic nitrogen deliveries. We spent years scouring the world for material and it was all gone. Dead. Ruined. All we had left were a handful of IES-clear survivors and an ageing population of first-gen infected."

"So the babies are the real donors? The women are just incubators?"

Victor nodded his head in confirmation. "Getting enough sperm was easy but the eggs, they were a different matter. Even with superovulation, there was no way we could ever keep up with the demand the Lottery system imposed on us, and the Lottery was the only thing stopping the country dissolving back into anarchy. Those tanks in the Cathedral? They're nearly all empty, just smoke and mirrors for the public - it's taken us years to get even a few months ahead. So you can keep your disgusted and self-righteous attitudes, this was the only way."

"If those women knew what you were doing, they'd-" Kate began to say, but Victor cut her off mid-sentence.

"If they knew?" he scoffed, "Of course they know! Everyone here knows! We all believe in the mission, that what we are doing here is necessary."

The IVFree man piped in. "If it's necessary, then why hide it? Why not be honest?"

Victor returned the man's stare with his own. "Because it's abhorrent. People don't even want to know how their meat is processed, how do you think they will react to this? What do you think will happen? That the masses will rise up and storm the clinics in a rage, chanting your slogans as they go? All you'll do is make them feel guilty, and they'll hate you for it."

His tormentor started to challenge Victor on his words, but Kate stopped him with a dismissive wave of her hand. "This isn't why we're here."

"No," replied Victor, at last seeing an opportunity to exploit. He knew from the early days of the clinics that the first rule of selling to a couple was to divide and conquer, home in and focus on who wanted it more whilst distracting the other. "That's not why *you're* here," he said, directing his answer to Kate before turning his gaze on the man with the needle. "Why *you're* here though is a different matter. I doubt that your organisation would send some lowly grunt to get me, so what are you? A lieutenant with an axe to grind?"

"You're right," the IVFree man replied almost instantly. "This is personal. My wife is dead because of you Dr Pearson. I'd imagine you don't remember the names Andrzej and Lucja Zawojski?"

Victor shifted uncomfortably in his chair and shook his head, the throbbing of his fingers suddenly increasing in intensity. "I don't even know you, let alone your wife!"

"We'd saved for years for the treatment," Andrzej said angrily. "Everything we had went into that pot, scraping here and there whenever we could. I still remember her face that morning when the time finally came to head to the clinic. I'd never seen her happier or more excited."

"So what happened?"

"She miscarried three months in. The doctors said it was just one of those things."

"Surely you were insured against that?" asked Victor, confused at the man's response. Non-complete pregnancies were usually open and shut cases for the claimants, which was why the premiums were so high.

Andrzej looked away in shame. "I never smoked in front of Lucja, ever. Not even before she was pregnant. But it was enough for those bastards to wriggle out of their responsibilities and invalidate our policy. Someone at that company probably got a pat on the back but we lost everything. Lucja said it wasn't my fault, that she didn't blame me, but I knew deep down she did. She couldn't even bring herself to look me in the eye after that." He paused briefly, trying to choke back tears. "A few weeks later she took her own life."

"How the hell is that my fault?"

"It's the system! You're the system!" Andrzej shot back. "Denying people treatment unless they're rich or win that corrupt lottery. I started IVFree to give people a shot at a chance that Lucja and I never had. The next generation is a right, not a privilege!"

Victor had to laugh despite himself and the danger he was in. "So is that what it's all about? Guilt? You can't handle that you were responsible for your wife's suicide, so you decide to crusade against us instead? What are you looking for, Andrzej? Atonement? Believe me, you'll never find it." His laughter was cut short though as the man strode over and leant hard on his bleeding fingers, making him cry out once more.

"That's enough!" exclaimed Kate, shock now starting to creep into her face. It seemed that the revelation was news to her too.

"I'm sorry," Andrzej replied to his accomplice rather than his victim. "I care about those people, about the world." He turned his attention back to the prisoner. "What do you care about Dr Pearson?"

Victor was about to say 'money and recognition' as he always did when asked that question, but the phrase turned sour as he went to speak the words. What had money got him after all? A large empty house, access to technology he had no interest in, and the finest high-class whores he could no longer perform with. Misery in luxury to be sure, but misery nonetheless. So no, not money. Recognition then; the adulation of his peers, showing all of those fast-track research fellows with their snide remarks and superior attitudes how good he really was, and how small their lives were in comparison. But was even that the case? He inspired mostly envy and suspicion from the research community, the fawning scientists clambering to shower him with platitudes quickly turning to tones of contempt the minute his back was turned, the result of a career built on lies and half-truths. So what then? There was only one thing he truly held dear, and she was lost to him long ago. The pain of the memory and Andrzej's words filled him with a rising anger. He no longer cared what the man might do to him next, and if the woman would or could stop it. "Screw both of you and your sanctimonious opinions," he cried. "How dare you judge me! You think because someone close to you died that makes you unique, gives you the right to do whatever you want? You have no fucking idea what loss is."

"And what do you know about it?" demanded Kate.

"More than you'll ever know," said Victor quietly, thinking of happier times as the fight started to go out of him. "I was married too once. It was years ago; we were just starting things up. The testing stations had identified a new batch of IES-clear patients and transferred them over. I watched them as they arrived, a bunch of lucky but unremarkable people. But then I saw her. Susanna. I'd never seen anyone so beautiful in my life, all dressed up to the nines like she was off to a formal dinner party. She was the daughter of some wealthy landowner, someone I would never even get to notice me normally no matter how much money I had. I loved her from that very second, and she became my world as we got closer in those first few months. She had brains as well as looks you see, helped me set up the donor programme, helped me shape the future. Susanna knew what had to be done, no matter what the cost was. 'God would be our judge' she used to say, 'we can only do our best for the world, and He will decide if it was right or not'." Saying it out loud made him realise why he'd been so easily captivated by Rowena. Susanna and she were two sides of the same coin, a perfect tempest of innocent charm and sometimes brutal pragmatism. But where he doubted Rowena would have the courage of her own convictions, Susanna was never afraid to put herself through what she expected of others. "I used to hold her hand every time she went into that room," he continued, tears of grief mixing in with those of pain, "and we'd cry together as she gave birth to those tiny children, knowing what happened next. Seeing her like that, having to watch her go through it again and again, it broke my heart more each day. So yes, I know plenty about it."

"They were your children?" asked Kate, her voice flat.

"No, they were from randomised donors, not that it made a difference. We could never be together, I'm a first gen'er like everyone my age and would have infected her. I used to lay awake at night wishing it were different, that we could be in love like normal people, but Susanna would never have allowed it. The programme was too important to her for that. But do you know the worst of it? My dream came true!"

The IVFree man snorted with indifference but Kate, at least, seemed attentive to his plight. "What happened?"

"At first, we thought the pain was just a side effect of the treatments, that it would pass after a while, but then it got worse and worse. Ovarian cancer they said, gave her six months tops when they found it had metastasised. The treatment made her useless for the programme and I got my wish. We got married and we were happy, for a little while at least. Then she was gone, and I was alone." Victor let out a large sigh but his breath was caught by the throbbing pain in his fingers. "So go ahead Kate, ask your questions and get it over with. I don't care any more."

Kate walked over to his chair and leant down close to him, so their heads were at the same level. If she felt any sympathy towards him after he had bared his soul, she hid it well. "We can skip ahead a few steps. I know that Emily was pregnant."

"How do you know that?" Victor asked, his eyes widening, startled by her statement. "No one knows that. Did one of the nurses talk?"

"No, I worked it out myself," she replied, "and I think you killed her because of it."

"I didn't kill her! Why would I do that?" Victor said, flabbergasted by her response. Did she not understand the significance? "I thought you just blamed me for IVS failing in our duty of care towards her."

"You killed Emily to protect your company," Kate replied accusingly. "If there was a cure you'd be out of business."

Victor let out a laugh of derision. "Yes, in about eight generations time when I'd be long dead and past caring! For someone who seems intelligent Kate, you really have no idea about commerce. You think that mending the gene temporarily is expensive? Imagine how much we could charge for a permanent fix! Forget statues, they'd build entire cities in my name! I'd be the true saviour of the human race rather than just a patch-up mechanic."

"Then why is she dead?"

"I have no idea," he lied. No matter what dilemma he was in now, it would be nothing compared to Caden's wrath if he betrayed him directly.

"And before you ask, no I don't know how she was still pregnant; her genome sequence was normal."

Andrzej fished around in a pocket for something, which for a heart-stopping moment Victor imagined was a gun, but it turned out to be just a large folded piece of paper which the IVFree man passed to Kate.

"That's because you were looking in the wrong place," the woman said slightly too triumphantly as she held the paper up to his face. "What does this mean?"

"Where did you get this?"

"It's from Emily's ovaries. She had a botched treatment and it did this to her before she was assaulted by some bastard first gen'er. What does it mean?"

Victor studied the images and stacked sequences of letters intensely through the gloom of the room, hoping for inspiration, hoping that they would be satisfied with an answer and spare him more pain, but no flash of genius was forthcoming. The lies and false modesty he had built up and relied on over the years were stripped away now, leaving him naked and raw. So he just said what he saw and hoped it was enough. "Is this from a tumour? You've got multiple mutations in there and the sequence counts show more copies than there should be."

"Yes we know that already," said Andrzej, playing with the needle in his hands, moving it rhythmically between his fingers. "How does it work? What does it mean?"

"Without the context I can't tell," replied Victor, his breath quickening. "It could be doing anything. I don't know."

"How can you not know? You're the world expert on this!" demanded Kate, her tone almost as desperate as his.

"This level of mutation should just stop the gene from working at all. I'm a transgenics specialist, not a pure molecular biologist. I don't know!"

He never got a chance at his next stall, as Andrzej held down Victor's hand as he struggled hopelessly to escape, this time plunging the needle directly into it and out through his palm, scratching the arm of the chair with a screeching sound as he cried out in agony once more.

"I DON'T KNOW!"

They didn't believe him. Victor frantically searched for an answer, any answer, as his tormentor pushed the weapon embedded in his victim's hand to the side slightly, producing an excruciating scream. He had to give them something, anything to make them stop. He had to give them that name. "Tobias!"

"What? Who's that?" asked Kate, clearly confused by the revelation.

"Tobias Heath!" Victor cried as the needle was removed. "He was my old mentor years ago. Tobias is the real expert on this. He'll know what it means, what it does."

"Does he work at the clinic?"

"No. He's rotting in some care home on the south coast. Eastbourne."

"If he's the expert then who are you?" questioned Kate, throwing a look at her accomplice.

Victor looked away in shame and humiliation, broken at last. "A salesman. I'm just a salesman."

Andrzej went to plunge the needle into him once more but Kate stopped him, her voice trembling. "Don't. I believe him."

"I'm sorry about Emily, I really am," Victor sobbed. "Why did she run? We would have taken care of it, quietly, legally, no one would have ever known. She could have had a family with her husband and been happy. Why did she run?"

"My sister would have considered it a miracle, a gift from God no matter the circumstances," Kate replied, her eyes full of lament. "She'd waited all her life to have children, there's no way she would have just given it up voluntarily."

Her explanation cut him deep to the core, an emotional wound much deeper than Andrzej's needle could ever penetrate. Victor could feel Susanna's gaze upon him, her disapproval and disappointment obvious at the decisions and choices he had made since her passing. The compassion, the people and purpose of the donor programme had been ripped away, turned to ash, and replaced by cold unfeeling balance sheets and profit margins. But perhaps there was a way to help, to unburden the weight of the chains around his neck. Not a direct betrayal, but a nudge in the right direction at least. "I didn't kill your sister, but I would imagine whoever did doesn't care about money; they care about something else entirely," he said, but judging by the look of shock on her face, it seemed Kate had figured it out before he'd even finished his sentence. "I'm sorry," was all Victor had left as he heard the IVFree man rustle for something in his pocket.

Kate leant over and whispered into Victor's ear. "I'm sorry too."

He felt a sharp scratch on his neck, and then nothing.

*

Victor awoke and found himself alone in the darkness, his arms and legs now released from their bonds. A sudden sharp and then continuous fiery pain in his left hand put his ordeal back to the fore as his nerves fired up again, making him vomit his breakfast over the floor. He staggered to his feet, making it to the door before stumbling through it into a dimly-lit corridor with familiar-looking signs on the wall. He hadn't been lying about the tracker, but now he understood why it hadn't activated and why no one had come to his rescue. He was in the old maintenance basement. He had never left the clinic.

It was then he heard the alarms.

Escape

Kate's head was still spinning at the revelations from Victor, as she and Andrzej made their way purposely away from the sub-basement room where their captive was now slumped, unconscious in his chair. Her sister's words kept echoing around her mind and she couldn't shut them out. How could she have been so wrong, so naive?

Patrick and Andrzej had been right all along, she could see it now. It wasn't about money; it was about control. And that meant they were in even more trouble than she'd initially thought. As they reached the end of the corridor and waited for the lift she paced around frantically, trying to clear her head of the waves of confusion pounding against her brain. Water, valves, turbines. Capture, questions, justice. Plan, action, consequence. She had been so sure and set on the path before her that she had not even considered the reality of what happened afterwards if she was wrong. Victor was supposed to confess to Emily's murder, beg forgiveness and turn himself into the authorities whilst she and Andrzej disappeared beyond the SafeZones to a new life together. But all that had been torn away, and now she was lost.

Her partner turned to her, his face unreadable. "You think I went too far back there," he said, wiping a small trail of blood from his fingers and down the side of his shirt. It was a statement rather than a question.

"No, it had to be done," replied Kate, as if simply saying the words would convince herself of the fact, or make her feel any better. The emotion-fuelled anger that had boiled over a few minutes previously was wearing off now, replaced by the sickening remorse of having interrogated and tortured a man innocent of the crime she had pursued and condemned him for. A pathetic and wretched man, guilty of many things to be sure, but none of which was her place to act as judge and executioner for. Something else was bothering her too, a betrayal much closer to home. "You should have told me about what happened to your wife," Kate said, feeling more hurt than she'd realised.

"Yes, and I'm sorry," replied Andrzej turning away. "Back there, I didn't mean that to happen. But hearing him mocking us and our grief, I just lost it."

His apology didn't work. "Did you actually want to help me, or was I only ever just an opportunity to you?" Kate leant past him to hit the lift call button needlessly with her fist.

Andrzej took her hand in his and looked her straight in the eyes, his own a picture of regret. "Of course not. All this, I did it for you, for us. You have to believe me."

Kate wanted to more than anything, but the wound was still too raw so she avoided the question. Forgiveness would come in time she was sure, but they had more pressing matters at hand. "So what happens now?"

Andrzej, who clearly had about as much of a clue what to do next as Kate, paused for thought before responding. "Pearson gave us a name; Tobias Heath, and it wasn't one he told us willingly. Our next move should be to get to him and see if he can help us."

Kate nodded in agreement. Whoever this man was, he was important to Victor Pearson, important to unlocking the secret of Emily's pregnancy and any hope for the future. The Government she had supported and so vigorously defended throughout her adult life had deceived her, conspired against her and played her for a fool. The walls she had built against the doubts, and the evidence she had ignored had come crashing down around her the moment Victor had said those words. IVFree and the hope of a cure were now all she had left, or Emily would have died for nothing.

"I didn't have much of the sedative left so we don't have much time," Andrzej explained, as the doors of the elevator slid open with a rusty creaking noise and the pair slipped inside, "and we'll need a distraction."

The logistics parking section was just one level up and a short walk, much to Kate's relief, as she tried to shake the imagined scenario of a now awake and enraged Victor Pearson pursuing them from her mind. The area was thankfully empty of people, the only inhabitants being stacks of boxes on wooden pallets and large bags of linen, one of which had spilt its contents of soiled sheets over the floor. Andrzej, who passed his jacket to Kate to wear and cover her uniform, found what he was looking for on the wall by some disused lockers and pulled the small red handle down from its enclosure, resulting in an ear-piercing wailing noise as the fire alarm burst into life.

"Let's go!"

The alarm had the desired effect. As Andrzej drove slowly out of the parking area and into the daylight, a sea of people emerged from the clinic building while supervisors in yellow jackets attempted in vain to usher them to the correct holding areas, away from any potential explosions. The security guards at the front gate were similarly preoccupied directing a group of arriving clients, and impatiently waved the laundry van around the barriers and out of the clinic campus. Andrzej waited until they were out of sight, then slammed his foot on the accelerator and headed off at speed. They soon reached their junction and veered off down one of the unmarked roads, the suspension crunching and complaining as it bounced over the pitted and crumbling tarmac. They were free, for now at least.

After several minutes of avoiding fallen trees and corners taken at a speed the chassis of the van was not designed for, Andrzej eased up his right foot, much to the relief of Kate who was keeping a nervous watch on the climbing needle on the engine's temperature gauge. Her car was hidden in an abandoned village a few miles away, but it would be of no use if the van broke down before they could get there. She couldn't feel even remotely safe until they'd switched vehicles and put some distance, both physical and mental, from the events she was still grappling with in her mind.

"We should get changed as soon as we get to the car," she suggested, "it'll be easier to blend in when we make it to London." The proposal was sensible but hid her real intent; the blood on Andrzej's uniform was a constant reminder of what they'd done and it was making her feel nauseous.

"I don't think that's going to be possible," declared Andrzej glancing left then right at the wing mirrors with increasing concern, "we're being followed."

"Is it the police?"

"I don't think so, they'd have their lights and sirens on by now if it were," he replied, lurching the van forward and wrestling with the wheel as the vehicle threatened to understeer into a hedge. "There's a small town not far from here, we can try and lose them there."

***

Joe Parker was on his way to the clinic to oversee the security for Mrs Schoier's next visit when he got the call. It was a garbled half-message from the Repro office, the remote countryside location making the phone signal weak and interspersed with static. He managed to get enough of the gist of it, though, to order the driver of the car to put the hammer down and get to Highpoint in double time. He felt an unusual feeling of elation, breaking out a rare smile and clenching his fists in silent celebration. After a long string of failures, this was his chance.

The car, a luxury German model designed for a different era of travel, screeched to a halt at the main gate. Victor Pearson was standing there, looking as white as a sheet, and clutching his left arm as he shielded the hand from view. The conversation with the CEO and the security guards was brief, to the point and full to the brim with information. At last, they had a name and a face to IVFree, and he was within their grasp.

"Should we call for backup or the local police?" the driver, a dark-skinned and muscular man called Maahir asked, as they sped off in the direction the guards had indicated.

Parker shook his head and muttered something about a lack of time and his total faith in Maahir as a pursuit driver. In reality, his motives were much more selfish; no one was going to take this prize from him no matter what was at stake. This Andrzej, whoever he was, was his and his alone.

*

Kate gasped out in fear as the van lurched to one side, accompanied by a grating and scraping sound of metal on metal as the pursuing vehicle punched unsuccessfully against their flank. Luckily, the weight of their transport, which up until now was a handicap slowing them down, was now their best defence. Some nimble work on the steering wheel by Andrzej kept their path straight as the other car swerved around dangerously behind.

"It's only a matter of time before they fishtail us, or the tyre goes out," said Andrzej in a barely-level tone as he fought with the controls. "The town is just ahead. Hang on!"

The SafeZone boundaries here were, unfortunately, in much better condition than in her home city, with bright yellow metal barriers and concrete posts sectioning off the narrow country approach road into several solid chicanes. Combined with the sprinkling of fresh snow making the road greasy, they proved more than a match for Kate's driver as he weaved and lurched the van around the obstructions, smashing off the rear bumper on the way. Their pursuer had no such problems and was on them again in seconds, this time attempting to barge them into one of the small shops by the road, and giving little care for the pedestrians scattering wildly for cover. Andrzej tried a different tactic, suddenly slamming on the brakes and sending Kate flying forward towards the windscreen until the seatbelt caught her, knocking the wind out of her before wrenching her back to her seat. It had the desired effect, sending their hunters hurtling off ahead without them as they quickly headed down a side street and into the winding maze of a half-abandoned residential area.

After a few hasty turns, which Kate hoped would not send them down a blind alley, Andrzej slowed down briefly as he reached over to the glove compartment. He pulled out a heavy-looking object, which was wrapped in an oily towel. Kate was shocked to find it was a pistol.

"Do you know how to use a gun?" Andrzej asked, handing her the weapon with one hand whilst trying to weave around some large bins with the other.

"No, of course I don't!" replied Kate, feeling the weight of the weapon as she tried to keep it as far away from herself as possible, as if it were a dead animal. "Why do you even have one?"

Andrzej turned the van sharply down yet another side street as the road got ever narrower. "After what happened to the old HQ, Patrick thought it would be a good idea to get some protection, just in case. He knows some people out beyond who deal in those kinds of things. I've left the safety on; just point it at whoever you need to get out of the way, they probably won't know how to use one either."

That wasn't very reassuring, but before she could argue he slowed down, pulled over to the side of the road and told her to get out. There was no time for goodbyes. Kate leapt out of the car, concealing the gun in her jacket pocket as Andrzej roared off into the distance. Not waiting to check if the other car was following she ran as fast as she could towards a small gap between two buildings, gasping for breath as her heart pounded and threatened to explode from her chest. Stopping briefly to recover once out of sight, a wave of panic washed over her as her rational brain regained control. She had no money, no transport and no clue where she was. What the hell did she do now?

*

Joe swore loudly as their car shot past the ailing van, and Maahir had to take evasive action not to mow down a group of pedestrians who were too stupid to get out of the way. The street was too narrow to attempt any flash manoeuvres, so they had to quickly dive down a side street. The gearbox crunched and screamed as the driver slammed the stick into reverse and accelerated hard back around the corner, before hitting the brakes and heading off towards their quarry, leaving a trail of smoking rubber behind them.

The housing area was a labyrinth of side streets and potential wrong turns, but fortunately, their prey had left a breadcrumb trail of broken bits of bodywork and light fittings for them to follow. As they turned a corner where a boarded-up pub with a rusting sign stood, their prize finally came back into view. Before they could reach them, however, the passenger door of the van swung open, a woman jumped out and then sprinted away.

"Should we stop?" the driver asked as the van accelerated hard into the distance.

"No!" shouted Joe impatiently. "She's not important, keep on the driver. We can get the local plods to pick her up later." They were too close now for any distractions, and too close for failure to be an option.

*

As she peered nervously around the corner of the alley, Kate saw potential salvation across the empty street. A woman, a few years older than her with greying hair tied in a bun, had just approached a rusty green car that made Kate's look new in comparison, and was struggling to push some furniture onto the back seat. Calmer now, the fugitive considered her options. It didn't matter what she did now, her freedom and possibly her life were forfeit, and all that remained was not getting caught. She couldn't just steal the car from in front of the woman, however, nor could she simply pull out the gun in full view and take a hostage. If there were any witnesses in the surrounding houses, then the police would be on her in moments. Andrzej had given her a chance and she couldn't blow it in the first few minutes.

The woman had nearly finished loading her cargo now and would be gone in seconds, and the only plan forming in Kate's head had Hugo's words of 'be convincing' echoing around it. If she needed help, then she needed to look the part. Grabbing herself by the throat, she dug her fingers deep into her neck and pulled down hard, wincing as her nails gouged a red path along the contours of the flesh. Next, she scraped her forearm along the rough brick of the alley wall, grazing it into a puffy and angry rust colour. Taking the band from her ponytail, she quickly ruffled her hair loose and smeared the blood that was now seeping from her neck and arms over her forehead. "Help me!" she cried, staggering out of the shadows, and heading as rapidly as she could towards the woman.

"Oh my God! Are you okay?" the woman called to her, instantly stopping what she was doing and heading in Kate's direction.

"Some men attacked me! They took my purse!" replied Kate in as shocked a tone as she could muster.

The woman put her arm around Kate's shoulder, giving her a supportive hug as she gestured with her free hand towards the house opposite. "Come inside dear and I'll call the police."

"No!" cried Kate too quickly, which caught the woman off guard. But it was a good point; why wouldn't she want the police? Then an idea struck her. "I need to get to the hospital. Now!" she pleaded. "They punched me in the stomach and I'm pregnant. It really hurts. Please, help me!"

It had the desired effect. "Oh of course my poor girl!" the woman said as she guided Kate to the passenger seat of the car. "I'm Gaby. Always here to help a critical worker like you," she said, drawing her eye to the uniform under Kate's coat. "It's only a short drive, probably quicker than calling an ambulance anyway. Are you a nurse there?"

"No," replied Kate, wary in case Gaby asked her for directions. "I'm from Highpoint. I just came off shift and was visiting a friend when they approached me. Before I knew it they'd thrown me against a wall and were hitting me until I dropped my bag."

"What scum!" said Gaby angrily as she started the car and drove off at speed. "Don't worry, the police will get them and the bastards will get what's coming to them."

Kate acknowledged the woman's concerns. Putting an unborn child in danger through violence was a very specific law which the perpetrators paid for with their lives, regardless of whether they were ignorant of the victim's condition or not. She felt guilty about lying to this friendly and helpful woman, but there was no need to continue with her ruse no matter how well it had worked, especially as they could reach the local hospital at any moment. Taking a deep breath, Kate reached into her coat pocket and pulled out the gun, holding it on her lap and pointing it up at the woman's head. She prayed that Andrzej was right and it wouldn't go off accidentally.

Gaby shrieked and shook with fear, her knuckles turning white as she gripped the wheel. "What are you doing? I was trying to help you!"

"I'm sorry. I'm not a bad person, but I'm in a lot of trouble," said Kate, trying to keep the woman from becoming hysterical. "I don't want to hurt you, but I need you to drive south towards the coast. Can you do that for me?"

The woman nodded her head jerkily, not daring to look Kate in the face. "Are you on the run?"

"I am now."

***

Kate slowed the car to a halt by the seafront, a short walk away from the domineering large white building with countless square sash windows overlooking the beach. A quick stop at a local phone booth and the directory listings within it had given her an address for Tobias Heath, which turned out to be a converted hotel whose glory days seemed to be long over. The use of Dignity and the commencement of the Retirement Act had all but closed most of the homes down in recent years, but a few remained to care for those rich and stubborn enough to cling on to life beyond their ability to look after themselves, and continue to be a burden to society. At least, that's what she used to think, but as she'd been wrong about pretty much everything else up to this point, who knew what the truth really was?

The needle on the fuel gauge mirrored her options. This was it, the end of the line. If Victor had been lying they'd never get close to him again, and all this would be for nothing. Perhaps this was what she deserved, throwing her life away over an obsession just like her sister had. She inhaled the salty air, the freshness briefly taking her breath away. To her, the coast was a place of work, of bustling industry, dirt and noise but here everything was quiet, the gentle roll of the waves against the sand giving a sense of calmness to all that surrounded it. The biting wind had dropped, and the angry dark clouds that had been threatening more snowfall had dissipated for now, which made her feel a little better about abandoning her hostage a few miles out of town. It was far enough to delay Gaby in calling the authorities, but not too far to leave her dangerously exposed to the elements for long. She had enough guilt on her hands as it was, without adding hurting innocent strangers to the list.

The interior of the building was as dilapidated as the outside, with shabby carpets and a faint odour of human excrement permeating the air. There was no one at reception so she just walked into what passed as the lounge, where several old men were sleeping in large armchairs and ignoring the television in the corner.

"Hello?" she asked loudly, "I'm looking for Tobias Heath." There was no response, so she tried again with the same result. Feeling frustrated, she spun around to head back to reception, only to be confronted by an ancient-looking man in a wheelchair. He was being slowly pushed towards her by an enormous male nurse, who had piercings in his head and a sleeve of tattoos on his right arm.

"I'm Professor Heath," the man in the chair replied through a croaky toothless voice, running his fingers through wispy grey tufts of what hair remained on his head. "Who are you, girl?"

Kate took off her jacket as if her uniform would serve as some kind of identification, taking care to secure the gun in case it fell on the floor in front of them. "My name is Kate, Victor Pearson sent me," she lied. "He'd like some information about something."

"Go away child," the old man spat, "if that piece of filth wants to speak to me, he can come himself!" He gestured to the porter who then began to wheel him back out of sight. "Good day to you. Don't come here again."

"Wait!" cried Kate. "I lied, I'm sorry. He didn't send me, I was torturing him and he gave your name up. He said you could help me."

The old man lifted his arm and was stopped dead in his tracks. "Well, in that case, welcome my dear!" he said, his expression changing from disdain to a beaming smile as the large nurse turned him back around. "Put some tea on please Barney and find some cake, our guest here has come a long way I'm sure."

As the huge man vanished off in the direction of the kitchen, Tobias leant forward and peered at Kate through his thick-rimmed glasses. "You must have hurt him a lot to get him to say my name. Good for you!"

"Nothing he won't recover from," replied Kate, quietly hoping that was actually the case. Whatever wrong Pearson had done to this man in the past it wasn't because of her. "I'm sorry but I might not have a lot of time. I have some questions about the IES virus."

Tobias sighed deeply. "What did Victor tell you?"

Kate glanced around, but nobody else in the room was either awake or could probably hear her anyway, and even if they could they almost certainly wouldn't care or comprehend it. "We may have found a permanent fix, a cure, but when we confronted Dr Pearson he didn't know how it worked," she said in a hushed voice. "He said you were the real expert on the virus."

"Well of course I am," the old man replied succinctly. "I designed it."

The murderer and the thief

Kate stared in disbelief at the frail old man, her mouth agape. She had thought perhaps he was a spurned and betrayed partner from years ago, but she hadn't imagined anything like this.

"It feels strangely liberating to say that out loud," Tobias said to no one in particular, before snapping his attention back to Kate. "Come, girl. I think this is conversation best taken outside in the fresh air." He pointed to the wheels of his chair. "You can drive."

Kate rolled the old man and chair out of the building and into the sunshine, her head full of questions but nowhere to start. As they crossed the empty road and onto the promenade, she settled on simply asking, "Why?"

"Interesting choice," replied Tobias. "I would have gone for 'how' personally, but that's scientists for you."

"That was my second question," Kate retorted flatly, starting to feel the weight of the wheelchair starting to get away from her as the path sloped slightly downhill.

"Well, the 'why' is all about context," the old man said, gesturing at the water's edge as the crashing waves fizzed against the shore. "You have to appreciate how things used to be before to understand our motives. The world was dying you see. It probably seems incredible to your generation living in these half-empty cities, but when I was your age girl the human race was crumbling under its own weight. We got so good at curing disease and prolonging life that people just starved to death, or killed each other over resources instead. Insects can form new colonies, even parasites can find new hosts but we had nowhere else to go and nothing else to support the growing population. Even the democracies had begun to envy what their neighbours had, and that envy turned to distrust, and distrust to hate. After that, it was only a matter of time before they all turned in on each other. We wanted to stop the madness before they did."

Tobias suggested a diversion to the nearby pier because the view was better, as Kate tried to imagine the world as it once was. She'd seen films, heard the stories and read books on life before the plague, of course, but the flavour of the moments, the stress and tension of people crammed together like rats in a sewer day after day were unfathomable to her. So instead she asked, "Who's 'we'?"

"I can't even remember where we met, it was some virology and epidemiology conference somewhere in America I think," Tobias replied, his few remaining teeth chattering slightly, as Kate pushed his chair over the rutted threshold of the pier entrance and onto the boardwalk. "It was after a few too many drinks at the bar one night after an overlong platform session. The four of us got chatting about the state of the world and population control came up. A few scribbles on the back of a napkin and several whiskies later we'd got the basics down of how it could be done. Purely theoretical of course, but the idea had worked on mosquitos to stop Dengue Fever, so why not on humans? We went our separate ways and that was that, but I couldn't let the thought go, and after a while, the idea began to consume me. I contacted the others again and we agreed to take it further. We'd make a virus and test it in some cell lines, just to see if it could be done."

Kate was so intrigued by the story that she didn't notice the cluster of cars appearing in the distance, instead guiding Tobias further up the pier, through the old penny arcade games aisle and past a couple taking it in turns to use the fixed binoculars to spy on a boat on the horizon.

"Oh, you should have seen it girl, a perfect and beautiful piece of synthetic biology constructed with a single purpose. We designed it to look completely natural; no linker sequences, no markers, nothing that would trace it back to a lab. It was a work of art."

"Art?"

"Perhaps the one true art, the act of creation."

Tobias looked out over the guard rails at the pier's edge, whilst Kate looked nervously at the large gaps between the gnarled boards by her feet which threatened to suck her down into the icy water below. Unaware of the men now searching her abandoned car and asking passers-by about the whereabouts of its owner, she encouraged the old man to continue his tale, fascinated to know how they'd taken the leap from thought to action, from water to valves to turbines.

"We became aware of a small company experimenting with a new antibiotic they'd derived from soil bacteria, to treat drug-resistant tuberculosis," said Tobias. "Fortuitously they'd just got permission for a small clinical study in India, which was perfect for our little trial. We infiltrated their staff, contaminated their stocks and the virus replicated unseen in the bacteria. We designed it to lay in wait you see. You can't just sterilise an entire experimental cohort, someone is going to notice, but the next generation? The study would be well finished by then and no one would be checking up on them. Well, apart from us that is, to make sure things were progressing as they should. Phase two would be to introduce it in stages where the problems were the worst. Instead of war and famine, there would be a gradual decline in the population down to manageable numbers that the local resources could support. It was a perfect solution."

Kate knew where this was going. "And then the Death came."

Tobias smiled ruefully and nodded. "And then the Death came. The new antibiotic was the only thing that would touch it, so they expanded the production to an unimaginable scale. They sent it to every corner of the world and our little experiment went global before we had a chance to stop it." He stared sadly out to the sea, his breath condensing in the chilled air. "We wanted to save humanity, but instead, we just sealed its fate. It turned out nature knew what it was doing after all. We should have trusted it."

"Why didn't you admit what you'd done?" asked Kate in disbelief. "You could have helped develop a vaccine or treatment, help stop it before it took hold?"

"Fear mainly," replied Tobias. "The world was just pulling itself out of the furnace, can you imagine what they would have done to us if they found out? As soon as we realised what had happened we purged everything; designs, sequences, computer records, all of it. Well except for me anyway, instead I just collected up the data and locked it away in the back of my filing cabinet in my lab. I don't know why I didn't destroy it all, perhaps part of me wanted to be caught and I was just too much of a coward to turn myself in. The others all died in the plague, either of the disease or the chaos during it, and someone had to keep an account of what we'd accomplished. Rather fitting really."

Kate didn't notice the red dot on her back, distracted instead by a missing link to the chain of events that had brought her to this place. "What does this have to do with Victor Pearson? Did he help you?"

Tobias laughed. "No, he would have been a small child at the time. He's responsible for many things, but I can't lay that at his feet as well. Victor Pearson was a postdoc in my lab years later, always full of enthusiasm but lacking in vision, a failing that he tried to make up for with business acumen. That's probably why everyone hated him, wanting the academic plaudits and the corporate profit at the same time. Don't get me wrong, he's a skilled technical scientist, but even as a dictionary is full of words it still can't write poetry. I'd give Victor a problem to solve and he'd pursue it night and day until it was done. But to ask him to take the next step, the leap of faith to a new discovery of his own and he was lost."

A second dot now joined the first.

Kate shrugged her shoulders. "So what happened? I presume you didn't tell him?"

Tobias grimaced and shook his head. "Of course not! It must be twenty-five years ago by now, Victor had asked for some old papers and I'd absent-mindedly given him the key to the cabinet. When I checked the next morning frantically for the file it had gone, the bastard had stolen it! My notes, computer disks, biotech access cards, all of it. Everything was gone. Victor may not be a genius but he was no fool either, he knew what my notes were and what they represented. I presumed he would go to the police; I spent countless sleepless nights waiting for that knock on the door by the authorities but Victor was too canny for anything as trivial as justice! No, instead he set up a fertility clinic with someone else's money, and 'discovered' the virus just before the scale of the infertility problem became apparent. He patented all of my research to stop anyone else working on it, sold his treatment to the world and they proclaimed him the saviour of the human race for it!"

"At least he developed a treatment," replied Kate, surprised at herself for defending the man.

"It's easy to reverse engineer something when you already have the user manual and surround yourself with the best people in their field," spat Tobias. "What he did was nothing. Less than nothing."

Kate reached into her jacket pocket and fished out the now creased and dog-eared piece of paper. "Well if it makes you feel better, Victor couldn't work this out. I was told it's the sequence of the gene IES breaks, and whatever's different about it stopped the virus from working."

"Good God girl, do you think you could have printed it out any smaller?" complained Tobias as he squinted through his glasses at Isaac's analysis. "That's very odd. Is this from a tumour?"

"That's what Dr Pearson said."

Tobias made a snorting noise. "Well, I'm glad I taught him something at least. I'm amazed that with this level of mutation anything worked at all. The gene sequence is usually highly conserved; even synonymous mutations can stop it working properly. It's one of the reasons we chose it as a target in the first place. How did this happen?"

"It was a gene therapy treatment," was all Kate could remember.

"Whatever happened here I doubt it was what was intended," said Tobias in a distracted tone as he stared intensely at the paper. "Ah yes, I see it now. It's the duplications. Instead of two mutated copies, you have four copies mutated in different places, but each part contains a separate domain that's intact. It may be that's enough to stop the virus from cutting the gene up but still allowing enough functional protein to be produced."

Kate had no idea what any of that meant, but it sounded hopeful at least. "So it is a cure? We can use this?"

Tobias passed the paper back to her and sighed. "Therein lies the problem. Imagine four bits of string with beads on them in a very specific order, but there's no way of telling from this data which mutation goes with which to make it all work. It would be like doing a jigsaw with no idea what the final picture was or how the pieces you have fit together."

Something triggered in Kate's mind and her heart leapt. "What if I could get the picture?"

"Well, that would certainly help," replied Tobias with a smile, before his expression turned to alarm. "Do you know you have a red laser dot on you?"

Kate looked down and spun around as the dots now converged on her torso, their origin clear as a gruff man flanked by armed guards walked out of the shadows of the arcade.

"Kate Adams!" the man barked as if were an order. "Surrender yourself to our custody or we'll kill you where you stand. You have ten seconds."

For a brief second Kate thought about going for the gun in her jacket before quickly thinking better of it; she'd be dead by the time she'd put her hand in her pocket. Then she thought about jumping over the edge to escape, but the water was freezing and in any case there was nowhere to go. The pier and its tempting views had turned into a blind alley, a trap with no egress apart from through the armed men slowly advancing towards her. "Thank you for your help, Tobias," she said in the few seconds she had left, not daring to turn around to face him in case they opened fire on them both. "Don't worry, I won't tell anyone about your secret, I'll just say I kidnapped you."

"Thank you for the nice chat, and no need for concern," he replied simply, "but you should probably be going now. I think that cake will have to wait for another time."

Kate slowly complied and put her hands in the air as the guards rushed over and pushed her roughly to the floor, knocking the paper from her grasp and bashing her head against the wooden planks of the boardwalk, before pulling her arms behind her back and binding them with metal restraints. As she lay dazed on the ground, she caught sight of Isaac's cure catching the wind, blowing it off the pier and into the frothing salt water below. She thought back to the divers at the power plant as she was dragged to her feet and marched back through the pier with a gun barrel digging into her back. But this time, it was her swimming through the maze of pipes and into the turbine blades. She'd been right about this place when she arrived; it was the end of the line.

Choices

Kate stared dispassionately out of the car window as the countryside gradually gave way to concrete and industry, the restraints that forced her arms behind her back making her neck sore as she strained it to sit up. She was on her way back to London at least, but these were not her familiar and comforting streets that flew past in a blur. Darkness had descended and the snow had begun to fall again, drifting in the wind and turning everything it touched into an encroaching alien landscape. It didn't seem to slow down the car, however, making her secretly hope that they would crash and she could make her escape into the night. It was a hollow fantasy, though; the driver was too highly skilled for such accidents, despite the older man sitting next to him constantly distracting him with triumphant re-enactments, and proclaiming that 'two in one day' was an achievement that his bosses should better appreciate. It was that last comment which made Kate sick with fear and concern, even though she desperately tried to appear outwardly in control of herself and her plight. It could only mean one thing; that they had Andrzej too. Unless, of course, it was a ruse to make her feel hopeless and easier to break. Perhaps she could cling to that hope to give her strength for whatever happened next.

As Kate tried to push the thoughts of interrogation out of her head, the car pulled into a side alley and slowed to a stop, the men surrounding her alighting first and then ordering her out. The man called Joe, who seemed to be in charge, opened her door and pulled her from the vehicle. Kate thought briefly that they intended to shoot her there and then, but that made no sense when they could have done that in the isolation of the countryside, away from any prying eyes. Her deductions were confirmed a few seconds later when a large steel door in the wall opened from the inside. She was then quickly shepherded down a series of rusty metal stairs, the cold air and dampness making them awkward and slippery. This wasn't a police station. Wherever she was they didn't want to advertise the fact that she was there, and that was the most unnerving thing of all.

"Someone here would like to ask you some questions," the man called Joe said, as they reached the bottom of the stairwell and into a small holding area with unpainted brick walls, and doors to rooms without windows. "Do yourself a favour and tell them what they want to know. It'll be a lot less painful," he added with a grin.

The other guards dissolved away to their normal duties until it was just the two of them heading down to the last room on the left. Kate felt her legs nearly give way as Joe's words echoed around her mind, sending her heart and imagination racing to what horrors awaited behind that door. Was it a meat man with a bloody leather apron replete with a hack saw and knives, fresh from the slaughterhouse and wanting something else to carve up? Or maybe a crazed Victor Pearson with a bucket of starving rats hell-bent on revenge no matter what questions she answered? She didn't get to dwell on it for long, at least, as the burly man opened the door, grabbed her by the arm and pushed her through over the threshold.

None of the nasty and gruesome things Kate's terrified brain had conjured up beforehand awaited her on the other side, however. Instead, there was just a metal desk table with a chair either side, one of which was occupied by a beautiful young blonde woman. The woman was wearing a red evening dress with a matching handbag, that looked to Kate like it would cost about a year's wages back at the power plant.

"Hello Kate," the woman said with a smile and upper-class accent, as Kate was thrust down into the chair opposite, her arms still locked behind her back. "I apologise for my slight overdressing. My husband and I were at a charity function when I heard of your plight. My name is Rowena and you are a guest here at the Repro Ministry security facility. I would like to ask you a few questions if I may?"

Kate sat there in dumbfounded silence, looking around the room for the charade to end and the men with instruments and strong fists to storm in, but none appeared. Rowena turned to the security man instead. "Mr Parker, our friend here looks frightfully uncomfortable, can you release her arms please so we can speak like civilised people? The door is locked behind us; she cannot go anywhere."

"I don't think that's a good idea ma'am," was the response.

Rowena's smile faded slightly before she tipped her head to the side slightly in deference. "You are right of course, Mr Parker, security is your expertise after all. I suggest a compromise then; Kate, are you right or left-handed?"

"Right," replied Kate, suddenly dreading her reply, but again no bad came of it. Instead, the security man released her bonds briefly before handcuffing her left wrist to the chair and leaving her right arm free. She stretched it out instinctively, glad to be able to move it again and ease the cramp.

"See, is that not better?" said Rowena as she thanked the man for complying. "I have to say, I have followed your exploits for some time now Kate and I have been very impressed, so I was keen to meet you at last. You managed to single-handedly infiltrate a group that none of our people could get anywhere near and you have allowed us to accelerate our programme by several years. So whether you meant any of it or not, you have our sincere thanks."

Having heard Rowena's name, Kate now recognised her from various gossip columns in the independent papers Brianna often read back at IVFree. She tried to remember what the headlines had said about the woman in front of her but they mostly seemed to be about appearances with people in power or at posh parties, nothing that would give her an edge. Perhaps she should act tough, try to take control of the situation and swing it to her advantage? After all, if Rowena was just a vacant socialite then the woman might feel in over her head when challenged. "I want to see my representation," she demanded. It was the kind of thing characters in the films Michael used to drag her to see used to say, and since she couldn't think of anything else it was as good an opening salvo as anything else she could muster.

"Absolutely," was Rowena's instant reply. "We would not be much of a Government if we did not follow our own rules. And if you were still part of a simple pressure group handing out leaflets, that is exactly what you would be entitled to. However, since you and your friend Andrzej's escapades with our good friend Doctor Pearson you have managed to upgrade yourselves to full-on terrorist status, so the rules have changed somewhat."

Kate felt her heart leap, and then sink down again as she thought of him in a room like this one. "Andrzej is here? What are you doing to him?"

"Yes, he is here," said Rowena in a slightly harsher tone, "and as to what is happening to him? Nothing good I am sure. My husband has many great qualities but, well, patience is not one of them. I am afraid your man is not quite the hero you may think he is. He gave up your location, after all."

"This is pointless," said Joe, who had begun to pace around the room impatiently behind Kate, making her even more nervous. "Give me five minutes alone with her and we'll get your answers. She's just a terrorist, not worth your time ma'am."

"Oh I do not think so, I think she just got her head turned by a charming face and took the wrong path," Rowena replied before turning to her prisoner. "Is that not right Kate? But I am afraid he does not love you, he never did. He was just using you to get to us; typical man trying to control things he does not understand. You do not owe him any loyalty, Kate."

Kate didn't want to believe the woman, she wanted to tell her that Andrzej would only say such things to protect her, but even in her head it rang hollow. How could she possibly defend against it when that seed was already planted in her own mind? She remained silent, confusion and hurt replacing the fear of physical pain, for now at least.

Rowena's smile returned. "From your records it seems you have been a big proponent of the Government until recently Kate, until things changed for you. So we come back to the beginning again. I would like to ask you a few questions if I may, starting with the location of the IVFree base, and what you were doing in Eastbourne? But you must tell me the truth Kate. I cannot help you if you lie to me."

Silence.

Rowena sighed quietly and reached into her handbag, pulling out a portable phone and making a call. "Hi Sweetie!" she said cheerfully to the voice at the other end. "Yes, everything is fine. Oh, you know; girl stuff. Really? That is wonderful darling. Great! I will see you later then." She hung up the phone and replaced it back in her bag. "Someone to see you, Kate."

The next few moments seemed to a take an eternity, Rowena's gaze never leaving Kate who felt compelled to look away, despite her efforts to try and control the situation, a battle she rapidly realised she was losing. The silent war was shattered by a loud knock at the door which Parker opened, pulling in a figure from outside and parading it in front of them. It was Andrzej's height and build, it was wearing Andrzej's clothes but the face was almost unrecognisable, a beaten mush of red and purple swollen features, struggling to stand unaided. Only the eyes betrayed his true identity, and they were full of sorrow.

Rowena ignored his presence, continuing to address Kate as if were just the two of them there. "Where is the IVFree base? What were you doing in Eastbourne? Please, you must tell me."

*

The ringing in Kate's ears was fading now, but the involuntary shaking of her body and the fuzzy darkness around her peripheral vision was only brought into relief by Rowena's fingers frantically clicking in front of her eyes.

"Kate? Ah there you are, I thought we had lost you for a minute there," Rowena said cheerfully, glancing briefly down at the table. "I am glad I wore a red dress now."

Kate followed Rowena's gaze down at the desk which was splattered with blood and tried to recall what had just happened. She remembered the man called Joe reaching for the gun on his belt and raising it to Andrzej's head, Rowena smiling and tipping her head slightly, then a loud noise, a splash of liquid across her face and the taste of tin in her mouth. The dreaded realisation began to creep slowly over her as she turned to see the body slumped in the corner, the hole in what remained of Andrzej's head seeping blood slowly over the floor as his executioner stood over his corpse, smirking.

"Right, where were we?" Rowena said out loud to herself as if nothing had happened. "Ah yes. Where is the IVFree base? What were you doing in Eastbourne?"

Kate, her wide-eyed and terrified body now shaking again, snapped her attention back to the blonde woman, survival more than loyalty, however misguided it may have turned out, now taking control. "I don't know where they are," she said, her voice trembling, "they moved after we went to the clinic in case we got caught. I don't know where they are!"

"You see, not so difficult was it?" replied Rowena gently. "Do not worry, I believe you. You are just confirming what we already know. And why were you in Eastbourne?"

"Victor sent us there," said Kate, the information now pouring out of her regardless if she wanted it to or not. "We were looking for a man called

Tobias. He had information on the IES virus we wanted. He had worked on it in the early days."

If she had picked up on the small lie by omission the blonde girl didn't acknowledge it. "Ah, the old man in the wheelchair? So he was not a random hostage after all." Rowena turned an accusing glare at Andrzej's murderer. "A pity really you did not question him when you had the chance."

"Is he okay?" asked Kate.

Rowena shook her head. "Dead, unfortunately, but not by our hands before you think the worst of us. No, by the time Mr Parker here had sent one of his men to question him, the poor old dear had taken enough Dignity to floor an elephant. You should really work on your conversational skills Kate."

Kate ignored the insult and found herself feeling sorry for the old man. She had been the priest for his final confession, a story he had waited years to tell the right listener in confidence, and now she was about to spill it all to this evil woman whenever she asked.

Rowena, however, didn't seem interested in a history lesson, instead indicating to Parker who stood so menacingly close to Kate that she could feel his breath on the back of her neck. "You are doing so well, Kate. Do not worry, not long to go now. I have just one more question. You started on this path because you wanted to know about your sister, and I think you just got in with the wrong crowd. Things got out of hand and you got swept along. I understand. Not your fault at all."

Kate found herself nodding in agreement despite herself. Perhaps this woman was right. Perhaps she was just an innocent victim of someone else's crusade, caught up in a maelstrom of false hope and a feeling of wanting to belong.

"But things happened and you found something out. Some information. What happened to your sister? What happened to the cure, Kate?"

Upon those words, a door suddenly slammed shut in Kate's brain stopping her in her tracks, quickly followed by a voice screaming from inside her not to tell this woman the truth. But she had to say something, to give an answer Rowena might believe and not have her killed there and then. Luckily, an interpretation both Victor and Tobias had supplied gave her an option. "She had cancer, a tumour in her ovaries," she replied slowly in case she tripped over her own words, before gaining in confidence as the lie took a life of its own. "I don't know where she went to get it diagnosed but knowing my sister it was one of those off-the-grid places. Emily was so desperate to have children and she knew it would make her ineligible for the Lottery or treatment if anyone found out."

"I am sorry about that," said Rowena sympathetically. "And thank you for telling me, your friend held on to that one despite what they did to him. Shows where you were in his list of loyalties I am afraid. So, her cancer somehow stopped the virus?"

Kate tried to ignore Rowena's cruel observation but it still hurt nonetheless. "I don't know how it worked. We only had a piece of paper of DNA sequences she'd kept but we didn't know what it meant. Dr Pearson didn't know either. He sent us to Tobias for more information, but I lost it at the pier when I was arrested. It's gone."

Rowena shot another accusing look at the security man. "Is this true?"

Parker shrugged his shoulders like a teenager in a feeble attempt to show indifference. "Possibly, it was crazy out there. She may have dropped something when we apprehended her."

"Well, that is a shame," said Rowena quietly.

Kate found some inner strength, fuelled by the man's dissension. "Andrzej said you don't want a cure."

Rowena looked surprised, repeating Kate's words back edged with disappointment. "Andrzej said. Why would I not want a cure? Why would I not want that for my children?"

"You'd lose control if anyone could reproduce," Kate replied, her voice now more confident. "You wouldn't get to decide."

Rowena laughed harshly. "That sounds a bit paranoid to me, especially with the Lottery system choosing the winners at random. Does it to you Kate? In reflection? Away from that group and its people influencing and distorting your views?"

Maybe it did.

Rowena continued, pressing her advantage. "Did you know that cults depend on peer pressure Kate, on the charisma of their lead, preying on the feelings of wanting to belong in their marks? IVFree draw in impressionable and desperate women to their cause, women like you and I Kate if our circumstances had been different. They change them, alter their thinking, make them conform, make them dissent against the authorities trying to help them. Did they try and change you Kate?"

Kate thought back to her reading habits, the newspaper she had read for years now cast aside in case it offended her new friends. But that had been her choice, she knew what the group represented and she'd skirted around the edge of the abyss without falling in. She'd needed them and they'd needed her, a simple business arrangement. Or at least, that is what she'd thought at the time.

Rowena broke the silence again. "Mister Parker, could you pass me your gun please?" she asked politely, noticing and then flicking off a drying spot of blood at the end of a few strands of hair draped over her shoulder, making a passing comment about split ends as she did so.

The security man looked shocked and confused. "Ma'am?"

"Your gun, Mister Parker. Please do not make me ask again." Rowena said, her tone now tainted with menace. The man did what he was told. "Funny how such a small thing can make such a big mess," Rowena said as she turned the gun over in her hand, her voice returning to giggly playfulness. The innuendo was lost on Kate, however, who turned away to look at the 'mess' her captor was referring to, as Rowena continued to play about with the weapon out of view and Mr. Parker dragged the body to the corner. Part of her still hoped this was a ruse, a clever arrangement of smoke and mirrors designed to get her to talk, and now that she had a secret door would slide back and Andrzej would be standing there, bruised but alive and able to tell her how much he needed her.

"He is not going to get up again I am afraid," said Rowena sympathetically, "but just to let you know that there are no hard feelings, my turn to talk."

And with that, she passed the gun to Kate, who suddenly realised why her right hand had been left free. The girl had been toying with her the whole time, manipulating her and the narrative like a cat taunting a trapped mouse for sport. Rowena picked up on her thoughts and confirmed her suspicions. "You do not strike me, Kate, as someone who enters a situation without knowing how it is going to pan out. Neither do I."

Kate pointed it at her tormentor without a second thought. "Perhaps I should just shoot you, like you did Andrzej."

"I do not think that would be a good idea," Rowena replied calmly. "As you can probably tell I am the only one here stopping Mr. Parker and his friends outside from raping the answers out of you, whether you have any or not. Plus, the good Lord did not bring me this far just to die here I am sure." The blonde girl glanced up at the security man. "In any case, it was not me that killed your friend, he did."

"You gave the order!" Kate snapped back, the weapon giving her courage.

"Did I? All I did was smile."

Kate sat there frozen, confusion making her head spin as the ringing returned to her ears, the weight of the gun making her hand begin to shake. If she wasn't careful she'd pull the trigger by accident anyway.

Rowena hadn't missed a beat, however. "You see, Mister Parker here has a long history of doing things off his own back without asking. For example, not so long ago we asked him to stop a woman about your age escaping from the Highpoint fertility clinic. She was pregnant you see, and no one knew how. This idiot decided to blow her brains out instead."

Kate turned to face the man who looked horrified. "You told me to stop her, so I did!" he pleaded.

Rowena ignored him. "So feel free to pass judgement on him, Kate. Nothing bad will come of it, I promise you."

Kate swung the weapon around, pointing it instead at Parker who had backed away and was now rooted to the spot.

"If it were me, I would want revenge," Rowena said in an encouraging tone, her eyes greedy with anticipation. "Everything that has happened to you, all of it was due to that one incident, I feel. And all because of him."

Maybe Rowena was right. Maybe it was all his fault? Kate felt the anger inside her build and boil, a plugged volcano of buried and repressed emotions ready to explode; her mother for leaving before her time, her father's drunken inability to cope with life, her sister's obsession that got her killed, and finally Andrzej's body on the floor, unable to ever know how she felt about him. She'd pushed it all down for years, and now it wanted out. A lifetime of rage and grief amplified exponentially, and focused to a single point on her finger.

Kate looked the man square in the eyes, and pulled the trigger.

Consequences

Nothing happened.

As the man stood there and let out a sigh of relief, Rowena yelped and clapped her hands together. "I was wondering if you had it in you, Kate, and you did! Now you know it too."

Yes, Kate agreed silently, her body shaking. She now knew she was a murderer. The fact that the man was still alive didn't change that. She had wanted him dead. She had pulled the trigger.

"Still, even the most faithful have their moments of weakness," said Rowena, reaching over and taking the gun from Kate's quivering hands. "I took the clip out when you were not looking. There are some things even I will not trust God with."

Parker, however, looked incensed. "What the fuck are you doing you stupid bitch?" he cried, "I don't give a shit who your husband is, don't you ever pull crap like that again!"

Rowena ignored his raging. "You see Kate, incompetence and failure I can ignore as long as the intention is good, but this man made my husband look foolish in front of his peers and weakened his position. Weakened my position. And that cannot go unanswered," she said, pulling the ammo clip from her bag and sliding it into the grip of the pistol with a satisfying *click* sound. "You can consider this an olive branch Kate, our commitment to making things right."

There was no maniacal laugh as Rowena slid back the top of the barrel to load the chamber, nor any cry of joy as she aimed and fired the weapon. Just the sound of Joe Parker clutching his chest and crumpling to the floor, followed by a nauseating gargling sound as he tried to breathe through the blood in his throat and the hole in his lungs. Kate tried to feel something for him as he lay there dying but couldn't; all she had left for him was hate. She had killed him already and meant it, and if Rowena's gesture had meant to lighten the load from her it had failed. The bullet had just been delayed a while.

"It has been lovely meeting you Kate, but I am afraid my time is up," Rowena said, placing the gun back into her bag and swapping it for a compact mirror, which she quickly used to check her makeup and admire her reflection. "I have something I need to do tomorrow but we will talk again soon, I promise. Someone will be along presently to escort you to your room." She got up and glided elegantly to the door, gently tapping on it and throwing a sympathetic smile to Kate as she left. Rowena was true to her word and four guards entered soon after her departure, two men to take Kate to a small cell with a bed in one corner and a slop bucket in the other, and two more to manhandle the dead bodies onto a trolley. If they were shocked or saddened by the death of Mr. Parker they didn't show it, instead making jokes and predictions about who would get the dead man's job next.

*

Kate sat on the edge of the bed with her chin in her hands, the thin and stained mattress doing little to stop the metal springs from digging into her. She had attempted to keep the trauma of earlier events at bay by concentrating on aligning the pillow with an equidistant gap between the walls at the corner, but it proved to be a minor distraction at best. At least the disorientating spell Rowena had cast on her was fading now, the distance giving her clarity through the fog of confusion and self-doubt. Kate's mother had often lectured Emily and herself about the Devil tempting souls down a dark path with fine promises and exotic gifts, but the description she would always give was wrong. It was not a fire-breathing demon with goat horns and hooved legs, it was a beautiful woman in a red dress and a captivating smile. A fallen angel capable of twisting truth and lies into dark reflections of themselves and imposing its will on those it had favoured. Kate wondered how many others had fallen under Rowena's beguiling charm; she would not underestimate the girl again.

She had tried to sleep, but no matter how she tried to compartmentalise or suppress it, the image of Andrzej lying there dead on the floor kept worming its way back to the fore, whether she had her eyes open or not. Was she destined to suffer the same fate as her father, unable to move on from the horror she had witnessed? Would the pain fade in time or grow and amplify, condemning her to endure a loop of events for the rest of her life in which there was no escape? Presuming, of course, that the rest of her life would be longer than the day or so it took Rowena to get back from whatever she was doing to resume her torment. It had taken only a few minutes and some carefully chosen words to turn Kate into a killer, who knows what horrors the woman had planned for their next encounter?

No, this wouldn't do at all. Kate got up and paced in what small space the cell allowed, pushing out any thoughts of impending judgement and things she couldn't change. No more moping about like a spurned and love-stricken schoolgirl, wishing things were different; he was gone and all the wishing in the world would not bring him back. She knew her own mind about Andrzej, what he meant to her and she to him, and no amount of poison that the blonde woman poured into her subconscious could alter that. Only one thing mattered now; finishing what the two of them had started together around that table in IVFree. She had to be strong, to resist, to seize her moment in a game played by someone else's rules. Water, valves, turbines. Plan, escape, mission.

But that was for tomorrow. Tonight, she would grieve for him. In the dark, where no one could hear, and no one would judge.

***

Victor bounded up the snowy path towards the clinic with the joy of new purpose in his stride, the pure white of the flakes giving everything a soft, cleansing and virgin glow. The ground staff had been tardy this morning but it didn't matter, nor did the stabbing pain in his heavily bandaged hand. The doctors had told him it would hurt for several weeks as they pumped too many antibiotics into his arm, but he didn't mind. It would serve as a constant reminder that it was time for a change, a new beginning. He'd been writing and practising the speech in his head since the previous night and it was perfect; a rapture designed to inspire the staff and a rousing chorus to make them feel motivated again and care about something other than money and perks. Fate had given him a second chance, Susanna's spirit had given him a second chance and he intended to grasp it with both hands.

All of it came crashing down, however, the moment he saw Janet pacing around anxiously outside the main gate. Something was very wrong.

"Your phone wasn't working!" his assistant cried as he approached, brushing off the growing mound of snow from her shoulders that indicated how long she had been waiting there.

Victor apologised; in truth he'd turned off his portable phone and left the landline off the hook all night, not wanting to be disturbed as he worked tirelessly on his proclamation. It seemed that had been a mistake, for he'd never seen her so agitated. "What's the matter?"

"The politician! That slime ball and his wife arrived about an hour ago with a load of armed guards and just waltzed in. They said they were taking over."

Victor slammed through the doors and marched into the main clinic building with his blood boiling, the optimistic mood of earlier long forgotten. He pounded up the stairs, ignoring the throbbing in his head as his heart tried desperately to keep up with the demands placed on it, and crashed through into his office. The politician was sitting at Victor's desk, toying with the boxed shilling by passing it between and around his fingers. He was flanked by two no-name burly Ministry security guards, making Victor wonder briefly what had happened to the one he usually brought with him.

"Hello, Pearson. Something I can help you with?" Caden asked nonchalantly as he picked up the picture of Susanna and leered in appreciation.

"What the hell is going on here?" Victor demanded. "Why are you in my office, and why did Janet say you were taking over?"

Caden paused as if trying to recall the name. "Oh, the dragon with the acid tongue. Yes, she was correct."

"You can't do this! This is my company!" Victor cried, making a move towards Caden before the sight of the guards going for their guns stopped him in his tracks.

"No, it's the shareholder's company," Caden corrected him, "and when the Board of Directors heard what had been going on here, the non-existent security which resulted in your abduction? Well, they were more than grateful for our help."

"I need to speak to them myself."

"That time has passed I'm afraid, but don't worry you'll still be in charge of the science, of course," said Caden in a tone that came across as patronising instead of reassuring. "But the direction and oversight will now fall under my wife's remit and you'll be answerable to her from now on." The politician grinned an insincere smile and gestured to the walls with open arms. "I'm sure she'll even let you keep your little office here."

"Rowena? What the hell does she know about genetics?"

Caden laughed at the Salesman's apparent ignorance. "She's been running her father's business in his name since she was eighteen and I seriously doubt she knows how to strip down an engine. Business is business, after all."

Victor tried for a delaying tactic, something that would hold things up until he could regroup and consolidate his position. "Do you have this in writing? I can't just allow anyone free movement around the clinic based on their word, no matter who you are."

The politician was way ahead of him. "Of course," Caden replied, passing Victor a piece of paper. "I'd expect nothing less from someone wanting to protect their assets. You'll find everything here is signed and correct."

Victor took the document, scanning it carefully for any ambiguity or loopholes he could exploit. There were none, so he tried a different tactic, one that would allow him to exert some control over the situation. "Then at least promote Dr. Chaudhri," he pleaded, "I've been grooming him for a senior role for a while now; no one knows this company and our outposts better than him."

Caden was unmoved by the perfectly reasonable argument, though, dismissing it with a wave of a hand. "Don't worry, Rowena can make the big decisions, to do what's necessary for the good of the company and the country."

The look of badly-disguised guilt on Caden's face as he uttered those last words filled Victor's head with horrifying alarm. "What do you mean? Caden? What has she done?"

Victor looked past the man and out of the window behind him to the exercise fields. Even in this weather, he would expect some of the IES-clear to be jogging or at least playing in the fresh snow, but the area was completely devoid of them. "Where are the donors?"

"As I said, what's necessary."

Victor didn't bother asking any more questions. Instead, he turned and ran.

*

Victor sprinted down the corridors, ignoring the strange looks from the blurred faces that flashed by as they rushed to get out of his way. He made it as far as the entrance to the male donor wards where a red-headed nurse blocked his path, her face a picture of confusion and panic.

"Doctor Pearson! Chrissy Douglas, senior nurse. What's happening? Has the Government taken over? They said you'd been replaced?"

Victor was not surprised at her apparent revelation; nothing travelled faster than the speed of gossip. "Don't worry, it's all a big misunderstanding," he lied as he tried to look past her and into the ward areas. "Is everything okay? Are the donors still here?"

"No!" Chrissy cried. "I was on my way up to try and find out what was going on. It was Rowena Schoier from the Repro Ministry, she turned up and took them all!"

"And you let her?"

"I had no choice!" Chrissy replied getting more agitated by the second. "She had all the correct access codes and proper authorisation forms. She said she was in charge now."

"Over my dead body," said Victor in a voice that failed to convince himself let alone anyone else.

Chrissy instinctively stepped back and allowed him to enter the ward entrance, where a small group of junior nurses was stood around in a state of confusion, nervously chatting to each other in hushed voices. "I tried to warn her about the male donors' unpredictability but she didn't listen," she continued. "I phoned downstairs and the women are all gone too. She said she was taking them to the Cathedral."

*

Puffing heavily now, Victor ignored the cold and the snow as he burst out of the rear doors and headed out towards the small security hut, the perimeter of which was empty of guards and eerily silent. He knew why without even needing to investigate further; the giant extractor fans had been turned off. Once through the unmanned and open security gate, he found the bottom of the stairwell was draped in complete darkness, except for a small yellow emergency light on the far ceiling. The beam slowly rotated, illuminating a solitary female figure dressed in a long white fur coat and matching hat in a soft glow. She stood silent and still at the entrance to the Cathedral, her eyes transfixed through the small window in the door. If the politician's wife noticed Victor's presence she didn't acknowledge it until he was nearly upon her.

"It was just as you said," Rowena remarked, her voice wispy and distant as she continued to stare into the room beyond. "They were all fine one moment, and then they just... stopped."

"What have you done?" asked Victor, his voice shaking, his eyes not wanting to follow her gaze, not wanting to confirm his worst fears.

"Disabled the fans and opened the nitrogen supply pressure valves," she replied simply. "A helpful man showed me how. He is in there too." With that she turned her attention to the access panel next to the door and briefly played with the controls, which rewarded her with a klaxon alarm and loud whirling noise as the fans within the Cathedral started their initiation cycle. A few moments later there was a rush of air as the door unlocked and the emergency light blinked out, replaced by the harsh and regular fluorescent strips signalling a return to normality. Rowena quietly stepped into the opening as Victor followed her, still too dumbfounded and shocked to say anything else. Today was supposed to be the day when everything changed, and now it had.

There were dead bodies everywhere. Some had simply fallen where they stood when the signal to breathe in from brain to lungs was suddenly no longer there. Others had panicked at the sight of their comrades suffocating in an invisible odourless gas and ran while they still could, creating an ever-increasing pile of corpses up towards the ceiling in a desperate attempt to get to fresh air. The stampede had done them no good, though, for all had perished. In one corner, away from the others and slumped against one of the cryogenic tanks, sat two figures in a comforting and final embrace as they waited for their turn to die. Victor recognised them instantly and his heart broke at the sight; Hugo and Ariane, together at last.

Rowena made it to the centre of the room before she seemingly snapped out of her trance and turned to face him. "You have been holding out on us Victor, what really goes on in here. I have seen the files on the donors, the real stock numbers, everything."

Victor tried to comprehend what had happened but it wouldn't go in. He had lived through the Death and seen things that still came to haunt his dreams decades later, but at least they had been done as a result of the disease or fight for survival. This was on a different level of horror. "What have you done? You've killed the future!"

"No, I have unchained it," retorted Rowena in a voice so self-assured it was frightening. "In a few generations, most of the population of the country will have been related to these people. And who are they? Just random subjects with no special talents who were just lucky enough not to get a disease, that is all. Inferior stock to be sure."

Victor started to back away. "They were human beings!"

"Come now Victor, you do not strike me as the sentimental type," replied Rowena as she tip-toed her way through the bodies towards one of the storage tanks and checked the display on the side. "They were a means to an end, and nothing more. You said yourself their presence was mainly an economic issue. We do not need these people."

"But the costs without the donors? We simply don't have the resources to offer a full zygote treatment for everyone!" he pleaded. "It'll bankrupt the company, there'll be riots in the streets when people can't get treatments, just like in France. And they'll blame me for it!"

Satisfied that the display on the tank was appropriate Rowena turned to Victor and lightly pressed her finger to her lips. "Do you know your biggest failing Victor?" she asked, pausing as if to choose her words carefully. "It is that you realised your ambitions and then you stopped, just like most men. You went halfway up a mountain and were satisfied with that because no one else had made it that far. Caden was the same until I showed him the true path and unlocked his potential. But to answer your question, we will recall the majority of our staff from abroad and triple the costs to the outreach stations. That should minimise the impact on our own country, the one that matters."

Victor was appalled. How could she even imagine such a thing? "But we have contracts! Treaties with the foreign Governments!"

Rowena looked unconcerned, brushing some hair behind her ear with her hand. "Ink and handshakes. They have suckled from our breast long enough I feel; time for them to be weaned and stand on their own. But you are correct, we will still need donors for the Lottery. Our constituents like what they are used to, after all, and it will help avoid difficult questions."

Victor tried a different tack, to try and get her to listen to reason, as if that would make any difference after the fact. "Where are you going to get that much material from? Volunteers won't be enough."

Rowena had an answer for that too. "We have thousands of people queuing at our borders every day wanting to come in. We will pick only the very best, of course. They want to contribute to our society? Then let this be how."

"People will notice. They'll start asking questions."

"We will bus them into the facility at night. Do not worry, there will be no need for your staff to get their hands dirty. My teams will see to the initial collection."

Victor didn't need to ask what would happen to the 'donors' after their seeds had been harvested. "That's inhuman!"

"You murder unborn children, Victor, I hardly think you are in a position to take the moral high ground. Oh, do not get me wrong, I fully support your methods, just as you will support mine."

"When the public finds out about this, they'll-"

"Do nothing," Rowena interrupted. "The general populous care only about their own. You could burn the bodies of outsiders in the next street and the inhabitants would only complain about the smell. You survived the plague Victor, I am sure you know the truth of that more than I."

"And what happens in thirty years' time when there are no more donors at the doors to pick from?" asked Victor, desperate now for any glimmer of hope that the path she had set them on could be changed.

"We know a cure is possible now. I have full confidence in your team's ability to discover and recapitulate it by then. But just in case, we can start a new donor colony with the very best of what we find and just fix the gene each generation and treatment as we go. We can worry about the money later."

"The other countries and city states won't stand for this, you know that."

Rowena was unfazed and started to pace softly around Victor in a large circle. "Do you know what happened to Moses and his followers after the Exodus?"

"Yes. God punished them for their lack of faith and made them wander the desert for forty years."

"No Victor, Moses and the Israelites did not wait in the wilderness for a generation without an aim. They were breeding an army, the best God could provide. An army full of hard working, strong and loyal troops capable of crushing their enemies and cities on the path to the Promised Land. War is inevitable; the longer they wait the stronger we become and the weaker they will be. But today, tomorrow, twenty years from now it makes no difference to our plan. To His plan."

"Which is?"

Rowena stopped her pacing and stepped towards Victor until her face was inches from his, her fragrance as intoxicating as ever despite the death around her. He thought for a moment she was going to kiss him but at the last second, she leaned over and instead whispered, "Empire."

Non-random

Victor stumbled out into the daylight, his head spinning as the reality of events finally caught up with him. Everything he had worked for, strived for, sacrificed his soul for, had been ripped from him and torn asunder in a matter of minutes. He traipsed around behind the small building away from any watching eyes and leant back against the wall, resting his head against the cold bricks. He sniffed as the tears came and looked to the sky for salvation but none was forthcoming. He had been forsaken and no amount of overdue prayer would change that. The donors had been under his care, they needed his protection and he'd failed them on the eve of their renaissance. Wiping his eyes on the back of his sleeve, he took a series of long deep breaths as he struggled to regain his composure. No one could see him like this, he had to remain strong for his staff if nothing else. They would be looking to him in these uncertain times for guidance and support and he had to be there for them. The new regime certainly wouldn't.

Victor stood tall and strode out from behind the building, which was when he caught a view of Caden in the near distance heading his way, the Repro security guards a short distance behind him. The sight of the politician made something inside of him snap and seizing his chance, he marched at speed towards his quarry, punching the man hard in the face and knocking him to the ground before the guards had time to react. He silently thanked his previous interrogators for leaving his right hand unmolested as the security men grabbed him and struck him in the stomach, forcing his arms behind his back and manhandling him to his knees on the frozen path. Caden picked himself up and dusted down his suit, spitting a mouthful of blood onto the snow and splattering it with crimson. He looked down at Victor as one of the guards took out his gun and pointed at the Salesman's head.

"I can see you're upset, so I'll let that one pass," he said, rubbing his swelling cheek with his hand as a red mark appeared. "but try anything like that again and they'll pull the trigger, 'saviour of humanity' or no."

Victor felt the wetness of the snow soak into the knees of his trousers as he was pushed harder into the ground. "Your wife's a fucking psychopath, did you know?"

"No need to be rude," Caden replied, the rest of his face turning a similar shade to his developing bruise. "And don't confuse pragmatism for a lack of planning or recklessness, it gives her a clarity of thought so often missing in politics. Rowena is completely devoted to me, this country and to the future."

Well, two out of the three I'm sure thought Victor.

Caden, however, wasn't finished. "So are you going to be a good little man and play nice or do we need to be looking for a replacement, perhaps that Dr Chaudhri that you mentioned earlier? Your choice, you're not important enough now that I care either way."

It wasn't a decision Victor needed to dwell on, especially with a gun pointed at his head. He doubted the alternative would result in a long quiet retirement somewhere after what he'd seen. "I'll play nice, Mr. Schoier. My staff will need some sense of continuity and reassurance."

"See, that wasn't so hard was it? We all do what we must, to get what we want in life," said Caden as he turned to leave, before suddenly stopping and clicking his fingers together, as if to recall a memory. "Oh, by the way, we caught the couple who abducted you. The woman is still alive but the man died during interrogation. He tried to escape."

Victor gave a mock display of concern then satisfaction, but in truth he didn't really care how Andrzej had died nor the politician's crude attempt to cover his own back; he had much bigger concerns. "And?"

"What would you have me do with her? Rowena seems to have taken quite a shine to the woman, but I'll leave the final decision to you."

Victor was unimpressed at the feeble attempt at appeasement; was it supposed to make up for what they'd done? But however much he wanted to throw the offer back in the politician's face out of spite, he needed something else even more. He needed redemption. He needed someone out of the political and clinical system that he could rely on to follow their own path, and do whatever it took no matter what the consequences. He needed an ally, or least a co-conspirator, but that would be of no use if she was swinging from a rope or worse, so he took a gamble. "Aren't you supposed to be the Government of second chances?"

A smile slithered over Caden's face. "You see! You and my wife have more in common than you think."

***

It was five days before they came for her. Kate had spent the time in her cell staring at the wall, working on her story and trying to sleep away the monotony as much as possible. At least she was happy in her own company she mused; Emily would have gone stir crazy in a matter of hours without someone to talk to. The only human contact Kate had was the shifty-looking guard with a goatee beard who came in briefly twice a day to give her meals, change her toilet and leer threateningly at her, while she curled up in a ball on the bed and pretended to look terrified. On the last visit, however, he seemed to lose interest and glancing down at herself Kate couldn't really blame him. Her clothes had begun to reek of sweat and grime, her hair was greasy and matted, and the lack of any toilet paper had meant the area of her that the guard may have been keen on was apparently not so appealing any more.

Kate had been asleep this time when the door opened and jerked her awake. There was no clock on the wall, therefore the only way to determine the passage of time was the meal deliveries and her own circadian rhythm, so either one of them was out of kilter or this was something different. She wasn't wrong; three men entered this time and grabbed her before she had a chance to react, pulling her out of the cell and marching her, in silence, down a long dark corridor. She ended up in a small, cold and damp room which was empty apart from a shower head poking out of the ceiling, and a small drainage hole below. There was no curtain or screen to hide behind, so she undressed in front of them and stepped into the tepid water as the youngest of the three guards, a male barely out of his teens, tossed a bar of soap, a bottle of shampoo and a flannel in her direction.

The water felt good despite the temperature, a cleansing stream washing away the trauma and lingering dirt as the men looked on. Kate faced the wall and tried not to look down or display any reaction to the guards as the congealed clumps of Andrzej's blood in her hair ran down her body, twisting around the floor on its way down the drain. Everything now depended on her ability to suppress her reactions and hide her true intentions, and there was no time like the present to start.

A few minutes later and shivering in a towel, Kate was taken back to her cell which had been cleaned in her absence if the strong smell of disinfectant was anything to go by. She looked at the bed where some clean underwear, a pair of high-heeled shoes and a pretty-looking dress with a flowery pattern had been placed, alongside a very expensive looking handbag. It was not her style, but she was grateful at this point for anything that wasn't a soiled stolen nurse's uniform, and if Rowena wanted to make a pet of her then a pet she must be.

"You have five minutes," her normal guard said as he closed and locked the door behind him.

Kate had barely finished getting changed when the cell opened again and a man in an immaculate blue suit strolled in and looked up and down her with a nod of approval. "My word, don't you look a picture," he said. "My name is Caden Schoier."

"I know who you are," Kate replied flatly.

"Well, that makes things easier. Rowena apologises she can't be here in person but her new role is taking much of her time. She's the new CEO of InVitroSolutions," he said proudly.

Kate laughed inside. The new Deputy Minister, one of the most powerful men in the country being reduced to an errand boy by his domineering wife. It did raise one question, however. "What happened to Victor Pearson?" she asked.

"Oh don't worry, you didn't kill him, not physically anyway. He will be concentrating on the science side of the business from now on. You have my thanks for that, it would have taken us years to wrestle the company away from him without your intervention."

"And of course, being a democracy you can't just take over what you want when you want," said Kate, slightly more sarcastically than she meant and instantly regretting it. She was treading a fine line here and it depended on getting people like him on side.

"Quite," replied the politician humourlessly. "We have a surprise for you, Miss Adams, if you'd like to follow me."

Kate had no idea where the elevator was headed, but up seemed like a good direction and the fresher air wafting in from above was a welcome relief after the squalid conditions she'd endured the past few days. She wasn't sure what she expected as the door slid open, but it wasn't a large opulently decorated room with wooden cladding on the walls and a gold leaf flecked coffered ceiling.

"Welcome to the Ministry of Reproduction," Caden said. "Or at least, the public face of it," he added. "I prefer my team to work behind the scenes, away from prying eyes."

As they wandered the halls of power with the guards keeping a respectful distance, Kate now understood her attire; she looked for all intents and purposes like just another visitor or VIP having a tour of the Ministry or on her way to a meeting. Presumably, dragging someone in chains in the open to wherever she was ultimately headed would raise some eyebrows, or at the very least unwelcome questions, so she played along. It wasn't as if she could run away anyway, even if there was anywhere to run to, she would turn her ankles over in seconds wearing the shoes Rowena had picked for her. Caden kept up the charade by pointing out various aspects of the department and giving a brief history of its inception, until they stopped at a large oak door with intricately painted panelling.

"So here we are Miss Adams, the office of the Minister for Reproduction," he said too loudly, knocking on the door as a small group of people came towards them. Checking the coast was clear once they had passed by he leant over and spoke softly into her ear. "My wife is lonely I think, despite the sycophants that fawn around her, so I've put myself out on a limb for this. But if you make me look foolish or weak for that, then your last few days with us will soon feel like a memory of heaven. Do you understand?"

"Yes," replied Kate, feeling her pulse quicken and blood begin to drain from her face, as the game she'd been playing in her head suddenly felt very real.

"Good," said Caden, as he withdrew from her personal space. "Oh, I have a message from Dr Pearson for you. What was it now? Ah yes, I remember: 'I meant what I said at the end'. What was he referring to?"

"He said he'd come after me," Kate lied. If she couldn't even manage a simple casual deception, then she might as well head back to her cell now.

In truth, she wasn't sure exactly what Victor was trying to do or tell her, but that was a problem for another time.

Caden made a small snort of derision. "Figures," he said, walking away as the oak door swung open and a tall elegant woman emerged, gesturing Kate inside.

Kate heard the door click quietly behind her as the woman left her standing alone on the threshold of a spacious office, the decor matching that of outside, with the addition of dozens of old oil portraits adorning the walls. At the far end, was sat a large old man in a black pin-striped suit with the gold chain of a pocket watch hanging from the breast pocket, his bushy moustache and eyebrows barely compensating for the thin comb-over of hair on his head. He was deep in thought, pouring over the contents of the letter on his desk through a pair of fine-rimmed glasses, adding his own notes in the margins with a black fountain pen. Kate was unsure he had even heard her enter, for he failed to acknowledge her presence.

"There are no guards in here," she said out loud by accident, the days of solitary confinement catching her out.

"Do I need any?" the man asked, continuing to not look up from his work.

Kate shook her head. "No."

"Good. Then come and take a seat, I'd offer you some tea but I only have one cup."

Kate did as she was asked, hanging her bag on the back of the finely carved antique chair as the Minister poured out some black tea into a small china cup, the steam swirling out and mixing with the fine dust in the air. "Caden says that you show great promise," the Minister said, taking a sip of tea. "Or at least, his wife does, which means he does too."

Kate reminded herself about keeping eye contact, lest he mistakenly took it as a sign of deception. "Is this why I'm here?"

"No, you're here because Caden Schoier is a coward, unable to make a decision unless he has someone else to hang out to dry if things don't go his way," the Minister replied curtly as he patted the arms of his leather chair. "But if he wants to sit here one day he'll have to stick his neck out eventually, rather than skulking about and scheming in the basement."

Kate was about to agree and insult the Minister's junior but thought better of it. Alternatively, trying to speak out in Schoier's favour would just come across as insincere at best, and anger the man in front of her at worst. She needed him on side, and silence seemed the best option.

"You see, Miss Adams," the Minister continued, "given the choice between freedom and execution for terrorism, only a fanatic would choose the latter. You're clearly not one of those, but that doesn't mean that you're worth saving. It might just be easiest to put you back where you just came from and send you to trial and execution as a lesson to the others. Safer for everyone that way."

Kate's heart leapt into her mouth. "So what do you want me to do? How can I prove it to you?"

The Minister contemplated her question for a moment. "I've read some of your group's propaganda, it had some interesting analysis on the Lottery. Can you remember what it was?"

"Yes," said Kate, seizing the opportunity to distance herself from IVFree. "They said it was fixed. I told them it was impossible."

The minister stared at her quizzically for a few moments and then took another sip of his tea. "They were correct, though. The Lottery is rigged."

Kate stared at the table, her mind racing too much now to concentrate on social protocol. The Minister sat the cup down on its saucer, wiping the rim with a handkerchief. "I'll tell you what Miss Adams, why don't you convince me what they believe about your potential. You tell me how we do it and we'll talk further."

Kate closed her eyes and tried to see the processes; the jigsaw edges first, the water flowing from sea to valves to turbines to power. A stream of events in time one after the other. The ticket, the number, the draw, the shuffling, the prizes. But random events could not predict random events, players could not be pre-filtered out based on an unpredictable outcome, the numbers had no tricks. Perhaps the Minister was testing her, to see if she'd fall into line and confirm the impossible.

"The guards will be here any second, Miss Adams."

Her mind was stuck in a loop again; input, process, output, input, process, output. She tried to relax, the valves shut and her mind blanked briefly, and for a brief second a memory of Michael and an argument about him doing the jigsaw middle first came to the fore.

Then suddenly she understood; the valves opened and the water flowed again but this time in the opposite direction.

Output, process, input.

Turbines, valves, sea.

Prizes, draw, tickets.

"You don't fix the draw; you fix the allocation. The draw isn't live."

The minister sat forward in his chair, the expression on his face unreadable, except for a slight raising of his bushy eyebrows. He leant back again and smiled. "Very good."

Now it was Kate's turn to ask the questions. "But how do you choose who wins?"

"Hard working and moral parents have hard working and moral children. Filth breeds filth. Those worker assessment forms and appraisals you endure each month? They're not just a pointless exercise in bureaucracy, they're a census of who's most deserving. You won the top prize Miss Adams I'm told, so I'd imagine that your scores were very good. It's one of the reasons you're sitting here and not being executed right now."

Kate thought back to Patrick's scatter graphs, his missing variable laid bare at last. "So what happens now?"

"That depends," the Minister said. "What do you want, Miss Adams?"

It was the chance Kate had been waiting for, to grow her lie within a stack of truths. "I want IVFree to pay," she replied instantly, as she stood up and leant over the table towards the figure in front of her. "They filled my sister's head with dreams and promises, made her ignore the cancer growing inside her, made her run when she should have stopped and asked for help. They didn't bless her with a future, they signed her death warrant and then they took advantage of me when I went to them for information. My life is ruined because of them, so give me a chance and I'll help you crush them."

"And how would you do that?"

"I told Rowena I didn't know where they were and I was telling the truth. But I know how they operate and what's more, I know how to find them."

The barracks

Victor cursed as the speeding pickup truck hit a pothole concealed under the snow, sending it bouncing up in the air and dangerously close to the ditch. The driver, a surly man in a military uniform of a style Victor didn't recognise, laughed and calmly fed in some opposite lock to put the squirming vehicle back on the straight. One of the tyre chains had broken earlier and his escort had simply ripped off the one from the other side with a cry of "keep on trucking!", and carried on regardless. The Salesman let out a sigh and pretended not to be nervous as he checked that the strip of paper in his coat pocket was still there; his days of first class business travel were over it seemed. Still, at least the large padding on his hand was no longer necessary, and the replacement plasters gave him just enough room to put on a glove. He was glad of the protection; the mitt lessened the sharp stinging pain of the cold that was threatening to re-open the hole in his palm.

Despite Victor's mood and the temperature outside, the destination, wherever it was, was going to be worth the journey. She would be there, and whatever chaos he still needed to patch up back at the clinic after Rowena's spree of genocide, this distraction was a small price to pay. The official story was that the donors had been moved to a secret location due to heightened security concerns, and as the new collection facility was not up and running yet, the clinic would be using the frozen banked samples for a while. It was a pretty good lie considering, and if his staff had any concerns or doubts they kept it to themselves. If that silence would hold when the new tissue samples started arriving, though, was another question entirely. The lab staff were not stupid; they could tell the difference between embryonic and adult ovarian tissue as clear as night from day.

"Home sweet mother of home!" the driver suddenly declared as they drove past a village speed limit sign that someone had recently crashed into, judging by the angle it was at, before swinging the vehicle left through a bricked gateway and pulling up by a security barrier.

Looking beyond the gate to the hive of activity beyond, Victor couldn't decide whether he was intrigued or alarmed. There were dozens of people in uniforms like his driver's, differentiated only by the words in large yellow letters sewn onto the back of their dark jackets. Some were unloading supplies from large military trucks, others were running in formation or gathered in small groups, listening intently while their superiors barked information at them. There didn't seem to be a rail track or station anywhere nearby, Victor noticed; whoever these people were they didn't want anyone else to see what they were doing. "Where are we?"

"ReproSec training facility sir," the man replied as he handed his identification card to the man at the gate. "It was an army barracks before the Death, but we moved in a few weeks ago. There's not many of us yet, but we're growing in numbers every day." Once through the security detail, the driver pulled the truck up outside a T-shaped concrete and brick building overlooking a small parade square, and announced that they'd arrived. "Follow me please sir, I believe the others are already there."

The meeting room had changed little from its military origins, the plain concrete walls and exposed wooden floorboards complementing the modest decorations, and thin windows that did nothing to stop the cold and damp seeping through. In the centre of the room, gathered around a large table covered in paper notes, stood four figures deep in conversation. The politician and his wife were easy to spot, despite the long coats and hats disguising their features, but he didn't recognise the large and muscled military-looking man with black tattoos creeping up his exposed neck. Standing at the far end, however, was the reason for Victor's presence here; Kate Adams, adorned in black and white combat trousers and a black jacket with 'intel' written on the front, pointing out some locations on a map to the tattooed man.

He had one chance and the longer he waited, the more contrived it would look, so before anyone could stop him Victor marched over and launched himself at Kate, grabbing her by the throat and wrestling her down to the floor as he shouted obscenities at her. The army goon was on him in seconds, dragging him away as he cried out and flailed his arms around, but Victor had already done what he needed to. As Kate got to her feet her shocked gaze met his stare and he glanced down to the pocket in her jacket, compelling her to instinctively move her hand there and feel the note he had just planted. It was a huge risk; if he was wrong she would betray him instantly and that would be the end of that, but since he had nothing much more to lose it was a chance worth taking. Luckily his instincts landed on firm ground, and Kate just continued with her shocked persona act.

Caden, however, just looked disgusted at the whole incident. "Right, have you got that out of your system now Pearson or do I need to have the guards restrain you for the rest of the meeting?"

"Indeed," agreed Rowena softly, her little trophy wife act back in full effect. "Please calm yourself, Victor. What is past is past. We all want the same thing here."

Victor tipped his head in deference and sat back down, smiling inside; he was pretty sure they didn't. He had seen the fire and passion in the IVFree woman's eyes close up back in that dark basement, and how far she was prepared to go to get what she wanted. That wasn't something one simply gave up when a better offer came along. If he knew what it was she was up to then perhaps he could help.

"Why is he here?" Kate asked, dusting off some floor dirt from her jacket.

"You've given us a starting point Kate," Caden explained. "Victor is here to narrow that search down. Don't worry, we can trust him to keep a secret."

They thought they owned him, and on that, they were gravely mistaken. Still, Victor surmised, it would make his role in this easier. "And what search is that?"

"Kate here is going to hand IVFree to us," said Rowena, beaming like a proud parent.

Victor looked confused. "I thought you killed their leader? That high-standing pillar of society who stuck needles in my fingers."

"If only it were that simple," replied Caden. "IVFree is an idea, a way of thinking and we gave it a martyr to hang on its banners and herald in its songs." He reached over to take Rowena's hand tenderly, as if to absolve her of any blame. "A necessary measure to be sure, but they'll have a new leader now, and we have to crush them completely before this cancer spreads again. They keep moving bases to evade us, but Kate has given us a potential anchor point."

"Which is?"

"Liquid nitrogen," replied Kate, as if it were the most obvious thing in the world. "They need to keep replacing it every couple of weeks or so, according to what I saw there and the research I've done since. I know they are getting it smuggled to them by someone in Cambridge, but I don't know who."

"That's where you come in, Pearson," added Caden unnecessarily.

"They're harbouring the head of their illegal IVF clinic branch in their base," explained Kate, pre-empting Victor's question about why a pressure group needed such a thing. "His name is Isaac Arrington and apparently he used to work for IVS. He has a vat of material, which I guess he's collected from various volunteers and IVFree's been using it to fund their activities."

Now it was Rowena's turn to look confused. "Sorry to interrupt Kate, but seeing you Victor just reminded me of something. Victor, I thought you said it was not possible to store infected eggs and sperm? You said that the virus kills the cells if you do that?"

Victor glanced over to Kate, who looked like a startled rabbit caught in the headlights. The lies she was telling for whatever her game plan needed was rapidly unravelling in front of her, and he didn't fancy her chances with any further pointed cross-examination from Mrs Schoier. He needed to take control of the situation before Kate dug herself into a hole she couldn't get out of, and it did at least give him an opportunity to show his intentions with some half-truths of his own. "That's true," he said as casually as he could, putting his arms back over his head to hide his now-sweating palms, and drawing the attention of the others away from Kate's growing distress. "But I can guess what's really in that dewar. I fired Isaac because we found he'd been stealing straws of donor sperm and selling them on the black market, thinking we wouldn't notice. The backstreet clinics then had to only fix the broken egg rather than both copies of the gene in the zygote, which is easier and cheaper. It seems that theft went much deeper than we realised."

Caden sneered. "I did wonder where they got their money from for all those leaflets," he said, glancing at his wife who appeared satisfied with the explanation, before he turned his attention back to Victor. "So, as we were saying Pearson, this is where you come in. We need names of possible contacts that this Isaac is dealing with."

Victor tried to dredge his memory for likely candidates, but most of his conversations with the man that weren't directly about the day-to-day work seem to revolve around whichever pretty girl Isaac was infatuated with at the time. Perhaps that was it? He swiped through stills of past encounters in his mind's eye, replaying memories as if they were reels on a film projector, but nothing leapt out at him.

Caden, however, was running out of patience, drumming his fingers heavily on the table. "Anything at all Pearson? Any clue we might use to take down these animals?"

That last word shot a bolt of electricity through Victor's brain, striking some rarely trodden synapses and bringing a past discussion from years ago to the fore. "Actually, I do have a thought," he said at last. "Tricia Wallace."

Caden stopped drumming. "Who's that?"

Victor sat up in his chair, glad to have an attentive audience again. "She's a veterinary researcher based in Cambridge, that Isaac met at a conference a few years back and kept in touch with. They co-authored a couple of papers together if I remember. She was studying increasing genetic diversity in various farm breeds by using gene editing in embryos. It would certainly mean that she has ready access to liquid nitrogen, plus the other reagents Isaac would need to run his clinic."

His skills as an orator hadn't diminished at least, he was pleased to note as Rowena, tempted by the hook in front of her, began to hang attentively on his words, especially when it involved something close to her heart. "Genetic diversity?"

"Yes, the problem is that most of the animals were eaten during the plague, and consequently there is a very limited gene pool to keep stocks breeding healthily. Tricia was mutating the major histocompatibility complex as well as some other immune response genes, to help future generations to fight infection and- "

"Yes yes I don't really care about that," said Caden, cutting Victor off in mid flow. "Why is it that scientists can't discuss anything without going off on some tangent? Anything else you know about this woman?"

"Sorry no," replied Victor feeling slightly deflated, "apart from she has really nice hair apparently, if that helps." He smiled ruefully; if Isaac had spent as much effort on his work than he did chasing women, he'd probably would have been running Highpoint by now.

"Should I bring this woman in for questioning Sir?" asked the military man, in a voice that filled Victor with trepidation. "We'll extract the location from her no problem."

"No!" cried Kate a little too quickly, "I mean, they may be expecting her any day now. If she's a no-show then they might panic and make a move before we're ready."

Rowena signalled her approval as she curled a lock of golden hair around her finger. "Kate makes a good point gentlemen. Surely a more subtle approach is required here? We can observe this Tricia from a safe distance and follow her until she makes contact with the terrorists. Then, once we have their location, Mister Harris, you and your men can go in and do what you do best."

Victor was still trying to nail down why Kate had bothered to lie about something as odd as the contents of a liquid nitrogen tank, when her next statement made it as clear as day.

"I should be there in person, to help guide the attack."

There was something in that dewar she needed and didn't want any of the others to know about, and based on their previous encounter Victor had a pretty good idea what it was. He stayed silent, wondering how Kate had explained away her sister's pregnancy without arousing any suspicions. The last thing he wanted to do was ask a stupid or naive question and blow the whole thing wide open.

Harris made a face that showed just what he thought of Kate's idea. "Do you have any experience in combat ma'am? If they're armed as you say, when it hits the fan out there you could get hurt or worse become a liability to my men."

"Yes Kate, Mister Harris is correct," said Rowena. "I think it is safer if you stay here."

Kate looked frustrated for a brief moment, before quickly composing herself to counter the military man's argument. "None of your men know who you're dealing with. You won't be able to tell the lieutenants and foot soldiers from the vulnerable women who are probably now just stuck there and scared for their lives. You don't want another bloodbath like the last time you went after them." She turned to address Caden directly. "Think of the PR victory you'd score by rescuing them and bringing the hard-core followers to justice! I can point out to Harris' team who to focus on, and who's no threat to them. But only if I'm there."

She can think on her feet, at least Victor thought, impressed by the performance. If she was lucky it might not get her killed in the coming days.

As Harris and Kate started a heated discussion on who was right and who was wrong, Rowena gazed into her husband's eyes with a look and a smile that no man on Earth would have said no to, and the decision was made.

*

Kate made it back to her quarters before letting out a large sigh and splashing some fresh water onto her face. It was a small and functional room but she had her own washing facilities, a luxury in the functional surroundings of the barracks fitting of her new position. Rowena and Caden had made her a consultant for the newly formed intelligence wing of the Repro security force, to provide information on her former comrades that would lead to their capture. This room and a few other perks were her reward; thirty pieces of silver paid in advance to show good faith in her hasty promises. She was on probation though it seemed, still not officially part of the chain of command with no real power in decision making and, therefore, leaving no hole to fill if she were to fail.

She'd adorned the room with various familiar items to try and give some sense of comfort and safety, a difficult task to achieve when every distrustful face she saw was a potential spy attempting to uncover any hint of treachery on her part. Her superiors had allowed her to briefly go home to pick up some things so she'd grabbed some books, poured her jigsaw back into its box and rescued her vacuum flask from a sink full of unwashed plates. The cat was nowhere to be seen she noticed, and judging by the mouse droppings on the sill of the half-open window it had been absent for some time. Like her, it had moved on from this place to a new home with new people to purr at and manipulate for food and attention.

She felt into her jacket pocket and pulled out the paper that Victor had planted there earlier. She'd hoped originally to appeal to his sense of avarice, but his recent message from Caden and the performance just then suggested that something had changed. As she read the note it was clear what that was.

"...The donors are dead. She killed them all. I need your help..."

And underneath was a single instruction: "write in the amino acid code."

Kate tore the paper to tiny shreds and smiled as she flushed them down the toilet. It wasn't just her fight any more.

Assault

"Three-hundred yards to target sir," the corporal said as he squinted up at the creased map in the faint pre-dawn light. "The hospital should be off on the right at the next junction."

Harris thanked the man for the report, making Kate wonder if either of them had noticed the rusty road sign above them offering the same information. She kept quiet, however; the others had made it quite clear at the beginning of this operation that she was only there at their sufferance, and smart-arsed observations were unlikely to ingratiate her to them any further. The last thing she wanted was to be left behind for getting in the way.

Harris took off his helmet and rubbed his hands over his shaven head, before pointing at a long-abandoned coffee shop with no front window. "We'll wait there to regroup until the others are in position. Phillips, go tell the others. Quietly."

The man with the map slunk off to the rest of the team who were hanging back in the side street. Harris had apparently picked his twelve best for the frontal assault on the assumption that resistance would be light and disorganised at best. It didn't matter if the enemy had guns, he had told Kate arrogantly a few days previously, if they didn't know how to use them effectively or work in a team. As the others joined them and Harris went through the plan one more time, Kate took off her backpack and stayed away in the corner. Slurping some tea from her flask, she pretended to not be interested as she listened intently to their updates and conversations. She was glad of the drink, feeling the heat of the liquid spread out from her core, bringing life back into the extremities that her gloves and boots had failed to protect from the biting cold.

"So, thanks to Miss Consultant here," said Harris, shooting a look of disdain at Kate, "the rules of engagement have been set out explicitly by Mr Schoier. Anyone unarmed with their hands raised gets shown the exit for the support teams to process. Those with guns get one chance to lay them down and surrender, but any asshole opens fire on us then we take them down hard. Lethal force unless Adams says they're important enough not to kill."

The others all turned to stare at her, making Kate suddenly feel very self-conscious. It wasn't the fact that she was responsible for curtailing their fun, however, that filled their eyes with disgust as their gazes lingered longer than necessary. To them she was a traitor, the lowest of the low, selling out her friends to save her own skin or advance her own standing with their superiors. Part of her agreed with them; perhaps she should have gone out in a blaze of glory back at the pier, or attacked and killed the Minister while chanting the IVFree mantra before the guards could stop her? But basking in guilt and self-loathing was a luxury she couldn't afford at present and would have to wait until this was all over, one way or the other.

As Harris finished his summarising, the other squad members, dressed in the dark colours of ReproSec with armour and guns to match, dissolved away from the group. Kate tried her best to look busy as they stopped to check their equipment, or disappeared further into the building looking for a place to relieve themselves. They looked like soldiers and they behaved like Kate imagined soldiers would do, but most of them were not from the military she had learned, and barely seemed more trained than those they were up against. The one the others had nicknamed 'Butch', who Kate had assumed was a man until she heard her speak a few minutes previously, wandered over and offered her a cigarette from a half-empty and creased up packet.

"Smoke?" Butch asked in a surprisingly feminine voice, dismissing Kate's refusal. "Oh don't worry it's fine, ReproSec ain't gonna worry about LifeChoice or any shit like that. We can drink, smoke and screw around as much as we like, don't make no difference to us."

Her candidness made Kate smile at least, and she took the gift in the spirit it was offered. "For later maybe."

"Don't know what their problem is anyway," said Butch, gesturing rudely in the direction of the others. "We get to kill some terrorists thanks to you and that other guy. What's his name again?"

"Victor Pearson," replied Kate. Butch's observation was correct, though, it was Victor's insight that had allowed them to track down the IVFree base so quickly. Finding Tricia Wallace was simple enough, and just a few days after the observation team had set up their efforts had been rewarded. The researcher had loaded up one of the University vans with a liquid nitrogen dewar and some boxes of dry ice one night, and headed off to the outskirts of London. Kate had not been involved herself in case any of the IVFree members were around and tipped the others off, or at least that was the official line. The real reason she guessed was that they still didn't trust her not to run back to her former group the moment their backs were turned.

Butch misread the look of concern on Kate's face for something else. "Don't worry, you stay behind us when the shit starts to fly and we'll look after you."

It was a nice sentiment so Kate decided to play along. "I don't think Harris trusts me," she said, looking away, "I didn't even get a gun."

"Do you know how to use one?"

"No, not really."

"Well then!" Butch laughed, "you're more likely gonna kill yourself by mistake. Saw that a few years ago when I was still in the service, before I got sent down the mines."

Kate was shocked, although not totally surprised, that the Repro Ministry would be recruiting straight from the prisons. "You were down the mines?"

"Yeah, for shooting my asshole of a CO for trying to screw me without asking nice first," Butch replied casually. "Anyway, guns. Some idiot maggot decided to look down the barrel to see if his pistol was jammed and held the gun by the trigger - we were scrubbing the damn wall for days afterwards! Hold on, tell you what," she added, reaching down to her belt and extracting a small handle grip with two metal prongs on the end, "take this. Just stab it into whatever you want to stop moving for a while."

Kate thanked the woman and clipped the weapon to her belt, but the rest of their conversation was curtailed by Harris' radio blurting into life as the other teams reported in and ready. It was time to go.

*

The hospital looked much larger in real life than the drawings and photographs they found during the mission planning had suggested. It was a vast oblong monolith of steel and brick, with two wings separated by a glass-fronted central atrium and concourse. The surrounding buildings kept a respectful distance giving the site an isolated and superior aura, which despite the years of neglect looked surprisingly intact. Thankfully, the overgrown trees and decorative hedges had let loose over the same period, giving the advancing troops some cover as they slowly approached. Kate had learned about the history of their target during their preparation. It was known colloquially as 'The Deathspital', a state of the art medical facility that had never actually cured anyone. It had the unfortunate timing of being built just as the Death had started to bite, and was opened in a hurry to increase capacity as the infected started to overwhelm the other hospitals in the area. No one who had entered had come out again, including the unfortunate medical staff who had also succumbed to the disease they were desperately trying to stop. As the squad moved carefully and deliberately through the deserted street in the soft dawn glow, Kate wondered if the curse would still hold true by the time the sun set again.

"One hundred yards. Keep behind the hedges!" Harris ordered with a whispered shout as one of the squad found himself out in the open and dangerously exposed, before ducking back out of sight cursing under his breath.

Kate found herself running a cold sweat as they inched closer to the building's perimeter, despite the freezing temperature. She thought with all that had happened to her then fear would be a thing of the past, but it seemed it didn't work that way. Harris' plan was to snake around the side of the building to the main entrance, before fanning out his men inside and clearing rooms as they went. The spotters from the other squads, who would remain outside to mop up any attempted escapes, had identified an area near the rear of the hospital where there was apparently power, so a frontal assault and a flanking manoeuvre was considered the best approach. Kate had no idea if it was a good plan or not; if they were spotted before they were in position, then her former group members would have plenty of time to get entrenched and mount a defence.

Butch picked up on her anxiety. "Don't worry lady, I used to know a guy who pissed himself before every fight. Fearless bastard after that! You stay behind me and it'll be okay."

They reached the paved garden area in front of the main entrance without any resistance or confrontations, the squad scattering out behind some trees that shielded them from the expansive glass facade of the atrium. Kate peered out from behind her protector as they crouched down and

Harris scuttled towards the doors. Apart from a reception area and a couple of kiosks, the interior of the concourse was dark and bare, the walls littered with the skeletons of old vending machines long since smashed and emptied of their contents. Two wide and sweeping stairways flowed from either side of the central area up to the top mezzanine level, where a large balcony dominated the area below, but before Kate could see what was up there Harris signalled to the others that all was well and they made their way inside.

The atrium was eerily quiet, which somehow made Kate even more nervous. If they were catching IVFree unawares she would expect to see or hear some activity in the distance. Harris pointed to the large hallway that intersected the rear of the concourse and gestured at Phillips. "Take five men, go left and spread out, the rest with me."

"Yes sir," replied Phillips. "Stevens, White, Ali you're with me. You too, Bu-."

Then the back of his head exploded.

The shot had barely finished ringing out when Butch spun around, grabbing Kate by the shoulders and throwing her like a rag doll behind the safety of the kiosk before diving forwards herself to the bottom of the reception desk.

"Ambush!" cried Harris, as further shots were fired from the balcony and three more of the team crumpled to the floor. The rest of them scattered for what cover they could find, firing blindly at their invisible assailants. The tattooed man swore loudly as he frantically let off a few more quick rounds from his rifle. "Kill them all!"

Butch, however, just had a look of resigned annoyance on her face as the wood from the desk area splintered all around her. Rather than firing back, she reached behind her back and pulled out a grenade. "Pineapple!" she shouted, throwing it with frightening precision hard and high into the depths of the balcony. There was a brief silence and then the mezzanine exploded, sending a shockwave through the room and shattering the glass behind them.

Kate, now curled up in a protective ball with her ears and face covered by her hands and elbows, shook the daze of the concussion from her head and looked around as the gunfire and shouting recommenced from both sides. It was now or never. Spotting a door to her left, she seized her chance and ran for it, hoping to God that it wasn't locked or more people with guns weren't on the other side waiting for her. She was lucky on both counts, crashing through and over the threshold as a bullet ricocheted close behind her. Gasping for breath and massaging some life into a badly bruised wrist, she turned left away from the main corridor, scouting the cubicles as she went, the sounds of war becoming more distant with each step. Isaac had to be here somewhere, and she needed to get to him before the others did.

A glimmer of hope offered itself as she turned a corner and headed deeper into the Accident and Emergency section; a flash of shadow behind a closed office door at the far end. Kate strode towards her target, the thought of the prize overriding her sense of self-preservation and the concern that there was a potential enemy behind every wall. She was running out of time fast, and being over-cautious wasn't going to help if she failed in her mission.

Opening the door as quietly as she could, Kate slipped inside, hoping to catch whoever was skulking behind it unawares. But instead, she found herself staring down the barrel of a gun, the owner of which was the last person on Earth she wanted to meet.

"You traitorous bitch!" cried Patrick, his features twisted with fury. "You sold us out!"

"Yes," replied Kate. "It was necessary to finish what we started."

Patrick waved the gun threateningly at her, his voice incredulous. "It was necessary? Getting us all killed was fucking *necessary*?"

"You gave them all guns, Patrick! What do you think would happen when they used them? You should have just surrendered!"

"Don't you dare turn this on me!" raged Patrick. "You brought the soldiers here, Kate! And where's Andrzej? What happened to him?"

Kate looked away, not wanting to look the man in the eyes and admit the truth. "Dead. They murdered him in front of me."

"And yet here you stand, safe as houses and in a Government uniform. Why shouldn't I just shoot you?"

Kate half-wondered herself why he hadn't done so already, but he was always one to gloat before he acted. She looked around; she needed a distraction fast, but only one thing came to mind. "Your gun. It has the safety on, you know."

Patrick just laughed at her feeble attempt to draw his attention away. "It's a Glock, it doesn't have one. Why are you here Kate? To make sure they kill all the right people? To identify our bodies when you've finished slaughtering us?"

"I'm here for Isaac."

A voice, belonging to a shadowed figure that Kate had not previously noticed in the corner, suddenly spoke up. "Isaac?"

"Don't believe a word she says, Brianna," warned Patrick, turning his head briefly in the woman's direction.

It was all the time Kate needed. Her hand shot towards her belt and grabbed Butch's gift as she lunged at Patrick before he could react, burying the metal prongs deep into his side. There was a loud noise of electrical sparking and a strong smell of ozone as Patrick started convulsing uncontrollably, his fingers locking around the gun and firing a round off into the air. His face contorted in agony and his jaws locked together, preventing him from screaming as he fell to the floor. Kate followed him down, pushing the weapon harder into his flesh as he hit the floor and stopped moving.

"You killed him!" Brianna cried.

"No, he's just unconscious," Kate reassured her as she prised the gun from Patricks hand, noting his chest gently rise and fall. "We need to get him out of sight, and then you need to get out of here."

Brianna, however, didn't move. "Is it true what he said? Did you betray us all?"

Kate paused, choosing her words carefully. "Andrzej died chasing a dream, Brianna. I'm here to complete the work we started. But to do so, I had to give them something. I had to give them IVFree, to sacrifice the present for the hope of a future. I'm sorry, it was the only way."

Tears ran down Brianna's face. "He's really gone?"

Kate nodded sadly. "Yes, and it'll mean nothing if I don't get to Isaac before the soldiers do. Isaac has the key to everything. Where is he, Brianna?"

Brianna wiped her eyes with her sleeve, her voice sombre. "He's in the Pathology section on the other side of the hospital. End of the main corridor and down the stairs."

Right through where the battle was still raging. "Thank you," said Kate, grabbing Patrick's legs and dragging him behind a desk area with some struggle. "Now you need to get out of here before the others catch up; they won't listen to reason now. Go through the ambulance station and head out with your hands up. The other teams will take care of you. Tell them you're scared, tell them you're just a frightened woman who got in over her head."

As Kate turned to leave, Brianna grabbed her arm to stop her. "Wait, not everyone wanted to fight. There are others here we need to get out too."

"Show me."

*

Kate followed Brianna at pace as she ran out of the Emergency department, before screeching to a halt at a crossroads and peering nervously around the corner to the main corridor. It was easy to understand why; the gunfire was getting closer again. Kate could even make out Butch shouting encouragement to her squad mates, and despite her current predicament, she was glad the woman was still alive. The only thing protecting Brianna and her from the violence was a single set of fire doors, which burst open just as they were about to head out, quickly followed by three IVFree members who dived for cover behind some metal wall cabinets as a hail of bullets buried themselves into the wall beside them.

Kate took a deep breath. The longer they waited, the harder it would be to cross undetected. "Ready?" she asked a terrified Brianna, who nodded tentatively. The dim light and smoke from the fighting obscured their presence, at least giving them a chance as they leapt out into the firing line.

They made it halfway across before Brianna screamed as a bullet hit her in the arm, sending her spinning like a top as she hit the floor. Kate rushed over, pulling the woman to her feet by her other arm and stumbling with her to the other side of the hallway and out of danger. "It's not too bad," she said reassuringly, glancing at the wound as Brianna slumped down against the wall, her face wincing with pain and shock. In truth, Kate had no idea, but the fact that the blood was seeping rather than spurting suggested it hadn't hit anything vital.

"My legs feel like jelly," said a very grey-looking Brianna as she struggled to get up, protecting her wound with her free hand. "The others are just up ahead, let's get there before I pass out."

Kate helped Brianna up through the twisting maze of the old Diagnostics Department where the others were hiding. Her original pitch about saving innocent women had simply been leverage on Rowena to let her on the mission, but now that the opportunity had presented itself she could actually deliver on that promise. Perhaps the act would help re-address the balance of what she had done? The rational part of her doubted it, but it was a start at least. There were about twenty of them in all, a few men but mostly women, huddled together behind some lab benches and bits of old equipment no one had bothered to steal over the years of neglect. Some were crying while others were trying to console them and telling them to stay strong, but all of them looked terrified out of their wits, especially when they caught sight of Brianna's injury.

"Kate, is that you?" asked a young blonde woman who Kate remembered as being called Amy.

"Yes. I'm here with Brianna to get you out," confirmed Kate before glancing down at the uniform that the others were staring suspiciously at. "You're going to have to trust me. There should be a way out back through the ambulance station, the troops will arrest and process the women, but you'll be safe. Brianna will tell you what to say."

One of the men who Kate didn't recognise piped up. "What about us?"

"You'll go prison most likely even if you openly condemn IVFree, but you'll be alive."

"You want us to denounce our friends?" the man said angrily. "Screw you!"

"Fine!" snapped Kate, and pointed back towards the hallway. "The soldiers are back that way killing them all. If you want to join them then go ahead, knock yourself out."

The man fell silent.

"That goes for all the rest of you too!" Kate warned, her voice cold and rapidly running out of patience. "You have one chance to get out of here, so take it now before you're trapped for good. I won't be able to protect you if that happens and the soldiers won't care if you're armed or not by now."

Kate hurried back through Diagnostics with the others now in tow and towards the main corridor, where she hoped the fighting had moved on, since reaching the ambulance station meant crossing it again. They'd barely gone twenty yards, however, when a loud explosion up ahead rocked the walls and ceiling around them, causing her charges to dive for what cover they could find as the corridor shook, and lumps of plaster and roof piping descended on them. Harris' team had apparently got frustrated with breaking the IVFree defences on that side of the building and simply thrown all of the grenades they had at them instead. But whatever the cause, their way was blocked.

Kate swore before turning to Brianna. "Is there any other way out?"

"Yes, back the way we came," Brianna replied, "there's a fire exit but I think it's locked up."

It was.

They reached the fire door to find a heavy chain crudely wrapped around the handles and sealed by a padlock. Kate rattled it in the vain hope that rust would have weakened the links but it was to no avail. They couldn't go back the way they'd come and heading off deeper back towards the front atrium would most likely get them killed. A few of the group gasped or whimpered in fear as they realised they were stuck, their frightened faces looking to Kate for salvation, their previous distrust at her uniform forgotten.

An idea then struck her. Taking Patrick's gun out from her belt Kate pointed it at the lock, turning her head away and grimacing as she pulled the trigger too hard. The recoil made her arm jump but it had the desired effect and the padlock shattered as the bullet struck. Amy helped her unwrap the chains and flung the doors open, the morning sunshine flooding in and bathing the hallway in light as the others hurried out into the cold to the shouts and demands of the soldiers outside.

Brianna was the last to leave, having sent the man she was using as a prop out before her, the jacket sleeve on her injured arm now sodden with blood as she struggled to keep standing upright. "Good luck Kate," she said sadly, "I hope it was worth all this."

Kate silently agreed. She hoped it was too.

EP-001

Kate made her way carefully through the rear labyrinth of the hospital, trying to avoid any turning that would lead back to the main corridor and the continued fighting. She was lost in moments, the smoke from battle-born fires obscuring her vision and scouring her lungs. She stifled a cough as she skulked towards what hopefully would be the old Pathology Department, scared of giving herself away to either side in the struggle. At a hallway intersection she came across two bodies riddled with bullet holes, a smeary blood trail originating from around the corner indicating where they had fallen. On closer inspection Kate realised that she had known these men quite well, both happy and gregarious members of the second tier of command, now reduced to lumps of meat and offal. What she didn't notice, however, was the figure emerging from the shadows of a doorway opposite her. It was a girl barely out of her teens, her torn clothes grubby and smeared with blood, her arms struggling to hold up the shotgun she was pointing at Kate.

"Stay away from me!" the girl demanded, her hoarse voice little more than a whisper.

Kate raised her hands by her head. "Don't worry, I'm not going to hurt you. Why didn't you hide with the others?"

"I wanted to help. Patrick said you'd kill us all anyway."

Kate was shocked at the girl's appearance, but the blood didn't seem to be hers. "What happened to you?"

"I was on my way up the back stairs to the balcony when it exploded. A few of us managed to escape but they hunted us down." The girl pointed a shaky finger towards the corpses. "I hid under them!" she cried, "I pretended to be dead until the soldiers gave up and went away. Does that make me a coward?"

"Listen to me," said Kate as the girl stumbled slightly, the weight of the gun unbalancing her. "None of this is your fault. You need to get out of here, just drop the gun and I can show you the way. What's your name?"

The girl did what she was asked. "It was empty anyway," she said, wiping tears from her eyes. "My name is Tess. Please, I just want to go home." She walked out into the open hall towards Kate's outstretched hand, but she'd barely made it two steps when a shot rang out from far down the passageway. Tess reached up to her throat, her eyes full of confusion, and then collapsed to the ground as Kate thrust her hands to her face to block out the scream trying to burst out of her lungs.

"Clear!" a voice called out. "Think that's the last of them in this section."

"Let's go!" said another voice which sounded like Harris. "Head for the pharmacy and then we'll loop back and smash through the blockade in Pathology to mop up the rest."

As the voices retreated into the distance, Kate looked down in horror at the poor child whose soft gasping had now ceased. The girl had been right; it wasn't Tess' fault, it was hers. But falling apart now wasn't going to change anything, only strength and focusing on the task at hand mattered now. Kate squinted across into the gloom and realised why the girl had taken her by surprise; she hadn't emerged from a doorway to another part of the hall, it was an emergency fire stairwell that headed downwards. The sign above it filled her with hope for the first time, a way to bypass the fighting and give her a head start on the others. It was a back entrance into the Pathology Department.

Kate tiptoed her way down the steps, sneaking past the back of the barricade whose occupants had their focus firmly towards the main corridor entrance. The hallway in this section had power, at least, the temporary lights hanging crudely from cables attached to the walls casting harsh shadows in the blackness of the windowless basement. Under the assumption that Isaac's equipment would need electricity, Kate followed the wire trail deeper into the laboratory block. Her intuition was rewarded as she approached the laboratory a few rooms down; pacing around nervously from wall to wall between a bay of benching, his bushy hair a clear giveaway to his identity, was Isaac.

He caught sight of her military uniform and was about to cry for help when a look of recognition shot across his face. "I know you," he said too loudly, "but I don't know why."

Kate put an index finger up to her lips in a silencing gesture. "Hello Isaac, it's Kate, Emily Palmer's sister."

Isaac let out a sigh of relief. "Of course it is! Nice garb, by the way. Are you undercover, spying for IVFree?"

His relaxed demeanour was short-lived, however, as Kate shook her head. "Not exactly. I'm here for the biopsy you took of Emily's ovaries. Where is it?"

"Why would you want that?" he replied in a voice full of bewilderment. "As I said before, it's useless without a research lab to decode what happened to your sister. And you'd still need millions of pounds to develop it into anything, even if Victor did tell you what it meant."

"No, you're wrong," said Kate, "it's the key to everything. It's the picture of the puzzle. And I'll have all the resources I need to solve it."

Isaac's expression turned to one dripping with disgust. "So you're working for them now? The Government? Were you always?"

"No, they know nothing about this. I'm here to finish what Emily started," said Kate, as the guilt started to pour out of her uncontrollably. "Everything I've done here, everyone I've betrayed, everyone I've lost, it was all for her. Our parents died and I never comforted her. All those years I could see she was in pain and I did nothing. She was raped and I never even knew! I need that sample, Isaac, it's all I have left. It's all I have left of her!" Kate felt her knees tremble and fought to stay on her feet as the stream of emotion turned into a cascade. "Please, tell me. I have to try and solve it or all this was for nothing. She died for nothing!"

Isaac slumped down over one of the benches, his elbows on the worktop and head in his hands. "It's in the mortuary," he said sadly, "down the end of the hall and turn left. All the cryogenics are in there. Seemed apt somehow. You want vial EP-001."

"Thank you," said Kate, and pulled out her gun.

"What are you doing?" Isaac exclaimed as she levelled the weapon at him, "I told you where it was!"

Kate stepped towards him, the weapon pointed at his head, her fingers twitching at the trigger. "I'm sorry Isaac, but I can't risk you telling anyone else what happened, or what you did to her. If you talk then everything Andrzej fought for is lost, they'll kill us all and his revolution will be over before it started."

Isaac backed away into the corner of the bay, sliding down against the wall in an effort to get as far away from her as he could. "That's some very odd logic there Kate," he said in a quivering voice, "destroying IVFree in order to save it."

It was nothing that Kate hadn't already argued about with herself a hundred times before. "IVFree died with Andrzej," she said dolefully. "He was its heart, everyone knew that. Time for a fresh start, a new direction."

"I won't tell anyone, I promise!" Isaac begged, now crouching on the floor and making himself as small as possible, not daring to look her in the eyes. "Please!"

"I'm sorry."

Kate aimed down at the figure at her feet. She had pulled the trigger before, surely, this time, it would be easier? She focused on reliving those feelings of hate she had experienced back in that interrogation room, closed her eyes and tried, twice, to fire her gun. But the rage that had threatened to overwhelm her before was gone, replaced instead by just a dull numb throb of sorrow. But even worse than that, seeing him cowering before her made her feel strong, powerful and superior. Rowena would have killed the man without hesitation or remorse, but she was not that woman. She lowered the weapon.

"If I remember, Isaac, you like theatricals?" she asked, trying to think on her feet. The man just stared at her, either too shocked or too relieved to speak, she didn't know which. "Well, I need you to act out a story for me. Do you think you can do that?"

Isaac nodded slowly.

"Good," said Kate, as softly as she could. "I need you to pretend that you're not a genius."

That made him smile at least, as a glimmer of his personality came back to the fore. "Oh, I'm not sure I could manage that."

Kate returned the smile. "The Repro Ministry doesn't know how Emily got pregnant, just that she was. I told them it was a tumour, and as far as they know you're just some opportunist parasite working for IVFree, who Victor fired for stealing donor sperm. He's already confirmed that story."

"Victor? He's in on it too?"

"Yes. He's going to help me cure the world."

Isaac raised an eyebrow. "Well that is a surprise, I can't imagine him doing anything that didn't directly benefit Victor Pearson. Can't you just let me go?" he added hopefully.

"No, you'll be safest here," replied Kate. "If you run they'll shoot you down. Barricade the door and I'll tell them you're no threat."

"And what happens to me then?" Isaac asked, pulling himself up onto to his feet as Kate walked away towards the door.

Kate briefly thought about fabricating a story to make Isaac feel better, but honesty seemed the best path. "If you tell them what I told you to, then you'll just go to prison. I'm sorry there's no other choice. I need a win to get me closer to the inner circle, and if you start boasting about how you cured my sister it's all over. They won't believe that you don't know how it happened, and they'll stop at nothing to find out."

Isaac let out a sigh. "Death versus torture versus prison. Not much of an option I guess. Promise you'll visit me?"

Kate was about to reply when shots started to ring out down the hallway, followed by shouting and volleys of fire in return. Isaac stirred into action, grabbing a table from the corner and dragging it towards the door. "You'd better go, Kate. They'll be through any minute."

Kate turned to leave, before realising that the mention of Victor had reminded her of something. "Isaac, do you know what the amino acid code is?"

"Yes of course," he replied. "It's one of those things they drummed into us at University for some reason."

"Good, I need you to write a message for me."

*

Kate raced away as the sound of gunfire intensified behind her and headed for the large double doors at the end of the passageway, hurrying past some broken elevators which had once ferried the dead to their refrigerated resting places. It seemed odd to her that the mortuary was hidden away in the darkest corner of the basement, as if the hospital designers were embarrassed that a building designed to prolong life might occasionally fail in its task. The morgue itself was empty, apart from some portable lights illuminating four large slab tables in the centre of the grey vinyl floor, each arranged at right angles from the other like spokes of a wheel. Each wall was covered from floor to ceiling in small doors, making Kate briefly wonder if the lockers had ever been emptied of their contents after the Death had struck the place down. Her focus, however, was drawn to the table nearest her, upon which sat various cardboard boxes full of laboratory equipment, flasks, tools and some battered-looking polystyrene packaging.

Resting up against the slab was an old and battered wheeled trolley, which instantly caught Kate's attention. For on it was sat her prize; Isaac's liquid nitrogen dewar. She approached it in a trance, as if the moment was an intangible dream and would fragment and dissolve if she moved too abruptly. She was shaken out of her rapture, however, by the sudden realisation that the shooting in the background had stopped.

She was out of time.

Rushing over to the table and throwing her backpack to the ground, Kate grasped and tore off the lid of the cold container, pulling out the insulating bung and casting both aside on the floor. Smoke billowed from the open top and rolled down the sides, the nitrogen boiling away and obscuring Kate's view as she tentatively reached inside with a gloved hand. She felt the coldness burning through the mediocre insulation in seconds, but it was just enough time to locate the metal handle and pull out a metal storage rack full of small tubes from the icy depths. Kate threw off her soaked glove, placed the rack on the slab table and searched frantically through the box of tools until she found a small metal ladle. Feeling sweat start to bead on her forehead, Kate reached for her backpack and retrieved her vacuum flask, tipping out what small amount of tea remained down a small sluice drain embedded in the floor.

She could hear voices now, shouting to each other that the way ahead was clear.

Seizing the polystyrene box, Kate tore a few small chunks from it and stuffed them into the flask, lining it as best she could and praying it would be enough. She then turned her attention to the rack of samples, hastily scanning through the crudely written labels in such a rush that she completely missed EP-001 on the first attempt. Cursing loudly, Kate plucked the tube from the holder and placed it carefully in the flask. Next, she withdrew a measure of freezing liquid from the dewar with the ladle and poured it slowly over the tube, praying that the glass inside the flask didn't shatter under the strain. Hearing no cracking sounds, she quickly plugged the top with another chunk of polystyrene and screwed on the lid of her flask as tightly as she dared, in case the pressure of the expanding gas proved too much and the whole thing exploded in her hands.

The sounds of footsteps now joined the voices.

Sliding the package and its precious cargo as delicately as she could into her backpack, Kate quickly re-inserted the rack and retrieved the lid from the dewar, just barely replacing it before the door behind her was kicked open and the soldiers piled in.

"Stand where you are!" one of the men barked. Kate put up her hands and turned to face them, only to find their guns trained directly on her.

"Wait!" said a voice behind the shouting man, who Kate recognised at once as Butch. "Hold your fire. It's Kate."

Harris, his face crusted with blood from a cut over his eye, barged his way past the others to the front. "What the fuck are you doing here?"

Kate feigned annoyance and picked up a box of Isaac's flasks and tools. "While you have been out killing everything that moves, I've been doing what I was supposed to. I protected the women Mrs Schoier was concerned about and I've captured the fugitive Isaac; he's holed up a few rooms back."

Harris didn't look impressed. "And?"

"And, Mrs Schoier wants the samples he stole from Dr Pearson destroyed," Kate replied, hoping that the explanation for her being there was enough and that Harris wouldn't check later.

"Well then, we wouldn't want to disappoint her now would we?" Harris said with a sneer of contempt as he walked over to the dewar, kicking it as hard as he could and sending it flying off the trolley and smashing onto the floor. The lid flew off and the contents spilled out, the remaining tubes popping and cracking as their contents began to spoil in the sudden change of temperature.

Harris watched the dissipating cloud of liquid for a brief moment and then turned to what remained of his squad. "Come on, let's get out of here."

Kate sat outside on a snowy bench with the box of cryogenic tools by her side, while the other soldiers reported back for debriefing, medical treatment or aided in processing what few prisoners they had taken. Patrick was not amongst them she noticed, making her wonder if he was still unconscious or had gone down fighting in a heroic hail of bullets. She glanced over as Isaac was led out, his wrists in restraints but his head held high despite his predicament. She hoped he would be okay and that they would not be cruel to him, but most of all she hoped he could keep their secret. The sun was out now, shining through a gap in the surrounding buildings and warming her face with what little heat it could provide. She thought of Andrzej, wondering if his spirit would forgive her and if the ends could ever justify what she had done here today. But more than that she thought of Emily, the children her sister never had the chance to love, and if what happened next would ever offer any redemption for either of them. And at last, the tears came. Tears of joy and relief, tears of sadness, grief and loss, all mixed together until she didn't know which were which any more.

She didn't know how long she had been sat there when Butch approached and gave her a friendly pat on the shoulder. "Hey don't worry about it," the woman said, mistaking Kate's grief for fatigue from the battle. "Most of the guys who didn't crap themselves back there will be crying to their mothers tonight. First battle's always the worst. Especially if it's the last!" She laughed loudly at her own joke and even managed to inspire Kate to crack a smile despite herself. "See there you go, it's not so bad after all. Hey, do you have any of that tea left?"

Kate's eyes went wide with shock. "No, sorry," was all she could manage. What if the woman decided to push the issue and demand to see the empty flask?

Butch, however, just laughed again. "Don't worry I'm just messing with you. Come on, I saw a bottle of whiskey going around somewhere."

Kate nodded in agreement. That seemed like an excellent idea.

The long game

The Alpha Block indoor garden was usually a tranquil place of reflection, its scattering of round tables and comfortable chairs offering solace, or a quiet chat between friends. Its cobbled stone floor was patterned in gentle waves and the walls lined with large potted trees, adding to the airy aura of calmness and serenity.

Today, however, it couldn't have been more different; the peace replaced with a chaotic throng of security, journalists and people of influence. All were jostling with each other to get the best view, or to position their microphones and tape recorders to ensure that no question was overlooked or soundbite missed. Victor stood at the back in the shadows, strangely content and relaxed about not being in the limelight for once. He had other things on his mind.

The echoing noise suddenly reduced to a respectful hush as the politician and his wife entered, taking their places alongside each other at the podium at the end of the courtyard. Both had beaming smiles. "Thank you, ladies and gentlemen, for coming here on such short notice," said Caden, his voice exultant and full of confidence. "As you may be aware, the Ministry scored a major victory yesterday with the dissolution of the terrorist network known as IVFree, including the capture of the head of its illegal clinic arm; the man known as Isaac. In addition, we rescued many innocent women who'd fallen victim to their dogma, or had been lured in by their false promises." Caden paused to allow the enthusiastic ripple of applause to die down before continuing. "But that's not why we've asked you here today. Our close relationship with InVitroSolutions continues to thrive and grow with its new head, Rowena Schoier. And to this end, we have come together to give this joint statement."

Rowena turned to her husband excitedly, playing to the crowd as the anticipation in the room built to fever pitch. "As a result of one of our recent expeditions, we are very proud to announce the discovery of a brand new source of IES-clear donor material!" The crowd erupted into shouts, ovation and questions as Rowena raised her hands and appealed for calm. They fell silent immediately. "Fifty years ago, the Swedish Government initiated a project set deep underground using automated and state of the art technology, to ensure the survival of plants and animals in the event of a cataclysmic disaster. They took samples of every type of life they could find, storing seeds, gametes and DNA safely away for posterity. But what wasn't made public at the time was that they also included humanity on that list. It was a true modern-day Ark, lost for decades after the Death, and we've found it!" The congregation burst into a rapture again and this time, she didn't bother to wait for them to quieten down. "Thousands upon thousands of male and female samples from a wide range of different races and backgrounds, allowing us to match children with parents closer than ever before!"

Caden seemed to realise that his wife was getting all of the attention, which Victor guessed probably wasn't helping his ministerial power play. "It truly is a great day for our great country," the politician proclaimed, "helping ensure our future and protect our way of life."

"Of course, I cannot take all of the plaudits for this," Rowena said, bowing slightly. "The real credit should go to my predecessor and our current head of science, Dr Victor Pearson."

None of the crowd bothered to turn to look for him. It was an excellent play thought Victor, deflecting all possibility of being accused of glory hunting whilst still being the face that everyone associated with the news. It was all a lie of course, albeit a brilliant one, and a deception he was glad not to be a part of inventing. He'd lived through enough of his own.

He never heard the rest of the announcement, as Janet approached and tapped him on the shoulder. "A big woman from the Repro police dropped a box off for you at reception," she said in a whisper. "She said it was from a Kate Adams; some stolen equipment they'd rescued from IVFree apparently. No idea what's in it but it had 'urgent' written on the side so I've put it in your office."

Victor was breathless as he hotfooted it into his office, his racing pulse nothing to do with the dash to get back. He carefully closed and locked the door behind him before turning his attention to the box sitting on his desk, sliding his thumbnail through the brown tape on the top and opening the lid excitedly as if he were a child again at Christmas. There were some miscellaneous tools of little interest, but what really caught his eye was the silver-coloured vacuum flask propped upright in the corner. Attached to it by some sticky tape was a piece of paper with the word 'GluMetIleLeuTyr' scrawled hurriedly across it, and under that in a different ink colour and style, was a telephone number. Victor had wondered if Kate was perceptive enough to understand his previous communication and it thankfully looked like she had. He tore off the note, grabbed a pen and translated it into its one-letter protein equivalent, his hands trembling with excitement as the meaning became clear.

The message spelled out EMILY.

He slowly unscrewed the lid and took out the polystyrene plug, releasing a hiss of pressure and freezing smoke which briefly burned at his hand and took his breath away. Taking a pair of metal tongs from the box, he dipped them into the small amount of liquid that remained, withdrew a small tube and held it up to his eye level. Inside the tube was a tiny lump of frozen tissue. Victor stared at it intently, as if trying to decipher its secrets. Somewhere buried in its mutated and scrambled DNA was a key to the future and he was going to find it, however long it took, and no matter how much it cost. He had to appreciate the irony of it all; Rowena had banished him to the lab while she took control of his company and basked in his previous achievements, but now being back in the lab was the only place he wanted to be. Snorting slightly, he carefully replaced the sample in the flask, re-sealed the lid and picked up the phone.

Kate was in the barracks mess hall struggling to use the tea machine, when a voice from the doorway caught her attention.

"Lieutenant Adams!" Butch stated clearly with an official tone that made Kate grin inside. "Ma'am, there's a call for you in your office."

Kate had yet to get used to her new title let alone her new job, but the gruff woman seemed to have adopted her after their encounter with IVFree, and was making sure the transition was as smooth and pain-free as possible. Kate's superiors had been impressed with her performance in the hospital, so much in fact that a whisper in Caden's ear from his wife had resulted in Kate's instant promotion into the higher echelons of ReproSec's new intelligence division. Harris was apparently furious with the decision but it didn't matter, he would do what he was told like any good soldier. In some ways her new assignment couldn't have been more convenient; her apparent aptitude meant that she had been tasked with bringing down the other illegal back-street clinics, which she was more than glad to do. But most importantly, it would mean legitimate regular access and meetings with Victor without rousing any suspicion, time they could spend discussing more pertinent subjects. She found the phone's receiver off the hook on her desk, waiting for her to respond. "Hello?"

"Kate? Victor Pearson. I got your package, thank you for returning my things. Everything seems in order, I'll make sure it's all put in a safe place."

Kate felt a rush of elation flow through her body. She wanted to cry out, to proclaim to the world what was coming, but then she and the phone line were probably being monitored closely. "That's good," she replied instead, in an as flat and uninterested tone as she could manage.

There was a pause at the other end of the line for a few moments, before Victor's voice again filled her ear. "Oh, and by the way," he said casually, "you never did claim your Lottery prize. I imagine you're very busy and I have a few details I need to sort out here, but in a few months' time maybe you might want to think about an appointment?"

Until now Kate hadn't given much thought to the mechanics of how their new world would begin to shape itself, but now it was finally here she realised that she was the only logical choice. "You know what? That sounds like a good idea. Thank you, Dr Pearson, I'll speak to you soon," she replied, and hung up the phone.

Victor leant back in his chair and let out a long sigh. Smiling, he reached out for the ring box sat on his desk and threw it hard across the room. He watched as the box cracked open against the wall, and laughed as the old shilling flew out and landed in the waste bin waiting below.

Kate stared out of the window into the empty parade square and softly stroked her belly. For the first time since the police officer had come to her door and broken the news about her sister, Kate saw the path clear in front of her. No more doubts, no more hesitation, no more compromises. They would have to be careful, for their new crusade was still just a delicate embryo of two frail and fragile cells. But like any new life, they would grow, develop and differentiate, become a breathing and unstoppable organism so much more than the sum of its parts.

She would live out Emily's dream for her in the only way she knew how, because Andrzej had been correct. Hope was not a reward or a commodity to be traded amongst those with means. Everyone should have the opportunity to see the future in their children's eyes, because as IVFree's mantra declared; the next generation was a right, not a privilege.

Links and community

Thank you for reading! If you enjoyed this novel, please rate it at Amazon and Goodreads:

Amazon UK

http://www.amazon.co.uk/gp/product/B01AG6XJC8

Amazon US

http://www.amazon.com/gp/product/B01AG6XJC8

Goodreads

https://www.goodreads.com/book/show/28532142-in-vitro-lottery

For more information about the author please visit:

Facebook

https://www.facebook.com/edryderauthor/

Twitter

https://twitter.com/Ed_Ryder7

Blog

https://edryderblog.wordpress.com/

Want to know more about gene editing and genetics? Then pay a visit to my website at www.gene-editing.org

Printed in Great Britain
by Amazon